GUNPOWDER ALCHEMY

THE GUNPOWDER CHRONICLES

JEANNIE LIN

GUNPOWDER ALCHEMY

Print: ISBN: 978-0-9909462-4-3

Publishing History

First edition: InterMix eBook Edition / November 2014

Second edition: Jeannie Lin Edition / September 2017

For inquiries, contact Jeannie Lin using the e-mail contact form at:
www.jeannielin.com

PROLOGUE

Q*ing Dynasty China, 1842* A.D.

The Emperor waited on his golden throne.

The Hall of Supreme Harmony was a place of grand ceremony and state occasion, too ostentatious for an audience of one, yet Chief Engineer Jin found himself alone before the Son of Heaven. In accordance, he had worn his best court attire: a silk robe embroidered with the bordered red banner of his ancestral line.

The Forbidden City was closed at night to all but the royal family and the Emperor's closest attendants: the palace eunuchs, the imperial guard, the harem of concubines and consorts. Despite the ordinance, Jin Zhi-fu had been summoned in this late hour to appear before his sovereign.

Jin lowered himself to his knees and placed both hands before him, pressing his forehead to the tiled floor once, then again. Three times three. Nine times for the proper kowtow. When he was done, he waited with his head lowered, staring at his hands laid flat on the ground before him. His left arm from the elbow down was fashioned from steel bones and copper muscle. Gold-tipped acupuncture needles connected the contraption to his nerve endings, allowing metal to take the place of what was once flesh. A small price to pay in service to the empire.

He was not allowed to rise or speak until addressed directly. The silence went on, and his heartbeat grew louder in the absence of sound, pounding with great force until the cadence of it filled his ears.

The Emperor's voice rang through the assembly hall like a clap of thunder. "Do we not outnumber the foreign ships?"

"Yes. Imperial Majesty."

"A hundred men for their ten."

"Yes."

Jin closed his eyes and breathed slowly. He counted each throb within his chest. Each one had become painfully significant. It was said the heart could continue pulsing for a full minute even once the soul had fled.

"Why was the Western fleet not destroyed?" the Emperor demanded.

The imperial commissioner had guaranteed success. Each of the senior ministers had assured the same, as well as the grand admirals of the imperial navy. Yet here he was, the humble chief engineer, to deliver failure.

"The cannons held Wusong for days." Jin tried to project as clearly as he could with his head bowed. "But the Western gunships—"

The Emperor cut him off with an impatient noise. He didn't want an explanation, and from that moment, Jin knew he had only been summoned for one reason.

The Ministry of Engineering had heard rumors of powerful weapons from the West. His men had worked to secure the ports. They had outfitted the forts with cannons and an arsenal of gunpowder and explosives. The nautical division had developed superior sails so the war junks could maneuver without equal through wind and water.

Yingguo, or England as the foreigners called their land, had countered with something his engineers had never seen before. Iron-clad devil ships had roared into the harbor to tear through the war junks as if they were made of paper. The Middle Kingdom had been defeated by a fleet of steam and iron.

The Son of Heaven was perfect and infallible. If the empire had failed, then someone else, someone mortal and imperfect, was to blame.

The chief engineer could protest his innocence. He could blame the greater men who had come before him who had underestimated the English threat, but he, too, had remained silent for the sake of pride. A thousand years of pride. He had allowed the imperial navy to sail against the superior Western fleet to be destroyed and, even worse, humiliated.

"The failure lies with this unworthy servant," Jin conceded.

A sound of rage bubbled from the Emperor's throat. "Remove this man from the Emperor's sight."

The Forbidden Guard appeared from the recesses of the hall to take him. Jin's mechanical arm froze as their rough grip displaced the control needles. They dragged him from the hall with his feet scraping helplessly over the tile.

Perhaps his death would be enough. The engineers who served him could be spared. And his family—He prayed his family would remain unharmed. His wife had watched him with haunted eyes through their final embrace. Soling, his ten-year-old daughter, had curled her slender fingers tight over his as she'd walked with him to the front gate.

She was growing so tall now. He'd somehow missed that part, with the war with the foreigners taking up all his time. He would only be able to watch over her now in spirit.

Jin Zhi-fu emerged from the hall to the towering shapes of the Forbidden City and the stark night sky above. He was nothing more than dead weight now, a burden, a thing as the sentinels pulled him further into the hidden depths. His body grew slack and his knees refused to hold his weight.

He was afraid to die after all.

The war was already over, though no formal surrender had yet been issued. Jin had known it since Canton fell a year earlier. More strongholds followed: Tinghai, Ningpo, Wusong, Shanghai. A slow death sentence of a thousand cuts, slice after relentless slice. It was ill omen to speak of failure, so no one had said anything. They had all of them remained so very quiet.

1

Q*ing Dynasty China, 1850 A.D.—Eight years later*

I felt heat rising up the back of my neck as I walked past the center of the market area. Past all the places where any respectable young woman would be found. Everyone knew what lay at the end of the alleyway. We liked to think that because it was at the edge of our village, that dark little room was hidden. A secret thing. If no one spoke of it, it didn't exist.

By the same rule, everyone knew there was only one reason anyone went out there.

Though there were no eyes on me, I could feel them all the same. Linhua was small enough that there were no secrets. It was small enough that people didn't even pretend not to know.

The back door was buried deep at the end of the lane. As far as I knew, no one ever used the front entrance. I knocked twice and stepped back. After a pause, the door slid open, the corner grating against the dirt floor. The man who stood behind it gave me a wide grin. "Ah, Miss Jin Soling."

A sickly sweet smell wafted into the alleyway. Though faint, the pungent floral notes were unmistakable. Our village wasn't large enough to have a grain store, yet we had an opium den.

"Shang," I greeted.

Cui Shang was thin, long in the face. I knew he was ten years older than me and his father was a widower. Once, a generation before, their family had worked a plot of farmland, but now the Cui family had no other trade besides opium.

"Are you here to try a pipe with me, Miss Jin? It will take away all your burdens; remove that worry line always hanging over your brow. You might even be pretty without it."

I held out my palm to display the two copper coins, half of my earnings from Physician Lo that day.

"I have this week's payment."

"That's not enough," he said.

"This is how much it always costs."

Shang scratched the side of his neck with one bony finger. "Don't you know? The runners have raised their prices. News is there was a fire in the docks in Canton. Several large shipments of opium were destroyed."

"I haven't heard anything of it."

He shrugged. "It's the truth."

I kept my face a mask. He was trying to play me like an old fishwife in the market. "This is all you'll receive."

Shang tried to stare me down, his lip curling into a scowl. Straightening my shoulders, I stared right back even though my pulse was racing. I was taller than most of the other girls in the village, but at my full height he was still half a head taller. Though constant opium use left him gaunt in appearance, he was still stronger than me.

I had my needle gun in my pocket, a spring-loaded weapon I kept with me when I had to travel on the lonely roads that surrounded the village to tend to patients. If Shang tried anything, all it would take was a single dart in his neck or torso to immobilize him, but I couldn't draw with him so close.

With a shrug, he disappeared into the den while I shifted my weight from one foot to the other. It had been a long day. Old Lo had sent me far out to the edge of the rice fields for the monthly visit to farming huts. Now it was late and my family would be holding our evening meal to wait for me.

Ten minutes passed by and he had not yet reappeared. I loathed to go inside, but I was prepared to do so when he finally emerged.

"I had to give you a smaller amount," he announced with even less of an attempt at politeness than before. "You can't expect any special treatment, acting so superior all the time."

Without argument, I held out the cash, which he took after thrusting the packet into my hand. Inside was a pressed cake of black opium. I slipped it into the pocket of my jacket and didn't bother to say farewell before turning to leave.

"*Manchu witch*."

He spat on the ground behind me. My face burned at the insult, but I didn't stop. I hated knowing that in a week I would be back.

By the time I reached our home, I was still livid. We lived in a small village, and the walk wasn't nearly long or strenuous enough for me to forget.

My family lived in three small rooms surrounding a patch of dirt where we attempted to grow vegetables. I hesitated to call it a courtyard. The moment I set foot inside the front gate, the scent of cooking rice floated from the kitchen. I also heard a wail coming from one of the sleeping chambers: "*Soling, Soling, Soling...*"

Each call of my name pierced into me a little bit less. I went to the kitchen even though the cries grew louder.

Our maidservant Nan was at the stove, stirring a pot of congee for our evening meal. My eight-year-old brother Tian had his head bent over a notebook at the table. The flicker of an oil lamp illuminated the pages.

"I am sorry I'm late," I told them.

"No, no need to be sorry," Nan soothed. "Everything is still hot. Come sit."

The old maidservant had been with us in Peking. She'd stayed with Mother and me when we'd relocated to Hunan province. There had been other servants with us then, though they had gradually drifted away. We could no longer support other servants besides Nan. By now, she was family.

Tian closed his notebook and laid it onto his lap as soon as I sat down. The third chair remained empty.

"How was school today?"

"Good," Tian mumbled.

From the sleeping chamber came another cry. "Soling!"

I pushed on. "What did you study?"

"We practiced calligraphy."

Tian played along admirably, though he kept his head down as he spoke. Nan ladled rice porridge into two clay bowls and set them before us. I picked up my spoon but set it down when I heard my name again, this time accompanied by a low moan.

"Go to her," I said quietly.

Nan nodded and I slipped the cake of opium from my pocket into her hands before she left. Tian spooned the watery rice porridge into his mouth even though it hadn't been seasoned yet.

It had been less than a day since we ran out of our supply. Nan had prepared a pipe for Mother last night before she had gone to bed. When there was none in the morning, she refused to eat or even drink. She claimed she was too sick to keep food in her stomach and had gone to bed.

We had gone without opium for almost two days once. I had tearfully begged Mother to stop, and she had even more tearfully agreed. After ten hours, she started crying that her skin was alive, that it was being torn away. I don't know who broke first, me or her.

And now Mother was getting worse. I tried to deny it, but she was getting worse.

I stood to finish setting the table myself. Nan had prepared a plate of fried bean curd, sliced thin so the portion would stretch further. There was also a tiny dish of salt and pickled vegetables from our cellar.

Only when I was near the stove did I notice the bruise on my brother's cheek, on the side he'd kept painstakingly turned toward the wall. I sat down again. Using my chopsticks, I picked up slices of bean curd to drop into his bowl.

"You need to eat more, Tian. And stop getting into so many fights," I reprimanded.

He bent his head lower. I knew it wasn't his fault, but I scolded him anyway. So he could at least save face.

My brother wasn't weak. He was just too quiet, too serious. He was different. Our family was different. When we came to Linhua village, the rumors were already circling, most of them true. We were from Peking, exiled, disgraced Manchurian aristocracy among Han villagers. No matter how long we lived here, that was all we would ever be.

"Will you look at my drawings, Soling?" Tian asked once he was finished with his bowl.

"Show them to me."

I tried to be kind to him now after scolding him earlier. An uneasy peace had descended over the house. No more cries came from the sleeping chamber, but Nan hadn't yet returned.

I stacked the bowls beside the wash bin while Tian retrieved his books. He sat down and opened his notebook, turning the pages carefully by one corner.

A pang of emotion took me by surprise. My brother hadn't even been one year old when we lost our father, yet there was so much of Father in him. In the way he bent his head over the page and the deliberate, thoughtful way he touched the world around him. Tian would pick up stones and turn them over and over, before setting them back down exactly as he'd found them.

Tian had hardly known Father's expressions, yet whenever my brother bent over his sketches or his lessons, there was the same wrinkle across his forehead. The same look in his eyes with a crease in the corner as if his mind were a thousand *li* away.

The drawing showed a crane by the water with wings partially unfolded. I moved my chair to get a closer look. It wasn't a pretty picture, nor one infused with majesty or emotion. My brother's sketches were studies in structure; of shapes and their joinings.

"Very good."

He was old enough to wear his hair braided into the queue required of all male subjects of the Qing Empire. I tried to touch a hand to the nape of his neck, a gesture that Tian seemed to hate lately. He gave an impatient shrug and I withdrew, trying not to feel hurt.

While Tian continued to work on his sketch at the table, I finished clearing away the rest of the dishes, making sure to leave enough food warming for Nan. She usually ate by herself once we were done. For some reason, it was important for her to maintain that faint boundary between master and servant.

"I'm going to be taking a trip tomorrow," I told my brother once the kitchen was tidied.

"Where to?"

"Changsha with Merchant Hu. Now time for bed."

Tian didn't move. "Why Changsha?"

"This is an adult matter."

That meant that there would be no more discussion. He was still my little brother, and with Mother—with Mother the way she was lately, I was the head of the household.

An eight-year-old boy shouldn't need to worry about the price of rice and eggs. When I was a child in the capital city, clothing had appeared like magic. I was never afraid that the dinner table would be empty.

Tian closed his notebook and rubbed his thumb over the spine in disappointment. He was growing old before his time, watching and listening to all around him. This village was too small for him.

My brother belonged in the academies of Peking, studying mathematics and the sciences. He should be groomed for the engineering exams once he reached manhood. It was in his blood, but it wasn't possible. Not here.

"To bed, Tian."

My voice cracked. My brother didn't seem to notice, or at least pretended not to. Good boy. He brushed the back of his knuckles over his bruised cheek, tucked his books and writing case close to his side, then headed out toward the room that he shared with Nan. I watched him disappear into the house while I breathed the evening air in deep and let the coolness of it sting against my skin.

Sometimes, through the mist in the autumn or while my eyes were closed at night, or even while they were open and staring at the herbal cabinets in Lo's shop, I could almost see the gilded buildings of Peking; the sprawl of the city with its towering pagodas and sparkling ponds. Once more, I walked through the hallways of the Ministry of Science as I'd done as a child. I could smell the sharp, chemical perfume of the laboratories.

I needed to wake up. *Wake up.* Even though I knew I was no longer sleeping.

Beyond the walls of our humble home were the tiny shops and homes of our farming village. Thatched rooftops, dull wooden hovels. Narrow streets of packed dirt and straw.

The house was quiet now, which meant Mother wouldn't stir for several hours. Maybe when she woke again, I could get her to eat something.

With the oil lamp in hand, I went to the storeroom beside the kitchen. The space was kept desolately clean with the bins and jars mostly empty. Even mice sought better prospects. The basket in the corner held a layer of rice that was no more than a finger deep. The entire province was feeling the aftermath of a poor growing season.

The wooden panel at the back of the storeroom creaked as I pried it open. I wedged my arm through the opening and rummaged around until my fingers wrapped around a solid object.

Over the last years, we had gradually sold and bartered away our family treasures except for the few trinkets kept hidden here. I pulled out a bundle wrapped in green silk.

Brushing away the dust, I untied the cloth. The light from the lamp flickered across the polished steel inside. Even after all this time, it remained untarnished.

A puzzle box, my father had called it. The cube was the size of a large grapefruit and appeared to be made of several panels all welded perfectly together.

I rotated it in my hands, running my fingertips over the surface. On first glance, the sides appeared uniform, but as I turned it, the light reflected off to reveal a geometric pattern of shaded squares and diamonds. Yet the metal was smooth to the touch and seamless to the eye. Only the right combination would open it.

I tightened my grip and the honed edges cut into my palms. When the Emperor had stripped my father of his title, all of his inventions and records were seized and destroyed. His name was removed from the records of the imperial exams.

The imperial guard had come to our house after Father's arrest and ransacked his personal study. The metal puzzle box had always been kept upon his shelf, but on that day, it wasn't there. I found it later, forgotten in a trunk of clothing that had been hastily packed.

All I had left of Father was this trinket. I found the secret panel and slid it forward, activating the mechanism inside. With a whir of gears, the box shifted and opened only to reveal another closed compartment. A puzzle within a puzzle. I had loved this box so much when Father had first shown it to me.

"It's very valuable," Father had warned, putting it up high so I couldn't snatch it up in my little hands whenever curiosity struck.

The memory faded, leaving only the threat of tears. I pinched two fingers to the bridge of my nose until the stinging in my eyes went away. Enough. There was nothing else to be done about it.

What good were such memories anyway?

I had decided what needed to be done earlier that day when Old Man Lo had counted out my earnings. He wasn't stingy. On the contrary, he had given me more than my share.

Physician Lo was a generous man who operated on the old tradition by which his patients only paid him when they were well. Thus he always had a stake in bringing his patients back to good health.

Payment only sometimes came in the form of copper cash. Often he would be paid with a cup of rice or a quantity of salt or eggs. Whatever the villagers had to spare. Lately food was scarce and, as could be expected when the elements were unbalanced, sickness was common. For the last month, every coin Lo sent my way had been charity and I knew it.

I had gone to the provincial capital of Changsha several times before. Usually when we needed to sell something that we had brought with us from Peking. There was no market for finery in Linhua.

Someone in Changsha had to be willing to pay something for Father's box this time around. It was the only thing we had left of any value.

2

The next morning, I waited until Tian had left for school before preparing for the trip to Changsha. There wasn't much to take, as I would only be away for two days.

I brought the puzzle box from the storeroom and placed it into my satchel along with my acupuncture case. Then I dressed in Nan and Tian's room so as to not disturb Mother, who was still sleeping. Over my usual plain robe, I put on my mandarin jacket, fastening the long row of cloth buttons down the front. It was made of sturdy, serviceable black cotton and adorned with a single looped pattern of embroidery along the border. A quick pat down of the bun at the nape of my neck assured me that all the hairpins were fixed in place. I hoped it made me appear older.

Smoothing my hands over the jacket one final time, I slung the pack over my shoulder. I had to use a bucket of water in the kitchen as my mirror. I appeared to be a strong, serious woman with business on my mind, didn't I? Not a young, desperate girl pretending to be worldlier than she was.

Before going to the gate, I stopped and pulled aside the

curtain to the adjoining chamber. Mother lay on her side in her pale sleeping garments. She wasn't asleep as I had thought. Her eyes were aimed listlessly into the corner.

"I'll be back soon," I said softly.

My mother remained still, not acknowledging my presence in the least. I hoped that meant she was at least comfortable and not in pain, but I wasn't certain. I let the curtain fall back in place and stepped quietly away.

Nan was out sweeping the leaves at the front of the courtyard. I pressed a small purse into the old woman's hand. The last of our household savings.

"Only two pipes a day no matter what Mother says," I said in a low tone. "Make her drink her tea and take food in between. And don't let Tian wander too far after school."

Nan nodded. She had been with us so long that she understood things without them being spoken aloud, but I told her anyway.

Outside the gate, I could hear a wagon rolling to a stop. Merchant Hu had arrived with his shipment of goods packed into the back. My gaze swept once more over the small courtyard to make sure I hadn't forgotten anything.

"I'll be back tomorrow," I told Nan, knowing that I was drawing out the inevitable.

"You be careful, my young lady."

The way Nan addressed me was more affectionate than formal. Still, it sounded strange to my ears. I was no lady.

I greeted Hu, whom I knew from his visits to the herbal shop whenever he came to town. As I climbed up onto the driver's seat, my stomach was a tangle of knots.

Two days was not so long. Afterward, I would have new stories to tell Tian, and Mother would hardly realize I was gone. Old Man Lo could get by without me for a couple of days.

Some of my anxiety had faded once the wagon pulled away

from the village, though my shoulders remained tense. By the time we were on the open road, however, the immense weight had lifted from my shoulders and even the air seemed clearer.

But then I was stricken with guilt. I was actually relieved to be leaving Linhua behind, if only for a little while.

THE ROAD to Changsha was plagued with ruts. I found it reassuring that the path was well traveled, though we hadn't seen anyone on it since leaving our village that morning.

I sat beside Merchant Hu while he held the reins over the pair of mules that pulled the wagon. An iron fire lance rested between us, within easy reach.

Summer was coming in fast this year and the sky was mercilessly clear. The sun glared down, baking the earth, and not a single cloud or shade tree provided any relief as the wagon rolled along.

One of the wheels caught on an uneven patch of road, and I gripped the bottom of the wagon seat, trying to keep from jostling against Hu. He wasn't quite a stranger, but he wasn't familiar to me, either. All I knew was that Old Man Lo trusted him. Hu was a frequent visitor to our village as he transported goods from the major market areas to our dusty square.

"Have you been to Changsha, Miss Jin?" he asked.

"Once."

"No need to worry. We should be there long before nightfall."

I nodded, keeping my eyes on the road. The only news we heard of the provincial capital and the surrounding countryside came from merchants like Hu, and lately the reports hadn't been reassuring. Years of drought had turned many of my countrymen to banditry. A traveler could be killed for nothing more than the handful of rice while outside the safety of the cities.

"Old Lo speaks of you like a daughter," the merchant continued. "'She is quite focused,' he tells me. 'Clever, too.'"

I shifted uncomfortably, not certain how to react to such praise. "Old Lo has always been very kind."

Hu was doing me a favor by allowing me to ride along to Changsha, and I at least owed him a little conversation to pass the time.

"What are you bringing to sell in the capital?" I asked, glancing back over the many sacks and crates packed into the wagon.

"Oh, odds and ends. I pick up salt, oil, other staples from Changsha and then cart them to the far corners of the province. Nothing fancy," he said with a chuckle. "But I've done well enough. One wouldn't think so, just looking at me, would they?"

He tapped his chest twice in boast.

Hu was middle-aged, plump around the middle and large in manner and gesture. In this time of famine, Hu certainly wasn't going hungry, but I didn't begrudge him his success. His profession required that he travel through the province in a constant cycle of buying and bartering.

Another wagon approached from the opposite side as we neared a junction in the road. Reflexively, I lowered my hand into the pocket of my jacket to grip the needle gun.

Hu glanced over as my shoulders tensed, but the wagon passed by with merely a nod from the driver to us.

The merchant laughed. "Seeing rebels everywhere, Miss Jin?"

I'd heard too many stories of bandits and rebels roaming the countryside. "Have you ever seen any?"

"That filth prefers to hide out in caves far in the mountains," Hu said dismissively.

They said the rebels were wild animals, long-haired and savage. They were traitors who had rejected the authority of the imperial court and lived in lawless squalor. If that was true, why did we keep hearing that more had joined their camp?

"In any case, their quarrel is with the imperial government. You and I, us common folk, we have nothing to fear."

Despite his assurances, Hu set a hand upon the fire lance beside him. The weapon was an ancient one, effective against a single foe, but hardly a threat against a band of rebels. My own gun could only load two needles at a time, each filled with a strong dose of sleeping potion. It was enough to slow an attacker or stop him completely, but once again, an unsuitable weapon for a large-scale attack.

In Linhua, we listened to reports of brewing rebellion as tales of some far-off land, nothing that could affect our lives. We were more concerned with the price of rice and salt and cooking oil. But out here on the open road, all the stories suddenly loomed large around me.

We stopped midday and Hu set about building a cooking fire to brew tea. I had finished tending to the mules when I noticed the merchant clutching his shoulder.

"Is your arm bothering you today?"

"It's always worse on travel days." Hu rotated his arm, working the joint. "Too much sitting in one place."

Hu periodically visited the herbal shop seeking a remedy for the ache in his shoulder. An injury from his youth, he said. It was how I had first made his acquaintance, though it was Physician Lo who usually tended to him.

He continued to massage his shoulder, wincing until I had no choice but to offer.

"Do you wish for me to see to that, sir?"

I knelt in the grass and pulled aside his sleeve to press two fingers to the pulse point at his wrist. I wasn't as concerned about his heart rate as I was the flow of qi through him. The course and rhythm of internal energy through the body was the source of all Lo had taught me. I could sense where the merchant's muscles had stiffened, blocking the flow of qi along the meridians of his body.

"I can try to lessen the pain," I offered.

"That would be very good of you, Miss Jin."

At the very least I could release some tension from his shoulders. It would be repayment for taking me to the city.

I pulled out the acupuncture case from my bag. The hinges were tarnished and the wood worn smooth near the latch—Old Lo had given me the set he'd used as an apprentice.

A diagram with all of the commonly known acupuncture points had been affixed to the inside. Slim wire needles were arranged in rows of varying length and thickness, and inserted into bands of silk to keep them in place.

Rolling up his sleeve, I selected one of the thinnest needles and cleansed it with a vial of alcohol. I pressed against the meridian along Hu's arm with the pad of my thumb to stimulate the flow of energy before inserting the tip just into the skin above his elbow. Hu didn't flinch from the contact. Likely he felt nothing at all other than a faint tingle at the insertion point.

I'd first learned about the mysteries of internal energy when my father had a mechanical arm fitted in place of the one he'd lost in an explosion at his laboratory. After the acupuncturists had attached the needles, he'd reached out to hold my hand. The steel fingers were surprisingly gentle and I was captivated.

"The shoulder has been much better under your care," Hu complimented.

"You should thank Physician Lo, sir."

All I'd ever done for Hu was assist. I focused on fixing the second needle opposite the first one.

"I hear from Lo that business is slow lately," he continued.

"These are difficult times for everyone."

"Especially with the devil *Yangguizi* at our ports."

I nodded absently, keeping my focus on the needles. What foreigners at the trading ports had to do with business in our village was beyond me, but it was easy to blame the foreign devils for everything. There was the failure of the crops year after year, the spread of the black poison opium down every river and stream. The white ghosts were even blamed for the recent earthquakes that shook the region. I myself didn't have any opinion about the *Yangguizi*. As long as they remained far away.

"Fortunately business has been quite good for me," Hu said with a small laugh. "More than enough for an old bachelor such as myself."

His pulse jumped beneath my fingertips and I glanced up. For a moment I caught an odd look in his eyes before he looked away.

Lately, the merchant had been coming by Old Man Lo's shop quite frequently, complaining of this ache or that pain. Despite the fact that Linhua was removed from major trade routes, Hu had been by twice in the last month alone.

"I have been thinking hard on this." He gave a nervous cough before continuing. "You are a very talented woman. And not really so bad to look at."

The third needle slipped from my fingers and I scrambled to catch it. My cheeks burned as I tried to regain focus. Did Old Man Lo know he was sending me to be courted? The physician didn't strike me as a matchmaker, but Lo had suggested the merchant would be able to take me to the capital. And Hu had happily agreed.

"You must be teasing, Mister Hu."

"Now, Miss Jin. You are no young, innocent girl. We can speak plainly, right?"

My stomach churned as I applied the last needle. I really wasn't so old. Only eighteen. But to the villagers, I was already passed over, left behind. I had taken up a trade, and a somewhat improper one for a woman.

"Old Lo told me as bright as you are, he feared he wouldn't be able to keep an assistant for much longer," Hu said soberly.

Was my mentor truly so eager to marry me off? I didn't want to be anyone's burden, let alone that of Old Man Lo, who had taken me under his guidance all these years.

Merchant Hu must have considered himself truly generous considering me as a bride. If I had thought marriage was at all a possible solution, I would have hunted down a suitable match years earlier.

My options might very well be reduced to marriage to the merchant or enlisting to work in the factories.

"Mister Hu, you are a good man—"

"*Aiya!*" he exclaimed, waving his hand to save me from having to explain. "I've spent most of my life haggling one deal or another. I already know from your tone what your answer is."

"I don't mean any offense."

"No offense here. Too thick-skulled." He tapped his temple good-naturedly, then grew serious. "But think on it, Miss Jin. It's not a bad arrangement."

"I'll consider it," I replied, but merely out of politeness.

When I spoke again, I tried to keep my tone neutral; as if a man three times my age hadn't just proposed marriage. As if it wasn't the best offer I would ever receive.

"Leave the needles in for the next half hour," I instructed. "I'll brew some tea for us."

I used the task as an excuse to keep my head bent and my gaze averted. Once the water was steaming, I poured some over the tea leaves in the ceramic pot and set the lid in place.

The merchant wasn't being unkind. No one would think a match odd despite the difference in our ages. Hu had been courteous to me and was a man of some means. Though my father had once been the head of the Ministry of Science, our family had been reduced to the lowest of peasants.

The tea was ready, and we shared a simple meal of cold steamed buns with the merchant managing with only one arm. Afterward, I set about removing the needles and cleansing them over a lighted candle.

Hu flexed his arm. "Much better. I'm very grateful."

I nodded my acknowledgment. Two days couldn't be over quick enough.

"Why are you going to Changsha?" he asked after we had packed our belongings and returned to the wagon.

"I'm visiting our great aunt," I murmured.

"I didn't know Miss Jin had relatives in the provincial capital."

Immediately, I regretted the lie. The villagers of Linhua knew we were from Peking in the north. I suspected they also knew the unfortunate circumstances that had brought us to this province.

After a few minutes back on the road, I closed my eyes and pretended to sleep. It was unfair of me, I know. Hu was making what would be considered a respectable proposition. Most of the men in town simply looked through me as if I didn't exist. They didn't exist for me, either.

I was beyond the ideal age for marriage, and what good reputation I had was worn thin. I tended to strangers alongside Physician Lo; men who were not of my immediately family. I stayed awake late into the night and exercised no sense of propriety. And I was Manchurian. Unsuitable in every way.

Lo sent female patrons to me when they needed to discuss their ailments, but I tended to men and women when the need arose. Hardly proper or ladylike, but it was the only way I knew to support my family. I had stopped thinking of how I appeared to others until Hu's proposal.

I had been engaged to be married once. My mother and father had arranged it when I was only ten years old. My husband-to-be was eight years older than me. One of Father's associates from the Ministry. He was hardworking, Mother had told me. He was clever and earnest. After Father's disgrace, the betrothal had quickly and quietly dissolved.

I would never marry now. Becoming a merchant's wife might provide security for me, but who would take care of Mother and Tian?

The young girl who had once hoped for things like marriage

and family remained back in a dream realm. There wasn't any part of me that wasn't tired and worried all the time. The haze curled around me again, hiding away those fragile hopes that had once been a part of another life. Memories I couldn't hold on to, yet refused to forget.

3

The provincial capital of Changsha was protected by a fortress and enclosed in a towering wall of brick and stone. Cannons lined the upper rampart accompanied by armed sentries at the watchtowers.

Our wagon passed through the arched gateway in the indolent simmer of the afternoon. Hu was reluctant to leave me alone in such a large city, and I had to insist and insist again before he finally bid me farewell. We parted at the edge of the main market area after making arrangements to meet up again that evening.

I didn't want him hovering over me as I tried to pawn my family's last treasure. Part of me was still too proud.

Stalls and shops crowded both sides of the avenue, and for the first few moments, all I could do was stare, at a loss. I'd told the merchant I'd been to Changsha before, but it had been at least a year ago and never alone.

The river divided the city in half, and the market was located on the east bank. The market was roughly divided into sectors, and our maidservant Nan had been an expert at forging through them. I navigated through the streets much more tentatively, passing by cages of chickens and vats of fish on ice. Stacks of cabbages and onions lay wilting in the later hours of the market day. The adjoining area held bolts of cloth and embroidery thread.

Lo had written down an address for me, and I dug into the pocket of my mandarin jacket to retrieve it. He'd also given me some brief instructions that made no sense now that I was in the clutter of the city. One could waste a day wandering through these stalls.

I pushed beyond a display of rugs and shoes and caught sight of mechanical rigging at the end of one lane. A lattice of metal slats and bolts stood out against the surrounding wooden buildings. When I ventured closer, I saw a lot filled with equipment. Ploughs and threshers lay in lifeless heaps beneath the sun along with an odd collection of wheels and cranks.

The lot was empty of any customers, but there was a man riding atop one of the machines. It was made of interlocking iron segments that moved together in a fluid motion. An array of small wheels allowed it to roll along the ground.

Using a set of levers, the driver directed the machine toward the corner of the lot. The front of it coiled and swayed like a snake. Black smoke coughed out from the belly, spewing fine ash into the air. I could taste sulfur on my tongue.

With a final sputter, the wheels grew still and the operator climbed down from the seat. His queue was tightly braided and looped around his neck to keep it out of the way. He pulled a scarf from within his tunic and used it to wipe his hands, though they were still black with powder and grease when he approached me.

"Young miss," he greeted.

I was transfixed by the machine. "I've never seen one like that."

He grinned and his teeth gleamed white against the black residue that covered his face. "Is that a northern accent I hear?"

I tensed as he looked me up and down. He merely sounded

curious, but ever since the Emperor had conceded the ports to the *Yangguizi*, Manchurians were even more hated. With my feet unbound, my particular manners and even my speech, I couldn't escape where I'd come from.

"My family is from the capital," I replied before deflecting attention back to the iron beast. "What is this machine used for?"

"Excavation," he explained, politely enough. "Down in the mines there are narrow tunnels that need to be cleared. This one has a problem with its engine."

These machines were great hulking beasts with hard, sharp edges; nothing like the sleek creations I'd once played with in my father's workshop.

The inventions of the capital had been clever and surprising and unexpectedly beautiful. No such aesthetic existed here. The machinery of the south was all about labor and productivity, yet I was still fascinated. The excavator moved with the rumble of a gunpowder engine at its heart, much like the ones my father had worked on for the Emperor.

A twinge of nostalgia warmed me. "Do you repair engines here?"

"When needed." He tucked the rag into his belt and took a closer look at me. "Strange to see a young woman so interested in mining equipment."

I hadn't meant to become so distracted. "I'm looking for the —" I read from the slip of paper. "The Bao Zhen Curio shop."

He gestured to the street just behind the lot and I thanked him.

This section featured a string of repair and secondhand shops and was much less crowded than the central part of the market. I searched the signboards until I found the shop Physician Lo had recommended.

The shelves were crowded with brass microscopes, windup clocks and compasses. A layer of dust indicated most of the items had been forgotten. My fingers itched to rearrange the shelves into some semblance of order.

In the center of the floor, a circle of eight bronze toads sat with their mouths open around a central urn. Over each toad hung a dragon holding a ball.

The design sent a wave of nostalgia through me. A larger scale model of the classic earthquake detector had decorated the center of the main courtyard of the Ministry of Science. When the ground shook, a mechanism inside the urn released one of the balls into the toad's mouth. The location of the ball would indicate the direction of the quake.

I saw that one of the metal spheres had indeed fallen from a dragon's mouth, perhaps from the last quake we'd felt just a few days ago

"To the southwest of here," a raspy voice intoned. "Luckily nothing but mountains there."

The owner sat behind the counter, drawing smoke from an elongated pipe. He blew it out in a languid stream while I approached.

"Sir, I work with Physician Lo from the village of Linhua."

He gave me a nod that could have meant he recognized Lo's name or that he was simply acknowledging that I was speaking.

"He told me you would give a fair price," I continued undaunted. I had to be bold. I had to be unwavering.

I placed the puzzle box onto the counter and stepped back, trying not to let my anxiety show. After merely a glance, the shopkeeper pushed the steel cube back at me with a solemn shake of his head.

"But sir—"

"I have no need for such an item." He took another pull and released the smoke from the corner of his mouth.

I hadn't even had a chance to open the box. "Perhaps the honorable shopkeeper would be interested to see what lies inside?"

"No." The smoke swirled in a hazy curtain between us. "Not worth the trouble."

"Trouble?"

He tapped the box with the end of his pipe. "This is a foreign invention, hmm? Trouble."

"I don't understand."

The shopkeeper sniffed at me, which served as his only reply.

"Thank you, sir," I said, my throat tight. "If you would tell me where else I might go?"

"No one around here will take that. At least not anyplace a proper young lady such as yourself should ever go," he drawled with a touch of amusement. It was the same dismissiveness I'd endured for years.

"Are you speaking of a ghost market?" I demanded.

I'd heard the nighttime markets were unregulated and often involved the pawning and selling of treasured items.

"Better to try the Academy."

He leaned back and returned his pipe to his mouth. His gaze focused on the door as if I were no longer there.

Stubborn as I was, I prowled the rest of the lane, seeking more pawnshops. The other places yielded much the same result with usually less conversation. The brokers would take one look at the puzzle box before waving me away.

At one counter, I swore I saw interest in the woman's eyes. The moment she met my gaze, the look was gone.

"Selling something like this is too difficult," she said. "Be very careful, miss."

The art dealers in the city refused me as well. With each stop, my spirit sank deeper. I had held on to this prized possession as a last hope, but my dream was turning to dust in my hands. It was only my own sentiment that had given this box any value. I blinked back tears of frustration when I saw that I had returned to the first curio shop once again.

The sun was setting and the merchants had begun to pack

their wares. I was supposed to meet Mister Hu at the sixth hour beside the central exchange before sundown, but I wasn't ready to give up yet. There was still the Academy, as the first shopkeeper had suggested. Perhaps the box wouldn't fetch as high of a price among scholars, but I couldn't return empty-handed.

I crossed a bridge over to the west bank of the river and followed the walkway through a wooded park. The late hour cast ominous shadows between the trees, and the buzz of cicadas filled my head. I hurried back onto the streets as fast as I could.

Pedestrian traffic was sparse on this side of the river. The sky was growing dark faster than I had anticipated, and before long, the last of the daylight had faded, leaving me in a maze of streets and alleyways.

It was only then, in the quietness of the evening, that I realized someone was behind me. When I quickened my step, he remained at close quarters, lurking like a shadow.

My pulse jumped and the hairs on the back of my neck rose. How long had he been following me? Long enough to know I was alone and unprotected. I turned sharply around the corner, positioning myself so I could see who was there. It wasn't long before a man emerged around the building.

Stories of abductions and enslavement flooded my mind. But this wasn't some sinister port town. Our village was just a day away. I had sat across from my brother this very morning.

I wound a path through the alleyways, my chest tight and heart pounding. With trembling fingers, I drew the needle gun from my jacket. My palms grew damp as I fumbled for the trigger and prayed. Please let him go by.

He didn't. The man was still behind me. Closer now.

I broke into a run. Buildings swept by on either side. I was in the middle of a crowded city and there had to be someone nearby. Footsteps pounded behind me, and I shouted for help until my throat was raw, but it was no use.

My hand froze around the needle gun. My lungs were burning. I couldn't go on much longer. I had to make my stand now while I could still fight.

I spun around as a dark, hulking figure closed in on me. Raising the weapon, I pressed the trigger out of reflex, firing one shot after another.

The needle must have struck home, because my pursuer stopped to claw at something near his face. I remained stunned before him, my arms still outstretched. I'd only fired at wooden dummies before.

Within moments, he stumbled to the ground. With a sharp exhale, I forced myself to run.

The market. My only chance was to get back to the other side of the river and out in the open, but I didn't make it farther than ten steps. A solid mass struck me and my vision blurred as I hit the ground. My hands scraped over dirt and the gun clattered out of my hands.

Rough hands grabbed at me and I couldn't breathe. Couldn't see. I tried to scream again, but no sound came out. Someone was on top of me and I had to fight. Had to.

"Stop," a deep voice commanded. He shoved me hard against the ground and sharp bits of gravel cut into my cheek. "It will be worse for you if you resist."

I heard the clank of iron as my wrists were locked behind me. My attacker dragged me onto my knees while another man held a lantern up to my face. That was when I realized I wasn't surrounded by outlaws.

The two men wore dark uniforms and headdresses that were easy to recognize even in the dim light. They were city police and I was under arrest.

~

My head was bowed, knees pressed to the stone floor of the

holding cell with my wrists cuffed behind me. I could hear a strident voice, demanding answers, but I didn't dare look up.

"What is your name?"

I answered but was trembling so hard that the interrogator couldn't hear me.

"What is your name?" he repeated, the question striking against the bare walls.

"Soling," I said again, trying to raise my voice as much as I dared. "Family name Jin."

My stomach twisted. Why hadn't I just stayed in the marketplace?

"Who did you come here with?"

Biting down on my lower lip, I shook my head. "No one. I came alone."

I didn't dare think of the consequences if I was caught in the lie, but I couldn't bear to implicate Hu. He'd done nothing wrong. I'd done nothing wrong, either, but I remembered how it had been when imperial soldiers had swept through our house after Father was arrested.

Anything I said would only make it worse. There was no way to set things right once accused.

Fear was a sign of weakness and weakness was a sign of guilt. It was best to do nothing, say nothing. I kept my eyes lowered and tried to think of home. Of my brother, Tian. Of Mother.

"Do you know that smuggling weapons is a crime punishable by death?" the interrogator prodded.

My heart stopped. "W—weapons? But I wasn't—"

"Speak up!"

"You're frightening her."

A new, calmer voice came from outside the bars. My gaze flickered up briefly to see a tall man in a high-collared jacket standing outside the cell. He was dressed in black from head to toe, his robe devoid of any insignia. The moment he spoke, the interrogation ceased. It was clear to me who held the authority here.

He stroked a long, sharp beard as he regarded me, and I ducked away, realizing I had been staring for too long.

"I commend you for your dedication, Lieutenant, but the girl doesn't look like a bloodthirsty rebel to me."

"The reports from Thistle Mountain claim the rebellion boasts men and women in their ranks. Children as well." I stared at the pair of boots that came to rest before me. "What is a woman doing alone in the capital? And her feet aren't properly bound."

Manchurian women were forbidden to bind their feet in the custom of the Han. Yet these men would now use it to condemn me?

"Please." I spoke to the dirt floor, but I hoped the newcomer could hear the sincerity in my tone. "I am loyal to the empire. I have no weapons."

"Quiet!" the lieutenant barked. His boot stomped alarmingly close to my hand where it lay pressed to the floor, and I shrank back.

"So she was asking many questions in the market?" the tall official interrupted.

"And she was transporting that strange device."

"Indeed. Look up at me."

Despite the direct command, I hesitated. The tone that I had at first considered soothing now rang cold.

When I tilted my head back, I saw the two men staring down at me. The man in black was the elder of the two, a senior in age as well as rank.

For his advanced age, his face was unexpectedly smooth. This was a face that rarely smiled. A face that rarely showed any emotion at all. He wasn't defending me; he had simply not yet decided.

He held out his hand to reveal the puzzle box. "How did you get this?"

"It was left to our family by my father."

"And how did he come to possess it."

"I don't know."

He raised his eyebrows sharply, and it was enough to make my pulse jump in fear.

"A...a gift. It's just a box." I prayed they would just take it and let me go.

"Just a box," he repeated slowly, turning the steel cube around in his hands.

"Rebel spies are somehow infiltrating our cities. Getting past the defenses to take the guards by surprise." Once again, the lieutenant's questions were aimed at me. "What's inside? Explosives? Poison?"

"Nothing. Nothing like that. I...I don't know what's inside." At least that was true.

The man in black halted the questioning with a flick of his hand. I inched back as he neared only to have the lieutenant growl at me to remain still. I was more afraid of the quiet one.

"Weapons can take many forms nowadays," he said. "Family name of Jin, you said?"

"Yes, sir."

"Jin Soling."

I didn't like how my name sounded on his lips. Sharp, cynical. Still, I nodded obediently.

"You are not from around here, Miss Jin."

I didn't dare say anything but the truth. "I was born in Peking."

He spoke to me then in a language I hadn't heard in many years. It took me a moment to recognize the words. He was speaking Manchurian, the language of my ancestors.

The official was asking me why I was so far from home.

"Forgive me, sir. I don't know enough to answer in Manchurian, but our family was exiled."

My face burned hot with shame. All these years, but the humiliation of being thrown out of the capital had not faded. I felt all the more a criminal now for it.

He returned to the more common dialect of the region. "I must tell you, young miss, it appears you've made an effort to attract attention. A woman traveling alone and wearing those"—he looked me up and down—"mannish clothes."

It was becoming apparent who, or what, the man in black was. The lieutenant had similarly deferred to him without referring to him by title, and Manchurian was only spoken in exclusive circles within the imperial court. The man had to be a senior official or a member of the Forbidden Guard. The Emperor's secret police.

If I was afraid before, I was terrified now.

"The city guards feared you had brought some mysterious weapon into the city." His tone remained courteous, chillingly so as he held up the box. "This is certainly no ordinary trinket."

"It isn't a weapon, I swear on all of heaven. I can show you."

He tested the weight of the steel in his palm. "No, I don't think I will allow that."

"The box belonged to my father." If I thought that begging would help, I would have done so. I could think of nothing to do but reveal the whole truth. "My father was once the Emperor's chief engineer."

A light sparked in his eyes. "A bold lie."

I shook my head furiously. "I wouldn't dare."

Without another word, he swept out of the cell and my stomach sank. I'd made an awful mistake. Father had been denounced as a traitor. He was also known for his experiments with gunpowder.

When no one came back after several minutes, I struggled to my feet. The rope cut into my wrists. Trying to reposition my hands only made the pain worse. An hour must have dragged by, or at least I thought so. There was no way to tell time in here.

If they truly thought I was a rebel spy, would they interrogate me and force me to confess? Or would they have me executed and be done with it? I blinked back tears. All I wanted to do was go home.

When the door opened again, I breathed deep to try to compose myself. It was the man in black. The Manchurian.

"Miss Jin." He approached and I started as a knife flashed in his hand, but he moved behind me to cut my bonds. "I do apologize. With the rebel faction growing in strength, the authorities must take every precaution."

He stepped back and even affected a slight bow in apology. I didn't know how to react to the sudden change in how I was being treated.

"I can go then?" I asked meekly.

My wrists burned as I stared at him. He didn't appear so tall up close, yet his presence seemed even more menacing as he regarded me with a blank expression.

"Yes, you can go," he said, his tone crisp. "You will be coming with me."

4

I gripped the side of the sampan as the gunpowder engine propelled us through the water. Swarms of gnats hovered over the river's surface, and the lantern from the boat cut a swath of light through the haze. The Manchurian official sat beside me.

The vessel was large enough to accommodate the two of us along with a boatman at the helm. A guardsman stood at the rear of the barge with a rifle in his hands.

"Inspector, may I ask where are we going?"

The others referred to him as Inspector Aguda. I was right about his origins. The inspector traveled with an armed escort, and this was no fisherman's vessel. It sliced like a knife through the water.

Aguda glanced to my hands, which were clenched tight in my lap. "Rest easy, Miss Jin. You are no longer a prisoner."

Wasn't I?

My heart pounded so hard my chest hurt. The inspector wanted something from me, but I was too frightened to ask what it could be. The engine hummed along, and a cloud of sulfur smoke grew thick around us.

"How familiar are you with your father's work?" Aguda asked after a stretch of silence.

The hairs on my neck rose in warning. "I don't know anything of it."

"A shame. Of course, one could hardly expect a simple woman to understand something so complex," he said with a snort.

He was baiting me. I stared ahead, refusing to be caught. Yes, I was simpleminded. Useless and of no value to anyone. If Aguda would only be convinced of that and let me go. Instead the boat continued down the river, coughing on gunpowder and taking me farther away from home.

I took to watching the sway of the lantern hanging overhead and thinking of my family. They would be expecting me tomorrow evening, but I wouldn't be there to ask for my brother's report on what he had learned in school. Mother would lie in bed, unblinking as Nan explained that I hadn't come back. That I was gone.

Inspector Aguda stared into the night, his posture rigid like a temple statue. Whatever he wanted, it had something to do with Father, but I couldn't imagine what that would be. It had been eight years since his death. I just prayed he would let me go.

Eventually, I nodded off. I didn't know how much time had passed when I woke up, but my neck was sore and the sun was up. The sampan swayed gently in the river and the engine lay silent.

"Where are we?" I asked.

Some port that I wasn't allowed to know the name of. I remained beneath the protective awning while larger vessels surrounded the sampan. With no other explanation, Inspector Aguda ordered me onto a rope ladder where I half climbed and was half pulled onto the deck of one of the riverboats. The inspector followed immediately behind me.

Archers with crossbows were positioned all along the deck, and the ship had been fitted with cannons for defense.

"The rebels have taken to raiding ships along the river," Aguda told me. "But they wouldn't dare attack a ship of this class."

"If the rebels are such a threat, why not send the imperial army to be rid of them?" I asked once the inspector had directed me below deck.

"A mob of angry peasants and laborers are hardly worth the Emperor's notice," he replied. "Our empire faces a larger threat. A foreign enemy that has already invaded our shores."

A sleeping berth had been arranged for me, and Aguda left me alone with my thoughts. Did he believe that my father had some secret weapon that could help the Emperor in his war? What would happen when the inspector found out the steel box held nothing of use?

Food was brought to me at mealtime and tea in between. Otherwise I was left undisturbed for the remainder of the day. Gunpowder was too unpredictable for use in anything but the smallest of vessels, so the ship relied on wind power and the grace of the current as we sailed down the river.

I made several requests to speak with Inspector Aguda, but to my frustration, I was ignored as one day went by and then another. Only after three days did he come to the curtain that separated my sleeping area from the rest of the crew.

"Have you sent word to my family?" I asked him anxiously. Merchant Hu would have known something had happened when I didn't show up at our meeting place, but he was unaware of where I was or who had taken me. By now, he would have returned to our village with the alarming news.

"We have more urgent matters to attend to."

"But my mother will worry."

The inspector was unmoved. "Country first and family second," he droned. "Especially in a time like this."

I had to bite my tongue. Aguda held complete power over me.

"Perhaps when we reach our destination," he relented, though his dismissive tone was hardly any comfort.

"Where would that be?"

Inspector Aguda's answers, when he gave them, were always simple. "Canton."

"But that journey would take a week," I said with a gasp. A week with my family not knowing what had become of me. "Why must we go to Canton?"

A hollow feeling settled in my chest. My life was no longer my own. I was at the inspector's mercy.

"All will be made clear in time," was all he said.

I hated him. I hated the imperial authority that could demand everything from its subjects, every last drop of blood, and offer nothing in return.

But even thinking such things was akin to treason, so I kept quiet.

Several days later, I watched from the bow as the river funneled into a canal. A sprawling city loomed on the horizon, at least three times the size of Changsha. I was an ant lost on a mountain.

As we docked, Inspector Aguda gestured to me. "Come with me, Miss Jin. They're waiting for us."

Beyond his shoulder, I could see a row of warehouses along the water. From what little I knew, Canton was a crowded city at the mouth of the river full of brothels and gambling dens. It was also swarming with *Yangguizi*—or so the rumors said.

Inspector Aguda educated me on one crucial element in the last day of our approach. Our empire had been forced to grant access to the foreigners after our defeat. From their section of the port, they were able to sell and trade whatever goods they pleased and there was little the empire could do to stop them.

"Their commerce usually involves opium," Aguda said darkly. "It also involves the abduction of men and women."

My countrymen. Our people. What was becoming of our land?

I'd never seen a foreigner before, and they grew even more twisted in my mind. Pale, soulless demons. I searched for ghost-white skin at the dock, bracing myself for the sight. But only my own countrymen wandered among the boats.

Inspector Aguda preceded me down the plank and onto the dock. I stepped in-line alongside him, and a small escort of armed men joined us. I wished I had my needle gun, though it was hardly any protection in this strange place. It didn't matter. All of my belongings had been taken away: the puzzle box, my gun, every last coin I'd brought with me.

Aguda took the lead, keeping me close by his side. A rifleman slung his weapon over one shoulder and followed closely behind. Escape never entered my thoughts. Disobedience to imperial authority meant death.

A layer of smudge and grime lay over the area, from the flat stones that lined the streets, to the walls of the buildings. Even when we moved away from the water, the swampy smell of the docks stayed in the air. Businesses were laid out side by side and crammed together along the canals. Canton was a place where too much was happening in too small a space.

As we navigated deeper into the streets, the clinging dampness of the docks receded, though the air remained heavy. Aguda led us to what appeared to be a municipal building that rose three stories high. The signboard over the front door declared it as a trade office.

Inside, the hallways were swept and every surface was polished meticulously clean. I was taken to a room on the first floor where a female maidservant waited, a young girl of fifteen years at most. The building contained some sleeping quarters as well, it would seem. I looked to the inspector with a question in my eyes.

"Presentable clothing has been arranged for your use. Prepare yourself quickly," Aguda instructed before backing out of the room.

The girl directed me to a wooden tub that had been set up in a washroom. There she helped me out of my jacket and robe and loosened my hair from its knot. It had been a long time since I'd been attended to for a bath. I sank obediently into the heated water and let the steam envelop me like a shield.

Once the layers of dust and soot were removed, the maidservant returned to help me dress. I certainly wasn't being treated as a prisoner. I was being treated like an honored guest.

"Who is it that I'm preparing to meet?" I asked the girl.

She only shook her head and proceeded to help me into a deep green *qipao*. The neckline and hem were outlined by a border of dark brocade. A phoenix had been embroidered onto the front with the wings spread in flight, etched with vermillion and gold.

I ran my hands over the brilliant threads, and the touch of silk whispered memories to me. Once again, that distant dream.

Next the maidservant drew a comb through my hair before plaiting and tying it into an elaborate swallowtail knot. A fan-shaped ornament was pinned over my crown to complete the headdress. When she held up a mirror for me, an eerie feeling fluttered in my stomach.

I looked like Mother.

Or at least how she used to look. In Peking, she had prepared herself every day. She had always appeared regal to me; an empress in our home.

When we'd first come to Linhua village, Mother had tried to maintain her appearance even though we never had any visitors. She dressed us each day as if we were still in Peking, where we had to present ourselves accordingly as the family of a high-ranking minister. There were days when I believed our life would continue, that we would one day return, even though Father was gone.

I was so young then. So naive and full of empty wishes.

After she gave birth to Tian, Mother fell into a deep fog, and Nan became busy with the baby. At first the opium had been for the pain as Mother recovered, but soon she rarely left her room.

"It feels like everything happened so long ago," Mother had murmured to me. The cloying smoke formed a curtain between us. "All of this has happened to someone else. Someone who looks like me."

It was worse when Mother spoke from within the opium dream than when she said nothing at all. She had wasted away for years now and I had let her.

"My lady?" the attendant said, interrupting my memories.

I nodded my approval absently, and the mismatched reflection in the mirror nodded back at me. The maidservant went to open the door, and I saw Inspector Aguda stationed at the end of the hall.

"Miss Jin."

He bowed stiffly as I approached and then spoke in a hushed tone as he led me down the corridor.

"Remember to keep your eyes lowered. The proper address is the full kowtow. When you are done, wait with head bowed to be spoken to."

The fearsome inspector was reciting etiquette like a lowly retainer. He pushed open a set of double doors to reveal an empty reception hall. A single person emerged from behind a painted screen at the opposite end.

Curiosity made me forget the inspector's warning. I peered at the man dressed in the embroidered blue robe before me, trying to discern why I had been brought before someone so young. There was a hint of yellow cloth peeking from the edge of his sleeve, but I didn't know what to make of it. There was a sharpness about his cheekbones and his chin tapered to a point. The black eyes hardened as I met his gaze.

With that, the last of the fog around me lifted. I knew his face. I knew who this was.

"*Imperial Highness.*" With a gasp, I dropped to the floor and tapped my forehead against the wooden floorboards.

The man that stood before me, who I had so rudely stared at, was Yizhu, the crown prince of the empire. I pressed my head to ground two more times.

The doors snapped shut behind me while I kept my head down and tried to make myself as still and small as possible. I was alone with the man that would one day be our Emperor.

"Please accept the sincerest apologies of this most unworthy servant," I blurted out, not realizing until too late that I was breaking yet another rule of conduct: *wait to be addressed first.* Squeezing my eyes shut in horror, I sank even lower to the floor.

"Rise," the prince said after forcing me to wait for an interminable amount of time.

I did as he commanded and my knees shook as I heard the prince approach.

"Lift your head."

I was a puppet on a string, controlled by years of adhering to the strictest rules of etiquette.

"You are indeed the daughter of Minister Jin Zhi-fu," he pronounced. "His Imperial Highness remembers you."

I felt sick inside. Yizhu's father had ordered my own father's execution.

We had met once as children. A young boy had wandered into my father's workshop one day. He looked to be the same age as me, but I was taller. Without a word, he had reached for a model of a miniature rickshaw pulled by an automaton. I snatched the model away and started to scold the boy, but a pair of imperial eunuchs burst into the room.

They reprimanded me for offending an imperial prince and then called for a bamboo rod to be brought immediately. I was forced to hold out my hand and count out each blow as the rod struck. My father could do nothing but stand by while I was punished, and the eunuchs stopped short of breaking my hand, but I could barely move it for days.

I was only six years old.

"Master Jin was my tutor and a great man," the prince began. "He taught me many things."

"His Imperial Highness's kind words bring peace to my father's spirit."

Bitterness filled my mouth even as the words spilled out. There was no apology in the prince's tone, yet he knew my father had been blamed for the failure of an entire kingdom. There was nothing that could bring peace to his soul.

Yizhu gestured to the table at his side. "Inspector Aguda found these in your possession."

My acupuncture case lay open. Yizhu picked up one of the thin needles to examine it in the light.

"The Western devils believe that acupuncture is nothing but a folk remedy. Our weapons are primitive and outdated. We are easy prey."

He looked directly at me and I fought the urge to duck away.

As Prince Yizhu returned the needle to its place, I caught a glimpse of his expression. Lines of quiet anger cut deep, but only for a moment. When he raised his head, his look was impenetrable. To show emotion was a weakness.

"Do you think the *Yangguizi* are correct?" Yizhu asked me. "That our ways are ancient and misguided?"

I could sense the teeth behind the question, and I struggled to find a proper answer. "How can it be a mistake to follow tradition? Our empire is the greatest under heaven and always will be."

Yizhu laughed and the sound rang out flat in the chamber. "A good answer, Soling."

My palms started to sweat. I didn't like that the crown prince knew my given name.

"A perfect answer," Yizhu continued. "The same answer echoed by every minister and every general that serves the dragon throne. The same answer we have heard from every scientist since the blade fell over Master Jin's neck."

My chest squeezed so tight I could barely breathe. The crown prince was being cruel, but the Emperor's son could be as cruel as he wanted to be.

"But your father once told us something different," he went on. "He once said that we needed to build warships and cannons and flying machines to rival the ones we had glimpsed from the West. Our empire contains the men and the minds to surpass these fledgling kingdoms. Have you seen the land of '*England*' on a map?"

I shook my head. The foreign name was unfamiliar to me.

"I have, Soling. The size of it is smaller than Hunan province. How could anything so insignificant challenge us?" He was right in front of me now. I could feel his heated breath against my face. "Master Jin Zhi-fu warned us all that if we didn't act soon, it would be too late. That this tiny kingdom would bring us to our knees. Yet who could believe such nonsense?"

The silk of his robe swiped against me as he stalked away. Prince Yizhu suddenly bent over and squeezed his eyes shut, touching two fingers to his temple. Even the pained gesture appeared regal. He was quiet for so long that I began to worry, at first for myself, but then for him.

"Imperial Highness, are you not feeling well?"

He ignored my question. "It is not too late for us. Our empire understands the rise and fall of dynasties. We are the Middle Kingdom, the greatest empire under heaven."

What was I expected to do? Agree, just as he'd criticized me for doing moments earlier? Respond that the Son of Heaven would rule for a thousand years?

Some of the fire had drained from his speech, but he remained gravely serious. "My Imperial Father didn't fully understand the danger the empire faced. He made the mistake of trusting the words of his advisers and never seeing for himself. That is why this prince is here in Canton, this harbor of foreign devils and traitors. That is why he asked that you be found."

"Me?" I trembled at the sudden intensity in his eyes.

No one was allowed to speak ill about the Emperor. Certainly not a prince who could challenge his father for power. I was afraid now to find out what he expected of me.

"The prince finds himself in need of men like your father," Yizhu said.

Sadness swept over me. He didn't even realize the irony of it all.

"Father believed in serving the Emperor above all else." A lump formed in my throat. "But it's too late now. I'm not my father. I don't know half of what he knew."

"Your father continues to serve our empire," Yizhu proclaimed.

I looked up at him in confusion. "How?"

"His research was never destroyed." The prince's hard, black eyes met mine. "The Emperor failed to recognize your father's importance to our empire, but I will not make that mistake. I intend to continue his work to build an army. My own army."

5

I dug my nails into my palms so the pain would wake me up. I had to be dreaming because what Prince Yizhu was telling me made no sense.

After Father's execution, the imperial authorities had come to take everything: his writings, the inventions, all his sketches and scribblings. Everything was burned in front of the Ministry. Our family was left with nothing.

"Master Jin's research remains in the vaults of the imperial palace. The Ministry of Science has studied every last scrap of paper," Yizhu went on dispassionately.

The new Ministry. The one that had declared Father's ideas misguided and dangerous.

"Why?" My eyes stung with tears, but I wouldn't let them fall.

"Because knowledge is the true sword."

I could barely gather my breath to speak. When I did, the words came out strained. "If my father hadn't been—if he were alive, he would have devoted everything to your cause."

The prince's demeanor remained cold and detached. Royal blood truly flowed through his veins, and my pain was insignificant, anyone's pain was beneath him. "As I recall, Master Jin had many loyal disciples."

"Who were all purged from the Ministry," I replied bitterly, not caring if I drew his wrath with my insolence.

"The prince has heard that Jin treated his disciples like family. His daughter was well-known and accepted among them. As I recall, she was a frequent visitor to the Ministry of Science."

Yizhu fixed me with a pointed look. The injustice of our first meeting came back to me. I had been justified in scolding the little boy who'd so carelessly mishandled one of Father's works, but I'd learned that right and wrong meant nothing against imperial authority.

"Do you know the men who worked beneath your father? Would you recognize them to this day?"

I bowed my head in apology. "I was merely a child, Imperial Highness."

I had been pretending my childhood was from another life for so long, it was easy to lie now, even to the crown prince. That girl was someone else.

He snorted. "The prince wishes he had the luxury of forgetting."

Tension gathered in his jaw. His shoulders were raised and the cords of his neck pulled taut. Yizhu halted the interrogation and turned away, pressing a hand to his temple.

It was hard to think of the two of us as being the same age. At that moment, Yizhu was at once a young man and an old one. I noticed the pallor in his complexion and how his hands were clenched tight. How long had he been doing that?

My physician's training took over. "Is the prince not feeling well?"

I started to approach, but Yizhu flashed me a look that stopped me cold. With a single command, the doors swung open. Inspector Aguda entered and kowtowed to pay his respect before rising to stand beside me.

"Bring her to Engineer Chen."

Yizhu's abrupt change left me confused, but I admit I was relieved to be free of him. Every moment within the presence of royalty was dangerous. A single word could change my life and a single mistake could end it.

The crown prince was no was no longer watching us as we departed. His eyes were closed and he stood very still in the center of the room, as if willing the universe to stop moving.

My anger receded, curling up and growing quiet within me as we left the room. I wasn't worthy of judging the actions of an Emperor or a prince. Men of power had to make difficult decisions, Father had told me more than once. Decisions that could affect hundreds or thousands of lives.

Father had gone to the imperial palace that night without fear, while I had clung to his hand until the very edge of our courtyard where the servants had to pry me away. I didn't know anything about honor or courage. I was just a little girl who had wanted her father to stay.

The hallway outside was empty. Where was the entourage of attendants and guards who always accompanied the crown prince? Prince Yizhu appeared to be keeping his presence in Canton a secret.

The moment the doors closed behind us, Inspector Aguda spoke. "Do you recall a man named Yang Hanzhu?" he asked.

"No."

Instinct told me to lie and I'd done so without thinking. Of all my father's associates, I remembered Yang most of all. Uncle Hanzhu, I'd called him, though he was only ten years or so older than me. I could see him now, smiling at me crookedly, a mischievous gleam in his eyes.

"What comes first, Ling-ling? Smoke or fire?"

"No?" He went on regardless. "A man who goes by Yang has surfaced in the port cities of the empire. He's been reported in Canton, Macau, occasionally to the north as well. He appears to be a trader of some sort, but stays in the foreign concessions where we have limited authority. Our informers have been attempting to track him for nearly a year. We suspect he is the same chemist who served under your father. It is here that your assistance is required."

"But I told you I don't know this man."

Aguda was unperturbed. "He'll know who you are. Yang Hanzhu was fiercely loyal to your father. Your presence will draw him out into the open."

He pushed at the double doors at the end of the corridor. I was met by a study filled with shelves and shelves of books. A wave of longing hit me.

It was a library, like the grand book rooms in the Ministry I had explored when I was a little girl. Rows of shelves lined the wall cluttered with books and charts. Secret writings that contained so much undiscovered knowledge.

A desk was situated at the center of the room, and behind it sat a young man. To his left, I could see some sort of elaborate framework with the wings of a bird built out of rattan, but it had been set aside. Instead, my puzzle box was set before him. A spark lantern created a sphere of light that glinted off the steel surface.

The young man's eyes were hidden behind a pair of brass-rimmed spectacles that appeared unwieldy over his face. He wore an official black cap adorned with a mother-of-pearl ornament at the crown that denoted his rank. Beneath the headdress, his hair was braided neatly into a thick queue that he had thrown carelessly over one shoulder.

He was so absorbed in his endeavors that he didn't even glance up as Inspector Aguda ushered me inside.

The inspector cleared his throat. "Mister Chen."

The man shot to his feet and pulled off his spectacles. I saw now that they were for magnification rather than corrective purposes. His eyesight appeared undoubtedly clear, and an odd expression crossed his face when he focused on me.

He bowed stiffly with the spectacles dangling forgotten from his hand. "Inspector Aguda."

The address was spoken with care, with an effort toward formality.

"His Imperial Highness instructed me to bring Miss Jin to you."

"Thank you, Inspector."

Aguda retreated from the room, leaving me alone with the stranger. From his clothing, I could discern he was yet another imperial bureaucrat. He was of a lower rank, yet one still demanding respect.

Now that the spectacles were removed, his eyes revealed themselves to be a rich brown in color, set deep and serious. He had a prominent nose with a noticeable dip in the angle of the bridge that gave him an intriguing look.

His mouth pressed tight. "I apologize, miss. I don't believe the inspector knows."

I frowned at him. "I don't understand, sir."

He blinked rapidly, struggling for words. "What I mean is that —of course, you don't know, either."

Engineer Chen looked to be in his twenties, perhaps eight or nine years my senior. For a man who had earned a place in the crown prince's retinue, he seemed to lose his composure quite easily.

"My name is Soling, family name Jin," I offered, realizing we hadn't been introduced.

He sighed. Looking down, he folded the spectacles, one side and then the other with deliberate care, before placing them in the pocket of his mandarin jacket. When he looked at me again, a disturbing stillness had settled over him. A stillness that was not at all calm.

"Chen Chang-wei," he replied, then waited for my reply.

I had none. My mind latched onto his name, repeating it over and over.

Chen Chang-wei.

Chen Chang-wei was the name of the man I was supposed to marry. A man I had never seen, yet of whom my parents had always spoken of so highly.

That man was looking at me now, his dark eyes searching my face. His mouth lifted in an odd half expression that didn't know what it wanted to be. Was it acknowledgment or apology or something else entirely?

We both looked away at the same time.

His attention shifted to the puzzle box. "This is Japanese, made of *tamahagane* steel. The same steel used in their katanas." My heart was pounding so loud that his words all sounded like nonsense to me. I was standing next to my once-betrothed who was making a concerted effort not to look at me.

"See these here?" He ran a finger along the designs etched into the steel surface. "These patterns are a signature of the Yosegi region."

I came closer because it would have seemed odd not to. "Inspector Aguda thought it was a weapon."

The desk remained between us and I was grateful. There was a time, many years ago, when I had been insatiably curious about my husband-to-be. Now that broken promise remained like a chasm between us.

"The inspector is suspicious of everything," Chang-wei said, turning the box over and over in his hands. "Do you know how to open this?"

I nodded and took the box from his hands. As I ran my fingers along the surface, searching for the catch, I could feel Chang-wei's gaze on me.

A flush crept up my neck until the very tips of my ears burned. "You're in the Emperor's service?" I asked him.

"Yes."

My throat had gone dry. "All this time."

"Not quite."

The catch in his words made me look up, but I quickly ducked back down. I located the trigger panel on the box and slid the metal strip to the side. The action unlocked another panel, and then another one. Soon the gears took over and the box opened on its own in a series of whirs and clicks. We both watched the cascade of motion as if in a trance.

Chen Chang-wei.

I used to wonder what he looked like. I'd hoped, in girlish fashion, that he wouldn't be ugly. In the tradition of blind marriages, once our union was arranged, we weren't to meet until the wedding. I was banished from the Ministry from that day forward as well. Father had stressed that I was becoming a woman, no longer a child to run about the laboratories.

Now I knew that Chang-wei wasn't ugly, but I didn't know what else to think of him.

Though we were alone, I dropped my voice low. "Why does the crown prince want Yang Hanzhu?"

I saw a muscle twitch along his jaw. "When Yang was with the Ministry, he was involved in experiments with gunpowder. Special formulas that could be used for fuel."

"But we already have gunpowder engines."

"For small or midsized machinery. As we tried to scale upward, the mixture we used would become unpredictable. It wouldn't yield enough power."

"The last year Father held office, the Ministry had become devoted completely to the development of weapons," I recalled.

"Because of the war. The Emperor wanted more powerful cannons, but your father had another idea. He had seen what some of the Western ships were capable of."

The devil ships. But Father had refused to call them that.

"The *Yingguo* ships are powered by steam and shielded with

iron," Chang-wei went on. "During the invasion, it didn't matter how fast our war junks could sail. They were no match."

Realization sparked within me. "The empire has been building ships?"

"Armored ones like the foreigners have. And cannons and war machines as well. Though most of it is Crown Prince Yizhu's doing. He has made it his primary pursuit, and his imperial father indulges him."

I thought of all the factories that had been set up. The increased production in the mines. Farmers had been dragged from the fields and put to work by imperial decree. Even children were being summoned to labor at a young age. All of this had been done at the whim of a prince who had barely reached manhood?

Yet Prince Yizhu valued my father's work while the Emperor had not.

"The empire wants to take back our ports and expel the foreigners," Chang-wei explained. "But our own harbors are filled with foreign gunships now. We'll need a massive fleet to challenge them.

"Your father began to experiment with a gunpowder formula that was powerful enough to drive these large-scale engines. We have a reserve, but the supply is low and the factories haven't been able to replicate it successfully." He leaned closer, dropping to a whisper and speaking rapidly. "Prince Yizhu is not the Emperor's oldest son, but for now he holds favor. There are many conspirators in the imperial court who wish to see him discredited. If we do not show progress soon, all of our efforts will be for nothing."

If Chang-wei only knew what the crown prince's push for progress had done to us out in the provinces. Forced conscriptions, poor conditions.

"Do you know there have been two explosions within the factories in our province alone within the last three months?" I asked him. "Nearly twenty people were killed in an accident in Shaoyang. Many others were very badly burned."

I hadn't known at the time that the factories were trying to refine gunpowder. Father had lost his arm in a much smaller accident in his lab. The process was unpredictable and dangerous at best, and deadly when things went wrong.

At least Chang-wei appeared regretful. "Those deaths were a tragedy. I can only hope further accidents can be prevented."

I tried to absorb everything Chang-wei was telling me and was again swept up in a wave of sadness.

"If the Emperor had only recognized my father's vision sooner, then you would have everything you needed. Father wouldn't have had to die."

He was close enough that I could see the tiny creases at the corners of his eyes and the tightening of his jaw. A look of sorrow crossed his face. "I know."

Both of us fell silent. For a long time now, I had been trying to figure out why my father was sentenced to death. The Emperor had needed someone to take the blame, but why his chief engineer? And Father had gone like a general of some ancient army, falling willingly upon his sword.

All these years and I still didn't know the answer.

"So you're not trying to arrest Yang?" I ventured.

"No, we need his help. I just—" He paused and looked over his shoulder at the closed door. "I didn't think they would involve you."

Chen Chang-wei had not been surprised to see me. He seemed to have known who I was the moment I walked in the door. This after never having met, at least not formally.

"It was no accident that the secret police were in Changsha," I said accusingly.

"Miss Jin, you must understand—"

"The inspector was there looking for me?"

"Not you specifically."

But for my family. For some tie to my father that they could hold over Yang Hanzhu. Inspector Aguda had found me first and decided I was enough leverage for now.

"I knew I couldn't trust you," I muttered. "Any of you."

It wouldn't have been difficult for the secret police to hunt us down. We'd gone to Changsha because our servants had family there. They'd offered shelter out of loyalty. Over time, all but Nan had left and we'd retreated to the village of Linhua because it was more secluded. It had seemed a place where one could forget.

"You were the one who told the secret police about Yang, weren't you?" I demanded. "Did you tell them how close he was to our family? That he was one of Father's most trusted men?"

Unlike Chen Chang-wei, Yang had remained loyal to Father's memory. He hadn't gone back to serve the same men who'd turned on us.

"I did it only for the sake of the empire," he said gravely. "This is what Minister Jin would have wanted."

He turned his attention back to the puzzle box in front of us and I did the same. It was easier than having to look at him.

I didn't want any part of the Emperor's war. Our family had already sacrificed enough.

Reaching inside, I pulled on a hidden lever to activate the second sequence, and a series of panels folded open to reveal the inner compartment.

Chang-wei's gaze sharpened at sight of the device inside. It was a metal plate fixed with a series of knobs and bolts coiled with wire. He picked it up by the corner, holding it up to the light.

"Do you know what it is?" My anger was pushed back momentarily by my curiosity. I had wondered for years.

His brow furrowed. "I don't have any idea. The empire of Japan has made quite a few advancements in small-scale devices, but we've lost all contact with their engineering corps."

"I figured it must be broken. It doesn't do anything."

"Perhaps," he said, absorbed with inspecting the device.

The door opened, and with a deftness that surprised me, Chang-wei dropped the device down into his sleeve before glancing over his shoulder.

"Inspector Aguda."

He came up behind us, and his black eyes narrowed at the open puzzle box.

"A Japanese art piece," Chang-wei declared. "These were highly sought after by collectors several years back."

"What was inside?"

"It was empty." Chang-wei's tone betrayed nothing while my heart beat furiously in my chest.

"Empty?" Aguda echoed in disbelief, but the inspector always sounded skeptical.

"The box itself is rare and very valuable, though. Most likely Chief Engineer Jin received this treasure from the empire of Japan as a gift."

The inspector looked from Chang-wei over to me with one dark eyebrow raised menacingly. I thought of clear blue sky and tried to keep my expression as blank as possible.

"Have you told Miss Jin of our plan and why it is of the utmost importance that we have her cooperation?" Aguda's gaze remained fixed onto me as he spoke.

"It was your plan," Chang-wei corrected. "I'm not so certain this is the right course of action. Canton is very dangerous, especially the foreign settlement. I would be better able to handle myself if any situation should arise."

"Miss Jin is less likely to arouse Yang Hanzhu's suspicion," Aguda argued.

"I must formally object. I won't have her put in danger."

Chang-wei raised his voice for the first time, and even the inspector seemed taken aback. I remained silent through the exchange, confused by what was happening. First Chang-wei had concealed the device from Inspector Aguda, and now he sounded oddly protective.

Why would he care? Chang-wei wasn't responsible for me. Our arranged marriage had been dissolved when I was still a child.

"The crown prince has commanded it," Aguda declared.

The two men locked gazes. When neither backed down, I wondered who held the higher rank between them.

"If I help find Yang Hanzhu—" My voice came out weakly at first, and I cleared my throat before continuing. "If I help the crown prince, will our family name be restored?"

Chang-wei looked at me in surprise, but the inspector merely appeared annoyed. "It is not your place to make any demands here."

"Our family has lived in disgrace for these eight years." A new fire rose within me, spreading through my veins and giving me strength. "If no one else will speak for my father, then I must."

I didn't care for the Emperor's war with the foreign invaders. I only cared about my brother's future and my mother's well-being. If this was the only chance to help them, then I had to take it.

"If Prince Yizhu acknowledges my father wasn't to blame for the defeat and restores his name in the imperial archives, then I'll do what you ask."

"Is there anything else?" Aguda asked dryly.

I hadn't realized it was possible to negotiate for more. I swallowed before pressing on. "I want my family returned to Peking," I said, letting out a breath. Something told me that wasn't yet enough. "And I want our house restored to us."

Inspector Aguda laughed outright. "Maybe you should petition Prince Yizhu yourself, young miss. He might find it amusing that a peasant girl would be so bold."

"I am no peasant." I lifted my chin in defiance. I was tired of casting my gaze downward. "I'm of Manchurian blood, as you are. My ancestors served among the Eight Banners that founded this dynasty."

Rather than taking offense, Aguda appeared pleased. "See

now, Mister Chen? You can't say she doesn't have enough audacity for the task."

Chang-wei regarded me with a thoughtful expression. "Yang Hanzhu is known to be a very dangerous man. You must be careful not to trust him."

"I've always known him to be loyal," I countered.

"Why, I thought you didn't remember him?" Aguda pointed out.

I ignored his taunt. "What of my conditions?"

The inspector opened his mouth to retort, but Chang-wei interrupted him.

"Allow me to speak to Prince Yizhu on your behalf." His eyes were serious when they met mine. "I will do what I can, for the sake of your family. Your father was a great man who was always kind to me. I consider it my debt to him."

I didn't want to be moved by his words, but I felt a pang of longing nonetheless. My father had been more than kind. Father had promised me, his only daughter, to Chen Chang-wei. He had betrothed us to each other. Though the arrangement was nothing any longer, such bonds could not be so easily forgotten.

Chen Chang-wei, this stranger who was not quite a stranger to me, was the closest thing I had to an ally. Part of me wanted to trust him. I wanted to believe the man Father had chosen as my husband-to-be was at least worthy.

I looked to Inspector and then back to Chang-wei. "What do you need me to do?"

6

That night I stayed in one of the small apartments upstairs. The trading office was apparently a hideout for Prince Yizhu, who had his men stationed throughout the entire building. I was confined to a room, but at least there was a bed for me to sleep upon instead of a tiny berth on a riverboat.

After a slumber that was full of stops and starts, I awoke to blackness. A light tapping came from outside the door of the chamber, jerking me fully awake. It was early, too early for a visitor. The tapping came again, insistent.

I felt around for my slippers, then stumbled through the unfamiliar chamber with my hands out in front of me. The chill of the morning nipped at me through the light tunic and trousers I had been given.

When I finally opened the door, a faint halo of light greeted me. Chen Chang-wei stood in the hallway with a candle in hand. Thankfully it was dark and the door provided a shield. I shivered as I held on to it.

Chang-wei was fully dressed in his heavy robe and jacket. The material was dark in color and without adornment. Without the flicker of the candle he would have been completely invisible.

"There is something you need to know," he whispered urgently. The stiff politeness he'd maintained toward me the day before had disappeared. "Yang Hanzhu is no longer the same person you knew eight years ago. He's an outcast. An outlaw."

I rubbed a knuckle over my eyes. "Only because imperial authorities forced him out."

"Please reconsider," he entreated. "I said I would take your appeal before the prince. I'll do the same whether or not you cooperate with the inspector. I swear it."

"You'd have me defy the crown prince?" I asked incredulously, and Chang-wei fell silent. "We humble subjects don't exist to the Emperor or his exalted son unless we serve some purpose. Inspector Aguda went all the way to Hunan province to find me and bring me here. You and I both know the prince will have his way in the end."

The corners of Chang-wei's mouth turned downward at my irreverent tone, but he didn't contradict me. "You'll be outside the city wall," he warned.

"Aguda said I would be protected at all times."

"He can't possibly promise that. He has no authority in the foreign concession. Even the prince would find it difficult to exert any influence there."

He seemed so concerned and my pulse skipped. From the very first moment we'd met, he'd tried to protect me.

"Why did you hide the device yesterday?"

The shadows moved dramatically over his face, highlighting the definition in his cheekbones. "The imperial government is wary of all foreign implements and devices right now. I didn't want Inspector Aguda to have anything more to hold over you. If you want it back—"

"No, you keep it. I mean, for now." I stood there gripping the door, unsure of what Chang-wei had hoped to accomplish by dissuading me from going. I was at the mercy of the crown prince as much as he was.

What had happened to him when the Ministry was purged? And how had he come to serve the imperial court once more when all of Father's other men had been removed from office?

"Have you tried to contact Yang yourself?" I asked.

"I doubt he would respond favorably to such an attempt. We weren't—" He stopped short and started again. "Yang Hanzhu was highly ranked within the Ministry while I was no one of any importance."

Yet he was the one my father had betrothed me to. There was something missing here that I couldn't grasp.

Uncle Hanzhu had always made game of challenging my understanding of the world. *"What comes first? Smoke or fire?"*

Would Yang even still remember me? And even if he did, what sway could I possibly have over someone who had been evading the imperial authorities for years?

"Yang Hanzhu wouldn't do anything to harm me," I insisted, despite my doubts. "I'll tell him what you told me. That formula belongs to my father as much as it does Yang. He won't keep it from me."

Chang-wei looked less than convinced. Reaching into his robe, Chang-wei pulled out something from the inner pocket.

"At least take this with you." With a flick of his wrist, the fan unfolded. The candlelight reflected off an intricate web of silver spines.

"It's a bladed fan, razor-tipped along the edges," he explained. "If anyone gives you trouble, aim for the throat or the eyes."

He demonstrated with a quick swipe in the air that made me jump backward. Then he snapped the fan closed and turned it around to present it to me.

"A woman would be expected to carry a fan. No one will suspect anything."

The fan was surprisingly heavy in my hand. Carefully, I

unfolded it once more to give it a closer look. The spines were fashioned out of metal, then coated with lacquer. A painted border along the top hid the thin blades embedded between the silk.

Chang-wei seemed intent on protecting me in any way he could. It was hard for me to resent him.

"Mister Chen?" I felt too awkward to call him anything more familiar than that.

"Yes?"

"Can you help me send a message to my family? They don't know where I am and they'll worry."

"Of course I will."

"And if you could—" My fingers tightened over the door. "This is difficult to ask, but my family was waiting for me to return from the market after selling the box. I didn't leave them with much—"

"I will see that your family's needs are taken care of," he said graciously. "It would be my honor to do so."

The painstaking politeness had returned, but the candlelight flickered in his pupils, reflecting flecks of gold in them. Up close, alone with Chang-wei and embraced in darkness, I finally had my answer. It was the answer I had longed for since I'd known I was to be married to a young protégé of my father's.

My parents hadn't chosen poorly for me. I hugged my arms close to myself and did the one thing I'd always told myself not to do. I thought of what could have been.

"Thank you," I whispered, then ducked back into the room before Chang-wei could reply.

Inside, I leaned back against the door, eyes closed as I tried to catch my breath. After a pause, I could hear Chang-wei's footsteps retreating. I stayed in that same spot for a long time after they had faded away into nothingness.

~

By the first morning light, I was back on the streets of Canton in my "mannish" robe and mandarin jacket. My hair was once again in its austere bun, the same worn satchel slung over my shoulder. Inspector Aguda had also restored all of my possessions: the puzzle box, my acupuncture needles and my needle gun, which he had eyed with a look of amusement before handing it back to me.

Within the hour, I was alone in the bustling marketplace, or at least I appeared to be. I slipped into the throng and became just another head among many.

I thought of Tian and Mother as the crowd surrounded me. They would have to get by without me for a little longer, but if Chang-wei kept his promise. If Prince Yizhu could find it in his heart to be generous, then there was some hope for us.

Maybe bringing our family back to Peking wasn't the best solution, but it was better than wasting away in some backwater village. Mother could find comfort in her old surroundings among familiar faces. Tian wouldn't be conscripted to work the mines or factories.

For the first time, I had a purpose beyond survival. I had a chance to improve my family's fortune.

Despite Chang-wei's warnings, I wasn't afraid of Yang. In my heart, he was still Uncle Hanzhu to me. Despite all my promises to the inspector and the crown prince, I wouldn't allow Aguda to entrap him, either.

The doors of the shops were all open. Shoes and trinkets and bolts of cloth crowded the storefronts, displayed in such a way to catch one's eye. All manner of goods were traded through Canton.

"Don't look for my men. You won't see them," Aguda had instructed in his precise, clipped manner.

He had shown me a map of the city and traced out a rough course for me to follow. I threaded through the narrow streets now, over canals and bridges. A sampan glided down the waterway while I wove my way through the pedestrians along the bank. Before long, I found myself out of breath and realized I was racing through Canton. I forced myself to slow down.

A group of rickshaw drivers loitered at a street corner as they awaited their next fare. One of them knelt beside his vehicle, adjusting and applying grease to the gears that turned the wheels. He met my gaze briefly before spitting on the ground and turning away. One of the inspector's men?

I was too nervous. I had no talent for deception, but Aguda told me it wouldn't matter. If I was clumsy, all the better. I was so good at being conspicuous, and my goal was ultimately to be found.

Inspector Aguda had predicted rather smugly that it wouldn't take long for the news of my whereabouts to reach the elusive Yang.

"What comes first, Ling-ling?" Yang had asked me the last time I'd seen him. "Smoke or fire?"

It was a nickname that only he had used. A silly little childish name, but I didn't mind it from him.

Yang Hanzhu was young compared to most of the other members of the science corps. I'd overheard the others joking more than once how he was favored among the courtesans in the city. As a child among men, I hardly existed. I could dart in and out of the chambers of the Ministry of Science as if I were invisible. Yang was the only one who ever noticed me.

He had been standing in his laboratory, surrounded by oddly shaped glass containers. I was perched on top of a wooden stool and watching him with rapt attention.

All of the chemicals Yang usually worked with had been meticulously stored away for the day. Nothing was brewing or bubbling on the counter. There was only a small flask of clear liquid before him.

He'd held a joss stick over a candle until it ignited. "Smoke or fire?" he asked again.

"Fire!" I'd declared, proud of myself for answering so quickly. Had I been nine then. I suppose I would have been considered precocious at that age.

He waved the joss stick until the flame went out, then dropped a few pinches of what looked like sand into the liquid. I watched with delight as cloudy foam bubbled forth, but I knew there had to be more. Indeed there was. When he touched the smoldering stick to the foam, the end burst into flame once more.

I squealed with delight. Yang was a sorcerer, a trickster, the most interesting person in the world.

He blew out the small fire and handed the stub to me. "You try now, Ling-ling."

The stick ignited for me as well. Fire from smoke. This wasn't magic; it was wonderful and secret knowledge and I wanted it so badly.

Not even a year after that, Father was dead and Uncle Hanzhu was listed among the names of the condemned.

That was the other reason I had agreed to find Yang. If my father could be redeemed, then perhaps Yang could be redeemed as well. He wouldn't have to hide away like a criminal.

By the time I reached the warehouse district, sweat was pouring down my face. Tepid air rose from the canals and clung to me like a tangle of blankets that were neither comforting nor welcome.

It was the sort of heat that was on a constant simmer and made everyone think and move a little slower. I ran the edge of my sleeve over my brow. Workmen in muted grays and browns paused to watch me as I passed by. The bladed fan weighed down my front pocket, though it was hardly a comfort.

The story I was to use was the same one that had brought me to the market in Changsha. As Aguda had instructed, I headed to the noted Hongmen of the Thirteen Factories to make a deal. Though recognized as Chinese, the powerful guild-merchants maintained offices and warehouses near the waterfront.

Just beyond the wall were barbarian houses that the foreign traders occupied. My country, the land of my birth, no longer belonged to me and my countrymen. I was in a strange and alien land.

I slipped between two buildings and my breath stopped. For the first time, I had a clear line of sight out to the harbor. Out over the green gray waters lay a fleet of Western ships, alien in appearance with hard metal edges and massive hulls. Overhead, a fleet of airships crowded the sky.

The machines were unlike anything I'd ever seen. Clouds of steam billowed out from their depths as they hovered like iron dragons. Barbarian vessels had invaded both sea and air.

Chang-wei had said that the empire needed a grand fleet to defeat the *Yangguizi*. I could see now that we would need much, much more than that.

The blast of a steamship horn nearly knocked me off my feet. From our home in Hunan province, I had always heard that foreign devils, the *Yangguizi*, were being effectively held back behind the stone walls that circled our city.

But now it was clear to me the foreigners had completely infiltrated our gates. I looked once more to the floating steamships above, to the harbor that was thick with Western vessels.

These nightmare beasts in the sky were neither benevolent nor celestial. And there was no wall, no matter how high, that could ever hold them back.

7

For a long time, I could do nothing but stare at the foreign ships. My father's duty had been to defend against the Western invaders. He'd given his life to that cause, and here I was, taking on that same battle. But what could one person, one lone woman, do against such immense force?

I slipped back into the shadow of the alleyway; quietly, so as not to not disturb sleeping dragons. Winding through the lanes, I found my way to the front of one of the major trade offices that controlled the warehouse area. The signboard above identified the trade office as one belonging to Hongman Mingqua.

My first knock upon the door was met with silence. Fearing I was being too timid, I tried again. This time, a large, hulking figure opened the door. He stared at me with his mouth pressed into a disapproving line.

"May I speak to Mister Mingqua?" I began.

The man responded with something akin to a grunt.

"I have something to show him. Something of great value."

He looked down his nose at me. "What can you possibly have that is so important? The imperial crown jewels?"

"I will only do business with Mister Mingqua," I insisted.

The doorman snorted, his disdain evident in the curl of his upper lip. I held my ground even though I could feel my knees begin to shake.

Proper women did not approach foreign trading houses. They did not make demands or attempt to barter with the head merchants of the city as if the Hong merchants were nothing but lowly pawnbrokers.

The brute disappeared and returned a moment later. With a cock of his head, he invited me to follow him into the front room. Keeping a few paces behind him, I climbed up a set of narrow stairs and found myself in a study with windows that opened onto a view of the river.

An elderly man in an embroidered robe sat behind the desk. His head was covered by a silk cap and, as if he needed to boast of his wealth, there were at least three rings upon each hand. Gold and jewels peeked out at me from his fingers.

In truth, I was surprised to be allowed an audience. I had assumed I would be speaking to some clerk, not the head merchant himself.

Mingqua fixed his austere gaze upon me, taking my measure and then dismissing me all in one glance. He extended his hand out impatiently.

Fumbling, I reached into my bag to fish out the puzzle box. The metal felt cool against my fingertips as I set the box onto the desk. In the dimness of the study, the steel cube glowed as if emitting its own light.

The merchant's eyebrows lifted for the briefest of moments. "What is that?"

"A treasure from the empire of Japan," I said.

He picked up the cube and turned it over and over. "It opens?"

"Yes, sir."

"How?"

"I am not certain." Best to lie here. I didn't know whether

Mingqua looked favorably upon the imperial government. “It was left to me by my father.”

He shook the box. “Is there anything inside?”

“I don’t know, sir.”

Mingqua ran his leathery fingers over the surface to search for seams. I had done the same so many times. I knew he was met with nothing but smooth, cold steel. The craftsmanship was impeccable. That was the allure of the box.

“Five thousand yuan,” I demanded.

At the first mention of money, the grim-faced businessman returned. The elder merchant lifted his head. Quietly he set the puzzle box down and folded his hands before him as he contemplated me. “A bold price.”

As Mingqua ran his gaze once more over the steel cube, I feared my price was too low. Inspector Aguda had told me that the Hong merchants were some of the wealthiest men in China. What seemed like a mountain of gold to me was nothing to them.

“I cannot part with it for less,” I said when there was no response. There was little choice but to continue the ruse.

“You say this was your father’s.”

“A humble man of no consequence.”

Mingqua snorted at that. The beads of his necklace glinted as he leaned forward, and I saw that they were not beads at all, but pearls; an entire rope of gleaming black pearls.

He craned his neck toward me, peering at me with the eyes of a bird of prey. “Leave this place, young miss.”

My heart thudded in my chest. Was I so easy to read? He hadn’t spoken out of anger, yet the warning was there. Mingqua fell back into his chair. Raising his arm, he made a sweeping motion with the back of his hand. Sweep, sweep, away now.

Swallowing, I went to the desk to retrieve the puzzle box. His eyes cut once more to me with a sharpness that made me recoil. I shoved the steel cube hastily into my sack and retreated down the stairs.

Back out in the street, I could once again breathe. Before fear could take over, I found the next trading house. Then the next.

At one office, I was forced to wait outside for a long time before being summarily dismissed. Most of them shook their heads at me the moment I started to speak. Their business was with other merchants and traders, not girls trying to pawn off a trinket. For a few establishments, I was allowed inside where an appraiser of some kind looked over the puzzle box.

"It's worthless," one of them remarked before offering a mere fifty yuan in a careless tone.

I shook my head. Pleaded that my family was desperate and wouldn't the *Yangguizi* be interested in such an exotic piece?

Be clumsy about it, Inspector Aguda had instructed. Spread stories. The steel cube had been smuggled from within the Ministry of Science. It held secrets inside. The box and I were so out of place that gossip would spread into the concession.

There was no charity to be had. When I left the last of the trading houses, the afternoon was fading into evening. The foreign quarter appeared more menacing in the dark. I had heard stories about the *Yangguizi* with their pale skin and yellow hair. Did they truly look like ghosts? Were they large and barbaric and overbearing?

If Yang was really hiding on the other side of the wall, among foreign traders and smugglers, what kept Prince Yizhu from sending in the secret police to arrest him? Was it truly possible for an outcast to hide so carefully within the empire that even the imperial court could not touch him?

I retreated back toward the city proper, just reaching the outskirts of the warehouse district. A food runner was working the street, selling duck noodles. A portable cook stand was hoisted over his shoulders, attached to him like armor. When I hailed him, he came running.

"One bowl," I ordered.

He set down the stand and a stool and small table spun out from a bottom compartment.

"One bowl, duck noodles!" he cried out dramatically, then beckoned for me to sit. Perhaps he was hoping to draw more customers now that he'd hooked one.

With a few twists of the levers and knobs on the bamboo contraption, a pot of water started simmering over the cook stand.

I sat down to rest my feet. They were aching from wandering through the warehouses all day, and I hadn't had anything to eat besides a steamed bun from a street peddler at midday. Prince Yizhu had sent me out as bait, but they'd given me little instruction on what I was to do beyond the first day. Was I supposed to find my own place for the night? Would Aguda send me some secret message telling me what to do next?

It was hard not to be frustrated. I was carrying out the crown prince's orders, which meant I was to bite my tongue and obey. If His Imperial Highness had commanded me to walk barefoot over coals, I, as his most humble subject, was to do so happily.

They made it clear to me I was nothing but a lure, cast out to dangle prettily in water.

I knew I couldn't trust the prince or his retainers. I certainly couldn't trust Chen Chang-wei now that he was with them, wearing the imperial insignia. Our family had already given one life at the whim of the imperial throne.

For so many years, the story of the empire's defeat had remained fresh and jarring in my mind, the shame of that defeat having caused my father's death. I knew that the Emperor wasn't godlike and divine. After seeing the war machines of the West, I also knew our land had been invaded by forces beyond the Emperor's control.

We were no longer the Middle Kingdom. The center of the world around which all other nations revolved. Perhaps we never were.

As the noodles steeped, I pulled the steel puzzle box from my sack to look it over once more. Its appearance was cold and foreboding, but there was a terrible beauty to its flawlessness. I had attached so much mystery to this little contraption over the years, but apparently it was worthless aside from its sentimental value. I was able to hold on to my keepsake after all.

The thud of the cleaver broke me out of my reflection. The noodle man had a duck breast on his butcher's block, crunching through bone with each precise chop. Soon a steaming bowl filled with egg noodles and glistening slices of roasted duck was set before me.

The vendor's gaze flickered to the puzzle box in my hands before turning back toward his cook stove. I quickly stowed the cube back into my pack.

My stomach growled as the smell of food reached my nose. The dish reminded me of the soup Nan would make in the kitchen back at home. She would stew bones along with a mixture of dried mushrooms and herbs from sunup to sundown.

I couldn't help missing my family as I ate alone here on this street corner. By now, Tian would be wondering what had become of me.

There was a generous amount of duck in the bowl, and between that and the richness of the broth, I was unable to finish. I felt ashamed considering how scarce food had become in our village.

"How much?" I asked the vendor.

"One yuan."

I reached for my purse, but my fingers paused on the frog clasp. "Only one?"

"Yes, miss." He stood beside the table with his hands clasped behind his back. One yuan for such a generous portion? Canton was supposed to be wealthy compared to the dusty village where my family made its home, but did all the inhabitants of the city live in such excess?

I took the coin from my purse and placed it politely onto the table when the man spoke again.

"You're from out of town, miss?" He glanced once again at my travel pack and I nodded.

"There's a boarding house three lanes down." He gestured with this hand in the distance. "You'll see a lantern in the front. An old seamstress lives there."

That was when I realized how unusual it was for a noodle seller to haul his stand around in such a deserted area. More business would be found at the other end of the warehouse zone where the dock laborers congregated.

Aguda had claimed he would have his trackers following me. I looked to the lone beggar at the corner, then back to the noodle seller. Neither one appeared to be an imperial spy, though I supposed they would have been poor ones if I was able to detect them.

I thanked the vendor and started in the direction he'd indicated. The lanes and alleyways of the city appeared more ominous as darkness fell, and I began to walk faster. Despite Inspector Aguda's assurances, I didn't feel protected. I had my needle gun and bladed war fan tucked into my sash, but they couldn't do more than momentarily stun an attacker.

While I was watching the shadows for some hulking monster, I didn't anticipate the tiny figure that scurried toward me when I turned the corner. Small hands yanked my pack from my arm and started running down the lane.

"Hey!"

Instinctively, I ran after him. The thief was merely a child, even younger than Tian and certainly scrawnier. But his cricket legs carried him swiftly through the backstreets. After several twists and turns, I finally grabbed onto his shoulder.

"Keep running," he instructed as he turned to look at me. His eyes were clear and devoid of any fear of being caught. The rascal was barely breathing hard while I was panting. "Don't stop."

He looked beyond me to the end of the alleyway as if to see if there was anyone else chasing us. Shrugging his shoulder from my grasp, he darted toward a towering stack of refuse. Shipping crates had been piled on top of one another. The little thief slipped into an opening at the base like a mouse into the wall.

I hesitated, staring at the hole. The boy was no ordinary street urchin, and I had no idea where he was leading me. I couldn't be certain that he had been sent by Yang, but this could be my one chance. Taking a deep breath, I fell to my hands and knees and squeezed through crates.

"Careful, don't knock everything down."

The boy was crouched inside, waiting for me. Without another word, he turned and started scrambling through the maze of rubbish. Aguda's agents wouldn't be able to follow us. Even I could barely fit inside.

"Who sent you?" I directed the question at his feet as he wriggled in front of me. It was dark inside the heap and I started to doubt my decision to follow him, but there was no going back now.

"Talk later, miss."

We reached a wall and I was finally able to stand, but only barely. I flattened myself against the stone and crept alongside it. It was a lifetime before we were free and I could once again see the sky above me. I was standing in the corner of just another alleyway, staring at the back of a shop. We could have been anywhere in the city. I was completely at the mercy of this raggedy child.

He didn't look or sound like a child as he addressed me. "Those *guanfu* monkeys don't know the streets like I do," he boasted.

"You're with Yang Hanzhu, aren't you?"

"I don't know who you mean, miss." He adjusted my travel pack over his shoulder and beckoned for me to follow with a toss of his head. "But the captain wants to see you. Come on."

8

The boy called himself Xiao Jie and did appear to know every twist and turn within the backstreets. At some point, we dropped beneath a bridge and pressed ourselves against the base of it as a foot patrol passed by overhead. Little Jie waited until after the last footfall passed by before beckoning me into a drainage tunnel. I tried not to think of what was in the black and dank water beneath my feet as I crouched in after him.

We emerged with a view of the dock. There were vessels of all sizes crowding the waters as well as the floating airships above the harbor.

"They're not allowed to fly over the city," Jie said when he saw me staring at the hulking shapes in the clouds.

How long would that edict last? There was no force in the entire Middle Kingdom that could hold the foreigners back if they wanted to invade. Sadly, the last war had proven that beyond question.

Jie moved fearlessly toward the waterfront with me trailing behind. It was unsightly to be led around by a child, but I was afraid of the iron-clad vessels that towered over the water.

"They are faster than our war junks," I remember Father saying. "They are stronger. There was nothing that could be done."

Of all the things I could remember of my father, I hated that his defeat was the one detail that loomed largest in my mind.

The guttural sounds of a conversation floated from the other side of the dock. The words were alien to me.

"Is that *Yingyu*?"

"They call it 'Eng-rish,'" he told me.

"Do you understand it?"

Little Jie shook his head and kept on walking. At the end of the far pier, tucked in the shadow of two massive steamships, was the familiar site of an ocean junk. Its sails were masted and the wooden vessel floated restfully upon the water. Next to these Western boats, the junk looked ancient, yet proudly defiant. Its kind had survived a thousand years upon the seas.

"Our captain is aboard. He wants to see you."

"What is your captain's name?"

The little devil continued his habit of answering only when it pleased him. He hurried toward the ship. At the edge of the pier, he gave a sharp whistle and immediately a plank was lowered from the deck.

The boy stood back as I climbed the walkway. It was surprisingly steep, rising several stories off the ground. Little Jie scurried up much faster than I. On the deck, he took the lead again. I tried to take a quick look at the crewmen aboard, but Jie tugged my sleeve impatiently.

As we disappeared below deck, the men began to pull the gangplank back from the dock. I was trapped on a strange ship in the foreign concession, surrounded by strangers. At least they appeared to be my countrymen, but that didn't make me any less anxious. My hands were shaking as I stepped down into the hold. No matter what Prince Yizhu and Inspector Aguda had promised, there was no way they could protect me here.

But this was the way it had to be. Uncle Hanzhu had always been resourceful. If the ship's captain was the same man who had worked under my father, he had successfully escaped the purge that had swept through the Ministry. He had outwitted the secret police.

Little Jie rapped on a door to what I assumed was the captain's quarters. I held my breath.

When we were bid to enter, the sight that greeted me stopped my breath.

At the far end of the cabin was a writing desk. The captain stood in front, hands propped back against the surface. His posture, though relaxed, was rife with challenge.

I recognized Yang's eyes immediately; that hint of knowing laughter that always sparked within them. His look was a shrewd one, and I recalled his keen intelligence in the way his gaze analyzed me from head to toe. There was a hardness to him, however, that I didn't remember.

His face was the only part of him that was familiar to me. He was dressed in Western clothing. His shirt was white, a color not worn by our people except in mourning. It buttoned up the front and was left open at the collar. A vest was fitted around his torso with two rows of buttons adorning the front, and he wore trousers that revealed his legs, which were crossed at the ankles. More shocking than his foreign garb was his hair.

Yang had cut his queue completely off. What remained of his hair hung just above his shoulders. It gave him a reckless, dangerous look.

A man's queue was a quintessential sign of his loyalty to the Qing Empire. To remove it was to sever all ties with the Emperor. The act was irrevocable, and I felt a pang of sadness knowing he had willingly turned his back on his homeland.

"Uncle...Uncle Hanzhu?" I stammered out the honorific, though it sounded strange on my tongue. I didn't know how to address him other than with the name I had always used.

"Uncle?" His smile widened. "That makes me sound outright elderly coming from a young lady such as yourself."

My tongue cleaved to the roof of my mouth as he pushed off from the desk to come toward me.

"Soling," he acknowledged with a wink of one eye, an odd gesture I'd never seen before. A strange look flickered in his eyes. "Little Lingling. Not so little anymore."

His gaze rested on my face, and I could feel my cheeks heating. I was starting to think that some demon had stolen Yang's face. It was difficult to look at him.

I affected a stiff nod. "It has been a long time, Uncle. Are you well?"

"Uncle again."

I tried to clear my throat. "Mister Yang," I amended.

"So formal," he chided, shaking his head.

Yang Hanzhu was one of the youngest in Father's circle and a frequent visitor to our household. He had always been kind to me, but now every word out of his mouth seemed a challenge.

"How do you wish me to address you—"

"Why are you here?" he interrupted, his tone just on the edge of remaining pleasant.

"I—"

"This was what she was trying to sell to the Hongmen," Little Jie piped up. He fished through my pack, found the puzzle box and ran it eagerly over to his master.

Yang took hold of the box and waved the boy out of the room, leaving the two of us alone. He glanced once more at me before bending to inspect the gleaming steel.

"It belonged to Father," I said, my chest pulling tight.

"I remember." A heavy look crossed Yang's face as he inspected the marks on the steel. "Other than its craftsmanship, this piece has little value in and of itself. Worth perhaps a tael or two in silver to a collector."

His hands traced over the metal. Unlike Chang-wei, he knew

how to find the panel that triggered the opening sequence. The box came to life, gears whirring as the panels shifted to reveal the secret compartment. "What it held inside, however..."

He looked to me, but I shook my head. "It's always been empty."

Why had I lied to him? Perhaps it was because his appearance was still a shock to me.

I didn't know if he believed me, but Yang peered at the empty compartment for another few seconds before setting the cube aside.

"You were always so curious when you came to the Ministry, wanting to know everything." His tone grew fond as he regarded me. "You look as if you have a thousand things to ask me now."

I started to open my mouth, but he stopped me.

"Three questions; do you remember, Ling-ling?"

It was a game we used to play. I could ask any three questions, but only three. It wasn't that Yang was impatient with my inquisitiveness. He wanted me to learn how to choose my words with care.

"Why do you look like this?" I couldn't help staring at his Western clothing and the shorn hair that marked him forever as an outcast.

"I hate the Flower Empire," he answered simply, using the archaic name for our kingdom. The little crooked smile never wavered from his lips. "It forsook me long before I turned away from it."

I started to protest but bit my tongue. Hadn't I felt the same on nights while I lay awake, missing Father? Missing the life we once had?

"So you've turned yourself into one of them? One of the *Yangguizi*?"

"No." If possible, his smile became colder. "I hate them, too."

Yang uncrossed his legs and straightened, waiting patiently for my final question. He was full of secrets now, with more hidden levers and compartments than that puzzle box. Whatever connections or loyalties he'd once held were long gone.

I licked my lips, my heart pounding fiercely. "Am I in danger here?"

For the first time, I noticed a crack in his hard exterior. A look of shock crossed his eyes. "I would never hurt you, Soling. Why would you even ask that?"

I allowed myself to breathe easier, but not much. "You must have some idea of why I was sent here."

"I know who sent you," he acknowledged.

"The crown prince thinks you have Father's gunpowder formula."

His mouth twisted. "We worked on a thousand different experiments, a hundred different combinations."

"The empire needs that formula to power its warships to fight against the foreigners."

"The imperial court denounced our work and now they seek it like some elixir." With a snort, Yang uncrossed his legs and straightened, turning away to deposit the puzzle box into a drawer in the desk. "You have more reason to hate the empire than I. The imperial navy failed because of pride and ignorance, yet Master Jin was the one who paid with his head. Why do you want to help them?"

"I don't care about the Emperor's war. I care about my family," I told him truthfully. If we don't do anything, the foreigners will take it all."

My impassioned speech failed to move him. Lifting a long coat from the wall, he worked his arms into it. The seams were crisp and the material heavy in appearance. Buttons gleamed along the front. Nothing like the loose-fitting clothing of our people.

Yang moved away from me, toward the door. "Our land is already dying from within. All that matters to anyone anymore is profit."

"That can't be true. There's still honor and loyalty. Family."

"There is no secret elixir, Soling," he cut in sharply.

When I set out to find my old friend, there had been one last flicker of hope inside me, but it died as Yang regarded me sullenly from the doorway. In Father's workshop, he had been brilliant, always the one with new theories and experiments. He never gave up on any problem. He was convinced there was always a solution.

Like everything else from my past, Yang had changed. That spark of ingenuity and optimism inside him had burnt away.

"You've asked quite a few questions already, Soling. More than three." Yang regarded me with a grave expression. "I have a few questions of my own."

I swallowed, finding my throat had gone dry. "What do wish to know?"

"Did they promise you something or did they threaten you?"

The hard edge of his voice raised the hairs on my neck. I didn't know how to answer.

"To make you come after me, did they threaten you or did they bribe you? Whatever it was, I don't blame you, Soling. Under the rule of the Emperor, you are all his slaves—as I once was."

I shook my head. "I just wanted to help."

He returned and took my hand in his, the first time Yang Hanzhu had done such a thing. My heart beat faster.

"I was loyal to your father to the end. The Emperor's minions knew that and knew they could use you to draw me out. There was no other way for them to control me. I'm no longer their puppet."

"Then you won't give them the formula."

His lip curled. "Even if I had it, I wouldn't give it to those bastards."

"Then I was wrong to come." I slipped my hand out of his grasp and he let me go. "If you'll release me we can forget all this."

"The Empire won't let us forget," he said bitterly. "I won't let them exploit you."

I looked at him in shock. "You can't mean to keep me here?"

"It's the only way to keep you safe. I owe it to your father."

I thought of my family. For a brief moment, I considered pleading on their behalf to Yang. Maybe he could take us all in. Bring us to somewhere new, somewhere Mother wouldn't waste away breathing black smoke and despair into her lungs. Somewhere Tian might have a chance outside the factories.

But Yang was a traitor. He might even be a madman. He had bought his safety among the foreign devils in some illicit manner that I didn't yet know of. What I did know was that Yang belonged nowhere. This ship was his only haven, and he'd chosen that desolate path.

"Uncle Hanzhu." I used the honorific on purpose. "My father's execution devastated our family. For years, I felt betrayed. Lost. But this is my chance to redeem our name. It's your chance as well."

He stared at me long and hard. For a moment, I thought he might be considering my words, and I tried to imagine what it would be like if the Ministry of Science hadn't been purged. If the engineering corps had remained intact. What if my father and his most gifted disciples had been hard at work all these years, designing a defense against the foreign invasion? Chen Changwei, Yang Hanzhu, all of the others.

My hope was allowed to spark for only a brief moment. Yang straightened without a word and looked down at me.

"I have no need of redemption," he said before turning to go.

He closed the door quietly, leaving me alone in his quarters. For a long time, I stood where I was while the ship rocked beneath me, in exile within its mother country. When it was apparent Yang would not return, I tried the door and found it unlocked. There was no guard posted outside, either.

I shut the door once more and retreated toward the desk. It

was nighttime and I was in a strange port. Even if I had dared to navigate the foreign settlement by myself, I wasn't certain I wanted to go. Was I any better entrenched in Prince Yizhu's enclave than I was here?

What I did next didn't come without reproach, but I did it all the same. Yang had left me in his private cabin with his books and papers right before my eyes. He trusted me, and perhaps I should have valued that trust by not going through his belongings, but I had come here with a purpose.

I began sorting through his desk, sifting through journals, ledger books and maps. A route that dotted the coastline and skirted the waters of Japan had been marked upon one of the maps. Another route ventured as far as India. These were places I had heard of, but I had no understanding of where they were located or who the people were.

There was nothing I recognized as scientific in nature. Certainly Yang wouldn't have left me in here with anything valuable, but I had to try to seek out some clue. If I returned to Prince Yizhu empty-handed, I'd have nothing to negotiate with on behalf of my family.

After about an hour, Little Jie returned with tea and a plate of dumplings for me.

"How long have you been aboard this ship?" I asked him as he set the tray down.

"Oh no, miss! You won't pry any information from me."

With a devilish look, he was gone. I drank the tea and ate the plump dumplings, which were a mix of pork and shrimp, once again thinking of my family. The last of the rice would have run out by now. Nan was clever enough to perhaps barter away some small household items, but we had little left to trade.

Once I returned, I resolved to find other means of supporting them. I had become a burden to Physician Lo, and we had no need in the village for two healers.

The only options left to me were bleak: our family would be

reduced to begging, and Tian would be conscripted to work in the mines. I could marry Merchant Hu if he would still have me, but that was hardly a solution.

After the meal, I rinsed my mouth with tea and lay down on the bed. Blowing out the lantern, I squeezed my eyes shut, as if that could make my problems go away for just one night. Despite the difficulties we faced at home, I still wanted to be there. Safe.

The bunk was surprisingly warm and not uncomfortable. Before long, I started to drift as the activity of the day caught up to me.

I thought of Yang conjuring fire out of air. *Smoke or fire?*

There had been many questions I hadn't asked him. The remaining ones lingered in my head like the buzz of dragonflies.

If I had another three questions now, what would I ask him? What were all those shipments listed in his ledger book? And how did he get his hands on the exorbitant amounts of silver listed beside them? What had he been looking for inside the puzzle box? How had he escaped the purge when the rest of Father's disciples had been imprisoned and stripped of rank?

And finally, what had he done that was so unforgivable that it was better to cut off his hair and spend the rest of his life in exile?

9

I awoke to movement and the rush of the wind outside. The entire cabin was in motion, and it was no longer the rocking sway of the vessel upon water.

The ship had set sail.

I jumped from the berth and shoved my feet into slippers before bursting out of the door. No one stopped me as I flew up the stairs.

The too-bright sun blinded me the moment I emerged above deck. A gust of wind whipped over me, and I staggered at the wideness of the sky above and the breadth of the ocean surrounding us.

Water. There was nothing but water and blue sky as far as the eye could see. The horizon looked impossibly far away, and a hollow pit formed in my stomach.

Yang was moving calmly toward the prow of the ship while the breeze whipped the shorn ends of his shoulder-length hair about his face. I tried to catch him, but he was sure-footed at sea while each rolling wave threatened to topple me.

He finally paused to speak to his crewmen, with his hands in the pockets of his long coat as he looked out upon the water.

Though he had adopted Western garb, the others had not. Or rather, their mix of dress was neither recognizably Chinese nor Western.

"Yang Hanzhu!" It was rude of me to shout out his name like that, but I didn't care. I moved as fast as I could across the deck. "You can't take me with you. I have to go back."

He barely turned toward me. The wind blew through his hair as he kept his focus on the horizon ahead. "I can't let you go. The imperial authorities are having you tracked. They would have found me."

"I wouldn't have told them anything."

"Doesn't matter. They have their ways."

"This is kidnapping!" I sputtered.

"Not the worst of my crimes, by far."

Yang strolled down the deck, sparing a cursory glance at his crewmen as they went about their duties. I had no choice but to tag after him.

"Do you know the story of Admiral Zheng He?" he asked me.

He didn't bother to face me. I was familiar with this mood. Yang was acting as teacher, presenting a lesson.

"He was a statesman and an explorer," I replied darkly. "Song Dynasty."

"Admiral Zheng controlled the largest fleet of treasure junks the world had ever known. He traveled to the ends of the map, visiting wild lands across the sea. But apparently these voyages were not authorized by the imperial court. Do you know how the empire rewarded the admiral's glorious efforts?"

I wanted to demand once more that Yang turn his ship around, but there was no speaking with him until the lesson was done. "The Hongxi Emperor had Zheng He's ships set on fire," I replied begrudgingly. "And his voyages struck from the record."

Yang stopped abruptly to turn toward me. "The Emperor didn't merely destroy Zheng He's treasure ships. He was destroying his own fleet, crippling the imperial navy. Why do such a thing? Why cut off his own hands and feet?"

"Because the Emperor feared Zheng He's legacy would outshine his?" I ventured.

"Because he feared the knowledge Zheng He had gained. The admiral had opened up a window to the outside world, and the Emperor's advisers found the very idea dangerous—a world that extended beyond the Middle Kingdom. He didn't want his people to look outward. Ignorance, Soling. Ignorance and fear. Do you see why I can't help you?"

I shook my head. I didn't understand.

Yang exhaled sharply, composing himself. "Do you know the reason your father had to die? It wasn't because we were defeated by the *Yangguizi*. It was because when the first ports fell, your father tasked his most trusted men to analyze why we were losing the war. And when we found that it was due to the superior ships and weapons of the West, he advocated that we study their methods and adapt their ways to our own. And then he knelt before the Emperor and presented this report—a report that told the Emperor that his Majesty was wrong. He was inferior, he was not infallible, and his empire was crumbling. That is why Master Jin-fu was executed. For insulting the Son of Heaven rather than insisting that he would rule for a thousand years."

I stared at him, shocked into silence. My entire body had gone numb, and I felt the weight of a thousand stones pressing down onto my shoulders.

"That was why they wanted all of you," I said in barely a whisper.

Yang's mouth twisted cruelly. "Because of pride. Because to the Emperor, a thing said could be unsaid, if everyone who has heard it is silenced."

The worst of it was that everything Yang told me made sense. My Father would still be alive if he so intent on finding answers. I looked away, broken and defeated.

"And now there is a new Ministry of Science," Yang remarked quietly. "They build monuments to the Emperor to praise his greatness. Your beloved empire gains knowledge only to destroy it. They fear it more than anything else. Do not trust them, Soling."

But Chang-wei wasn't like that. Neither was the crown prince, who had been tutored by my father.

"Prince Yizhu is not like his father," I began weakly as I tried to explain what I had learned.

I argued and begged with Yang then, but mostly I was arguing with myself. Had I been fooled into believing the empire was worth fighting for?

Yang would hear none of it, not even when I asked to be left ashore to make my own way home. All this time, the crew continued with their tasks, paying me no mind as I followed at Yang's heels.

"Then what do you intend to do with me?" I demanded.

"I told you I would never harm you."

I don't know if I felt worse or better that he needed to tell me that. "But I can't stay on this ship with you. My mother and brother need me."

"You'll be returned to them."

"When?"

"When it's safe."

I stormed off to return below deck, shutting myself once more in Yang's cabin. Within the hour, I heard a sound that made me jump once again to my feet.

It was the whir of a mechanical engine down below. The rumble of machinery vibrated through the floorboards and filled my ears.

When I came above deck this time, I could tell without question we were moving faster. I could hear the chug and grind of the gears from deep below deck that propelled us forward.

Yang had lied to me. This ship only appeared to be a sailing vessel on the outside. Yang had a combustion engine and the gunpowder to fuel it.

The salt air breeze that had floated around me that morning now whipped by as the ship cut through the water. This time when I called out Yang's name, no one could hear me above the roar.

A quick search of the deck revealed he was no longer there. He had disappeared down below, and I went to search him out.

The ship had been fitted with a gunpowder engine, an engine powerful enough to propel it through the waves against the wind.

He stood at a worktable with his coat removed. He was wearing only a white shirt beneath, and his sleeves were rolled up to his elbows.

A shelf packed with books and scrolls lined the opposite end of the room. Another long table was set against one wall. The implements arranged upon it sent a pang of nostalgia through me. There were glass vials and containers of various sizes along with tools and burners.

I knew all the names because he had taught them to me, gifting me with sugared almonds when I named them all correctly. I had been a worshipful child in the presence of a doting mentor.

This was the man I remembered. He had papers fanned out about him in a semicircle, and a journal lay open, which he used to keep notes.

"You've built a laboratory on your ship," I said.

Yang looked up, his arm reclining along the worktable. "How else could I continue my work?"

With all his talk of turning his back on the empire, I was certain he had forsaken his practice as well. What use did a privateer have for the sciences?

"What is it you study down here?"

As I came closer, Yang straightened abruptly and closed his

journal. I caught the scrawl of a chemical formula before the pages disappeared beneath the leather-bound cover.

"A little of everything. Whatever catches my interest," Yang replied, casually resting the crook of his arm over the book. "Days out at sea can be very long. It helps to remain occupied."

At the Ministry, Yang had researched incendiaries and explosives. The alchemy of fire. I looked over the close quarters of the workshop. It would be madness to experiment with such materials here. My father had lost his arm in what was supposed to be a simple experiment. An accident here could set the entire ship aflame.

Despite the fact that I was being abducted—for my own protection, as Yang claimed—I found myself extremely curious about him and what had happened after he fled Peking.

"How did you come to be the captain of this ship?" I asked, offering a truce for the moment.

He took the offer. "My family has been in shipping for generations. Did you not know?"

I shook my head, feeling a bit shy. Yang had never mentioned anything personal about himself, and as often as I had hovered about him like a little hummingbird, I had never asked. He gestured for me to take a seat beside him and I pulled up a stool.

"I come from a line of merchants, quite humble," he said with a quirk of his mouth. "But wealthy. Do you know the foreign devils have a term 'filthy rich'? My family was wealthy enough to pay for an expensive academy education for their oldest son, the same type attended by better and more exalted names than mine. Our attempt to buy into rank and status."

"But you were accomplished enough to pass the entrance exams yourself," I protested.

"Soling. *Mèimèi.*"

So I had been elevated in status from an impressionable child to a little sister. He cocked his head and gave me a half smile that told me how sheltered he still found me. Amusingly so. I stiffened at his indulgent look.

"There is nothing money can't buy," he remarked.

I looked about the chamber. The laboratory appeared well stocked, and it had to have been expensive to have a laboratory built into a trading vessel.

"Do you still have ties to your family?"

"Of course not." His pleasant expression faded. "It is a good thing my ancestry was low enough to be beneath the empire's persecution. In any case, I'm dead to them as much as I am to the empire. I don't exist."

"But you're not dead." I started to argue with him again, but he froze me with a dark look.

"I'm suddenly valuable because I have something they want," he said, biting off the words. "Just like you're suddenly so *valuable*, after being forgotten for so many years."

I knew from Yang's tone what he was insinuating. I was only valuable to the crown prince as bait.

"Do you remember Chen Chang-wei?" I asked. "He's allied with the crown prince now."

Yang's eyes narrowed. "Engineer Chen."

I nodded, watching his reaction as I held my breath. He stood and reached for the waistcoat that had been folded and laid over the table.

"Chen Chang-wei," he repeated slowly, a crease appearing over his forehead. With great deliberation, Yang slid his arms into the coat and pulled it over his shoulders. "Do not trust that man."

"Why shouldn't I? Wasn't he also one of Father's trusted disciples?"

Yang shook his head. Chang-wei had claimed that the two of them had never gotten along and now I wondered why. I had only seen Peking and the Ministry through the innocent eyes of a child.

"Whatever he was to you once, that was all in the past," was all Yang would tell me.

Between Chen Chang-wei and Yang Hanzhu, I didn't know who to trust. They had both been in my father's inner circle.

Perhaps neither of them could be trusted. I had left home on what was to be nothing more than a two-day journey, but I had been taken against my will, not once but twice, to do someone else's bidding. If I had known I was to become a gambit to be tossed back and forth, I would have never set foot on the road to Changsha.

"Now let me give you a tour of the ship." Yang paused at the doorway and beckoned for me to follow. His demeanor was once again cordial. "You'll be a guest on board for at least a little while."

10

I spent mornings above deck, soaking in the sun and searching the horizon for land until the endless sight of water made me dizzy, but this morning I saw a dark ridge appear upon the horizon. After not seeing land for so long, my heart leapt.

"The Kingdom of Annam," Yang said, coming up beside me.

I didn't recognize the name and made a note to seek it out later on one of the maps in the main cabin. "Will we dock there?"

The bow of the ship was pointed to it as far as I could see. My abilities to tell direction at sea were poor at best. Nothing but the basics of north, east, south, west based on the sun.

"With these winds, we'll dock there by noon."

The engines below were silent and the red sails were unfurled above like a dragon's wings, angled to make full use of the wind. For a moment, I thought of the promise of land. Once I was no longer adrift, perhaps I could find a way to escape.

"My men and I will be making an excursion into the port, but I think it best that you remain on board during that time," Yang said with a sly smile as if reading my thoughts.

I might have pouted as I turned back to stare at the horizon.

The ridge grew darker as we sailed on, and within the next hour, I could start to see structures in the distance. A towering pagoda stood near the shore.

As we finally neared land, Yang and his crew prepared to head into the village. I watched him tuck a foreign pistol beneath his coat and slip a dagger in his boot.

From the main deck, I peered down into the town, taking in the ramshackle buildings and peddlers that crowded the docks. The people could have been Chinese, black haired and dark eyed, their skin burnished by the sun. The entire shoreline was a market area, baskets of fish, bushels of vegetables. As Yang and his men descended the plank, I noted they didn't transport any goods for trade or sale. One other crewman made some rude remark about a trip to the brothels, and I decided to retreat back to my cabin.

It was Yang's cabin in truth, but it had become my private area. The quarters were small, but much more spacious than the sleeping berths I had spied while roaming about. Once inside, I went to his collection of books and scrolls, and pulled out the maps.

I found Canton and then searched the nearby coastlines until I found Annam. For the first time in my life, I was outside the borders of my homeland.

Now that I could see the lands before me, I knew how foolish I'd been to think of escape. I had assumed wherever we were, the people around us had to be subjects of the Emperor and speak my language.

I left the cabin and walked along the lower deck past the sleeping areas. Most of the crewmen had gone up to the main deck to take in the sights and enjoy the brief rest while the boat was docked. I went to what had become my second hideout: the laboratory.

After spending three days at sea, I had managed to learn the layout of the ship. Initially Little Jie had followed me about, but after the first day, he lost interest and disappeared. It couldn't quite be said that I was sneaking about. Yang hadn't forbidden me from exploring. I had been to the laboratory a number of times to look through all the implements and journals there.

The worktables remained empty, which made me wonder what sort of studies Yang did there. Had he built the room to chase memories? The shelves in the laboratory were filled with volumes containing tables and lists of properties, but there was no record of any experiments.

The books in his quarters also told me nothing about Yang. He was very private despite living on a vessel surrounded by a crew of men. His shelf contained various writings he'd collected from the different lands he'd visited. Most of them in languages I couldn't understand.

I bypassed the worktables and equipment to go to the far corner. There was a door at the back of the room that was always locked. I inserted one of my long, thin needles into the lock to try to pick it, but was unsuccessful. I had no skill for thievery.

After my failed venture, I wandered back up to the galley where benches were arranged near the kitchen area. The cook provided me the usual bowl of mush. It had become more watery as the days went by and also lacked the bits of fried onion or salted egg that he sometimes used to add flavor.

"If we didn't have to leave so quickly," he grumbled, even though I hadn't complained.

I was the reason the ship had to flee Canton, so I kept my silence as I finished my meal.

When it was time to carry lunch up to the men, I offered to help. The cook hefted the large vat of porridge in his arms while I trailed behind with a basket containing the eating bowls.

"What about that one?" I asked, spying a smaller tureen left beside the iron stove.

"Don't worry, miss. That's for something else," he mumbled, huffing as he left the galley.

I followed dutifully behind. From the deck, I saw that another group had been sent ashore and was returning with crates laden with goods from the market below.

"Ah, better food tonight," Cook said.

The line started to form even before he set down the vat of porridge. I began to ladle out portions to the sailors as they shuffled by one after the other. The line was only halfway through when I saw Yang return out of the corner of my eye.

Yang disappeared below deck with a red lacquered case tucked beneath one arm. Even from afar, I recognized the indentation in the center of the case, which created a distinctive shape. It was a wooden pillow box typically used in opium dens.

I REACHED the door of the laboratory, it was locked. Yang and the goods he'd brought back on board had disappeared into that room. I had to know what was in them.

I thought of the ledger book I'd seen in Yang's cabin; all that money along with the various ports marked on his maps. Were they opium routes? I didn't want to believe it.

I tapped on the door and was surprised when Yang opened it without hesitation. "Soling," he greeted, his tone nothing but pleasant.

A solution bubbled behind him. When I peered over his shoulder, Yang made no attempt to block me. Instead he held the door open in invitation.

A distillation apparatus had been set up on the main worktable. Beside it sat one of the crates that had been brought from onshore. The lid was pried open, revealing a supply of green gray pods.

"Opium." I was unable to raise my voice above a whisper.

"Indeed." Yang fished one of the bulbs from the pile, turning it this way and that. "It's easy to find the finished substance but much harder to procure the plant itself."

My skin crawled at the sight of it. The pod was sickly in color, but more upsetting than its appearance was what I knew it could yield: the black poison that had taken my mother away from me.

"Why do you have it?"

Yang watched my face closely before answering. "For experimental purposes."

"Are you running opium?" This was no longer a child's game of question and answer. "Is that why the foreigners allow you into their ports?"

His jaw hardened. "Do you think I would peddle that filth?"

"Have you been running opium?" I demanded, shaking.

"No."

I stared at him, not knowing what to believe anymore.

"No," he repeated, stronger this time. "If I were running, would I have only brought three crates on board? And raw opium, for that matter?"

I tried to find fault in that logic and was unable to. Still, I wasn't convinced. "What is behind that door?"

He followed my eyes to the locked door in the back of the storeroom. Instead of countering with an explanation, Yang reached into the pocket of his coat and pulled out an iron key, which he placed in my hand.

"If you please." He beckoned me forward.

Warily, I fitted the heavy key into the lock. With an amenable click, the door swung open.

As soon as I saw what was inside, I felt foolish for accusing him. It was merely a storeroom.

The narrow space ran the length of the laboratory. The wall was full of little drawers on both sides, much like the medicine cabinet in Lo's herbal shop. Each drawer was meticulously labeled. I pressed my hand over my lips to stifle a laugh as I read through the names of rather mundane substances.

His eyebrows arched into a frown. "What's so funny?"

"I was expecting something unspeakable."

"A dead body, perhaps?" Yang obliged me with a sinister smirk.

It had been silly of me. I started apologizing profusely for insulting him, but Yang waved my worries aside. For the next few moments, he described how the chemicals inside were arranged, the most reactive ones lying inside the bottom drawers, the poisonous ones marked with a red dot beside the name. Then he handed me a flask of clear liquid as he collected several other reactants.

"It's a good thing that you question everything, even your dear Uncle Hanzhu," he told me as we returned to the laboratory. "And your hatred of the opium trade means you may find this current project of mine of some interest."

He demonstrated the proper proportions for mixing the solution. "I think it must be fate that caused us to meet once again. Everyone else on board this ship is a laborer or a sailor through and through. No one with an eye for detail or nearly clever enough to lend me a hand."

He checked the level of the solution and, apparently satisfied, set it down.

His confidence in me made me even more nervous. I had never assisted my father at the Ministry of Science. His work was dangerous, as anyone could see from his missing arm. I was wise enough now to know that the few times I had been allowed to mix chemicals, they were likely concoctions of water and salt Yang had provided to make me feel useful.

But Yang looked completely serious now. "I no longer study explosives or poisons or liquid fire, *mèimèi*. My work is now completely focused on one thing: the one substance that has destroyed our land.

"I don't allow it on my ship, except for this one purpose. I'm going to discover the source of this disease." He stared at the containers as if staring down an enemy. "And then I'm going to discover the cure."

"But it isn't a disease." As soon as I spoke, I thought of the last I had seen of my mother, unable or unwilling to move, her eyes blank. A feeling of helplessness crashed into me. "There is no cure."

"Our people have used the *minang* poppy for thousands of years," Yang pointed out. "As medicine or in the bedchamber as an aphrodisiac."

My face heated with embarrassment and I stared down at the opium pots. Some of them were ornate, grotesquely romantic in their rendering. Twisting dragons and lotus blooms encasing balls of black tar.

"What is it about the foreign opium that makes it so addictive to us?" he continued. "What makes the poison seep into our blood until we want it more than food or water? Something has changed over these last ten years, Soling. Anyone can see it."

"You think the foreign opium shipments have been tampered with?"

"Engineered," Yang replied with grim determination. "To make us into perfect slaves."

It was a wild theory, but he had always been known for such leaps in logic. In Father's circle, Yang had been the boldest. The one most willing to risk being wrong. My father had always been proud of him for it.

"Have you ever tried smoking opium?" I asked meekly.

I watched as his mouth pressed tight. "We all have at one time. But I wouldn't risk it again. Not after what I've seen."

He turned and started arranging the opium containers, pulling out a set of five. I noticed each was labeled with where it had been procured.

I wanted to believe his theory. If it was true, then someone else was responsible. It wasn't my fault that I couldn't wean my mother from the smoke or that she wanted to breathe it in more than she wanted air. It wasn't her fault that she had abandoned us.

I unbuttoned my mandarin jacket and folded it neatly aside. "Tell me what needs to be done."

For the next few days, I became absorbed with a series of tests and experiments. Dissolving dabs of the drug, heating the solutions, extracting impurities. At each step, we took notes. These figures and observations meant little in and of themselves, but Yang was constructing a larger picture. We worked side by side, and I was caught up in his quest and the relentless way he seemed to pursue it.

I forgot I was adrift at sea. At times, I even stopped worrying about Mother and Tian as I became absorbed in the work. The experiments gave me purpose, even if they turned out to be another one of Yang's wild schemes.

"There are plantations throughout the empire where the poppy grows like a weed," Yang would say as he heated the distillation apparatus. The coils and bulbs of glass were designed to separate out distinctive elements from within a compound. "Yet crops from India are in high demand. Cultivated from afar and dumped into our trading ports to be carried inland on riverboats."

Liquid evaporated and then condensed along the glass coils. Bit by bit, the batches of opium were broken down and trace elements identified. It was a slow, painstaking process.

"At first I thought it was different strains," Yang lectured, writing notes into his journal. "But regardless of the plant it came from, opium was opium. Concentrations of the chemicals may differ, but not enough to cause such dramatic effects. This made me consider additives. I'm convinced that in particular shipments, there is something more than opium in the dosage."

I had learned more about opium in the last few days than I had in my years apprenticing with Old Man Lo. Sap or resin from the opium poppy was boiled down to create the sticky black tar that was rolled into balls to be smoked. Whereas for centuries we had ingested the drug in soups and teas, smoking the opium had multiplied its effectiveness.

"Frighteningly effective," Yang declared. "Don't you see how all our weapons are useless? There is no cannon we can build large enough to defeat this. No engine fast enough to chase it away."

It was said monks would sometimes meditate watching drops of rain as they fell from leaves, the pattern providing a focal point. Yang stared at each drip from the distiller now as if similarly searching for answers.

I returned the current batch of samples to the tray and carried it back to the storeroom. After working side by side, Yang and I had eased into a comfortable routine. He was a different person in his laboratory. He was focused; less angry. I have to admit, the work chased away my sense of desolation as well. Even if Yang was delusional, it was calming to be able to search for an answer. For any answer.

All of the drawers in the far corner were labeled according to region rather than with a compound name. I began to place the present samples back into the Annam drawer and couldn't help scanning the entire cabinet. The highest of the drawers were just above my head, but I could still read the names painted onto them.

I was shocked to see how far Yang had traveled to procure his collection: Goryeo, Japan, Formosa.

There must have been hundreds of samples in here, maybe close to a thousand. Had he truly been tracing opium routes through the seas, going from one seedy port to another, collecting opium? He was convinced that opium shipments smuggled into our ports had been tainted.

It seemed far-fetched, but Yang was a scientist. He wouldn't make such a bold statement without evidence. What exactly had he seen to give him this impression? Had someone mixed the opium with some other more potent chemical?

I had to stand on my toes to return the control sample contained in a plain white jar. Finally, I managed to nudge the jar into its drawer with my fingertips, but lost my balance as I started to come back down. Out of reflex, I grabbed onto one of the drawers, which I inadvertently dragged open as I tried to regain my footing.

The clink of the glass inside turned my attention to the contents of the drawer. Nestled inside the long drawer were twenty slender vials sealed with wax. Each one contained a dark liquid that appeared to be blood.

11

If I was starting to become complacent at sea, the next day served to remind me that it was far from an idyllic existence. I showed up in the laboratory as I had done for the last few days only to find all the equipment had been stowed away. Up on deck, I saw the reason why in the churn of gray clouds overhead.

Even if I hadn't been able to interpret the skies, I would have known something was wrong immediately from the demeanor of the crew. Everyone was quieter than usual with heads down to focus on their duties.

Yang and I found each other at the same time. He came toward me while I wrapped my arms around myself. The air had become much colder than I was accustomed to, and I had nothing but my thin mandarin jacket, which was meant for the summer months. The gentle morning breeze had been replaced by an angry gust that whipped my hair against my face.

"You should be below deck, *mèimèi*," Yang said, touching a hand to the small of my back.

His tone was gentle, but I sensed it was to not alarm me. Drops of rain splashed against my cheek as he directed me back toward the stairs. I noticed one of the crewmen securing a length of thick rope around one of the masts. As I went with Yang back down below deck, I could see the sailors with their heads tilted up to stare at the gathering darkness above.

We returned to Yang's private cabin where he opened the door for me. "Have you eaten?" he asked, as if there weren't more important matters for him to concern himself with.

"A storm is coming."

"Commonplace for life at sea," he said dismissively, but I knew his expressions well enough after working in close quarters with him.

"It's going to be a bad one."

"One can never tell. But they can build quickly."

I knew he had to return to his crew, so I didn't burden him with more questions. Obediently, I latched the window to keep the rain from getting in and settled in behind the desk. I chose a book of fantastic tales to try to distract myself, but I had barely begun the first one when the crash of thunder made me jump.

My heart was beating so hard that each throb was painful. The floor of the cabin lurched beneath me. Never had I been more aware that I was floating in a contraption of wood upon a vast ocean.

Within minutes, a knock came on the door. It was Little Jie. He had brought food on a tray, but I doubted my stomach would allow me to eat the way the waves were tossing the ship about.

"Miss, don't be scared!" he piped up, though the pitch of his voice told me he was far from calm.

He set the food down and stayed in the cabin with me, which I was grateful for. "Have you been through a storm like this before?" I asked.

The rumble of thunder interrupted his reply. With a yelp, he edged closer to me. "No, miss. I only came aboard in Canton, just like you. What are you reading?"

We moved to the sleeping berth where we could huddle

beside each other, and, despite the flicker of the lantern as it swayed with the ship, I started reading. The first story I turned to was one about a fox demon seducing a scholar. I quickly found another story, one more suitable for a young boy. Jie made no remark. He just pressed closer, listening intently to every word as I began to read a ghost story. I was reminded of my younger brother Tian as Little Jie laid his head against my arm.

I wanted to curse the string of mishaps that had brought me onto this ship. If I hadn't gone to Changsha that day, I would still be home in our village. I didn't know what deities I needed to pray to, but I couldn't end here, swallowed by the sea.

I forced myself to turn the page, reading about a young man who was unknowingly haunted by the ghost of a maiden he had once fancied. Words came out of my mouth, but they had no real meaning. I was listening to the crash of the waves and the crack of thunder. The sear of lightning across the sky could be seen as a glow through the shutters.

"Why did the exorcist have to get rid of the ghost?" Jie was asking. He stared up at me, his eyes looking even larger set against his thin face. "Why couldn't they just let her stay near her family? She wasn't scaring anyone."

"I don't know," I said, wondering about the sadness of only being able to see your loved ones as a ghost. Would my spirit be able to find its way across the waves back to our village?

I had spent too much time aboard this ship, wooed by Yang's cause and slipping into a routine. How had I forgotten why I'd come in the first place?

I vowed that if I survived this day, I would do everything I could to get off this ship and return home to my family, as flesh and blood and not as a wispy ghost caught between worlds. I put my arm around Little Jie, who reminded me so much of my brother that my heart ached.

Another rumble momentarily drowned out the patter of rain

outside, but it wasn't thunder this time. The low sound vibrated the floor beneath our feet.

The gunpowder engine was firing up down in the hold. Despite the winds that battered the hull of the ship, it began to gain in speed. Was it possible to out sail a storm?

"Let's find another story," I said, sifting through the pages of the book. The boy Jie was looking up at me expectantly, and he seemed calmer when I read to him. It certainly calmed me.

I had just begun a story titled "The Tiger Guest" when a huge boom rattled the walls. Immediately after, I heard a sound that I could only describe as a ragged cough from an iron throat.

Jie clutched onto my arm. "What was that?"

The ship had ceased its forward movement and once more lurched on the waves. "The engine," I muttered, shoving the book aside and launching toward the door.

If the gunpowder engine had exploded, it could have taken a large part of the hull with it. Water could be flooding the hold at this very moment.

With my heart in my throat, I bemoaned the fact that I couldn't swim, but that hardly mattered. We were out in open water with a storm bearing down on us. This junk was life itself.

I had never been to the engine room, but I knew it was located to the rear of the ship. I stumbled through the hallway, navigating by lantern light.

As we neared the hatch to the engine room, I could smell the sulfurous stench of gunpowder. Yang appeared then as well, rushing down the ladder from the upper deck. He spared me only a glance before reaching for the hatch. His hair was slick with rain and his coat drenched.

A trail of smoke poured out from the opening as Yang disappeared. Grabbing one of the hanging lanterns, I went to peer down the passageway. The haze of smoke was thin, which I hoped was a good sign. Taking a deep breath, I eased myself down the ladder after Yang.

The corridor below was a narrow one. There were two chambers separated by a large iron cauldron. I chose the one where an orange light glowed through the crack at the bottom of the door. Tentatively, I pushed the door open and caught the middle of a conversation.

"I told him a hundred times," a gruff voice chided, the sound muffled behind a face mask. "The boy overloaded the cylinder. He gets overexcited."

The speaker was a stocky man wearing a leather apron and heavy gloves who stood half a head shorter than Yang. His face was darkened with soot, and the hair in his queue was noticeably gray. Behind him, a young boy of about fourteen years who was similarly clad and covered in soot apologized profusely.

Yang addressed the engineer. "Save the explanations, Liu. We need this running immediately."

It was the first time I had seen a working gunpowder engine. Whereas the junk was built of wood, its heart was steel, and intricately fashioned. The size of the engine was remarkably small, and the bulk of the chamber was taken up by cogs and moorings that connected the contraption to the rest of the ship. Black smoke billowed out of one of the cylinders now. I coughed at the grittiness in the air.

Both the men turned at the same time. The elderly man spoke first. "Is that—"

"Stay focused," Yang cut in, turning back to the engineer and his apprentice. "How fast can you get this engine working again? Without it, this storm will tear us apart."

As if to emphasize his point, the vessel suddenly rose, then dropped, leaving a sick, falling feeling in the pit of my stomach. I steadied myself against the doorway. "Is there anything I can do to help?"

Engineer Liu ignored me to bark at his apprentice. "Bring water! We need to cool the chamber enough for me to check the pistons."

I followed the boy as he scurried outside. I found two buckets against the wall while the boy lifted the lid off the iron caldron I had passed outside the engine room. It was used to store water. I remembered similar ones in every courtyard of the Ministry building, so that fires could be immediately controlled.

I thrust one of the buckets into the apprentice's hands before dipping mine into the cauldron. Water sloshed over the side in my haste and I rushed back into the engine room.

Engineer Liu was busy closing off a series of valves and gaskets. "Pour the water into that funnel there."

He pointed toward a receptacle high above my head, and Yang lifted the bucket from my hands before I could comply. Stepping onto a small ladder, he tilted the water over the funnel. I followed the network of pipes that snaked out from it, presumably carrying water to cool critical parts of the machine without contaminating them.

"If you bring the engine all the way down, it will take too long to power up again." Despite Yang's protest, he took the second bucket from the apprentice and tipped it in without argument.

"You worry about keeping this ship afloat, I'll worry about this beast!" Liu snapped.

I ran back out to scoop more water with the boy immediately on my heels. We repeated the process two more times before Engineer Liu chased Yang and me out of the room.

"Away with you. I need to concentrate."

Yang took me by the arm. He spared one tense glance back into the engine room before directing me up the ladder.

"We should get some air. Even with the ventilation shafts, it gets difficult to breathe in there."

Back up in the lower deck, I could tell that the storm had become worse. The commotion in the engine room had drowned out the roar of thunder and the crash of the waves. Most of the crew were gathered in the galley area and around the berths. A group of them had started a game of dice, likely to distract themselves just as I had with my strange tales. Conversations continued in a quiet murmur.

"There's nothing to do but wait it out until Liu fixes whatever he needs to fix."

I could tell Yang wasn't happy with that. He led me back to his cabin while Little Jie trailed behind us. "Did the engine explode?" the boy asked. "Is the ship on fire?"

Though the urchin had directed his questions to me, Yang took the liberty of answering. "No. And no. There was a miscalculation in the amount of gunpowder. One of the cylinders has been damaged, that is all."

Jie stared at him wide-eyed, not comprehending.

"Everything will be fine," Yang concluded, leaving it at that.

We had reached the captain's quarters, and Yang removed his coat to place it onto the hook. His shirt beneath it was only in a slightly better state. He combed a hand through his hair to push it away from his eyes. I would never become accustomed to how short it was.

"All these days aboard the ship and I've never seen Liu or his apprentice before," I remarked.

"Engines are complicated things requiring constant maintenance and care. One does not become an engineer without preferring seclusion."

I thought of the spider's web of pipes and gaskets in the engine room and the shelves full of spare parts kept on hand. With heat stressing the metal and soot griming the gears, the machine would have to be cleaned and calibrated.

There had always been a divide between the scientists and the engineers in the Ministry. Yang showed a typical scientist's wariness toward moving parts. In terms of rank, the scientists had also held themselves superior to the tinkerers who got their hands dirty working machinery. Scientists were more closely aligned to the illustrious scholars where engineers were akin to laborers.

At that moment, the ship lurched violently. Yang reached out to steady me as I stumbled, and I might have hung onto him longer than was proper. I was frightened, truly frightened that I would end up below these waters forever.

"How long do storms last?" I asked shakily.

A crooked smile flitted across his lips, which told me the silliness of my question, but Yang banished it immediately. "My ship has handled much worse," he assured gently.

"But you told Engineer Liu this storm would tear the ship apart."

"I was exaggerating to push him along."

"Or lying now to make me feel better," I argued.

"*Mèimèi*," he said quietly, in such a way that the words sounded entirely different; as if they'd never been spoken before.

My heart beat faster. I was standing closer to him than I was supposed to; staring at him longer than I should have been.

The moment was broken when I felt a tug on my hand. "Miss, the engine is running again," Little Jie said.

I could feel the purr of it down below; not yet the full roar as it was at full power, but building slowly.

"There." Yang ran his fingertip playfully down the bridge of my nose, grinning as if we were out of danger, though we were far from it. "Now let us escape this demon of a storm and find the sun again."

We did see the sun again, as Yang promised. On the day I saw the first ray of light break through the clouds, I stayed up on the main deck for hours. Everyone's spirits seemed high, and the crewmen greeted me in a more familial manner.

"The air after a storm always feels fresher," Headman Zhou told me. "The sun warmer."

Zhou was Yang's second-in-command, a surprisingly affable

man whose beard was just starting to gray. Despite his seemingly mild demeanor, he was unquestionably strict in enforcing the rules of the ship.

I had to agree with Zhou as I tilted my face toward the sky. Overhead, a large falcon soared through the air with wings outstretched. I was surprised to see it so far out at sea, but perhaps it had been blown out by the storm, just as we had been, and was now finding its way home. Its shadow momentarily passed over me, leaving me breathless with a sense of freedom and renewal. This was a good moment.

Yang was sound asleep down below. He had stayed up for nearly two days, coordinating between the ship navigator and Engineer Liu to steer the ship from the storm. I relinquished his cabin as soon as he allowed himself to retire.

I didn't mind lingering out here after being huddled away for so long. I even found myself looking forward to when we could return to the laboratory and continue our work. Yang's experiments had convinced me that he hadn't forsaken the empire. After the cannons and gunpowder had failed during the war with the foreigners, Yang had changed strategies. He was still fighting the war in his own way. Maybe it was best for the empire that Chen Chang-wei continued to build his war machines while Yang searched to cure the addiction that was robbing the empire of its lifeblood.

I didn't know what my place was in all this, but there was a restlessness growing within me. I could no longer stand back and do nothing. I could no longer remain asleep.

"Pardon me, miss."

Engineer Liu's apprentice stood behind me, head bowed with hands folded in his sleeves. I hadn't seen him since the first night of the storm and hardly recognized him save for his clothing. His face was scrubbed clean of soot and his face mask was pulled down around his neck, revealing a youthful face.

"My master apologizes for imposing, but he wishes to speak with you."

I was taken aback by the extreme formality. "Certainly."

Ducking his head, the apprentice hurried back down into the hold as if escaping the sun.

"What is your name?" I asked as I followed behind him.

"Benzhuo, miss."

"Your name is 'Clumsy'?"

"That is what my master calls me, miss. But only part of the time. When he's happy with me, he calls me 'Clever.'"

The gruff old engineer certainly seemed the eccentric type. I wondered if he had come up with a nickname for me after our brief encounter.

"How is everything down below?"

"As usual."

"The repairs weren't too difficult?"

"No, miss."

I made one last attempt at conversation. "How long have you apprenticed with Master Liu?"

"Three years."

Not once did he glance back my way as he answered, and I thought of Yang's remark that engineers tended toward being recluses. One would have to be a recluse to be shut up inside that tiny chamber for so long without going mad.

Down in the engine room, Liu was still checking and adjusting valves even though the machine was silent. As soon as the young apprentice delivered me, Benzhuo took hold of a rag and set about cleaning out some piping without needing to be told. Clumsy or not, he was very industrious.

Liu squinted at me through the glow of the lanterns while his hands finished their last task. "It *is* you," he said finally.

"I apologize, sir—"

"Ah, you don't remember me? Liu Yentai." The engineer pulled his face mask down below his chin and blinked at me expectantly. I could do nothing but blink back, trying my best to find some sense of recognition.

"I gave you a windup frog for your first birthday," he prompted.

My eyes lit up. I couldn't remember Liu, but I remembered the toy. It would hop about the room, changing directions in random fashion while I chased after it. At some point, our dog had pounced on it and damaged one of the legs. After that the frog would only hop in a sad half circle before the gears would grind to a halt.

Mother had put the clockwork creature away in a cabinet for safekeeping, promising Father would try to get it repaired. For all I know, it had been left in that very spot when we fled, forgotten like so many little things from our old life.

"You worked in the Ministry with my father."

Engineer Liu beamed proudly. "You look like your mother," he said with delight, waving a finger at me. "She was one of the quickest, cleverest minds I have ever encountered."

I was shocked. "Mother?"

"An accomplished mathematician in her youth." His hands had gone back to work on the machine as he spoke, as if the habit had become ingrained. "Without a doubt, she stood out among the candidacy that year."

"But women are not allowed to sit for the imperial exams."

Liu chuckled. "No, Miss Jin. They are not."

I listened in fascination as he recounted the tale of a reclusive young man who showed up to the academies. He kept to himself and his studies, doing as little as possible to attract attention—but so much so that it had the opposite effect. Especially when his scores emerged at the top of his class during the provisional exams.

"That young man was your mother!"

The story was so far-fetched, Liu must have invented it. I thought of Mother lying in her room with the shutters closed, her lungs filled with smoke. Who was this brash young woman the engineer was describing?

But then, I remembered how mother had taken control of our household after Father's execution. She'd swallowed her grief and found a new place for us to start anew before shutting herself away.

I was grateful to have a new image of her: young, reckless, brilliant. I secreted away this new knowledge like a gift.

The old engineer finished some adjustment and tapped his wrench lightly against an iron pipe, head tilted to catch the sound. "This is why men of science like Yang find this work to be so difficult. He keeps on telling me to write it down, each detail and step of maintaining this machine. But it is impossible to describe knowing the feel and sound of when the gaskets are tightened enough or the pistons need replacing. There is art to this. Benzhuo over there is only starting to learn all of this creature's tricks."

Benzhuo lifted his head at the sound of his name but immediately bent down again to keep on working.

"Yang wants to believe there is a clear answer to everything. An equation for the human mind. Our frailties must be chemical impurities, our flaws due to a predictable reaction. Not so." He sighed long and loud. "Sometimes men are weak. Sometimes fate is cruel."

It appeared that both Liu Yentai and his apprentice were sorely in need of rest, but the old engineer insisted that night was day and day was night down in the engine room. The chamber beside it was their private quarters in which the two of them caught snatches of sleep when the engine wasn't in use.

I left them shortly after, hoping they would use the opportunity to rest up.

When I returned to the second deck, Yang had awoken. I wanted to point out that he'd only had a few hours of sleep, but he was in a grumbling mood, so I brought him tea and a bowl of stew from the galley.

Yang was dressed and at his desk when I entered the cabin, though his face was still haunted by dark shadows. He hadn't shaven, giving him a rough appearance. There was a map spread out on the desk, which he was frowning at.

"The storm took us off course," he explained when I asked him what was wrong. "And also drained our store of gunpowder. We'll need to sail by wind power until we reach the next port."

He took the tea from me, giving me a grateful look as he took his first sip. Though I knew it was not a good time, I brought up the prospect of returning me to the mainland.

"As soon as possible, if you could," I added, which earned a small bark of a laugh from him.

"I can't have you fall into enemy hands."

"Our countrymen are not your enemy."

"They are," he said with a dark look. "In more ways than you can imagine. We are our own enemy."

I switched tactics, hoping for a better result. "You took Engineer Liu in during the purge."

He nodded. "We fled Peking together. I had my family's wealth; Liu had access to the Ministry's airship. There were others with us, but we all scattered to go our separate ways. We all knew that one day the empire would come after us to reclaim what it had lost."

Yang was trying to protect me, but there was a wild light in his eyes. I tried to explain it away as lack of sleep and the strain of fleeing the storm, but I began to doubt Yang's dedication to finding a cure for opium addiction. His determination had twisted into obsession, and I feared he would take the rest of us down that same path of madness.

12

By the next day, Yang and I were back in the laboratory. He came to ask that morning whether I would return to assist him and I agreed. Even though we fell into the usual routine, a rift remained between us.

We worked in silence for the first hour. I performed a series of tests on each sample, just as Yang had shown me, and only spoke when I needed to, which wasn't often.

"You know that you're not my prisoner," Yang remarked wryly.

When I looked over, he remained with his head bent to his task.

"But you won't let me go."

"Soling, after what I've seen—" He shook his head. "I have a sense that things are going to get worse quickly on the mainland."

"But you can't run forever. Surely there is still something or someone in all of China that you care about?"

Yang shook his head regretfully. "You can come with us," he offered after a pause. "We have need of a physician on board."

"But what of my family?"

"Bring them here."

He offered it so readily, as if it truly were that easy. I hadn't told him of Mother's addiction, and I doubted Yang would tolerate opium on board his ship. Even if he would, I didn't want my family stowed away, in exile from our homeland. We had already been living in exile all these years.

Our conversation was interrupted by the sharp ring of a bell.

"What is it?" I asked as Yang shot to his feet.

"Trouble," was all he said before leaving the laboratory.

I took it upon myself to quickly stow away all the chemicals and pack up the various implements. Back in the storeroom, my hand hovered over the drawer where I had discovered the mysterious vials of dark red liquid several days earlier. What was it that had launched Yangon this quest?

As I emerged from the lab, it seemed the bell had summoned everyone to the upper deck. The level was empty, and as I climbed the stairs, I could hear the hum of conversation from all the men gathered above.

Yang had a spyglass pointed to the sky. His crew surrounded him, waiting. Overhead, I could see the outline of bird.

"We're being tracked," Yang declared.

Headman Zhou came up beside him. "Is it pirates?"

A murmur rustled through the crowd. At the mention of pirates, every man on board had tensed. On a large ship equipped with cannons, I thought we wouldn't need to fear pirates, but I was apparently wrong.

Yang didn't answer. He called for Liu, and a moment later, the engineer appeared above deck, squinting in the sunlight. Yang handed the older man the spyglass.

"What do you think?" he asked, jaw clenched.

The small outline in the distant sky had grown larger in the time it took the engineer to make his way above. I recognized the bird was a falcon with its wings outstretched, just as I'd seen yesterday. After staring at it, I had the unsettling feeling that it was the exact same falcon.

How could I possibly know that? It was closer now and appeared larger, the details clearer in my eye. The outline of the bird appeared identical, as well as the markings on the head and tail.

"Pirates wouldn't have anything that intricate," Liu declared, targeting the bird with his spyglass. At that moment, the falcon cut through the air at an odd angle.

"The storm blew us off course," Yang muttered. "Gave them time to catch us."

"Who?" I asked.

With a sideways glance, Yang handed me the spyglass. It took a moment for me to focus it onto the dark silhouette in the sky, but when I did, I saw it wasn't a falcon at all. Or at least not a live one. The skeleton was fashioned from rattan, the wings from panels of silk. I could just discern the line attached to the carriage that trailed downward before disappearing against the pale blue sky.

It was a kite. An elaborately constructed kite.

"I saw that same bird yesterday," I told them, my chest tightening with dread. Yang swore beside me.

I didn't know what purpose the falcon served, but I knew someone was nearby, controlling it. Yang gave the order to ready for battle, setting his crew into motion.

"We're low on gunpowder," Engineer Liu reported grimly.

Yang barely blinked. "Use it for the engine."

I caught the wicked gleam in his eye before he went to join his men.

The old engineer turned to me with a slight bow. "You should come on down below with us, Miss Jin."

Though he was trying to be delicate, I could hear the warning in his voice. I took one last look on deck to see the sailors working at the riggings to angle the sails. Yang with his eyes fixed on the horizon.

"Are we under attack?" I asked, hurrying down the stairs after the engineer.

Liu threw an answer over his shoulder. "Only if they can catch us. No need for cannons when we have a ship like this. Our engine is one of the finest there is. One of the fastest on the sea!" he said with a zeal that was far from humble. "Faster than those heavy iron beasts the foreign devils sail."

"Is that who we're fleeing from?" I asked.

Liu either didn't hear my question or chose to ignore me. "Where is that lazy apprentice of mine?"

Benzhuo stumbled from his bunk as we neared the engine room. He was no longer covered in soot as he'd been when I first saw him, though his hands were still stained black. I imagined anyone who worked down here quickly became coated in a layer of gunpowder.

"More wood!" Liu barked. "We need to get the fire roaring again."

The lanky apprentice rushed out to obey his master's instructions while Engineer Liu gestured for me to bring him the set of bellows leaning against the wall. Then I was given my first glimpse inside the inner workings of the engine.

"This is a wood furnace?" I asked with a frown.

"The fire needs to be hot enough to ignite the gunpowder. But in a controlled fashion. See those embers?" The tinder inside the furnace compartment had burned down, but there was a visible glow beneath the ash. "We keep that layer lit, so that we can awaken the beast quickly should we need it."

Liu took the bellows from my hands and began to fan the embers, the thick muscles in his forearms flexing. All the while, he kept on talking.

"The devil ships use steam, did you know that? The real force behind them is the same as ours. They use fire to heat water. We use fire to ignite gunpowder. More power there! But takes a well-crafted machine to contain such forces. Engineer Chen knows that already."

"Chen Chang-wei?"

"Yes. Young Mister Chen. Another one of your father's prodigies. Chen was in the engineering corps like me. He's aware of the engine required to handle such heat. What he doesn't have is this."

Liu held up what looked like a drum plastered with red paper over the ends. I knew what it was before he said anything.

"This is the secret. Do you know the ancients used to mix all sorts of strange things in their powder? Realgar, saltpeter, honey . . . garlic, of all things! The alchemy of fire." With each proclamation, his voice rose higher dramatically.

I didn't realize I'd been holding my breath. "What's in this mixture?"

"I don't know. I just know to throw in the correct amounts and keep my head down if the situation looks desperate. I prefer not to touch the stuff myself. And you shouldn't touch it, either," Liu warned, waving a finger at me. "The making of weapons will not win this war. Your father learned that very tragic lesson, little one."

Benzhuo had returned with a wheelbarrow laden with firewood. He tossed a few of the logs into the furnace to feed the fire.

"Now powder!" Liu commanded, taking hold of the bellows once more.

The apprentice darted out of the room to collect more drums of gunpowder while I stood flat on my feet, wishing there was something I could do to help. After seeing that Engineer Liu was absorbed with his task, I followed Benzhuo to the far section of the cargo hold.

"Why so far away?" I was out of breath.

"The gunpowder has to be kept away from any spark that could ignite it, miss."

The old engineer and his apprentice seemed to wage an

ongoing battle with fire; how to keep it alive, how to keep it from devouring everything.

Inside the cargo hold, the gunpowder drums were stacked in crates with straw in between. With their earthenware containers and the red paper seal on top, they resembled jugs of wine. It occurred to me that Yang might very well have intended the powder to be disguised as a shipment of spirits.

Benzhuo hefted up of the crates and headed off toward the engine room while I only managed to lift one drum. My arms strained against the weight, and as I struggled to find my balance, I heard an odd sound.

At first I dismissed it as one of the creaks and groans of the ship as it rolled upon the waves. But I had become accustomed to those noises and this was different. Someone was thumping against the walls.

The sound was coming from down here, somewhere nearby. Though the noises were muffled, I thought I could hear a voice. There were no words, just a low moan as if someone were in distress. I set down the drum of gunpowder and tried to follow the source of the sound.

Outside of the storage area, there was a long, narrow corridor. I followed it, and the pounding against the walls became more pronounced. There was a chamber right beside the cargo hold. The door was unlocked, and I opened it with a trembling hand.

A chill entered my blood. There were large cells with thick iron bars on each side. Cages, with enough space for a man to lie down inside, but little else. The cells were all empty except for two.

At first, I thought these prisoners must have been locked down here for disciplinary reasons, but one of them stared listlessly, not even recognizing my presence. He was gaunt, the hollows of his face sunken and almost skeletal in appearance. I kept on telling myself to back away, get out, but my feet wouldn't obey.

The man closest to me slowly turned his head as if it took great effort. His eyes were black and endless, and my skin crawled as I realized I knew that look too well. It was the same gaze my mother fixed onto me when she was looking, not at me, but through me.

Without warning, he lunged at the bars. Startled, I fell backward and could do nothing but stare as his gaunt form came smashing at the iron cage. A bone-thin hand snaked through the bars to grasp at me. At that moment, the second prisoner also came to life.

They were little more than animals in a rage. The men shook their heads furiously, rocking back and forth, clawing at the bars and then at themselves. The one who had started it all had his face forced against the iron, mouth gaping open. His tongue, gums, teeth, everything inside looked black as if doused with tar. His fingertips, beneath the nails, had also turned dark.

I scrambled away, my hands scratching against the wooden panels in the wall as I tried to pull myself up. My limbs had forgotten how to function in the face of the horror before me, and I fumbled with the door for an eternity before I was able to drag it open.

As soon as I was out, I slammed the door shut, pushing my entire weight against it. The banging and snarling continued on the other side.

I ran down the corridor, trying to escape from the stench, the cages, the mindless rage. I saw Benzhuo at the door to the gunpowder room, staring at me. "We're not supposed to go back there."

His words barely registered in my ears. My thoughts were like a riot of crows seeking escape. All at once, I could see Yang in his laboratory. The vials of blood locked away in the storeroom. The extra portions of food that Cook always set aside.

Yang had imprisoned those men down below. He experimented with opium in his lab, but maybe it didn't stop there. Those two prisoners, the blankness of their eyes.. .

I didn't need to know what was happening to know there was something very wrong. I shoved past Benzhuo. Behind me, I could hear the captives shouting, their grunts more animal than human. Liu emerged from the engine room as I reached the stairs.

"Soling, wait!"

He kept on calling after me, trying to calm me down, but I took the steps as fast as I could. Even when I broke out onto the main deck, I couldn't stop running. Only the edge of the ship and the long drop to the ocean below stopped me.

Yang was mad. He was gifted and brilliant, but he had become insane in his fervor. I gulped in deep breaths of salt air as if I could cleanse myself.

There was shouting all around me as a great shadow coursed overhead, blocking out the sun. It was then that I finally glanced up and then over the water.

For a moment, I had forgotten that we were under attack. Another ship had appeared and had navigated close enough for me to see the red sails of the imperial navy. The prow had been carved into a dragon's head whose gaping mouth was aimed directly toward us.

The glider continued to circle overhead. Now I could see there wasn't a single cord attached to the rattan frame, but many lines that controlled the movements of the falcon as if it were a puppet rather than a mere kite on the wind.

The crew was focused on the approaching ship as well as the contraption circling us. No one paid me any attention, but when I searched out Yang he was looking right at me. There was a question in his eyes. His lips moved, and though I couldn't hear him above the shouts of the crewmen, I recognized the words.

Chen Chang-wei.

I recalled the elaborate rattan skeleton in Chang-wei's study.

The glider was his work. Yang had probably recognized that fact the moment the giant falcon appeared in the sky.

A few of the crewmen attempted to throw a spear through the glider, but the silk bird dipped and banked out of harm's way. A moment later, an orb dropped from the rattan frame and shattered onto the deck, not unlike the shell of an egg. A blue flame spread out from the remnants.

By the time crewmen gathered to douse the flame, another orb had been dropped on the opposite side of the deck. All the while, the dragon ship sped closer, black smoke spewing from its sides from vents hidden in the scales.

"Fire!" Yang ordered.

The boom of a cannon shot shook the deck. I staggered to my knees, hands pressed to my ears as I searched for cover. Rather than answer with cannons, the falcon released more of its incendiary orbs, splitting the efforts of the crew between controlling the flames and manning the cannons.

I ducked behind the main mast, realizing a moment later that my strategy wasn't sound. The falcon began attacking the sails with its firebombs. The engine remained silent beneath us. Engineer Liu hadn't gotten his "beast" fully functioning yet.

The next time Yang's ship fired its cannons, there was an answering volley from the approaching boat that shook the deck. The air filled with the tang of sulfur and the sound of splintering wood.

What if they destroyed each other? What if each ship dragged its crew down into the black waters?

Through the rush and roar of the battle, I heard my name.

"Soling!" The cry came again, louder this time.

The imperial ship now loomed large before us. I thought I saw a figure wave at me from the opposite deck.

"Get on," Chang-wei shouted.

The falcon glider swooped low across the deck right before me, clearing a path through the swarm of crewmen. As the men leapt away, the glider arched up into the air, sailing high before diving back down toward the deck.

"Get on," he said again. Chang-wei was asking me to do the impossible.

I glanced back at Yang, then traced the path of the falcon's flight over the water. Yang and Chang-wei were both keeping secrets from me, but when I considered the emaciated prisoners with their mouths stained black, I started running as fast as I could.

I heard my name once again right before I intercepted the glider. It was Yang this time. I should have kept my focus upon the glider and my one chance at escape, but something in his tone made me pause.

There was no threat there. No anger. It was merely an entreaty and. . . something more.

I turned to see the mystery box held out in Yang's palm. The steel surface gleamed in the sunlight. With a heft of his wrist, the cube was sailing through the air at me.

My arms closed around it out of reflex. I pulled the box protectively to my chest and felt the hard steel edge against my breastbone.

A moment later the falcon flew in front of me. I reached out and hooked my arm onto the rattan frame, pulling my feet into the carriage beneath the wings. In the next breath, I was flying.

The air rushed out of me and I clung to the frame as tight as I could. The skeleton formed a cage around me, and the flutter of the silken wing and tail feathers drowned out all sound. I could feel the rush of air over my face, and my heart thundered inside my chest. Louder than the cannons below.

I was in the air, inside a contraption that I knew was nothing more than a collection of silk and sticks. Yet weren't bones and feathers just as humble of materials? I wanted to squeeze my eyes shut in fear, but I also wanted to throw them open as wide as I could and stare at the two battling ships below, the tiny crewmen aboard them. The endless water all around. I was flying.

Gradually, the glider was being reeled in. As the imperial ship became larger and larger below me, I noticed that the cannon fire had stopped on both sides.

Chang-wei was there waiting for me as the falcon lowered to the deck. He held the control apparatus in his hands. It looked like a skein of cords wrapped around a sunburst of wooden knobs.

Several of the crewmen came forward and reached up with long poles to hook onto the frame to pull it the final distance. Chang-wei handed the controls aside as I lowered my feet to the deck.

"Are you all right?" he asked, reaching out to steady me as I untangled myself from the glider. My knees buckled when I tried to stand on my own and Chang-wei held on to me to keep me from falling.

"I thought we'd lost you." Chang-wei's hands lingered on my waist as he spoke.

When our gazes met, his expression was full of concern. Then something flickered in his eyes, and he quickly let go of me as if remembering we weren't alone.

"It is good to see you're safe."

His tone had become formal, and he took a step back for good measure.

"Shall we commence fire?" one of the navy men asked.

There was no chance to reply. I looked across the water to Yang's war junk and watched as some sort of netting was released from just beneath the ridge of the bow. White powder rained into the sea, which immediately began to churn and froth around the ship.

Yang tipped two fingers toward us in a brief salute before the entire ship and the surrounding waters became enshrouded in a thick, smoky mist. With a roar, the engine started up and the scent of gunpowder filled the air.

Old Liu had done his part, and the junk sped off, the whir of the engine fading away behind the curtain of fog.

"We can track them down again," suggested a man who appeared to be the dragon boat captain.

I glanced down at the mystery box, still hugged against my chest. Chang-wei watched silently as I found the trigger and set the gears spinning. The panels of the box folded open to reveal a square of folded paper inside, covered on both sides with neatly written notes and formulas. I couldn't decipher the script, but Chang-wei seemed to comprehend.

"There's no need to pursue them," he replied, turning the sheet of paper over. "We found what we were looking for."

13

The captain's quarters on the imperial dragon boat were luxurious compared to the cabin on Yang's vessel. Chang-wei brought me there so the two of us could speak privately, and I took a seat in one of the rosewood chairs. I still had my puzzle box in my hands with Yang's gunpowder formula tucked safely inside. Chang-wei had returned them to me after a brief inspection. Despite how eager the crown prince and his cohort were to seize the secrets, Chang-wei hadn't seized possession of the papers.

A servant brought tea. Awkwardly, I set the box in my lap as I took the cup. Chang-wei seated himself beside me, resting his hand over his knees. He still wore the state robes designating him as an imperial official just as the rest of the crew were in military uniform.

"Are you well?" he asked as if this were merely a social visit in my family's parlor.

"I wasn't harmed."

"Inspector Aguda promised me his men could track you through any part of the city. When they reported they'd lost you, I was—" His voice rose fiercely, and he made an effort to bring it under control. "I was furious."

It was hard to imagine Chang-wei losing his temper. He carried himself with so much control. Every action and word was well thought out. Perhaps that was why he was able to retain a position with the imperial government while Yang, with his brash attitude, had no choice but to flee.

Chang-wei drank his tea now while I did the same. He appeared deep in thought.

"So that is what Yang looks like now," he said after a while.

"Yang claims he's rejected any allegiance to the empire—but he did give me his formulas," I added hastily when I saw Chang-wei raise his eyebrows.

I hadn't meant to mark Yang as a traitor. It was difficult to tell where Chang-wei's loyalties lay, but I couldn't forget that he wore an imperial insignia.

"Yang Hanzhu gifted his work to you, not to the Emperor," he replied. "This was what we had set out to achieve, but I confess I had hoped for more."

"More?"

"We could have used Yang's knowledge and skill. He's a brilliant scientist, but it's clear to me that he has no desire to reconcile with the imperial court."

Brilliant scientist. I shuddered to think of what experiments Yang had engaged in. The subjects kept in cages, dosed with opium until their minds were lost.

"Yang did mention you briefly," I ventured.

"I'm certain he did not have favorable things to say." He set his tea aside, agitated.

"He told me not to trust you."

I watched Chang-wei carefully as we spoke. After my final discovery on Yang's ship, I had to look at everyone with new eyes.

He appeared wounded. "Soling, everything I've told you has been the truth. Even when Inspector Aguda wanted to keep information from you, I gave you the truth. You do believe that, don't you?"

He regarded me so intently that I felt my face heating. It was hard to decipher my feelings about Chang-wei. I had never known him beyond a name, yet we still shared so much of our past lives.

"I didn't realize there was ill will between you and Yang," I said, deflecting.

His tone became curt. "We've never gotten along."

"Why not?"

"Yang doesn't make himself easy to work with. He can be stubborn, disagreeable. His ideas are for his own glory, where we at the Ministry of Science should be working for the glory of our empire."

"You were right then, that Yang would only give up his secrets for personal reasons."

I still didn't understand what made him decide to relinquish the formula, but Yang was unpredictable. It gave me hope that he wasn't completely lost, but we'd never know now. He'd escaped once more to the seas.

Chang-wei looked to the box. "If I may have a closer look?"

He held out his hand, but I held on to the box and its contents. "After this, the crown prince will have no further use for me?"

"I don't suppose he would. You've done everything he's asked."

"I can go then, without any further conditions."

Given that I was on an imperial ship and at the mercy of the Emperor's men, a formula scribbled on a scrap of paper was a meager bargaining tool, but it was all I had.

"If that is what you wish. You've more than done your duty."

"And you'll keep my brother from the factories? My family will be taken care of?"

I knew I was asking for too much. The crown prince had

commanded me to take on this task. It was my duty. I had no right to demand a reward for accomplishing it.

"I told you I would help you if I could," he replied stiffly.

This time I did hand the steel container over. Chang-wei wasted no time in opening it to retrieve the contents. He unfolded the paper and held it up to the light. I could see from the ragged edge of it that Yang had torn it directly from his journal.

"Is that what you needed?" I asked when the silence became uncomfortable.

"We won't know until we test it," Chang-wei concluded. He folded the paper back up and carefully tucked it into his sleeve. "But this is promising. I have to get this to the Ministry laboratories in Peking."

And after that, the formula would travel to the towering factories churning with black smoke, where conscripted laborers would slave away producing the raw materials for the Emperor's war.

It really wasn't my concern. It was the sovereign's duty to wage war against the invaders. It was my duty to make sure my family was cared for.

"Mister Chen," I began.

"There's no need to be so formal—"

"It appears you have command of this ship."

"At the present time. The crown prince has granted me temporary authority."

I fixed my gaze firmly onto him, emboldened by the daring of my recent escape. I would no longer be kicked back and forth between two players like a feathered *jianzi*.

"Let me use this opportunity to congratulate you on your respected position as well as the promotion that this formula will likely earn you. Now, if you could tell me, Mister Chen, how fast can you get me home?"

I EXPECTED Chang-wei to make up some excuse or argue, as Yang had, that I needed to be protected. Instead he retrieved a scroll from the cabinet and unrolled it over the captain's desk.

"This is Canton," he pointed out. "This is approximately where we are."

I was surprised at how far the storm had swept us from the mainland.

"We'll sail to Shanghai," Chang-wei explained. "From there, I can transport the formula to the capital in two days' time. We can also arrange to have you escorted back to your village."

He didn't apologize for the fact that getting the formula back to Peking was his primary objective. Given that he'd promised finally to send me home, I didn't challenge him on it, even though there were many ports on the map that appeared closer to Linhua. I also didn't ask him whether we would part ways in Shanghai.

"Is this plan acceptable to you?" he asked me quietly.

Were we wondering the same thing? Is this how we were meant to end? We'd finally come face-to-face again to just say farewell once more.

Chang-wei and I were still essentially strangers, and it was impossible for me to read his mood.

"It's acceptable," I replied and that was all we said of it.

The voyage aboard the imperial dragon boat was admittedly more comfortable than my passage on Yang's ship. The vessel was more spacious, and I was given a private cabin that I kept to most of the time save for a daily outing above deck for fresh air.

A few days later, I was on deck watching the pattern of sunlight on the water when a shade moved over me. I knew it was Chang-wei even before he spoke.

"The sun can be harsh out on the open water," he said, handing me a parasol.

I looked up as my fingers closed around the handle. The handle was fashioned from a thin reed of bamboo, and the canopy had a peculiar pattern. It took me only a moment to place it.

"Your falcon glider!"

"He was no longer of any service in his original form."

"So you re-created him."

I was delighted to see how the rattan frame had been worked into the spines of the parasol, the panels recut and shaped to fit. The feathered pattern was still visible upon the silk, and I could see the outline of both eyes. Those had been repainted to look like the sun and the moon.

"But what if you had need of him again?" I protested.

"Then I'll make a new one, as the situation dictates."

His resourcefulness made me smile, but I kept my gaze focused out on the water.

"You know we no longer have servants to shield the sun at every step," I told him.

In Peking, my family had traveled in sedan chairs, hefted onto the shoulders of carriers. A fine lady such as my mother, the wife of a high-ranking official, would shudder to find her pale skin baked dark like a common peasant. But I was no stranger to the sun on my back. My feet were toughened with callouses, my hands similarly rough.

"I can't imagine what has happened to your family without feeling great sorrow," he admitted.

I sensed he was preparing for something more. Chang-wei always became painfully formal when something bothered him.

"You must be wondering how it was that I came to be where I am," he continued. "When so many others were stripped of their titles or branded as traitors after Wusong fell."

"Like Yang Hanzhu and Old Liu Yentai?" I asked, finally turning to him.

A frown creased his brow. "Old Liu?"

"Engineer Liu is traveling aboard Yang's ship as part of his crew. He mentioned your name."

"Liu was my superior," Chang-wei remarked with a hint of fondness. "A traditionalist from the older generation."

"He seems to think engineering is a combination of tinkering and feng shui."

Chang-wei chuckled. "There has always been a degree of mysticism and superstition within the Ministry of Science."

"And you're a non-traditionalist?"

I'd meant to tease him, but he grew quiet. I twisted the parasol in my hands, trying to find some way to recover the conversation. It was Chang-wei who spoke first.

"I don't want you to think I've benefited from turning my back on your father's memory. Or by exploiting the intimate knowledge I had of the members of the Ministry."

"There is no need to apologize—"

I wanted to tell him that the past was the past. That I was no one to judge him, but Chang-wei went on.

"I don't enjoy as much influence with the crown prince as it might seem, Soling. He trusts me, but only to a limited extent. I do what I can to keep your father's old acquaintances protected. Inspector Aguda wanted to come along on this voyage to hunt down Yang, but I was able to persuade the crown prince to only send me."

"Why are you telling me all this?"

"Because Yang told you not to trust me and I feel the need to defend myself," he said, scowling.

With a deep breath, Chang-wei settled his hands onto the ledge. He appeared so torn that my heart opened a crack for him. Though he had claimed to have been honest with me, I knew there was still too much I didn't know about him.

"Yang is a very dangerous man," he began. "Because of what he knows. If he were to sell his secrets to the *Yangguizi*, our efforts to build a resistance would be crippled."

"But Yang wouldn't," I assured. "He hates the foreigners."

I didn't mention that he'd confessed to hating the Emperor just as much.

"Yang docks at foreign ports. He sails among their ships, trades with them. The Ministry of Defense has considered having him arrested for that alone. I petitioned the crown prince to reconsider that and so many other charges, but it's a difficult position for me to argue."

He paused, his hands tightening on the wood. "Yang and I saw each other once after your father was gone," he admitted finally.

I frowned. What could that matter?

"I knew Yang Hanzhu could be found among the foreigners," Chang-wei confessed. "Because I spent some time among them as well. For that reason alone, our countrymen will never fully trust me."

When he straightened, the look he gave me was as serious as I'd ever seen him. "Shanghai has the largest international settlement in the empire. It's said that there are two cities: one that belongs to us and one that belongs to the *Yangguizi*. Whatever you may see or hear there—please remember I have the best interests of our kingdom in mind."

I nodded, not quite knowing what I was agreeing to. He left me then, and when I turned back to the waves, I could just make out the dark outline of the shore in the distance. As grateful as I was to be returning to dry land, our conversation left me wondering whether I had made the right choice fleeing back into the Emperor's grasp.

14

I was given two instructions upon disembarking in Shanghai. The first was to stay close.

"And don't trust anyone," Chang-wei warned.

The perils must have been real. He actually held a hand to the small of my back as we moved through the market area near the docks.

"We must go to the administrative yamen," Chang-wei said. "They'll help me relay my message to Peking."

The streets of Shanghai swallowed us, and I was shoved against Chang-wei by the swell of the crowd. From the sheer number of shops and teahouses, Shanghai had to be unaccountably wealthy. Anything could be bought here among these lanes. The market vendors spied the insignia on Chang-wei's uniform and immediately pressed close, holding out various trinkets.

Though I had heard the city was overrun with foreigners, I found myself surrounded by my own countrymen, through their style of dress was markedly different from Hunan province or even what I recalled from Peking. The colors were blinding, the designs ornate and the fabrics combined in a way I had never imagined: silk beneath leather, brocades and fastenings and buttons that looked like a puzzle in and of themselves.

A man crossed our path wearing a sash of imperial yellow, though it was obvious he was no more than a merchant. I looked to Chang-wei, but he registered neither surprise nor outrage even though the color was supposed to be worn only by those closest to the Emperor. This truly was a lawless place.

Chang-wei found the administrative compound and installed me just inside the gates after a quick word with the sentry stationed there. The building had the look of a fortress with so many armed guards patrolling the gates.

Whatever official business Chang-wei had to attend to took much longer than I expected. There was a long line of petitioners waiting to see the magistrate when we arrived. The line dwindled down by half, but Chang-wei still had not returned.

When he finally did reappear, I could see by his frown that something was wrong. Worry lines cut deep into his forehead, and he pulled me into the far corner of the courtyard before speaking.

"Rebels," he said in a low voice as if the word itself were a curse.

This was nothing new to me. "There are always reports of rebels and bandits on the road."

"This is something different. Something worse."

"Where?"

Chang-wei ran a hand roughly over his face, and I knew the answer then. My pulse jumped.

"Is Linhua village safe? Mother? What about Tian?"

"We don't know. Nothing is certain."

"What's happened? How many rebels could there possibly be?"

I knew I was demanding answers he couldn't possibly have, but I was not going to back down. I would walk the entire way home if I had to.

"Miss Jin, you can't go to your village. The rebels have taken over entire cities in the southern region of Hunan province. The reports say they've gathered an army."

"I can't just remain here and do nothing. I told Nan I would only be away for two days," I protested helplessly. How many days had it been now? Almost a month.

My eyes stung with tears, and I knew I wasn't making any sense. I didn't fear rebellion. I feared not knowing whether my family was dead or alive.

"We'll go to Peking first," Chang-wei reasoned. "I've sent a copy of Yang Hanzhu's notes to the Ministry, and the crown prince will be more than grateful for your contribution. You'll be protected in the capital while the Emperor raises an army to defeat the rebels. Once he has regained control of the south, we'll send out messengers to find your family."

I shook my head even before he finished. "My family needs me now. Our village could still be untouched."

Chang-wei's jaw hardened stubbornly, but I could be stubborn, too.

I wasn't going to hide in the capital while Mother and Tian were in danger. No one in Peking cared about people like us.

"If I lose them now, I may never find them." When we'd been forced to flee the capital eight years ago, there was so much fear and confusion. You went where you were told, hoping that fate would be kind.

"I can't let you go alone."

"There must be someone going south. A merchant caravan."

"No one is going blindly into rebel territory, Soling." In his agitation, Chang-wei abandoned polite address completely. He rubbed a hand over the back of his neck. "I can find out if the governor of Shanghai will raise a militia to provide support."

"I don't want to be dragged into the middle of a war. I just want to find my family."

I broke away from Chang-wei. I didn't want him to see me so

shaken. For the last years, I had been making decisions for all of us, but I didn't know what to do anymore.

"Miss Jin."

Chang-wei hovered just beyond my shoulder, not touching me. I didn't turn to him. I would not allow myself to face him until I had some plan to show him I wasn't giving up.

"There is someone who will go into Hunan," I murmured finally.

The thought made me sick to my stomach, but I swallowed my tears as well as my pride. I turned to face Chang-wei. Behind him, the official business of the yamen continued without interruption. For these citizens, the threat of rebellion was far, far away.

"Opium runners," I declared, forcing the words out. "Smugglers have routes throughout the empire."

Runners were able to travel along rivers and secret routes to deliver the opium to every corner of the empire. Like ghosts, they managed to evade the most diligent of enforcers. The opium trade had to be alive and rampant in a city like Shanghai.

"I won't put you into the hands of such vermin."

I started to argue, but Chang-wei silenced me with a tiny motion of his fingers. "I said I would not allow you to go alone."

Could he possibly mean...that this wouldn't be farewell?

"Let us go together," Chang-wei said, answering my silent question "There's no time to waste."

CHANG-WEI DISAPPEARED ONCE MORE into the inner offices of the yamen, and when he emerged this time, he was no longer dressed in official robes of state. Instead, he'd traded his uniform for an unremarkable dust brown robe, suitable for a clerk or a tradesman. It was a wise decision. Bureaucrats were not looked favorably upon in the countryside where we'd be traveling.

He managed to procure transportation from the yamen. The gears of the carriage whirred as the driver brought it to a stop before us. He extended a hand to help me up.

"Will you be punished for abandoning your duty to come with me?" I asked Chang-wei as he extended a hand to help me onto the transport.

"It can't be helped."

The calm, almost dismissive manner with which he defied the crown prince's order made me see him with entirely new eyes.

Chang-wei took command of the levers that controlled the carriage. I'd seen them in the streets of Peking, but had no experience operating such a machine. Our village still relied on mules and rickshaws for transport.

He directed the carriage toward the east section of the city wall. A large gate guarded what appeared to be another section of the city. Beyond that gate was the foreign concession.

I held my breath as we approached, certain the city guards would have us immediately imprisoned. On the contrary, the sentry hardly made note of us as we passed through the boundary. They sent us on our way with a solid tap against the side of the wagon.

Chang-wei drove the machine forward. "It's much harder for foreigners to come the other way into the walled city."

I glanced back over my shoulder, and my final view of the gate told another story. A guardsman was tucking a string of coins into his belt. I'd failed to even notice Chang-wei sneaking the bribe to him.

"Attached on the outside of the carriage, no need to ask questions," Chang-wei explained.

The moment we were through the gates, I sensed immediately that we had left our homeland behind. The buildings rose two or three stories in shapes that weren't ugly, yet struck me as alien and forced upon this place. The lines and planes were too sharp, too abrupt. Neat rows of windows and doors. The writing on the signboards was also unintelligible to me.

The foreigners were dressed in stiff and heavy clothing. I was stunned to see not only white-skinned people but also our own among them. In these streets, we were invariably the ones pulling the rickshaws, holding open the doors. Standing meekly in corners. Bowing.

"Have you been here before?" I asked.

Chang-wei maneuvered through the streets as if they were familiar to him. "I have. Not too long ago."

We veered away from the riverfront filled with Western steamships and clippers. As the wagon rolled deeper into the settlement, the sense of being disoriented, being ripped out of place, became even keener. This was China and it wasn't.

I could hear the Canton dialect, which, according to Chang-wei, had been adopted in all the port cities as a trade language. Those familiar words were drowned out by the harsh sounds of the *Yangguizi* tongue.

Among the boxlike buildings, there were a few familiar sights, but their features were exaggerated to the point of ridiculousness. We stopped in front of a building that resembled an ancient temple. Red columns graced the front along with a pagoda-like architecture that rose three tiers high. There were dragons painted everywhere, dragons on the walls, the columns, the steps. Is that how our country looked to them?

As I stepped down, Chinese attendants came to take control of the carriage. Chang-wei guided me into the pagoda. The main room featured an altar upon which a many-handed bodhisattva stood balanced in a dancer's pose. That was where the resemblance to a temple ended.

We had entered some sort of drinking house. Tables were arranged throughout the parlor, though at this time in the afternoon, only a few were occupied. I followed Chang-wei to a table in the corner near one of the long windows.

The hostess came to greet us, dressed in an enviable green silk that fit her figure as if it had been poured onto her skin.

"The Phoenix Pagoda welcomes you, sir."

I raised my eyebrows at the ostentatious name, to which the hostess arched an eyebrow right back at me. Her eyebrow was decidedly shapelier than mine. Like a moth's wing, as the poems described. Her entire face was painted to perfection: red lips, darkly lined cat's eyes, skin as smooth as porcelain.

"I do apologize, but women are not permitted here," she continued.

"And what are you?"

I meant the question honestly, but her lips pressed into a thin, hard line.

"She is my assistant," Chang-wei interjected, slipping something surreptitiously to the hostess. It might have been identification papers. It could have been money. Whatever it was, the woman's look of irritation was immediately replaced by the cool mask we had seen upon first arriving.

Chang-wei ordered wine and then asked for someone with a name I didn't recognize. I waited until the hostess was halfway across the parlor before speaking.

"This place has a brothel's name," I complained. "And if the name is 'Phoenix,' then why dragons everywhere?"

He hushed me, his brow knitting in annoyance. "I hope to find someone here who can help escort us to Linhua."

"Then we *are* seeking an opium dealer."

"Not every foreigner is a smuggler," he chided. "The associate I'm meeting here is a well-respected businessman in Shanghai."

I shot him a look. Perhaps Yang's views had tainted me. "What lucrative business does a foreigner have in Shanghai besides opium?"

The hostess returned with two glasses set upon a tray. She leaned in closer than necessary to serve Chang-wei his drink. Mine was set down with a heavy thud.

"Mister Burton will be here shortly," she announced in a syrupy-sweet tone.

Another single, pointed glance at me and she was gone again.

Chang-wei took a drink from his glass. The liquor was a dark honeyed color, yet the vapors from it were reminiscent of kerosene and chloroform. I left my glass untouched.

"Will the crown prince's associates be able to pursue you here?" I asked.

"The imperial government has little say in the treaty ports," he replied, not looking entirely pleased with it. "The crown prince will soon be informed of our success. This"—he paused to consider the word—"*excursion* is only a temporary detour. His Highness will have to reconcile the triumph of reclaiming the formula with my less than utter obedience afterward."

I looked down at my hands. "Why are you risking yourself to help me? You're under no obligation to do so."

"I am," he said quietly. "For many reasons."

When I looked up, he was watching me so intently I could feel my face warming. Had he at one time asked my father for me? Or had Father initiated the arrangement? I would always wonder why this man, out of all possible suitors. I would always be searching for what it was that had set Chang-wei apart.

And I would never know the answer.

"You took all the danger upon yourself by seeking out Yang and then being held captive on his ship," Chang-wei added hastily. "I couldn't let you face this danger alone."

"Thank you, Mister Chen."

He played with the rim of his glass. My fingers drew a restless pattern on the tabletop. The moment had become too personal for both of us. I inspected the surroundings as a distraction.

Despite the decor, which favored painted scrolls and silk screens, the place had a distinctly different feel from a native drinking house. The other patrons were all *Yangguizi.* They sat in strange garb, also a mix of Western and native clothing. Cigars filled the air with a cloying haze.

The discomfort of being pulled out of place and time persisted. I couldn't sit still. In contrast, Chang-wei was remarkably composed. He was at ease, wholly accepting of the surroundings, which, by their very appearance, refused to accept him. Chang-wei lifted the glass to his lips, sparing only a casual glance in either direction.

I tried to follow his example but coughed violently as soon as the liquor hit my throat.

"*Heaven and Earth*," I sputtered, my eyes watering. The stuff tasted worse than Physician Lo's bitter ginseng brew.

"You have to drink it slowly." Chang-wei patted me on the back, which was as ineffective as his advice.

"I *did* drink it slowly," I managed between coughs.

The other patrons were staring. I waved Chang-wei's hands away and forced myself to sit up even though my throat was still burning. I was met by a pair of blue eyes, clear as the sky.

Standing over me was the strangest man I had ever seen. I had heard the *Yangguizi* had blue eyes and golden hair, but the few I'd caught a glimpse of so far had been darker in coloring. I had just dismissed the tales of ghosts as an exaggeration, but this man was startlingly fair skinned. He was dressed in a waistcoat similar to what Yang had worn. The material was gray and somber, though his demeanor was anything but. His lips were parted in a grin that bared teeth and spoke of familiarity.

Chang-wei stood to greet him. Instead of bowing, the foreigner reached out to clasp his hand and spoke in a torrent of *Yingyu*. But the absolute shock was when Chang-wei responded back with equal fluency.

"Mister Burton doesn't speak the Canton dialect," Chang-wei told me after inviting him to take a seat across from us.

"Not true, Chen," Burton replied cheerfully in flat yet passable Cantonese. "After five years, even a barbarian can learn."

He faced me and affected an exaggerated bow. "I am called Dean Burton."

Burton told of how he had gradually picked up the dialect as part of his business, which I discerned was some sort of trading house. Chang-wei shot me a look when I asked him pointedly what goods he traded.

"Tea and silk," Burton replied readily, taking a drink of what had originally been my drink, but which I gladly relinquished.

His Canton dialect was rough and my ability to decipher it incomplete, as I was unaccustomed to hearing it from a foreign tongue, but the gap didn't seem to deter Burton. He proceeded to direct his conversation to me as often as he did to Chang-wei.

"Your country is very beautiful," the foreigner said. "I feel quite at home here now."

"It is good to hear that you've been made to feel welcome," I said with some effort.

"Are you from Shanghai, Miss Jin?"

"No, sir. I was born in Peking."

"Ah, the capital. It would be"—he paused to search for a word —"most fortunate to see the palace one day."

"Foreigners are not allowed in the Forbidden City," I reminded him coolly. "Nor are most commoners."

I wondered if he had ever gone beyond the boundaries of the settlement. Here the foreigners had built a replica of their homeland. A part of me couldn't forget that Burton was here because my father had fought and failed to prevent the Western invasion, but I tried my best to remain polite.

"I hear that John here has seen it." The foreigner grasped Chang-wei's shoulder in a brotherly manner. "You must be more important than we thought."

I was taken aback by the mispronunciation of Chang-wei's name. Burton called him that repeatedly as if they were longtime friends.

My overwhelming impression of the foreigner was that he

was *big*. Not so much in size. He was only a little taller than Chang-wei, but everything about him somehow seemed larger. His face, his hands, how loudly he spoke. Every expression appeared exaggerated, as if he held nothing back.

"How did you and John come to know each other, miss?"

"This is considered polite among Western people," Chang-wei interjected with a note of apology. "An exchange of personal yet inconsequential information."

"But isn't it quite consequential how we know each other," I replied, voice lowered.

"That is the difference between us. We consider most personal matters quite private, while they...don't necessarily feel the same."

The foreigner's attention darted back and forth between the two of us. "Hey!"

The utterance was a foreign one, but translated easily.

"Can you speak a little slower? I'm a *gweilo* after all." Burton followed his protest with another grin.

"I have come here for an important matter, Burton. You've heard of the gangs of rebels in the south?"

His smile faded. "Not gangs, John. An army."

"I think you must be mistaken."

After that, the conversation proved to be too tricky in broken Cantonese. Chang-wei switched to *Yingyu*, and I was left adrift in the flood of gibberish.

"The washroom is in the back."

I looked up to see our hostess standing over us. Chang-wei and Burton only spared her a glance before continuing their discussion.

"You asked me where you could find the washroom," the woman prompted. The silver dragon curled around her ear gleamed as she turned her head. "It's in the back."

"I didn't ask—"

With a bow that was more like a curt nod, she went to see to the next table.

Perturbed, I stood and politely excused myself before starting toward the back of the parlor where the hostess had directed me. She caught me with a glance over her shoulder before continuing with her rounds.

Chang-wei had warned me not to trust anyone, but compared to the white-skinned trader, this young woman didn't seem like a threat. Still, I remained wary as I slipped past the mock altar and the golden bodhisattva.

The washroom was near the back door. I had just entered the tiny chamber when the door swung open once more to admit the hostess. She leaned back against the washbasin, her jade green dress pulling taut over her figure, and folded her arms as she scrutinized me from head to toe.

I straightened. "What is this game you're playing?"

She turned the jade bracelet about her wrist once before bothering to reply.

"Elder Sister." Her gaze passed over my brocade jacket and down to my slippers. "It's obvious that you have a proper upbringing. I can hear it in how you speak. Especially in how you command that bureaucrat out there. Unless he happens to be besotted with you."

I could feel my face heating. "He's not besotted."

Her eyes narrowed at that. "Oh? Do you know your lover is a Western sympathizer?"

"He is certainly not my—not that."

"Chen is aligned with the *gweilo*." She was relentless. "I've seen him arm in arm with them more than once."

"That's none of my concern."

I tried to push past her, but she took firm hold of my arm. "You don't know anything about him, do you?" There was no animosity in her tone. "As one woman to another, be careful. The *gweilo* have come here to get rich; every last one of them. Some of them run opium, but there are goods worth even more than that. The men they can barter away as laborers, but the girls—especially the pretty ones..."

My blood chilled. Yang had accused the foreigners of poisoning us with opium to gradually turn us into a land of slaves, but we could also be enslaved without opium.

"You don't look to be Chen's mistress," she continued. "And it's obvious you aren't from Shanghai. There's no family to come looking for you if you were to disappear."

Suddenly all of Burton's polite conversation seemed sinister, inquiring where I'd come from, what had brought me here.

"Chen Chang-wei is a longtime friend of our family. I trust him." Did I? Of course I did. My instincts had chosen him over Yang out in the middle of the ocean.

"Then be wary of that man, Burton."

I started out into the parlor, but the woman stopped one more time to turn to me. "My name is Ming-fen. You may not believe me, but I speak to you as a friend."

"Jin Soling," I replied in turn.

"Be careful, Miss Jin. Newcomers to Shanghai can quickly disappear."

15

When I returned to the parlor, Burton had risen to take his leave. I stood back as the men shook hands and the foreign businessman departed.

Chang-wei appeared bright eyed at my approach. "Mister Burton has offered to hire bodyguards to take us to your village."

"I don't trust him," came my immediate reply.

He was taken aback. "I do trust him."

Ming-fen, my newfound guardian, watched with interest from the table in the corner. I could imagine how the cautionary tale she told me would play out. To her, I looked like a young woman lured into the arms of the lover only to be abandoned to the wolves in Shanghai. Sadly, I Suspected it was a common occurrence in this port city.

"Mister Chen, do you truly believe that your associate has become wealthy by purely trading tea and silk?"

"I believe he deals in many goods in the course of his business," he replied stiffly.

I glared at him. "*Chang-wei.*"

"I understand Burton likely has his hands in opium and there are plenty of our own countrymen who have done the same. But

Mister Burton and I have established an understanding. He is an ally here in this city. One of the few I can trust to help us."

I told him about Ming-fen's warning. Rather than dismissing my fears, he listened to me patiently.

"I can guarantee Burton is not involved in the coolie trade, Miss Jin."

"And the armed escorts he's hiring? Do you know anything of them?"

"He has contacts that I unfortunately do not have. Remember that you were the one willing to seek out less reputable parties to get you home."

It seemed like so much bravado now, lost in this strange settlement without a friendly face in sight. Chang-wei knew how to survive in this new place that had become our homeland, and I did not. Sadly, the one lesson I was learning quickly was to turn a blind eye when a blind eye was needed.

Otherwise there was nothing to see but rage and sorrow. And defeat.

BURTON ARRANGED for a room in one of the hotels along the river. Stone steps led up to the front entrance, which was graced by a pair of carved lions. Unlike the guardian lions I was accustomed to seeing, these were lions of the West, large and shaggy haired.

I stood back from the desk as Chang-wei spoke in a foreign tongue. There was some problem, and the exchange went on for longer than I had anticipated. At one point, the clerk's voice rose loud enough for me to hear.

"*No Chinese allowed*," he said, breaking out in the Canton dialect.

I tensed, but Chang-wei remained unfazed. He continued in a firm and composed manner. All I could discern from Chang-wei's response was Burton's name, but apparently that was enough for the clerk to begrudgingly hand over a key.

Chang-wei took my side as we ascended the staircase and spoke apologetically as he worked the key into the lock. "There is only one room. He assumed we were husband and wife."

He said nothing of how the clerk had tried to refuse our entry, but it must have been a source of shame for him. For a clerk to treat an imperial official, even a minor one, with such rudeness was unheard of. The foreign concessions stood on Chinese soil, did they not?

But I let the matter die for Chang-wei's sake, since he'd chosen to control his temper. It wouldn't do to complain when living off of someone's charity.

It also wouldn't do to complain when I saw that our room took up an entire corner of the second floor. It was the size of my family's house in Linhua, with a decadently large bed and a canopy overhead. Chang-wei made a point of avoiding the bed with his eyes.

The true luxury, however, was in the adjoining compartment.

"A bath!"

I had difficulty containing my awe. In Linhua, the bath was a large wooden tub set in a storehouse that had to be filled by hand with buckets. Most of the villagers frequented the public bathhouse where they took the trouble of supplying and heating water.

Here, the washroom contained a porcelain tub connected to a network of brass piping that snaked into the wall. Seeing it, I was nearly ready to apologize for ever doubting Dean Burton.

"Use this lever here." Chang-wei pointed to the metal arm at one end of the contraption and explained the controls for hot water as well as cold.

I was almost more interested in figuring out the clever system of pumps and water wheels that fed the pipes than actually taking a bath. Almost more interested.

Chang-wei worked the lever, and steaming water flowed into the tub only minutes later. Then he left me in privacy so I could sink into the tub, washing away the layer of grime and salt accumulated from the ocean voyage. It was hard to imagine that just that morning, we were aboard a ship.

After I was scrubbed clean, I stepped out of the washroom to see Chang-wei at the desk by the window. He was turned away, head bent to read from something hidden in the palm of his hand.

He had set the bamboo screen outside the washroom door for me. A package wrapped in brown paper had been placed upon the bed.

"What is this?"

Chang-wei didn't turn. I saw his throat moving as he swallowed. "I don't know."

I opened the wrapping to reveal a blue *cheongsam* dress embroidered with white flowers. There was also a tunic and a pair of loose trousers.

"Burton," Chang-wei replied before I had a chance to ask. I saw there was another package for him beside his arm. "He runs a store in the settlement along with trade routes."

I was grateful to change out of my battered clothing. There was silence on the other side of the screen as I fastened the frogs that ran along the shoulder of the tunic.

Even turned away, with the screen separating the two of us, these close quarters were unsettling. My heart beat faster and I took a deep breath before stepping out from behind the screen.

"If you will excuse me," Chang-wei began hastily.

"Of course."

We navigated past each other, me to the window and him to the washroom, all without meeting each other's eyes once. It was a wonder we didn't collide, we were trying so hard not to make eye contact. His sleeve brushed against mine as he rounded the corner of the bed.

I pinned my hair while listening to the metal creak of the lever and the rush of water. Then I allowed myself to think of my brother, something I hadn't done for a few days. I wondered if Tian was keeping up with his studies, if Nan was able to keep him fed. I wondered if Mother had come out of her stupor long enough to worry that I was away for so long.

Most of all, I hoped the rebels hadn't raided our village. Another few days, a week at most, and I would be home.

I started to nod off with my head propped onto one hand at the desk when the washroom door opened. Just as I had, Chang-wei disappeared behind the screen. When he came out, he was dressed in a loose steel gray robe; notably finer than the one he'd been wearing before.

It was the first glimpse I'd had of Chang-wei's hair loosened from its braided queue. Quickly I turned away, but I heard his tentative approach.

"Miss Jin, I apologize—" He held out a comb in one hand, which I saw from the corner of one eye. "If I could request your assistance."

Despite his formal tone, I could hear the rasp in his throat. My pulse jumped and, for some reason, my hands would not move.

"If this is unacceptable to you, I can ring for a valet."

"No," I said, rising quickly. "I can help."

It would be even worse to admit that being so close to him unnerved me so.

We arranged ourselves with him sitting in the chair while I stood behind. He reached over his shoulder to give me the comb, and my fingers trembled as I took it. For an entire minute, all I could do was hover with the comb poised in the air.

Chang-wei needed his hair braided back into the traditional queue that all male subjects were required to wear. I had done so for Tian a number of times, but he was my brother as well as a boy. For a man such as Chang-wei, this was certainly an intimate service reserved for a wife or a trusted servant.

I thought I heard him let out a breath as I sank my comb into his hair to part it. It was thick and nearly as long as mine, falling down past his shoulders. Seeing Chang-wei with his hair unbound rendered him vulnerable. At the same time, he appeared inexplicably unrestrained and masculine. I tried not to think of the contrast as I began to braid the three sections together, taking care to keep the queue even.

"Yang Hanzhu cut his hair," I said partway through the process. I don't know why that particular thought came to mind, but I had felt the need to say something and break the silence.

"Yang?" He sounded annoyed that I had brought our mutual acquaintance up. "I saw he had done that and knew then he was beyond reach."

Yang could never join with the crown prince or work on behalf of the empire. Once a man's queue was cut, he could never return as a subject to the throne. It was an uncompromisable symbol of loyalty.

I finished tying the end of the braid and stepped away.

"Thank you," Chang-wei said simply.

He turned the chair around to face me. With nowhere else to go, I sat down on the bed. The mattress was padded and soft, sinking low beneath me.

"Yang believes that certain opium shipments have been specifically engineered to be more addictive." I didn't reveal the other part, when I'd stumbled upon the opium addicts kept inside cages.

"I don't see why that would be necessary. The drug is addictive enough in its pure form."

"Yang claimed to have seen strange effects of opium usage. He told me he was searching for a cure."

The corner of his mouth twitched. "That sounds like the man I remember. His ideas were always grandiose."

It was easier to look at Chang-wei now. He was composed and formal. Yet I couldn't forget the feel of my fingers running through his hair or the sight of his back to me, broad shoulders tensing beneath my touch.

I kept on talking because I needed to keep talking. "Maybe Yang had a point. Fighting against ships and guns won't free us as long opium holds our land captive. That isn't the battle we should be waging."

"Ships and guns allow the *Yangguizi* to force opium upon us," Chang-wei argued.

"*Opium addiction* is what allows the *Yangguizi* to force opium upon us."

His jaw hardened, and for a moment I thought he would berate me for being obstinate. Instead, he sat back in his chair, hands folded before him thoughtfully.

"Whenever the Ministry had a problem to solve, your father used to bring a group of us together. Even if our area of expertise seemed unrelated. And not just department heads, but junior members as well. Yang's expertise was in alchemy; mine was mechanics. I was the youngest in the entire ministry and had yet to earn any respect. Your father's rule was that no one could take insult if someone disagreed, no matter what rank he was. The arguments would often continue late into the night," he recounted wistfully. A moment later, he became serious. "I need you, Miss Jin."

"M-me?" I stammered.

"Someone like you," he amended, to my disappointment. "Someone who is willing to argue with me. After your father was demoted, the Emperor promoted men who were better at giving the answers he wanted. Or perhaps the men who were promoted had learned to say what the Emperor wanted to hear in order to keep their heads."

Chang-wei had only been nineteen when he passed the exams and joined the Ministry. Only one year older than I was now. Eight years had passed since then, but Chang-wei seemed to have lived eighteen years in the interim. He seemed so worldly and experienced to me. His knowledge put the narrowness of my concerns to shame. I was dragging him away from an important duty to the empire so he could help me get home.

But fish could only see the water they swim in. And I, too, had learned from my father's example. The only way to keep one's head was to not stick it out too far. The empire rewarded loyalty by asking an even greater sacrifice. And it kept on asking and demanding more until there was nothing left to give.

16

We left the hotel for dinner, ending up in a narrow alleyway where we watched an automaton crank out egg noodles between its gears and rotary cutters. The vendor then fried up the fresh noodles along with a handful of scallions, chilies and spices. We ate while seated upon upturned crates.

It was street food, greasy and cheap, and the best meal I could remember having in years. We were surrounded by the laborers and servants who worked in the foreign concession tending to the foreigners. Though they were peasant folk, we had more akin to them than the *Yangguizi* who dined in the restaurants and drinking houses.

Yet Chang-wei didn't wish to return to the walled city. Here, we were temporarily hidden from his masters; one of the reasons he had removed his state robe. For what we had to do, it was better not to stand out as a government official.

Afterward, neither of us was eager to return to the hotel where we were openly unwelcome. Instead we walked along the outer bank of the river. Activity at the docks had slowed in the evening. Most of the vessels had moored for the night. Occasionally lanterns could be seen hung from the decks. Other boats were dark and silent as they swayed in the water. High in the skyline floated a line of airships tethered to the docking towers concentrated to the north of the riverfront.

"There are so many of them here," I murmured.

"And more every day. Our Middle Kingdom is a land of riches. For the taking." His tone remained neutral as he spoke. Chang-wei could be impossible to read at times.

"I still don't know what your stance is."

"My stance?"

"On the *Yangguizi*. On being robbed every day by them."

To the left of us were the major trading houses that had been established by the foreign merchants. Chang-wei had informed me that it was more than just *Yingguo* or England laying claim to our kingdom. There were trading houses set up by a land called "America" as well as the "Netherlands," but I thought of them all as *Yangguizi*.

"The situation is complicated." He strolled with his hands clasped behind his back. "The foreigners are entrenched here and have been for years now. You can see that with your own eyes. They can't simply be swept out like dust on a broom."

Though we were strolling out in the open, with the evening breeze on our faces, we felt secure that no one was spying on us. The foreign inhabitants of the settlement always cut us a wide path when they came near. We had also slipped into the Peking dialect, which was more natural between us. It had the effect of further shielding our conversation. Mandarin was much less common in the trading posts than Cantonese.

"It is important to know who among the foreigners wields influence. Who are the names who can get things done? Who can be useful allies?"

I remembered how Ming-fen had accused him of being a sympathizer. It was akin to being called a traitor in many circles. I mentioned that to Chang-wei and a dark look descended over him.

"It's not the first I've heard of it," he said tersely.

"But it's not true."

I was hoping he would deny it and reassure me, but Chang-wei continued to evade the question.

"Whether I sympathize with the Westerners is irrelevant. I'm trying to build a future for our kingdom, one where we can remain strong rather than one where we are forced to surrender more every day to our very invaders. That vision sometimes requires I make friends of our enemies."

"But it's dangerous to walk that line."

"I know," he returned, his tone uncommonly harsh. "I understand that very keenly, Miss Jin."

I'd somehow offended him. It was time to change the subject. "How did you meet Dean Burton?"

His frown didn't quite fade. "Aboard a ship when he was first traveling to Shanghai."

What sort of ship would have those two men together on board? I kept quiet, hoping to hear the rest of the story.

"He came to me and offered to pay for my services."

"What kind of services?"

"Burton needed someone to act as a guide in this exotic new land. He didn't know the language or the people. Didn't want to be 'duped,' as he called it. I had lost what little fortune I had after being dismissed from the Ministry of Science, so I accepted."

"So he was your employer?"

"I suppose you could say that. What he needed from me most was my honest appraisal of a situation, education on how to handle himself with potential business partners. All the small pieces that hold the large pieces together. He came to trust me over two years working together."

"And you came to trust him?" I asked.

Chang-wei didn't answer at first. When he did, it was only in a single word: "Enough. I trust him enough."

Something wasn't quite right about his story. "You said Burton hired you to be an interpreter?" I asked.

He nodded, and I patched what I had learned just that day together.

"Mister Burton couldn't speak any Cantonese at the time he met you, and you were surprised today that he had picked up a few phrases."

"That is true."

"Then how did he communicate with you?" I asked pointedly. "How did he know you could help him?"

I could see Chang-wei was caught from the way his expression blanked. "It must have been mostly through gestures. I had picked up a few phrases in his language."

I realized then why Chen Chang-wei did well for himself by remaining honest.

"You're a poor liar," I told him.

"Only when I try to lie to you," he said gently. "I should know not to do that."

He stopped to face me there on the riverfront. Behind him, I could see the flicker of the gas lamps used to light the street. The shadows danced over his face, highlighting his cheekbones and the line of his jaw.

"They call their language 'English,'" he began. "I spoke it fairly well by the time I met Dean Burton."

"Have you always known how to speak it? Where would one study it?" I asked incredulously.

"Before the war, it was only spoken here and there among the merchant class in China. There are a few missionary schools in the port cities as well, but no, English is not commonly studied among the scholar elite in Peking. I learned the language of the *Yingguoren* after being forced onto one of their ships."

It was a more polite term than *Yangguizi.*

I stared at Chang-wei, at a loss for words. After the final battle of the war, the Ministry of Science had fallen apart. Father had been imprisoned. So many of his men had been stripped of rank. Others had just disappeared.

"I was in the citadel at Wusong," he explained. "Directing the cannon fire. It was a failed endeavor from the start, as your father knew. But we had to fight to the end, which I did until the moment I was taken by the *Yingguoren*."

I had always assumed Chang-wei had broken our betrothal and turned his back on us like so many of Father's former colleagues. We had never heard from him again, and then Father was put to death and our family exiled. But Chang-wei hadn't abandoned our family. He had been captured by the enemy.

"What happened?" I asked.

"When I think back, I realize it wasn't the worst of outcomes. The foreigners needed a replacement for their engineer aboard one of the iron warships, so they seized me. Once we were out in the middle of the ocean, the *Yingguoren* didn't even need to keep me shackled anymore."

"You lived among them." I still couldn't believe it.

"I've even lived for a time in their capital. They call it 'London.'"

We resumed our walk, but Chang-wei was no longer the stiff, formal, restrained academic I thought him to be. He was a man of many secrets.

He told me how there was a section similar to this one in London, a part of the Western city peopled entirely by our countrymen. Some of them who had been forcibly abducted like him and others who had voluntarily gone to work aboard the iron steamships.

"That's why Yang distrusts me. We came across each other in India after I had been away for more than two years. It was like a dream, seeing a familiar face in a strange land."

"Were you able to speak to each other?"

"Only long enough for me to refuse to abandon the devil ship, as he called it, to join with him."

"Why didn't you go?"

"Why didn't I go?"

I shook my head, confused. "You could have escaped then."

"To become a fugitive with Yang? I had become an established member of the crew on the steamship. I even kept a residence in that great, gray city of London."

Chang-wei certainly sounded like a traitor who had abandoned his country. Had he adopted *Yingguo* as his new home? Why did he come back?

"Why didn't I go, Soling?" he asked again, this time a smile tugging at the corners of his mouth, teasing me. "I had been dragged onto a foreign warship against my will and thrown into a sweltering engine room."

My heart throbbed, the blood pulsing through my veins as it always did when a puzzle was thrown in front of me.

"Their engines—" The answer lingered on my tongue. The thought had not yet fully formed.

His eyes glittered as he waited.

I could barely breathe. "Their engines are not the same as ours."

Old Liu had told me their engines were powered by steam. Suddenly I understood why Chang-wei had stayed away for so long; why he had practically become one of the *Yangguizi*, even though his reputation would be forever blackened by it.

"The Ministry misjudged how quickly the *Yingguoren* war machines had advanced," he admitted. "We were defeated soundly because their devil ships were faster, their guns bigger. I had no idea how to run that ship they threw me onto, but I learned quickly. I learned everything I could about their machines, their steamships and airships. At one point, I was even allowed to visit the academies and workshops of London."

He spoke without a hint of boastfulness. What I heard instead of pride was hope.

Chang-wei leaned in close to whisper the next part in my ear. "They thought I was harmless. Because I appeared so young. Because of my size compared to them. Because I remained quiet."

A shudder ran down my spine as his warm breath fanned against my neck.

"There are those in the Ministry that believe we should turn away from the wicked ideas of the *Yangguizi*," he went on. "To those men, I'll always be a sympathizer and a traitor. But I went directly to the crown prince with all I had learned, and he agreed with me. To know your enemies is, and always will be, a source of great power."

17

The next morning, Burton met us by the riverfront himself to see to the final arrangements. To me, he was as cheerful as he had been the day before, both bowing to me as well as shaking my hand in the Western style as he inquired about how well I rested, did I find the clothes suitable, and were the accommodations to my liking.

To Chang-wei, he lowered his voice and they spoke at length with heads bent.

The armed escort joining us consisted of two brothers from a private security firm. They were assembled by the quay when we arrived and were easily recognizable by the broadswords at their sides as well as crossbows strapped onto their backs. They were covered at the shoulders, arms and knees by plates of protective armor that still allowed them to move freely. The sight of the mercenaries alone was a deterrent to any small-time bandits.

Burton returned to say his farewell at which time I made sure to express my deepest gratitude. Whatever the source of his wealth was, he was sacrificing a significant amount of money to get me to my family.

"I am in your debt," I said sincerely.

"My pleasure. *Joi gin*, Miss Jin."

He grinned as he gave his farewell, flat without proper intonation, but well-meaning nonetheless. His blue eyes flashed and for a moment I could see beyond his strangeness and understand how he was able to charm people. I felt shame for thinking he was just another one of the foreign devils before I understood his association with Chang-wei.

Despite the comforts in the international settlement, I was glad to begin our journey. We joined a small transport ship with a crew of four men who would take us down the Great River.

The riverboat cut through the water at a swift pace while the guardsmen positioned themselves on deck as lookouts.

"Are they always so watchful?" I whispered to Chang-wei. We had just left the outskirts of Shanghai, but I assumed any threat would only come when we were far away from the cities.

"They're paid well to do so," was his reply. "Burton attempted to find news of the rebels last night. Reports are just starting to come through to Shanghai. Before that, it was all rumor."

"He said they had an army?"

"Apparently there has been an increase in local skirmishes. A Banner garrison attempted to march upon the rebels to force them to disperse, but the Banner army has been unsuccessful. Reports on their numbers have been unreliable."

"How many?"

Chang-wei shook his head. "Some say several hundred to a thousand. In other accounts, ten thousand."

I stared at him in shock. "How could a force like that have amassed so quickly?"

"Rebellion must have been brewing for a long time," he replied grimly. "The discontent seems to have reached a critical point."

There had been famine throughout the province for many years now. In Linhua, my family had experienced firsthand the gradual whittling away of our resources. The growing hunger in our bellies. These last years had been a struggle for everyone.

Having grown up surrounded by the wealth of Peking, I understood the disparity between the two regions. To hungry peasants in Hunan, Peking appeared to be bloated with riches.

"How long before we reach Linhua?" I asked, trying to stay calm.

"This boat will take us as far as Wuhan in two days. Then we head south."

From river to river, we'd make our way to my family. Though the transport was fitted with a gunpowder engine that churned and groaned its way through the water, it wasn't fast enough for me. Nothing could be.

The first evening, we docked at a riverfront village and sought out food and news at the tavern. The main room was full of boatmen and merchants traveling both by the river as well as alongside it on land routes.

Talk of the rebellion was on everyone's lips, but it was a faraway thing.

"They call themselves the 'Long Hairs,'" the tavern keeper told us. "Because they've cut off their queues in defiance of the Emperor. For a long time now, they were held back in the region of Jintian, but they've overpowered the Banner garrison there and have been steadily moving north."

These were the rebel skirmishes we would hear rumors of in our village. The Banner garrisons were outfits of Manchurian soldiers stationed at major cities throughout the empire. They had evolved from the original factions under the great Nurhaci who had defeated the Ming to found our dynasty. My family could trace its ancestry to the Banner men.

"Have you heard anything of Linhua village?" I asked.

He'd heard nothing of it, but we were able to gather that the provincial capital at Changsha was untouched.

"If the capital is still standing, then perhaps nearby Linhua remains safe," I surmised.

But something in my heart told me it wouldn't be for long. We were in the heart of rebel activity.

Chang-wei listened to the news with little comment, though I could see his mood darkening as the night progressed. I asked him what was the matter, but he assured me it was nothing.

"Just thinking," was all he'd say.

There was only a single room left, and a small one at that. We were fortunate to be able to get it. There was no feather bed or hot bath to be found here. The room was little more than a closet, but it was kept clean and warm.

"You...you can stay here," I said.

Chang-wei had only set one foot inside before turning back to the door.

"I mean, it's no different than the situation in Shanghai," I amended, suddenly shy when I had never been shy. A hundred butterflies circled in my stomach.

In truth, there wasn't enough space here for us to remain reasonably apart. There was a single bamboo mat on the floor that was barely large enough for one person. Even if we retreated to separate corners, all we had to do was stretch out an arm and we'd be touching.

"I'll be back shortly then," Chang-wei said. "Get some sleep."

Once he was gone, I took the place closest to the inner wall, leaving the blanket for Chang-wei. We would be sleeping practically shoulder to shoulder, but I needed to stop making such a fuss over it. We had crossed over any boundaries of propriety long ago. Despite all that had happened, Chang-wei was a gentleman at heart, and I had been unsuitable for marriage long before meeting him.

Extinguishing the lantern, I turned my face toward the wall.

In the darkness, I prayed for my family. I prayed that our

village was too small, and too insignificant for anyone to take notice.

Rumors were that the rebels would take over a city and then scour the surrounding countryside to pillage for supplies and conscript more men for their army. Tian was only eight years old. They wouldn't force him to fight, would they?

The rebels might just kill him. And Mother and Nan, too, or worse. I prayed that if danger came, they would know what to do. But Nan was elderly and a servant used to taking orders. Mother had been asleep with her eyes open for years. Tian was clever, but he was just a young boy.

We had heard of rebels gathering at Thistle Mountain, but we'd made light of it in the village. Even so, I knew the threat was there. Why hadn't I given my family instructions on what to do? Or at least asked someone to watch over them? But then who would I have asked for help? We had no friends in our village.

By the time I heard the door creak open, tears were pouring down my face. I bit down hard on my lip and choked back a sob.

The movement at the door ceased. I imagined Chang-wei standing there and debating whether he should come in. A moment later, the mat rustled beside me. I had hoped that Chang-wei would just go to sleep, but instead I felt his hand on my shoulder.

He touched my shoulder lightly. "Soling, you're having a bad dream."

In the darkness, he sounded so close; so strong and caring that fresh tears slid down my cheeks.

Though I hadn't been sleeping, I acted as if I were. "I don't remember what I was dreaming about."

I muffled my reply against my blanket so he wouldn't hear how my voice trembled. It didn't help. Chang-wei reached for me, awkwardly turning my head against his shoulder. We were in a tangle of blankets and my hands were folded to my chest between us, but still he closed his arms around me.

"It will be all right, Soling."

I didn't want to cry anymore. I didn't want Chang-wei to know I was crying, but I couldn't help it. It was a long time since I had been held like that.

"Tian will be nine years old this year," I choked out. "He has a gentle spirit. When the village boys pick on him, he doesn't fight back. He just likes to draw."

Chang-wei nodded, even though I wasn't making sense. I felt his hand resting against the nape of my neck, his thumb stroking my hair. Though his touch was hesitant, it was reassuring to me nonetheless.

"Feel better?" he asked after a long time had passed.

I didn't think so, but I nodded against his shoulder. Gently, Chang-wei laid me back onto the mat and pulled the blanket over me. Then he settled on his side of the mat and said nothing more.

~

WE KEPT on hearing more news along the river. Sometimes during our stops for food or more gunpowder fuel, other times from passing boats.

The rebels called themselves the Heavenly Kingdom Army and apparently had won several victories against the Banner garrisons, not just one. They were marching northward, gathering followers as they went. One witness to the march called it a human wave. There were thousands upon thousands of followers, and wherever they went, the fighting was bloody.

The rebels were bent on amassing men, women and children into their service. Apparently women fought in their army just as men did. The only people who were not allowed to join were soldiers from the Banner garrisons or Manchurian city officials. Those they executed on sight.

I wanted to discuss this alarming news with Chang-wei, but

he spent most of the day with the ship's machinist, inspecting the engine.

At night, Chang-wei and I shared a sleeping area that had been curtained off from the rest of the men, though we did occupy separate berths. As I drifted off to sleep one night, I noticed him going to the trunk that Burton had provided to us.

Chang-wei pulled a wooden case from it, and I watched as he opened the lid. Inside was a firearm, small enough to be held in one hand. It was undeniably a Western device in appearance with a polished wood handle and an iron barrel. Right before Chang-wei extinguished the lantern, he inserted two bullets into the weapon and set it beside his pillow.

18

Wuhan was a major city with a bustling port. Like all of the places we'd passed, the river was central to all life there, and a concentration of establishments could be seen from the water. A pagoda watchtower rose high above the tree line, marking the city's location. We docked there around midday, and I learned why Chang-wei had been spending so much time inspecting the engine on the transport boat.

I followed him to a repair shop and junkyard where, after a brief negotiation with the owner, Chang-wei pulled out a folded paper from a pocket in his robe. He opened it to reveal a diagram and then began rummaging through the graveyard of broken and abandoned boats.

"What are you searching for?" I asked, glancing over his shoulder at the complicated schematic.

He bent to sort through a pile of what looked like piping. "Whatever it takes to rework the engine."

"Rework it?"

"Improve it. The body of the vessel is suitable. It's lightweight, mobile. The engine is serviceable, but old. I can make it more powerful. Get us to your village faster."

I imagined the ship being grounded for a week for repairs. "Are you certain this is a good idea?"

"Can you bring me that wheelbarrow?" Chang-wei rose with an armful of parts.

His mind was on his new grand scheme, and everything else amounted to the buzzing of crickets in his ear. I went to retrieve the wheelbarrow, and he set the assortment of parts inside before turning to a hunk of machinery on the ground before him.

"Or I might consider replacing the entire engine," he surmised.

After two hours, Chang-wei needed to borrow a mechanized cart to transport all of the spare parts back to the dock. The assembly plodded beside him like an obedient pack mule.

"Don't worry. I won't disassemble the engine until I'm certain the loss in time will be offset by the gains," he assured as I helped him carry his pile on board. For the heavier parts, he had to enlist the crewmen and the use of their pulley.

While he set up, I ventured into the marketplace to browse for lunch. The stalls provided a good selection of fruit, and I found a vendor selling fried cakes wrapped into a banana leaf. The smell of them made my mouth water.

As I wandered past the produce stands into metalworks and devices, I heard a shop owner hawking his selection of fire lances.

"Did you hear there was a rebel attack outside of Jingzhou?"

The news stopped me cold.

"Nowhere is safe anymore, my brother," the dealer went on. "These lances are forged from the highest quality iron. Easy to fire. Just aim and it will down any target at a hundred paces."

I waited until the prospective customer was inspecting the other weapons on the shelves before approaching. The sight of the hand cannons and various firearms laid out on the counter intimidated me.

"Sir," I began. "Where did you say that attack was?"

"The Jingzhou commandery, not three days from here by horse."

"I thought the rebels were still far south."

"Now, miss, don't you know that we're not dealing with a single threat?" The shopkeeper's gaze darted to his customer before returning to me, fearful that my remark might cost him a sale. "There have been uprisings throughout the Chang River valley. These Heavenly Kingdom rebels are rousing all the other scoundrels to action."

As alarming as this was, I told myself not to overreact. Most likely this attack was nothing more than a gang of local bandits and the opportunistic shopkeeper was using stories of rebel attacks to increase sales.

True to my suspicions, the crafty businessman took advantage of my presence in his shop. "Miss, you don't appear to be from Wuhan. If your travels take you far, you should consider arming yourself. A woman especially needs to be protected."

I shook my head and thanked him for the news. Even as I left the weapons stop behind, I could hear him calling after me, "I can make you a good deal!"

Uncertainty filled my head with frightening scenarios. When I found Mother and Tian, I wouldn't leave them alone again. I'd find a way to take care of them so we no longer had to cower from anyone, whether it be bandits or government officials.

There was a long alleyway in the next section. Looking down it, I saw two men heading into an unmarked doorway at the end of it and knew immediately what sort of establishment it was. An opium den.

The dens really were in every city, in the same places were citizens bought chickens and bolts of cloth. As the men turned to enter, I saw that it was two of the crew from our boat.

I kept on moving. It didn't matter to me what distractions they chose to pursue. All they had been hired to do was get us to Linhua village. Yet I couldn't help the sinking feeling in my gut.

The poison was everywhere and impossible to eradicate. Rice was scarce in Hunan province and the wells were running dry, but the supply of opium would continue to flow.

I RETURNED to where the transport ship was anchored after my round through the marketplace. My final purchase had been two cups of cold plum juice over ice from a stall near the docks.

The deck was empty, which I realized was fortunate. I hadn't thought to bring any refreshment for the crewmen. Then I remembered where I had seen two of them and I no longer felt remiss.

Chang-wei was at the rear of the craft. The hatch to the engine compartment was open, and scattered around it was a layer of metal pipes and cogs and screws.

"Careful!" he barked when I set foot into the area. "Every part has been laid out in an exact spot mapping to its original location."

He was sitting on the floor with a scroll laid out before him on which he was marking said mappings. A spark lantern rested beside him.

"I brought food," I said.

"Thank you. That's kind of you."

He sounded less than grateful. He was distracted, perplexed, his mind still entrenched in its task. I sank down in the corner, making sure to not upset any of the parts as he'd warned.

I spooned some of the sweetened ice and let it melt on my tongue as I watched him work. He continued sorting pieces, making detailed notes on the scroll at each step.

The ship was little more than a floating raft while Chang-wei tackled his engineering project, but I had to trust him. As I observed his meticulous approach, I realized Chang-wei was a master engineer; of an entirely different class than Old Liu Yentai.

Engineer Liu had treated his machine as one would a horse. He knew its moods and eccentricities. He petted it and fed it and listened to the noises it made. Chang-wei was a man of exacting standards. He wouldn't tolerate such unpredictability.

I thought it would be dark outside before Chang-wei looked up from his task, but a moment later, he carefully cleared a path and came to sit next to me. The cups of ice hadn't yet melted, so I handed one to him.

"So you decided it was worth the effort?" I asked, indicating the scatter of parts.

"I believe this will increase our speed significantly and only cost us an additional day here in Wuhan."

"With all this to put back together?"

"If I work all night," he added.

I couldn't help smiling.

"What is it?"

"When my father was working, he would often forget to eat or sleep."

Chang-wei returned the smile with a wistful look. "Master Jin was a good man. If you will forgive me for being so impertinent, he was like a father to me as well."

We fell silent beside each other. At home, we rarely spoke of my father, but his memory was with me all the time.

"You're very much like him in many ways," I told Chang-wei, then decided I was being too personal. "That was why I brought you lunch—so you wouldn't go hungry."

He took the fried cakes from my hand with a look that I might describe as fond. A ball of warmth floated like a spring lantern in my chest.

As we sat beside each other, with my lips cool and pleasantly numb from the ice, I grew very aware of every detail about Chen Chang-wei. There was the tiny crease in his brow when he was preoccupied with something. The shape of his mouth, which was too serious to smile often. His hand was resting on his knee, placing it in close proximity to mine. If I stretched out my fingers, we would touch.

Of course, we didn't touch. Ours wasn't that sort of relationship.

Did he ever regret what had been lost between us? Was that why he was being so kind to me? Maybe he was sorry to see how far my family had fallen.

At first I had thought that, betrothal or no, Chang-wei meant nothing to me. Over the last eight years, I barely thought of him as anything other than a name to be forgotten like the rest of our past. But now I couldn't stop thinking and wondering. For the first time since I had lost my father, I was allowing myself to dream of what could have been. But only in silence.

Chang-wei finished the humble meal I had scavenged together and thanked me. When he went back to work, he beckoned me to join him. With the diagram in hand, we began gradually rebuilding the engine together. Or rather modifying it to Chang-wei's specifications.

He instructed me on what pieces to hand over, what fixtures to use to rebuild individual modules.

"You have a good eye for detail," he said, though I suspected it was just empty flattery. I didn't mind.

Just as I'd suspected, we worked late into the evening with a short break to snatch dinner before it was back to affixing bolts and seals.

"You can go to sleep if you're tired," Chang-wei suggested after I yawned for the third time in a half hour.

"No, I'm fine."

I lifted the lantern up so he could see better. We had lit several other lanterns around the hold, and Chang-wei had put on his spectacles to magnify the tinier components.

Despite my valiant efforts, my eyelids began to droop within minutes.

"I've been thinking about your family," Chang-wei said as he finished tightening a bolt.

My ears perked up.

"Once we find your family, I'll take them safely to Peking," he promised.

"That's too much to ask, Chang-wei."

"You didn't ask; I offered. How else can I repay the debt to your father?"

How I wished he had given another reason. One that didn't have to do with debt and honor.

"Let us take care of one thing at a time," I insisted.

In many ways I was like my father, a person of concrete details, of cause and effect. What gave me comfort was a task in front of me, no matter how difficult. A problem that could actually be solved. It gave me no comfort at all to imagine the impossible.

19

I woke up to the crackle of fire, which snapped me awake, but it was only Chang-wei stoking the flame in the incinerator. All of the parts that had been littered throughout the engine room were now neatly replaced into the engine.

"Larger combustion chamber," he said proudly. "And a new piston system. Most of the parts were intact; they just needed to be fastened together."

I rubbed at my eyelids. "That's very clever," I said between yawns. I glanced about and saw a hint of daylight streaming from above deck.

I had excused myself for a nap and curled up in the corner to the ping and clank of his tools. After what felt like the blink of an eye, morning was here. Chang-wei must have not slept at all. He had dark circles beneath his eyes, but at the same time there was an eagerness that vibrated through him.

"Once the fire gets hot enough, we can introduce gunpowder into the chamber. Then we'll know for certain."

I raised an eyebrow at him.

"It's completely controlled," he insisted. "I fashioned an outer shield around the chamber. If the reaction becomes unstable, we'll be protected."

I didn't need to remind him how many of his colleagues, including my own father, had worn mechanical limbs due to gunpowder experiments gone awry.

"You may want to stand back a little," he said on second thought.

I retreated just outside the engine room while Chang-wei fed more wood into the incinerator, watching the needle on the gauge the entire time. When it tipped into red, he measured gunpowder into the chute and began turning the crank. A moment later, the engine roared to life.

I jumped with delight. "It works!"

Though his eyes shined with pride, he didn't celebrate yet. "We need to run it for at least half an hour. See how it handles the heat and pressure."

He pulled out a silver watch on a chain from his pocket to check the time. It was another reminder of his exposure to the West.

"Is the madman blowing up my ship?" The captain approached to look over Chang-wei's shoulder.

"Captain Deng." Chang-wei was still watching his clock but gave a brief nod anyway. "We're ready to take the ship on open water."

The engine rumbled as the valves and pistons chugged away. A system of pipes vented the smoke, leaving a faint smell of sulfur.

Deng apparently approved of what he witnessed. "The crew will be ready in an hour's time."

He left us to go above deck.

"It was generous of him to allow you to rework his ship," I remarked.

"I believe he can easily afford two new vessels with what Burton paid for this voyage."

"Generous of Mister Burton as well, then. He's been a great help to us."

"An old debt," Chang-wei said simply. "With the new improvements, it is my hope that we'll be in Changsha in four, maybe three days' time. I won't know for certain until we can clock the speed."

He pocketed his watch and pulled a lever to bring the engine to a stop. I noticed the firearm from the previous night had been hooked onto his belt.

"That's a foreign-made pistol," I remarked.

The design was markedly smaller than the hand cannons and fire lances used for protection in the provinces. There was something almost dishonorable about a weapon that could be so easily hidden.

Chang-wei seemed uncomfortable that I had noticed he was wearing it. He adjusted his robe so that only the handle could be seen.

"There is something you should be aware of for the next part of the journey," he began. "We may encounter some adversaries that we need to outrun. That's why I felt it crucial to fix the engine."

I was reminded of the news I'd heard at the weapons shop about other rebel factions becoming emboldened by the Heavenly Kingdom rebels. When I told Chang-wei of it, his expression darkened.

"As I feared, the danger is closer than we thought. The official report in Shanghai mentioned that the imperial supply lines had been disrupted, impeding the army's progress in defeating the rebels. I suspect there was more that wasn't being said."

"What would that be?"

"That supply ships are being ambushed on the rivers. The imperial army isn't faring nearly as well as they claim to be against the rebels."

"Why would the report lie?" I knew the answer before the last word had left my lips.

"To save face," Chang-wei confirmed. "Do you have your needle gun? Your war fan?"

I nodded. Thankfully I hadn't needed to use either.

"Only use them if you have no other choice," Chang-wei advised. "If we encounter any trouble, stay down below. Deng and his men are armed, and this ship should be able to outpace any river pirates on the water. We'll get to your village in time to keep your family safe."

The weight pressing down on my chest increased twofold. "You can't promise that."

"I will do everything I can. I can promise you that."

When we climbed above deck, the captain was directing a bleary-eyed crew. Only two were present with two missing. After sending the men off ship, the captain turned back to us.

"Apparently a few of my men have overindulged in their entertainments onshore. We'll haul them back and be ready in an hour."

I didn't feel it necessary to tell him that I'd seen the two missing crewmen at the opium den. That was their affair, not mine.

Captain Deng took his leave of us and we returned to our private quarter. The moment Chang-wei lay down on his berth, he was asleep. I was tired as well and had just dozed off when the sound of voices above deck indicated the crew had returned.

Drowsily, we went out onto the deck to see the two late arrivals. One of them had to be carried back up the gangplank by his arms and ankles.

"That last pipe sent him into a stupor," his companion was explaining. He looked haggard as he stood before his captain. "I kept waiting for him to wake up, but he could barely walk."

As fortune would have it, the opium smoker was the heaviest of the crew, a stout man they called Big Gao. Puffing from the exertion, they released him onto the deck in less-than-gentle fashion, but he didn't flinch.

I took the liberty of approaching him as the other crewmen caught their breath.

"When was his last pipe?" I asked as I pressed fingers to his wrist to find a pulse.

"Late last night. After the first hour, for certain."

"Any effect of the opium should be long gone by now."

Considering his companion had been in an opium haze as well, I couldn't rely on his estimate. Gao's pulse was weak, but when I lifted his eyelids, his pupils shrunk beneath the sunlight.

"Drag that lazy dog into his bunk," the captain said in disgust. "He's lost a day of wages and earned himself a thrashing when he wakes up."

With that, the captain straightened and composed himself before turning to us. "One hour, Mister Chen, just as I promised."

CHANG-WEI'S SUSPICIONS had me looking around every bend for an ambush, but the river was thick with boats as we left Wuhan. The new engine propelled us through the water at a good speed, and with our size, we were able to break away from the larger ferries and cargo ship and leave them far behind.

"You may have just made me a rich man!" the captain laughed.

"This is nothing. Just a small improvement," Chang-wei denied.

Deng gave him a sly, sideways look. "You're not just some lowly machinist, are you, Mister Chen?"

Chang-wei said nothing.

After getting my fill of the wind on my face, I went back down to check on Gao.

Everyone else on board was busy with their duties, so he had been left alone to sleep off the drug. He hadn't yet awoken and his breathing sounded shallow.

It was odd. Opium did cause lethargy and drowsiness, but it wouldn't render a man unconscious for hours. The two of them had likely been drinking as well.

Unrolling my acupuncture case, I pulled out a needle and pricked it to the man's hand. A harmless test that caused no injury, but his fingers should have jerked in response. He remained still. I tried a similar prick against his jaw, which should have caused his face to twitch even if he were in a drugged state.

"Is there something wrong?"

Chang-wei came up behind me.

"This seems to me like something more than opium smoke," I explained. "I want to make sure he's all right."

"He could still be drunk."

"I thought of that, but he's not reacting to anything." I clapped my hands close to the boatman's ear. "Wouldn't a drunk be quite irritable? Turn his face away from the sun or groan when his comrades dropped him? His friend said he's been out for most of the night already."

"That does seem unusual."

Chang-wei inspected the case with the acupuncture needles I had laid out. I realized this was the first time he'd seen evidence of my trade.

"You're trained as a physician?" he asked.

"I apprentice with our village doctor. It's how I keep my family fed."

He nodded, looking over the implements with fascination.

I hadn't been entirely honest. Aside from bartering my services and a few coins from Old Lo, we had survived by selling off our family heirlooms, but I had accepted so much charity from Chang-wei that I wanted to hold on to some sense of pride.

"Would you believe there's an opium den even in our dusty little speck of a village?" I asked him. "Most of us are poor, yet there's enough opium for the villagers to feed an addiction just like the wealthy in Peking."

Once the words started pouring out, I couldn't stop them. The person I was cursing was none other than my own mother. I could feel my heart growing colder and blacker. I hated that she had stopped living her life. I hated that I had needed to go to Changsha to barter for not only food, but enough opium to keep her docile.

"The drug is everywhere," Chang-wei agreed sadly. He looked closer at Gao now that I had voiced my suspicions. "There's little we can do for him but wait."

"Unless he stops breathing."

Chang-wei didn't reply. His look was one of resignation. "He chose his fate."

I was surprised a man of science would be such a fatalist when it came to the frailties of the human body.

"Have you ever smoked opium?"

He was surprised by my question. "It was common to indulge in a pipe at the entertainment houses in Peking."

I didn't want to think of what other pursuits were readily available at those establishments. There were prostitutes who made their entire trade on providing opium and the pleasures of the flesh in combination.

"What does it feel like?"

"Somewhat like strong drink." He ran a hand over the back of his neck, uncomfortable with the personal turn of the conversation. "But quicker. Your troubles float away and a sense of peace fills you."

"A sense of joy? Happiness?"

"No, not that." He struggled to find words while I watched expectantly. "People are right to call it a dream. Everything feels far away, like you're looking down from the clouds."

"And why not stay that way all the time?" I posed bitterly.

"Why would anyone want to come back to their troubles from the clouds?"

He came close, his hand brushing against my sleeve. "Because there are better dreams," he said quietly.

I couldn't understand why some people could let go of the drug so easily while others would smoke it until they wasted away. And what had happened to Big Gao, who, according to his companion had only a single pipe?

"Yang was testing opium samples from different ports," I brought up. "He was particularly interested in sources where opium was manufactured."

"Yang again," Chang-wei muttered.

I ignored his snide tone. "His theory was that some shipments had been altered or contaminated."

"As I said before, that theory is quite far-fetched."

I recalled the men Yang had locked up in his cargo hold. They had been listless and nearly catatonic until I arrived, at which point they'd erupted in violence.

"Have you ever seen opium induce a rage?" I asked Chang-wei.

He frowned. "I wouldn't say so. It has quite the opposite effect."

"My thoughts as well."

I looked at Big Gao again, lying eerily still as if dead. I checked his pulse again. The beat of it was still faint.

"I'll get a cloth to wash his face. Perhaps that will help revive him," I suggested.

After making sure I didn't need anything more, Chang-wei left to see to the condition of his new engine now that it had been running for an extended amount of time.

Over the next hours, Gao showed little improvement. He still didn't respond to light or sudden sounds. The pinpricks elicited no response. At times, his hands and feet seemed chilled.

His comrades came by to visit occasionally but showed no alarm at his state.

"Dumb Ox smoked so much he passed out," they jibed.

But by afternoon, he still hadn't roused, and I worried some more serious illness had befallen him.

Chang-wei came back to assist me as I opened Gao's lips to insert a bamboo tube. With Gao's head held up, I poured a small amount of water down his throat, careful of the fact that he couldn't swallow. Without water, he would further weaken, making it difficult for him to improve.

"Have you apprenticed with the physician for long?" Chang-wei asked as we set our patient back down.

"Four years now. Before that, I hovered around his shop, fetching and carrying for him. I stood by Old Lo while he administered remedies, and I watched and listened. He called me his little shadow."

The reason I'd followed the kind physician around was only partly due to an interest in healing. I'd been lonely in the village and looking for someone to fill the emptiness created by my father's absence.

Old Lo was knowledgeable and kind. He had the only collection of books I knew of in Linhua village. That was enough to earn the worship of a ten-year-old girl. At least it had been enough for this one.

Chang-wei set a spark lantern down on the floor between us as I sat down to resume my vigil. He took out a small bamboo case that fit in the palm of his hand and put on a pair of spectacles. When he opened the lid, there was book inside filled with tiny pages.

"What is that?"

"All my observations and findings," he replied.

"From your time with the *Yangguizi*?"

"Those as well."

The characters looked like tiny ants. "How can you read that?"

"A scholar's trick," he laughed. "The most desperate of us can include the entirety of *Classic of Poetry* on a side of a calligraphy box."

He took off his spectacles and handed them to me. The lenses magnified the writing so it was easily readable. Chang-wei had kept meticulous notes on his discoveries. On a few pages there were even drawings scaled down to minuscule size.

"I kept it hidden in a pocket I had sewn into my clothes," he explained. "And wrote down all the secrets I learned abroad. Now I keep it with me so I can always refer back quickly. I'm going to record the improvements I made on the engine into it."

"So you didn't surrender all of your findings to the crown prince?" I handed the journal back to him as well as the glasses.

"That would be foolish, given what's happened in the past, wouldn't you agree?"

Though most of the previous leading members of the Ministry had been demoted or removed from office, Chang-wei had regained a position of trust. He'd made himself valuable to the throne.

"Was it difficult for you to pledge your allegiance to the crown prince once you knew what had happened?" I asked.

"There was never any doubt in my mind."

"That is where you and I differ." I couldn't keep the bitterness from my voice.

"The Ministry did fail, Soling. We were defeated. We failed to protect the empire."

"But what of the warships and troops and cannons? What of the generals and diplomats?"

"We have all been punished," he said gravely. "All we can do is gather our strength and fight back."

I fell silent and he returned to the journal, using a stylus no thicker than a needle to write down his latest discoveries. I tried to weigh out Chang-wei's argument, but as much as I wanted our land to be free, I couldn't find it within myself to be so unshakably loyal. Our family had already paid its price.

While Chang-wei was bent at his work, I thought I saw movement from the bunk. I continued to watch and indeed, Gao's hand had twitched.

I rose and went to him, fully expecting him to stir and wake up, begging for water. But his eyes remained closed.

"Is this good news?" Chang-wei asked, staring down at the big man as I checked his pulse.

This was the first time Chang-wei had deferred to me as the more knowledgeable one.

"His pulse and breathing are stronger," I reported. But when I pricked his hand with the pin, he didn't responded. After a prolonged delay, his fingers did twitch again, and I noticed that the tips had started to blacken, just as I'd seen with the caged prisoners on Yang's ship.

20

The transport ship reached the juncture of the Yangzi and Xiang rivers in a day. A small trading settlement spanned both banks, and we stopped only briefly to gather supplies and more news. The rebel army, either through exaggeration or gathering sympathies, was growing rapidly. Reports from refugees of the last battle claimed it was a slaughter. With every story, my stomach clenched tighter.

"We're close. Changsha is only days away," Chang-wei assured.

I continued to tend to Gao, who was wasting away before my eyes. The broth and herbal medicine I poured down his throat wasn't enough to sustain a man for long. I brewed ginseng to quicken his blood, but it was nothing more than an educated guess. I didn't know what remedy he needed.

One afternoon, I was pouring Gao his dose of broth and medicine when his shoulder jerked. Chang-wei was tilting his head back for me and holding the bamboo tube to his mouth. The movement made us both jump. Chang-wei and I looked at each other with mixture of surprise and hope.

"Mister Gao?" Chang-wei leaned close. "Are you awake—?"

Gao's arm suddenly lashed out, catching Chang-wei across the face. As Chang-wei staggered back, Gao fell from the berth. His eyes flew open, but they were unfocused. His arms and legs began to thrash about as if struggling with an unseen enemy.

"You're safe. You're back on the ship," I tried to tell him.

Scrambling to his feet, Gao lunged at me, as if the sound of my voice enraged him. He knocked the bowl of ginseng broth from my hands, and the look on his face chilled my blood. He was crazed, mindless.

Chang-wei threw his weight against Gao, tackling the larger man to the floor. Despite having been comatose for three days, Gao fought like a wild animal. I fumbled for my needle gun and fired.

The needle embedded itself into Gao's leg. I could hear the rest of the crew rushing down. I fired again, this time hitting him in the chest.

By the time the crew arrived, Gao had gone slack and Chang-wei was struggling out from beneath the larger man. He had a scratch across his neck that had drawn blood.

"What happened?" The captain brought up the rear.

Gao was sprawled on the ground in a heap while Chang-wei and I were breathing hard.

"He woke up." My answer was a feeble one, but my hands were trembling and my heart beating out of my chest.

"He was delirious," Chang-wei added, pressing two fingers to his neck to check his wound. "He didn't know where he was. Couldn't understand anything we said."

The captain bent to inspect Gao, who was still again, but the drugged needle wouldn't subdue him for long.

"We need to restrain him," I said shakily. "To keep him from harming himself."

And anyone else.

The captain ordered the others to bring rope while we

explained how Gao had attacked us immediately upon waking up.

"Like a rabid dog," Chang-wei supplied.

"From smoking opium?"

The men turned him over to bind his arms and legs, and I saw that the spittle at the corner of his mouth looked dark in color. I pried his mouth open and saw that that his tongue was stained black, as if covered in tar.

"This isn't opium," I replied grimly.

I didn't know what it was.

CHANG-WEI INSISTED that I go above deck and get some air, saying that I had spent too much time trapped down below. Still shaken from the incident, I didn't protest.

One of the crew stayed with Gao while the others returned to their duties. By the time Chang-wei came to me, a bruise had formed beneath his eye and he had a handkerchief pressed to his neck.

"I can clean that—"

"It's just a scratch. Were you hurt?"

"No."

"Good."

He turned to lean upon the rail, staring out at the riverbank. "What do you think this is?"

"Gao appears to be suffering from opium withdrawal, but the symptoms are so violent. They've taken him over completely. Yet he didn't smoke any more than his companion."

The captain came up beside us on the tail end of the conversation. "Miss Jin, is my man going to survive this?"

"I don't know."

The truth was, I was afraid to say. What if Yang had been right that some of the opium shipments had been altered? What if tainted opium happened to reach the opium den in our village?

"When we next dock, I'll have to—"

The captain never finished his statement. The long shaft of an arrow embedded itself into his chest with a sickening thud. He was still staring at me, mouth part open, eyes wide. His hand reached up and hovered near the arrow, unable to decide what to do with it. This thing that wasn't supposed to be there.

I kept on seeing that stare, uncomprehending and final, even as Chang-wei grabbed me and shoved me onto the deck.

More arrows pierced the air. I could hear our crewmen shouting. The two bodyguards scrambled into position to return fire.

"Pirates," Chang-wei said through his teeth.

He was right next to me, pressed flat to the deck. The captain had fallen not far away.

"He's dead," I choked out.

My limbs had gone to ice. All around me, the crewmen were running for cover.

Chang-wei had told me get below if anything happened, but my body refused to move. He grabbed my arm.

"Stay low!" he gritted out.

Keeping my head ducked, I ran beside him as another of our crew staggered, stricken by an arrow. I thought Chang-wei would flee into the hold for cover, but he headed for the port side.

"I can't swim," I protested when I saw what he intended.

Relentlessly, he dragged me along. I glanced back once. The attackers had come upon us from three directions in small skiffs. Gunpowder motors buzzed as they circled. There were at least three men to our one.

"Take a deep breath," Chang-wei commanded.

He helped me climb onto the rail and squeezed my hand once before I slipped over the side.

As I plunged into the water, panic seized me. I tried to hold my breath, but water flooded into my mouth. The river had become a living, malicious thing as it churned around me. Kicking furiously, I tried to grasp for something. Anything.

Strong arms grabbed me and I clung onto them. A moment later, my head broke through the surface. I came up coughing, lungs burning.

I didn't know where the shore was, and my muscles were still tight with fear, but Chang-wei wrapped an arm around me.

"I won't let you go."

Fire lance explosions cracked the air. Chang-wei held on to me as he swam through the water using his one good arm. I found it was easier if I went slack and let myself be pulled along.

"When we get to shore, run for the cover of the trees," he said between labored breaths.

I forced myself not to think of the ship, the men who had been our companions. We just had to get to dry land.

When I felt the muddy bank beneath my feet, I thanked the Goddess of Mercy. Dragging myself from the water, I ran for the forest.

Chang-wei was right beside me. Our clothes were soaked through, but we pushed on until we were hidden in the canopy of trees. My lungs were burning, but when I stopped to catch my breath, Chang-wei pushed us on.

"The ship?" I gasped out as we ran.

"Gone."

The heat and rush of our escape had just begun to fade when we stumbled into a clearing.

And right into a circle of menacing-looking individuals, every one of them armed. Rough hands grabbed me from behind. Before I could think to kick or scream, they had stripped the needle gun and bladed fan from my belt.

I looked helplessly over at Chang-wei, who had drawn his firearm. The rebels backed away a step.

There was no doubt these men were rebels. Their queues had

all been cut away, and they wore weapons openly in defiance of imperial law.

"Let her go," Chang-wei demanded.

"It was you who intruded upon our gathering here, my friend."

The voice was unmistakably female, wellborn and cultured judging by the accent. The mob surrounding us parted to reveal a lady in her late twenties seated in a wheelchair with a steelwork frame.

I was surprised to see such a young woman speak for so many men, but her robe, though worn, was of expensive silk while those around her appeared to be laborers and peasants. Her feet were encased in impossibly tiny slippers. She had been subjected to the Han foot binding process.

Using a set of levers upon the armrest, she moved the mechanized chair forward. "We only sought to protect ourselves. And it seems we were right to do so."

Her gaze moved first to Chang-wei, then to me before settling back onto the pistol in his hands.

"We are merely travelers passing by," Chang-wei replied. "Release my wife and we'll go."

Though he communicated the ruse without pause, the lady raised an eyebrow at the sight of our wet clothing. Despite her wariness, she lifted her hand and I was immediately released.

I hurried to Chang-wei's side. He kept his gun drawn as he positioned himself protectively in front of me.

"We can't let them go," the tall man beside her interrupted. He wore a sword in his belt as well as a fire lance over one shoulder. I assumed he must have been her second-in-command.

The lady once again merely raised two fingers to command silence. "You will need to answer some questions."

"Ask, then."

Tension gathered along Chang-wei's spine, and I had to keep myself from holding on to him for support. Though they had released me, the rebels kept a tight circle around us. It was impossible for Chang-wei to shoot his way out. His pistol only held two bullets.

"Where did you get that devil's weapon?" There was a chill in her tone that set my teeth on edge.

"I purchased it."

"I believe you're lying."

"If that is what madame believes, then I cannot convince her."

Chang-wei remained as steady as ever, and I was reminded that he had spent years among enemies.

"We have no love for the *Yangguizi*." Gears churned as the mechanized chair moved closer. "Nor for the imperial cowards who bow down to them."

My heart beat painfully inside my chest. There was nowhere to run, and we were among lawless, desperate men.

"I care nothing for foreign devils or imperial authority," Chang-wei said. "The only thing I desire is our safety. The weapon and all our silver is yours in exchange for our lives. We'll speak nothing of you to anyone."

At that, the second-in-command once again spoke, his hard gaze pinning us. "If the Emperor means nothing to you, cut off your queue and join our cause. That is the only way to ensure you won't betray us."

Chang-wei's grip tightened on the gun. "That is not an option."

"You cannot shoot all of us," the woman said lightly.

He trained the gun away from her minions and onto her. "Then I apologize, madame, but I can certainly reach you."

The air thickened and every man reached for his weapon. Every crossbow was aimed at us, while the woman remained seated regally in her chair, her expression fixed in challenge.

"Wait!"

At first, I didn't realize I had spoken. I could barely hear my voice through the roar in my ears, but I pushed on.

"We can help you."

Chang-wei shot me a questioning look, but I had the leader's attention. I began speaking quickly, pulling the first thoughts that came to my head.

"We came from that ship, the ship your pirates just captured."

She didn't deny it, so I continued.

"My husband is a mechanic. If you look at the engine, you'll know the extent of his skill. He...he can be useful."

I glanced to the wagons and carts in their retinue, all of which looked to be worn and in ill repair. Chang-wei shook his head sharply, but I kept my focus on the leader.

She gave me a small nod of acknowledgment. "There is no need to shed more blood here today if you'll come with us peacefully. As to whether you wish to keep your head, that can be decided later."

At that, she looked pointedly at Chang-wei's firearm. Hardening his jaw, he lowered the weapon and tossed it to the ground before her chair. Her captain bent to retrieve it, his eyes never leaving Chang-wei's.

"I am only sparing your life because I have no wish to make your wife a widow," she told Chang-wei. "But remember this, *friends*. If you ever threaten me again, there will be no chance for her to negotiate on your behalf. Your throat will have already been cut."

21

Though our hands and feet were not tied, there was no doubt we were prisoners. The rebels surrounded us, and the guards at the rear kept their bows trained on our backs.

The rebels referred to their leader as Lady Su. She was accompanied by her captain and a cadre of forbidding-looking warriors. She led us back to the river, where I saw with dismay that our ship had foundered upon the bank.

One of the brigands approached. Not long ago, this same man had been firing at us from the skiffs that now surrounded the larger craft.

"The crew are all dead except for one found on a sickbed. Opium addict."

I bit back a gasp, surprised at the pang of sorrow that hit me. That was how quick death could be. Captain Deng and his crew hadn't deserved to die.

"I beg of you to spare the last man," I pleaded. "He's weak and helpless."

Lady Su looked at the surrounding forest. "Release him here? Killing him might be a mercy."

"Please, madame."

She gave me a look that was not unkind. "You have a soft heart. It won't serve you well in these dangerous times."

One of her machinists went on board to inspect the engine. He came back and whispered something in her ear.

The leader of the skiff pirates reported that it would take them an hour and an additional twenty men to get the ship back afloat. The lady assigned a party to stay with the ship while the rest of us continued on.

I didn't see what became of Gao; whether Lady Su released him or ordered him killed with the others. I was stunned by the cold cruelty of it. If we had remained aboard the ship, we would have been shot along with the others. Death dealt blindly by a flying arrow.

At least we had been spared for now, but for what purpose, I couldn't say. Chang-wei and I walked stiffly side by side. My tunic clung to me, and a chill from the wet material had crept into my bones. I was shivering, but comfort was the last thing on my mind. All we could do was wait.

The rebel camp was larger than I had envisioned. There were more than a hundred men. Sleeping tents had been set up with a ring of lookout posts around the perimeter. I sensed that they had been encamped for several days now. Clothes hung out on a line and there were several cooking fires burning.

As we entered the heart of the camp, a guard took me by the arm. "Lady Su wishes to speak to you alone."

Chang-wei tried to protest, but without his gun, he had nothing to threaten them with. They dragged him back as he called out my name.

"Tell her she can make any demands she wants of me," Chang-wei gritted out.

I was taken to the main tent, one much larger than the surrounding ones. At the entrance I was searched once to assure I had no weapons before being allowed inside.

Lady Su was in her chair, but positioned behind a wooden table. She beckoned with an elegant wave of one hand. "Please sit."

Seated we were eye to eye, yet I felt at a clear disadvantage. Aside from her delicate feet, or her "golden lotuses", as the Han people called them, her features were bold. She sat tall with her shoulders rigid and square. The lines of her face were well-defined with only a hint of feminine softness.

But it wasn't her appearance that intimidated me. When Chang-wei had pointed his gun at her, she had stared back fearlessly. Lady Su had made it evident that Chang-wei was the one who was cornered. He was the one who needed to be afraid, not her.

"I apologize that Chang—that my husband threatened you."

"He isn't your husband."

I swallowed, caught completely off-balance. "No. But...but we were betrothed."

I don't know why I chose to reveal that to this woman, a stranger. I no longer thought of us as promised to each other, and I was certain—I was fairly certain Chang-wei didn't feel that way, either.

"If not for you, he would be dead now," she said coldly. "Another body to throw in the river."

"Does a man's life mean so little to you?"

The words caught in my throat. I could see Captain Deng, his mouth open, eyes staring sightlessly.

"I was once married to a man. *His* life meant heaven and earth to me." When her eyes met mine, there was sadness in them, but no remorse. "He was the mayor of our region. A good man, murdered by corrupt rivals. The magistrate would do nothing to punish his killers, so I vowed I would do it myself. And I did."

"If his death has been avenged, then why—"

"Why do I still command this faction? Because my act of vengeance made me an outlaw along with all those who remained loyal and sought revenge with me. At first our numbers were small, but they grew as I found so many others who had suffered injustice from those in power. Men forced to work in the mines, farmers whose fields were confiscated by the state before they could be harvested.

"In the Heavenly Kingdom Army, it does not matter if one is a man or a woman. If one can lead, then men will follow. That is why I joined their cause. I do not take lives without purpose, but the men who follow me, they must see that I'm strong. I can't allow anyone to challenge my authority. Certainly not a *Yangguizi* sympathizer."

She placed the firearm onto the table between us.

"The bullets have been removed," she assured me. Even so, I didn't like having the gun pointed at me. "It took the most knowledgeable machinist among us some time to figure out how to open the chamber. Similarly, the engine on that ship is like nothing he's ever seen before. Your betrothed is more than a simple machinist. Who are the two of you and why are you here?"

"Please, Lady Su, I only wish to get to my family. He was only trying to help me get home."

"This is not an answer."

The sharpness of her reply silenced me. She might be a woman, but there was little softness to her ways. If there had been once, it had been bled away.

"He's an engineer from Peking." That much was true. I didn't tell her of his governmental position in the Ministry. Given the rebels' hatred of imperial authority, I thought it wise.

"Peking. I could hear it in his speech. Yours as well," she confirmed.

"He's no *Yangguizi* sympathizer. The firearm was only for protection."

"He is highly skilled. And connected with the throne in Peking, no doubt." She let out a slow breath, weighing her options.

"He's just...just an inventor. A man of devices and engines and machines."

"Wars are won and lost by such machines," she argued. "My men will see it as weakness if I let him live. Make your final farewells to him. I will see it done quickly."

The speed with which the decision came down stole my breath. Desperately, I reached for her hand. "Wait! I said we could help you. What if—" I stared at her chair. "What if we made it so you could walk again?"

"I can walk," she said through her teeth.

"Not without pain."

I knew it was only with a slow, tottering gait. Han women who hoped to marry well had no choice but to bind their feet from a very young age. Even in our village, where there was little chance of noble marriage, many families still engaged in the practice to mimic the upper class in hopes of securing a good match.

"The pain is there to remind me," Lady Su said stubbornly. "Of what it required in order to be suitable for my husband's family. Of how beautiful and desirable he considered me because of my delicate feet. Of what my mother and her mother also endured to have their feet bound."

Despite her bold declaration, I could hear the hint of longing beneath her resistance. "You must always address your men while seated," I pointed out. "That's how they always see you. I saw how the gears of your transport struggled over uneven terrain. Whenever the wheels slowed, your bodyguards had to slow their pace to remain by your side."

"And you say your betrothed is talented enough to change this? My feet have not been simply bound. The bones have been broken and reshaped, something a Manchurian like you would not understand," she said bitterly. "This is nothing like fixing an engine or the gears on a chair. It is nothing that *needs* to *be* fixed."

Lady Su had shown no emotion when she had been threatened or when she had condemned Chang-wei to death, but the emotion was there now, raw and naked for me to see. Her feet were a source of pride for her and of sorrow. Of so many things.

"Not fixed," I amended. "Enhanced. And you are correct that Chang-wei won't be able to perform this task. This is a personal matter, one for the woman's chamber and not something for a man to meddle with. That is why he will only be assisting. I am the one who will be giving the lady back her ability to walk, to stand tall beside the men she commands, to run if she so pleases. And all I ask for it is our lives."

22

"Biomechanics is an extremely specialized study," Chang-wei protested once I explained the situation to him. "I have no knowledge of it, and unless you've kept it from me, neither do you."

"I don't," I confirmed. "I never had the opportunity to study formally."

"Then how—"

Chang-wei hushed as rebels entered the tent to set down crates full of metal parts and fasteners. Lady Su had ordered an area set up with a makeshift worktable created from loose boards. Our tools had also been retrieved from the ship. When we were alone again, I opened the case containing my acupuncture tools.

"My father had a mechanical arm fitted to him after he lost his. Sometimes I would help him attach it. I remember the connection points and fittings. The principles of pressure points and nerve energies aren't completely unknown to me. And you build machines powered by engines, but you also know how to build structures with joints and ligatures. Figures that move as if they were alive."

A light dawned in Chang-wei's eyes as he looked from the acupuncture needles to the spare parts. "It won't be easy."

"We only have three days."

I don't know if he even heard me. He was already sketching.

Merely minutes later, he showed me a drawing of what would be a pair of mechanical slippers that would fit over Lady Su's feet.

"The device has to rise up to the knee," I advised. "We'll need the pressure points there to move the leg appropriately."

Slippers became boots.

"And they can't be too heavy," I reminded him.

"The material will need to be hammered thin. Steel and maybe aluminum. The metal is malleable, but not strong, but we can reinforce it by tempering."

For the moment, we were able to push aside that we were being held prisoner, but I made certain not to forget that we were dealing with killers.

We worked shoulder to shoulder, heads bent over the paper. With red ink, I marked out the locations of the pressure points along the lower leg.

"The feet will be the challenging part," I warned him. "Our feet have over a hundred pressure points. The controls will be very intricate, and Lady Su's bones have been reshaped."

"We should create a prototype first. So we know the principles will work."

Hours passed before they brought us food, but we had barely glanced up the entire time.

"We better eat," I suggested. "There won't be much rest for the next three days."

"If we truly are going to do this."

I stared at him in surprise, slipping a glance over my shoulder to make sure no one was listening. "What do you mean?"

He handed me a bowl of stew and took up the other, bending over it and making as if he were eating. "If we haven't found an escape in three days' time," he said in a lowered voice.

"There are over a hundred men here! Lady Su was ready to have you executed, but she agreed to spare your life in return for our service."

"You believed her?"

"Yes."

"Because she's a woman," he said dismissively.

"Because we spoke with each other at length. She didn't gain her position through lies."

"She's a rebel leader and a murderer," he reminded me. "It's obvious they've positioned themselves on water and land for a reason."

At the sound of footsteps outside, Chang-wei straightened and shoved some stew into his mouth. I did the same and we ate the bland meal in silence until we were certain no one was coming.

"There's going to be an attack," he continued. "And this is the northern arm of it. They're here to either cut off escape or any attempt to send supplies or reinforcements."

"Changsha," I murmured, feeling sick to my stomach. If the rebels had come this far, then what had become of the surrounding villages?

"In three days' time, we'll be caught in the middle of a war. That woman may spare our lives but force us to join her army as the price. That would be death for me, Soling."

"There is a chance she'll keep her word."

Chang-wei shook his head. "There is no chance. She can't risk releasing us this close to the battle."

Or appearing weak if she did. Lady Su commanded from a tenuous position. Her men had been intent on cutting our throats from the start.

"But you were so focused on designing the walking boots," I said in dismay.

"It gave me an opportunity to survey our materials." He gave me a sheepish look. "And perhaps I did get carried away with the challenge of it. What's wrong?"

I ran a hand over my eyes, forcing back tears of frustration. For the last few hours, I had lived and breathed in the comfort that I had negotiated our freedom. But we were still very much prisoners with our lives hanging by the barest of threads.

"We need to keep working on the solution regardless," I insisted. "If Lady Su suspects that we're plotting against her, we'll be executed on the spot."

"I don't think you realize how dangerous this game is—"

"I know it!" I snapped. "She was going to kill you, Chang-wei. She was going to kill you! You need to listen to me, please."

Lady Su had called me to her. She'd confided in me and that had to mean something. Chang-wei had saved my life by getting me off the boat. I had to believe that I could do something here in return. I had to believe this was a problem that had a solution. I just needed to find out what it was.

"ARE YOU AWAKE?"

Chang-wei spoke from beside me in the darkness. It was nighttime and the lanterns had all been put out. Though there was plenty of space in our tent, we chose to sleep close for comfort and security, even if it was only an illusion.

"I can't sleep," I answered.

"Me neither."

I could hear him turning toward me. His hand brushed against mine and I stilled.

"I think better when I can speak my ideas aloud," he confessed.

Though he was whispering, his voice filled every corner of my awareness. I clung to his presence, in my heart if not physically.

Make your final farewells, Lady Su had told me. It was the only leniency she had been prepared to offer, and a part of my soul had died in that single moment. I wasn't sure it would ever come back to life.

"You can say them to me. I don't have any ideas at all right now."

"Most of them will sound ridiculous," he warned.

"All right."

"First I thought of building a weapon, but I doubt there's anything I could do against so many. My pistol was no use, as we saw. I thought perhaps two weapons, so we both would be armed."

"Against an army of a hundred?" I returned.

"Yes, so I abandoned that thought. My next idea was armor that would protect us from their weapons. But I would never be able to hide it from our guards."

"Build it in parts that can be assembled quickly?" I suggested.

He made a thoughtful sound. "That might be possible. But in three days...building just a pair of biomechanical boots in that time is a sufficient challenge."

Oddly the discussion had a calming effect on me. I even formed a few ridiculous ideas of my own. "Can you build another glider? We can wait for a strong wind and fly out of here?"

Chang-wei chuckled. "Or flap our wings and take off like a bird does? Perhaps I could make boots with coiled springs attached."

"Springs?" I echoed, incredulous.

Absently, he drew a series of loops against my hand, sending a tingle up my arm. "We would build up a considerable amount of pressure and then unleash it all at once to propel us upward. We can use the boots to hop out of the camp faster than the rebels could catch us."

Picturing this made me burst out laughing, which was entirely out of place given how much danger we were in. I tried to stifle the sound and ended with my face pressed to Chang-wei's shoulder. He grew still suddenly.

I started to apologize and pull away, but he reached over to drape an arm around me, as if it were natural for us to embrace. It wasn't. His arm felt awkward and yet wonderful around me.

My pulse skipped and I closed my eyes to hold on to the moment. I was disappointed when he finally spoke.

"Soling, I have other ideas as well—" He broke off the sentence and his arm tensed about my shoulder. "Ones that are much more practical. They might even succeed."

"What are they?"

"These plans all involve me staying to create a distraction to allow you to escape."

"No."

"We have to consider it—"

"*No.* I wouldn't be able to go on without you."

"You would. You were clever enough to buy us time; you'd find a way through these woods. We're only a few days from Changsha."

"That isn't what I meant," I said, frustrated, yet unable to find the words to explain myself.

I listened to the rhythm of his breathing. It didn't matter that we were surrounded by a hundred outlaws. With Chang-wei beside me, I could think, I could hope, I could even laugh. Even though I was frightened and had no idea what to do, I wasn't lost.

I was awake. I was finally awake.

"We go together," I told him defiantly.

"All right," he said after a long pause.

"Swear it."

"I swear it."

23

The next day we started working from the moment we awoke. We set out to build a model first, using my measurements as a guide since I was close in size to Lady Su. Chang-wei drew out the pattern for the outer structure and began cutting out the shapes from thin sheets of balsa wood. To create the skeleton, he measured out lengths of bamboo. I worked on creating the delicate network of wires that would transmit the flow of qi energy from the acupuncture needles to control the mechanical limb.

It felt good to be working on my own creation rather than as an assistant. I became thoroughly absorbed in the endeavor, and when I next glanced up, it was late in the afternoon. Our lunch had been left forgotten at one end of the worktable. Neither of us had touched it.

We were separated from each other by a bamboo screen, given that I needed to be in a state of partial undress for my task.

I had changed into the blue cheongsam dress I'd been given in Shanghai. It was the only clothing I had that would expose my knee, around which I wove a net of wires. Locating the key acupuncture points, I inserted needles just beneath my skin to activate the meridians. There was no pain at the insertion points, just a tingling sensation that gradually spread along my leg as the qi began to flow.

"I need you to try on the model," Chang-wei called from the other side of the screen.

I glanced up my from my task to see a silhouette of Chang-wei lifting a large, unwieldy contraption. Poking my head around the screen, I confirmed that the boot was equally hideous in plain view. Metal scraps twisted around a bamboo cage that looked like it should be used to trap large rodents.

"It's as big as an elephant's foot," I complained.

"What does it matter what it looks like? As long as the joints move properly."

With a sigh, I removed the needles and lowered my skirt, smoothing my hands over the silk. As I came out from behind the screen, Chang-wei was kneeling to place the model boot onto the floor beside a stool. He glanced up briefly at me before returning his attention to the bolt he was tightening.

Then his head swung up to look again. This time his gaze lingered, sending a flush to my cheeks. The dress was cut to fit snugly around my figure. I'd twisted myself nearly into a knot behind the screen to work all the fasteners.

I nearly missed the stool as I sat down. "What do you need me to do?"

"Umm...here." He reached for my foot, his thumb brushing against my bare ankle before he thought better of it. "Just slip your...ah...foot in here."

I needed his help to manage it. Chang-wei held the contraption still while I tried to wriggle my leg inside. Once I was in, he adjusted the leather straps to secure the fit.

"The edges haven't been sanded down," he said, head lowered. "And without a forge for any serious metalwork, I had to fit together what scraps I could find."

He was making a concentrated effort not to look me in the

eye, and I couldn't help smiling. I quite liked it, as wicked as that sounded.

Chang-wei took me through a range of motions; flexing and pointing my foot. Rotating it. At each point, he paused to take notes. Finally, I stood so he could test my full weight against the springs beneath the bottom sole.

"What are your thoughts?" he asked.

"It's still a bit heavy—" I began.

"That can be fixed later. This is just a prototype."

"—and it's hideous, Chang-wei," I blurted out. "Lady Su's golden lotus feet are a source of great pride for her. We have to create something at least...pleasing to the eye."

"Golden lotus?" Chang-wei made a face. "This is meant to allow her to walk again. What does it matter how pleasing it looks?"

"It matters to a woman."

"She's a murderous traitor leading a rebel faction."

I hushed him lest the guards overhear us. "It matters."

With a sigh, he undid the straps. "I'll try to work on it."

Muttering something beneath his breath about form versus function, he placed a hand onto my calf to ease my leg out of the mechanical boot. It took special effort freeing my foot without breaking the model. By the end of the process, Chang-wei had my foot in one hand and the boot in the other.

His thumb rested against the bare arch of my foot. I gasped as he pressed lightly, sending a pulse that radiated through me. Abruptly, he let go, and I thought I saw some color in his cheekbones before he turned away.

"This is just a prototype," he said, setting his creation to the worktable. "There are things that need to be done, of course. It's just a prototype."

"You already said that."

"Oh?" He fumbled in his pocket for his spectacles and put them on.

"Chang-wei?"

"Hmm?" he replied, suddenly very interested in some joint in the external structure. As interested as any engineer could ever be in any connector.

I noticed that the tips of his ears were pink. It was endearing.

"Nothing," I replied, standing up to slip back behind my screen.

I really had nothing to ask. I just wanted to say his name.

WHEN I WAS BROUGHT to Lady Su's tent that evening, I carried a much simpler, much lighter design. Rather than encasing the entire foot, the construction now served as a support skeleton.

"The sole has a spring layer to support the weight of your foot," I explained.

As we only had time to build one, I had to demonstrate with only my right leg, which made it impossible to perform with any grace. I tried very hard to focus on the enhanced mobility to distract from my uneven hopping. Fortunately we were alone, so there was no one to witness my staggering.

"I cannot look like an invalid," Lady Su insisted. "Or a spectacle to be laughed at."

I mentally shot Chen Chang-wei a knowing look, even though he was at the other side of the camp. I was right that appearances were important and not merely for vanity.

"This is just a crude model," I assured. "But our construction is limited by the scrap metal provided. If we could have access to a forge to shape the steel as we see fit?"

"A forge?" she scoffed. "You are beginning to sound like one of those Taoist sorcerers whispering promises into an Emperor's ear, Miss Jin."

"The furnace on our ship might burn hot enough."

She arched an eyebrow at me. "So you and your beloved can attempt to sail away?"

My stomach fluttered at the mention of Chang-wei as my beloved. "He's not—"

"I'll consider it," Lady Su said with a wave. "Your ship is surrounded by our fleet now and manned by our crew. The threat of escape would be minimal."

I ducked my head to unstrap the boot. The lady had inadvertently revealed to me that there were more ships gathered farther down river. Chang-wei was right—they were stationed here as a barricade.

"If Lady Su will allow me to take measurements now. The final design will need to be fitted specifically to her."

Her mouth tightened and her spine grew rigid, but she gave a stiff nod. I knelt and took hold of a delicately embroidered shoe, feeling very much like a supplicant.

The shoe was only half the length of one of mine. Despite her wealthy background, she wore no jewelry or adornment. Those luxuries would have been out of place in the rebel camp, but her shoes remained extravagant.

Carefully, I eased her foot from it. I had never seen a woman's bound foot before, but I knew it was a very private, very personal thing. It would be offensive to show shock or revulsion. With a physician's detachment, I pulled the shoe away.

The foot underneath had been wrapped with linen, and, I was startled by how tiny it was. Her foot had been bundled up to the size of a fist.

Lady Su kept her face turned away as I unwrapped the linen. "No one has seen me since my husband."

The last words came out choked, and I forced myself to stay focused on my task. I understood from the depth of my soul that I was seeing this powerful woman at her most vulnerable.

I pulled away the last layer of gauze, and my stomach did a little lurch. Her foot hadn't simply been bound. It had been folded upon itself with the toes tucked underneath. The bones had healed into the compact shape, but with every step she would be walking upon broken toes, putting weight on bones that were never meant to be used in that way.

"I married well enough that I would never have to walk far," she said, her voice strained and proud. "I was to live a life of privilege, sheltered from hardship."

Silently, I began to take measurements. We would have to take a slipper and construct the boot around it. The contact points would need to be exposed through the material of the slipper.

That posed another problem I hadn't thought of. Not knowing what to expect, I didn't anticipate that many of the acupuncture points on her foot would be unreachable. The nerves might be damaged and inactive.

"I need to use my needles to test the flow of qi to the meridians," I said.

Lady Su nodded her consent and I retrieved my case.

"Do you know the leadership of the rebellion detests this practice?" she went on, her tone sharp and fierce. "Many of them are not of Han descent. Like your Manchurian Emperor, they consider foot binding barbaric. They would conquer a village and set the men and women to work equally. When they saw the Han women and their tiny golden lotuses, the rebels tore away the bindings and shouted for them to walk. They were free now, walk! Ignorant bastards thought our feet would simply regain their shape."

"You don't agree with everything the Heavenly Kingdom rebels stand for."

"I believe that I do not deserve to hang for avenging my husband's death. Nor should my men for challenging the injustices brought upon them," she replied sharply. "This is the path I've chosen. The men who serve me have chosen a similar path and trust me to lead them. The Heavenly Kingdom rebels and I fight a common enemy. That is enough."

I completed my diagnosis and began removing the acupuncture needles. "But when does it stop? When the Emperor is dead?"

"When we have built our own kingdom," she replied matter-of-factly. "We have seen it throughout time, dynasty to dynasty. This empire has always been a broken map of lands sewn together. It is time for this current dynasty to fall."

24

Something was coming.

Even from the confines of our workshop, we could sense it. The conversations we overheard were brief and clipped. I heard them speak of the walled city. Of a signal. Talk of the local Banner garrison rounding up a volunteer militia. There was a heightened level of awareness in the camp and a drawn out sense of waiting, waiting.

Lady Su's second-in-command came to the work tent in midmorning accompanied with four armed guards, two of them archers. For one sharp second, I feared the rebel leader had decided to execute us swiftly before the coming conflict.

"We're here to escort you to your ship. Prepare what supplies you need."

Chang-wei and I had discussed this contingency and already had our tools and materials planned. We loaded everything into a wheelbarrow, which Chang-wei had to man himself. He met my eyes pointedly as we started on our short trip, and I knew what he was thinking. Escape was ever on his mind.

"Keep your eyes open," he had urged last night, his voice

gentle in my ear. "If you find a chance to flee, take it. Don't worry about me."

"Would you run and leave me if the situation were reversed?"

He didn't answer. I already knew his answer.

As the men led us to the river with crossbows aimed at our backs, I doubted there would be any such opportunity. Lady Su had mentioned that they had a fleet assembled on the river and scouts positioned throughout the surrounding forest.

We passed by one lookout on the way to the ship. The boy was perched high up in the trees. He waved a signal to his commander, presumably that all was clear.

Before long, we passed a barge cruising in the river. Several smaller sampans floated nearby on either shore. Upon a passing glance, the vessels might appear unrelated other than fellow travelers sharing the waterway.

Chang-wei's gaze scanned over the water, taking every detail into account. "The lookout," he said to me beneath his breath.

"Quiet," the commander threw over his shoulder.

I wondered whether he had been assigned to this duty or if he had volunteered. Escorting prisoners seemed a menial task for a captain of the rebellion. But Lady Su was convinced that Chang-wei was dangerous. Maybe she knew better than I.

Chang-wei took one final survey of the river before returning his attention ahead.

Our transport ship was docked by the shore, though I could no longer consider it ours. As Lady Su had pointed out, her people now manned the helm. We were led aboard, where I looked into the scarred face of the new captain, the same man who had led the battle that had killed the former one.

The ship must have been his reward.

Down in the engine room, the furnace lay cold. After a sweep for any potential weapons, the guards carried our supplies down the stairs.

The commander cast the pile of scrap metal and odds and

ends a dismissive look before addressing us. "Get to work. You have until sundown."

The two bowmen remained by the entrance while we began our preparations.

I laid out our diagrams while Chang-wei worked on building the fire. An iron beam taken from a broken wagon served as our anvil. I made several trips above deck with a bucket to draw water to pour into our cooling basin. Within the hour, the coals inside the engine furnace were glowing red and I was wiping sweat from my brow.

We had cobbled together a set of blacksmith's tools: a hammer and iron tongs. The moment Chang-wei reached for the hammer, the guards lifted their crossbows, aiming them menacingly at him.

"How am I supposed to shape the metal without a hammer?" Chang-wei asked incredulously.

"Stay away from the stairs. If you come toward us, we'll fire."

Chang-wei made a point of staying as far away as he could.

We had already selected pieces that were as close as possible to the design requirements. Chang-wei now used the forge to refine and perfect the shape. With the tongs, he laid the first flat strip of steel into the forge. Once the metal glowed as red as the coals inside, he extracted it and placed it onto the beam.

I watched in fascination as he brought the hammer down over the steel. Each strike resonated through the engine room, and soon the clanging sound rang in my ears.

As the pieces cooled, I compared them against our measurements and tested them for fit. Once again, we became caught up in the work and forgot that we were prisoners. In the thick of it, we hardly even spoke to each other. We didn't need to. Quickly, we'd established a rhythm.

Around midday, food was brought to us. Nothing more than a few rice balls and weak tea, but we devoured them hungrily.

Chang-wei stood to return to work, wiping his sleeve over his forehead. He had removed his outer robe long ago. Without thinking, he started to remove his undertunic before stopping.

"I apologize—"

"I apprentice with the village physician," I said with a roll of my eyes. "I won't be scandalized by the sight of you."

Despite my bold words, I made a point of always having something else to focus on once his tunic was removed. The two, perhaps three times that I glanced over, I was fascinated by the muscles in his arms and shoulders as he wielded the hammer. Chang-wei's strength had always remained hidden beneath loose-fitting robes. I don't know what I thought he would look like unclothed, but it wasn't this.

I was fortunate the heat from the furnace hid any maidenly blush that might have touched my cheeks.

The engine room was sweltering by late afternoon. By then, the metalwork was nearly complete. The guards insisted we go above deck for fresh air before finishing up our work.

"I should bank the fire," Chang-wei said just as the guards were leaving. They were already halfway up the stairs, eager to feel a cool breeze. Chang-wei rushed back to far end of the chamber to seal the furnace door.

His movements were so quick that I almost missed it when he jammed a nail into one of the engine's gauges before moving on to join us at the stairs.

THE SKY WAS dark when we started our return to camp, and the commander was in a foul mood.

"I said sundown," he scowled.

Around us, the trees had faded into dark, looming shadows and the buzz of night insects filled the air. I wondered why they didn't light a lantern. We certainly had them with us.

Instead we picked our way nearly blind through the forest.

Chang-wei once again pushed the wheelbarrow while I kept close to him. The commander took the lead while the other guards surrounded us on all sides.

The group paused as Chang-wei struggled to push the wheelbarrow over a rocky patch.

"Hurry up."

"The ground is uphill this way," Chang-wei said, breathing hard. "And my arms are tired from the day's work."

I knew to be ready. Throughout the entire day, we had exchanged signs. When we had been given the order to pack up, Chang-wei had dawdled as he reloaded our supplies so there would be less visibility as the sun went down.

"You, take the wheelbarrow," the commander ordered. "Make it quick."

The guard to our left came to relieve Chang-wei, and my muscles tensed. That was a break in the protective ring surrounding us. Chang-wei had told me to look for such an opportunity. He would create a diversion any moment now, and I had to seize the moment and run as fast as I could, no looking back.

I started moving as soon as I heard the crash of the wheelbarrow.

"Worthless dog—"

An unexpected cry came from the rear guard, and I froze at the vicious snarl that accompanied it. This wasn't part of the plan.

Suddenly the guard was on the ground, wrestling with something large. "Help—"

His plea was choked off by a scream of pure terror.

The formation was completely broken. The other guards rushed to the fallen man's aid. The beast on top of him tore at him, but there was something wrong, something very wrong with the sounds it was making.

I tried to run but could only stagger a few steps. My heart was pounding too hard to think. I saw the flash of a blade before it plunged into the creature.

The thing howled with pain. Then I realized why its sounds had paralyzed me. They weren't the growls and snarls of an animal. They were cries of anguish, of very human anguish.

The knife plunged again. Someone sparked a lantern and a yellow glow flooded the area just as a hand grabbed onto me. I screamed.

"It's me." Chang-wei wrapped an arm around me. His face was streaked with dirt and he was bleeding beneath his left eye.

My heart sank. Our short-lived escape had failed.

The guards had surrounded us again, but their attention was on their fallen comrade who lay bleeding, a chunk of flesh ripped from his cheek. His screams split the air.

The creature that had been pulled off of him wasn't a creature, but he didn't resemble a man, either. He lay curled with limbs writhing as he struggled to get up. His body had wasted away to skin and bone, which made me wonder how he had the strength to attack so viciously.

He was still howling, a desperate, soulless howl as if his tongue had been cut out. When I saw his mouth, it was completely black like a pool of tar.

The guard who had wielded the knife now stood paralyzed as he stared at the thing before him. "What sort of demon is this?"

I clung to Chang-wei. Though the man was emaciated and his clothes torn to shreds, I recognized him.

"Gao," I whispered brokenly against Chang-wei's shoulder. My mind didn't want to believe it. I didn't want to believe any man could become like this, let alone someone I had known. And only in a matter of days.

The only culprit I could point to was the opium Gao had smoked. But how had he deteriorated so quickly?

The commander approached what was left of Gao with his

knife drawn. When he ended it in one quick swipe, we all felt it was an act of mercy.

25

"There was trouble yesterday," Lady Su remarked the next morning as I once again knelt at her feet.

Chang-wei and I had stayed up all night building the mechanical boots as well as discussing Gao's disturbing transformation.

"It was a madman who had become feral," I said. "We were all shocked."

In the confusion of the attack, I prayed no one suspected we had attempted escape at the same time.

"You tended to my man. The one who was injured," she went on. "I'm grateful."

"Anyone would have done the same."

"But not anyone would have had knowledge of how to bind his wound. Or ease his pain."

Something in Lady Su's appreciative tone raised my guard. Rather than continue the conversation, I focused instead on attaching the steel frame of the enhancements onto the lady's legs.

The final effect was a lightweight brace that ran along the backside of her leg down to the spring-loaded soles. Her feet were covered in silk shoes, with holes punctured into the fabric at the necessary contact points. The effect was more akin to jewelry than the original clunky design that had wrapped around her entire leg.

There were structural attachments at the knee and ankle and thin copper wires to connect the impulses from the acupuncture points to the metal frame. The boots would move with her, as if it were part of her own flesh and bone.

After testing the basic movement of her foot, I stood back. "Try to stand now."

She braced her hands against her chair and pushed up. Her jaw was tight with anticipation, and I found myself holding my breath.

Lady Su took one step and then another and then stopped. I started toward her to check the controls when I noticed there were tears in her eyes.

"I haven't walked like this, without pain, since I was a little girl," she said softly.

She began moving again, walking from one end of the tent to the other. Her gait was steady and even. "No more tiny lotus steps."

"Your weight is absorbed by the springs," I explained. "You won't feel anything."

"I feel everything," she disagreed. "I feel everything."

For the next moments, she walked, turned. Even ran a few steps. She made a small jump and the springs adjusted accordingly. When Lady Su sank back into her chair, her eyes were bright.

"I used to love to run as a little girl. I was so fast, I could outrun my brothers. We used to race by the river, while I imagined tigers chasing me," she told me, her voice thick with emotion. "You've given me a great gift."

I felt a prickling sensation at the corners of my eyes but ducked my head quickly. "I'm very happy to do so."

"You and your engineer as well, Miss Jin. Your skills are indeed very valuable."

The feeling of unease returned. When I raised my head, the lady was regarding me with a thoughtful expression and my stomach plummeted. "Three days ago, you promised me—"

"I know exactly what I promised," she interrupted. "I wouldn't think to destroy such talent."

"But you won't let us go."

"I can't." For a moment, she almost looked apologetic. "I know that you sense something is coming. Trust me when I say you are safer here than you would be in Changsha."

"Don't try to convince me you are doing this out of kindness," I muttered.

Chang-wei wouldn't stand by while the rebels attacked the city, and I knew he couldn't stand to live among traitors. Sooner or later they would force him to renounce his allegiance to the empire.

It's death for me, he had told me.

"Let Chang-wei go," I said. "And I'll stay."

Her eyes narrowed on me. "You're willing to sacrifice yourself for him?"

"Chang-wei is only here because of me. He has no part in this."

She shook her head gravely. "That isn't possible."

At that moment, a violent tremor shook the earth. I stumbled and Lady Su shot to her feet. The springs and stabilizing mechanisms within the boots adjusted, allowing her to maintain her balance.

"What is that?"

"Just an earthquake," she said, maintaining her composure better than I.

The ground lurched again, and it was as if someone had pulled a rug out from beneath me. I fell to my hands and knees as the earth rumbled. The sound of it was louder than I'd ever experienced in an earthquake. I swore I could hear the shift and grind of rock beneath me. There were screams from outside, followed by a shout of "Fire!"

Despite the unsteady ground beneath her feet, Lady Su glided smoothly to a trunk beside her sleeping pallet. I wondered if it was our invention that gave her extra stability.

I paled as she pulled out Chang-wei's firearm.

"I am making a mistake," she declared, looking pointedly at me. Then she turned the gun around and held out the handle. In her other hand, she held the rest of our traveling pack with my needle gun as well as the bladed fan. "Go."

I stared at her from the floor, stunned.

"Go," she repeated. "My men are occupied with other things. I won't send them after you."

Rather than dissipating, the shaking had become more violent. Dragging myself to my feet, I took the gun from her and shoved it into my sash.

"Stay away from Changsha," Lady Su warned.

She stood tall and straight, as proud as any warrior, and bid me off with a final nod. I stumbled from the tent.

Outside, the world was in chaos. A fire had broken out at one end of the camp. I realized with dismay that it was in the direction of the work tent that Chang-wei and I had shared.

With my heart pounding, I quickened my step only to be thrown sideways by the sway of the earth. I was tossed just as I'd been on Yang's ship in the storm, but the trembling was unpredictable. I had experienced earthquakes before, but none that were so prolonged.

The inhabitants of the camp had come out of their tents, many of which had collapsed. Most of the men and women were too stunned to do more than crouch and wait for the shaking to stop. As I continued on, the smoke thickened and I heard shouts of "Get water!"

Several tents had caught fire. My breath caught when I saw

that our tent was completely engulfed in orange flames. Chang-wei had lain down to get some rest before I had gone to present our creation. We had both been up the entire night. He was exhausted.

I couldn't move. I tried to cry out to him, but my throat had constricted so tight that I choked on his name.

"Why do you look so heartbroken, Soling?"

The familiar voice sank deep into my soul and I spun around.

Chang-wei was there, standing immediately in front of me. "Let's go," he said, taking my hand.

He started running with me alongside him. I held on tight to his hand even once the rebel camp was far behind us.

WE STAYED AWAY from the river where the rebels had positioned lookouts. Instead we moved deeper into the forest, using the trees and dense brush as cover. Occasionally there were slight tremors from the earthquake, but the shaking subsided for the most part.

"One might say it was divine intervention," Chang-wei said, handing me back my travel pack.

Inside were my acupuncture case and clothes. Lady Su had returned our weapons, allowing us to defend ourselves, but my father's box was gone. A pang of sadness hit me deep inside. I had so little left that had belonged to him. The puzzle box was something I could hold and touch, but perhaps it had served its purpose. It had led me to his two disciples; to Chang-wei and to Yang Hanzhu, who was now sailing upon the seas on his own mission of redemption.

As I slung the pack onto my shoulder, I realized something. "How did you have enough time to pack?"

Chang-wei met the question with a bland expression that I now recognized as him pretending to conceal something that he really wanted me to discover. "The capital is due south. We'll need to move quickly."

When I had left, my needles had been strewn all over the worktable. We had been doing final calibrations on the boots. Not only had he packed all of my belongings; he had packed his belongings as well.

"You set the fire," I deduced.

A flicker of satisfaction crossed his eyes. "It wasn't hard to smuggle enough gunpowder from the engine room."

I had caught Chang-wei sabotaging the engine while we were using the furnace. I interrogated him about it now.

"All the gauges and sensors have been tampered with. The first time they attempt to fire up that engine, it will rapidly overheat and become unusable—if it's able to run at all. I removed a few key valves as well. I couldn't allow my work to be used by traitors."

"I would hate to make an enemy of you, Chen Chang-wei."

A small smile touched his lips. "That would never happen."

I believed he truly could have escaped the *Yangguizi* if he had set his mind to it, even while across the world in London. Instead, he had remained to gain their secrets. I remembered that I had one of their weapons tucked into my belt. Having it in my possession made me uneasy, so I gave the pistol back to him. He opened the chamber. "I hope I'm not forced to use this."

"Lady Su promised me she wouldn't come after us. She has other matters to tend to."

Grimly, Chang-wei hid the gun in the front of his robe. "Matters of treason and insurrection."

We knew for certain that Changsha would soon be under attack. What we didn't know was whether we could get there in time to warn the city. And even if we did, was it too late for us to stop it?

26

Exhaustion came on quickly. I'd had little food and no sleep, and we were hiking through a wooded area where there were no paths to aid us. Though the rush of our escape fueled me through the morning, by afternoon I was walking in a trance. Chang-wei didn't look much better. Over the last half hour we barely spoke a word to each other as we trudged forward.

We slept using the brush to conceal us, too tired to even designate one of us remain awake to keep watch. It was a small blessing that Lady Su hadn't sent anyone after us as she'd promised.

Over the next two days, we traveled when we could and rested fitfully. Our journey was plagued by more earthquakes. There was one the next night and a few small tremors as we made our way through the forest during the day.

"We've had many in this area over the last few years," I told Chang-wei. "They've contributed to the growing unrest among the villagers."

Along with the string of dry seasons and bouts of famine,

earthquakes were signs of ill favor from heaven. Lady Su wasn't alone in believing that it was time for this dynasty to fall.

"Folk beliefs can be very powerful. Some are so strong, they attain the level of prophecy," Chang-wei replied. "Do you know one of the earliest functions of the Ministry of Science was predicting where in the empire there had been an earthquake?"

Father had told me the story of the invention of the earthquake detector, the circle of toads or turtles or dragons, each holding a brass ball in their mouths. I enjoyed hearing it again from Chang-wei. It passed the time and distracted me from the growl of my stomach.

"Whenever there was an earthquake, the ancient emperors would immediately dispatch a deputy to go investigate and assess what damage had been done," he recounted. "These men certainly must have seemed all knowing, riding from the capital to the far provinces faster than news could carry."

"Now the imperial court doesn't appear so divine and all-powerful."

Chang-wei wiped a hand over his brow. "We are the sorcerers and soothsayers now."

But the engineers and scientists of the Ministry were far from all knowing. The *Yangguizi* held dominion over us in our own homeland, and we didn't have the weapons to chase them out. Or perhaps it was the will to fight that we lacked.

What if our next ruler wasn't crown prince Yizhu, or even a rebel usurper, but a conqueror from the West?

It was a soul-wrenching thought.

"We should have considered making mechanized boots for ourselves," I remarked dryly to lighten the mood. "I can feel every step over these last days in the ache of my feet."

"I can build you an automated carriage," Chang-wei suggested.

"Better a flying machine."

"With bones of made of twigs and wings feathered with leaves."

I could only manage the barest of smiles, but there was a warmth building in my chest. A single candle in the darkest night seemed to shine so much brighter. That was what Chang-wei's presence felt like to me as we labored on toward the walled city of Changsha.

THE FORTIFICATIONS of Changsha emerged from the horizon like a sunrise. At first I couldn't believe that we had finally made it. If I could have run to the gates, I would have.

Chang-wei stopped me as we came closer. "Is the city already under siege?"

"No force could have taken Changsha so quickly."

It was the largest city in the province and protected by a large, well-equipped garrison of soldiers. The gates appeared barricaded, and the banners continued to fly overhead. The surrounding area was clear of any enemy encampments, but we were alone on the road, which in itself was a sign of trouble. When I had last come to Changsha, the roads were crowded with the various wagons from farmers and merchants bringing their goods to the thriving market.

Fortifications at the river entry points had been increased. War junks clogged the waterways, and the city's cannons were trained upon the water. I wondered if Lady Su had intended to sail her fleet down the river from the north. But the size of it had been small compared to the force before me. Lady Su's rebel fleet had been sufficient to guard the juncture of the waterways, but I doubted it was strong enough to attack the city.

As we neared, I considered the sheer size of the capital. Changsha was protected by a high wall made of stone. Nothing less than a full-scale army of thousands could take it.

But some accounts claimed the rebel army had grown to that size.

A small number of people had gathered at the front of the main city gate. They had fled from the nearby villages to seek protection in the capital. I asked of Linhua village, but no one had news.

"All the villages nearby have emptied," one farmer told me. He had come with his wife and two children. "The rebels are raiding every place they encounter for supplies."

For a moment, I considered continuing on to our village. I had to know if my family was safe.

"If they fled, they'll be inside," Chang-wei pointed out. "We must be patient."

At noon, the gates crept open. An armed regiment waited on the other side to search the refugees for weapons. Even the smallest of daggers was confiscated.

When the soldiers reached us, Chang-wei spoke before the search could begin. "I'm an imperial official with the Ministry of Science. I must speak with the governor."

"Do you have any identification papers?"

"They were stolen. By a rebel faction that took us captive."

That wasn't entirely true, as I'd seen Chang-wei remove any means of identification from his person, but the statement certainly captured the guard's attention. Unfortunately, it also made the soldiers wary of us.

"I have a firearm in my possession," Chang-wei said calmly when they began to pat down his robe.

They seized the gun and clamped shackles over our wrists.

"Perhaps you should have gotten rid of the foreigner's weapon once we reached the city," I whispered sharply as we were lead to the administrative compound.

"It got us an audience quickly, didn't it?" he returned, jaw tight.

What it did was get us an audience with the rats in the prison block. The soldiers locked us into adjacent cells where they left us alone.

Chang-wei propped himself in the corner, eyes closed, while I was too restless to sit still.

"Refugees have come from the surrounding villages." I paced from one end of my cell to the other. "My family could be here in the city, but they have no idea I've returned."

"Then they're safe. For the moment, at least." His eyes were still closed.

"Are you meditating?" I demanded, my temper starting to simmer.

"Just trying to think. It's hard to do so with you there distracting me." He opened one eye to peer at me. "You're pretty when you're agitated."

The compliment, thrown out so carelessly, was out of place for Chang-wei. My pulse skipped, but I couldn't think of anything else to do but scowl at him.

He merely shut his eye and settled back against the wall for a long wait.

"I just wish I knew for certain," I said with a sigh, finally allowing myself to sink down onto the stone floor. "Do you know this all started in Changsha?"

It had been a long journey being dragged away from home, then out to sea, then back again.

"Do you regret any of it?" Chang-wei asked.

I let my head fall onto my arm, face tilted to regard him. When I had come to pawn Father's mystery box, I didn't know that Chen Chang-wei even existed other than as a name in my past.

"No," I said finally. "I was locked away before. The world had become small around me."

And now it was a vast and endless place of cities and oceans and foreign lands. I didn't know what the future would bring, but I would face it with my eyes open.

"I suppose you are locked away once more," he said, glancing at the cage around us. The corner of his mouth twisted wryly.

"This? This is just temporary. Aren't you going to build some clever device to get us out?"

Chang-wei held out his hands, still clamped in irons, and turned them over to display two empty palms. "For you, I'd try."

Even now he could make me smile. He came over to the wall of bars that separated us. We sat shoulder to shoulder waiting for what would come next.

Less than an hour had passed when someone came to stand before our cells. We shot to our feet at his arrival, and my cheeks flushed hot at being found in such an intimate pose.

The man was dressed in a dark robe and an official's cap decorated with a peacock's feather. A minor functionary.

"What is your name, sir?" he asked.

"Chen Chang-wei."

To my surprise, the official turned to me and asked the same.

"Jin Soling."

I looked questioningly over at Chang-wei as the functionary took a scroll from beneath his arm and unrolled it to scan through the contents.

Chang-wei returned my look with a shrug of his shoulders, then addressed the newcomer. "I am an official of the sixth rank in the Ministry of Science," he began, straightening his shoulders with authority. "If there is any doubt of who I am, I request an audience with your governor during which I can present myself formally and prove my claim."

The functionary looked up from his scroll. "There is no need, sir. We know who you are." He rolled up the scroll and bowed at the waist at the prescribed angle. "We received a message from the crown prince two days ago asking of your whereabouts." His bow to me was not as low, but still notably respectful. "His Imperial Highness asked about you as well, Miss Jin."

27

Without further delay, we were released from the prison and led into the main fortress.

The functionary introduced himself to us as Zuo Zongtang, the governor's chief adviser.

"We wondered why the crown prince would send someone from the Ministry of Science here, but then we started hearing about the march of the ghost army."

"Ghost army?" It was the first I had heard of it.

"Yes, miss." Zuo turned to address me directly. He had a manner that was efficient without appearing abrupt. "The rebels have taken several walled cities in the region, but we cannot figure out how. Reports from any survivors of the attacks have been confused. There are stories of storms and floods, thunder and lightning and the earth splitting. One moment they're facing a hundred men. In the next, there's suddenly a thousand. All we know is that cities with formidable defenses have fallen after brief and brutal battles."

"We heard nothing of this in Shanghai," Chang-wei replied, frowning.

"It's all happened very quickly. Faster than the relay stations can send the news."

"And what news there is has been very confused," I remarked.

I glanced over at Chang-wei, who gave me a knowing look. Had the imperial government been trying to hide reports of their defeat from the rest of the empire?

We reached a set of stone steps and began to climb high up into the fortifications. A war council had assembled atop a tower overlooking the surrounding landscape. From all four directions, the area looked clear.

A group of distinguished-looking men was gathered around a table. High-ranking officials and generals, from the look of them. The two of us were still in rumpled clothing and covered by a layer of dust from the road.

Zuo made the necessary introductions, and I undertook a round of bowing and greeting that left me dizzy.

"We apologize for our mistake." The Governor addressed Chang-wei as he spoke. "If any offense was taken, please know that it was not intentional. When the message spoke of an imperial engineer, we thought your arrival would be more...auspicious."

"My arrival here is a matter of coincidence," Chang-wei admitted. "I had informed His Imperial Highness of my intentions to travel to this region. But now that it appears your city is in danger, I swear to provide as much service as I can."

They went on to relay what they knew. The rebels had been steadily sweeping northward, ravaging villages and cities like a swarm of locusts. Their numbers were growing, and they had gathered an ample supply of gunpowder and weaponry.

"Upon taking a city, all officials are promptly executed and citizenry conscripted into their army or into work camps," one of the head generals reported. He looked about the table. "We know that defeat means death."

I paled at the grim report. "Excuse me, sirs. But if this humble servant may ask if the village of Linhua has survived?"

The men looked at me as if I were a horse that had started talking. I immediately felt foolish and small for worrying about my family.

Chang-wei came to my aid. "Forgive us. We have come far searching for my companion's family. They may be one of the many refugees sheltered within your walls. If I may trouble you to assist her?"

"I can do so." Zuo once again stepped forward. "If you will come with me, miss."

Chang-wei gave me a reassuring nod as the governor's assistant directed me back toward the stairs. As I turned to go, I could hear the discussion resuming behind me. Despite the warnings that they would soon be under attack, the scouts had only seen small bands of rebels. There was no sign of a massive army that would be required to defeat the city militia and breach the walls.

As Chang-wei's voice faded, I felt hollow, as if something vital had been taken away from me. We had been side by side for a long time now. Long enough for me to feel a sharp tug in my chest as I was led away.

He'd fallen in so quickly with the city authorities. Chang-wei was loyal to the empire, without question. From the moment he had spoken to the war council, his fate had become tied with theirs and also to the fate of this city.

I would find my family, and we could flee or hide or be forgotten among the sea of refugees from the countryside. For Chang-wei, from here out, to fail was also to die.

~

"WE KEPT record of all the arrivals," Zuo explained to me once he'd led me down to the administrative offices. "But the process became less orderly as time went by and more refugees poured in. There was the matter of the approaching army as well as unrest within the city that needed immediate attention."

He lifted a heavy book from the shelf and set it onto a desk. Flipping to the last recorded page, he traced the columns with a finger.

"Linhua village. We took in twenty-four from Linhua—that is all it says here. They were resettled in the northwestern section of the city."

Relief flooded into me. There was some hope my family was among them, or if not, the villagers would at least know where they had gone. Everyone knew everyone in our village.

I thanked him graciously. Zuo took note of the exact ward where the refugees had been placed before directing me out into the yamen courtyard.

A mechanized sedan chair awaited us there. I looked around for a driver, but Zuo helped me onto the seat before climbing up beside me.

"The northwest section," he murmured to himself.

In one hand, he held a slip of paper on which he'd written several coordinates. The control board looked like an abacus with wooden beads that slid along thin copper wires. But rather than forming columns like they did on a counting abacus, the paths crisscrossed over the board like a maze.

Zuo moved one of the beads into a position near the upper left corner of the board. The rotors beneath the sedan whirred to life, and we sailed through the streets, passing pedestrians and horse-drawn carts to our left and right.

I noticed more yellow strips of paper plastered onto the walls and street corners than I had seen the last time I was in the city. Motorized cleaners hopped along the street tearing them down.

"Filthy propaganda," Zuo muttered. "The automatons remove them and the next morning those scoundrels put them up again."

"Scoundrels?"

"There are citizens within these walls who support the rebel cause. Those are the enemies we must watch, Miss Jin. The ones from within."

"Is there a large enough contingent for them to launch an attack from inside?"

"That is certainly a threat we have considered," Zuo admitted. "We don't have enough constables to scour the city and have had to recruit volunteers."

I was surprised by Zuo's openness. Bureaucrats were known to paint a pretty picture when caught in dire circumstances. It was bad luck to bear unfortunate news.

Zuo seemed a capable administrator, and I felt bad for taking him away from his duties. When I suggested he allow me to search for my family on my own, he wouldn't hear of it.

"I can't leave a proper lady to wander the streets without an escort. The increase in population has caused several problems to emerge. Temporary shelters were erected along the main streets, but our clerks could not keep track of every name nor where they're squatting. These conditions have bred a certain degree of lawlessness in the refugee wards."

Zuo took over the control knobs now that the sedan had reached its prescribed destination.

"We'll go to one of the local teahouses. Many have been converted to temporary shelters."

We passed by a house with a red strip plastered over the front gate. At first I thought it might be more anti-imperial propaganda, but then we passed another one. This one appeared as if it had been boarded up.

"What are those?" I asked.

"Sick houses. Infection spreads easily with so many living in close quarters; an unfortunate consequence of taking in so many from the countryside."

He spoke without condemnation. It was yet another detail to be handled. I was about to ask Zuo what sort of sickness they were suffering from when the sedan stopped across the street from a three-story building.

The upper floors were packed with people. Clothing hung from the balconies, and even the entranceway was crowded with squatters.

I dreaded having to disturb so many people to search for my family, but to my good fortune, a familiar face emerged from the teahouse.

"Old Man Lo!"

I climbed down from the sedan and raced toward him. The elderly physician started when he saw me.

"Soling, child!"

I reached out to clasp his arm. "I'm so happy to have found you. Do you know where my family is?"

My directness could have been seen as impolite. Physician Lo was my mentor, but it had always been a quiet, formal association.

Lo took no issue with it. "All here," he said, waving in a general direction with one hand. "They will be happy to see you."

I took his medicine bag from him, much as I always had, and brought him back to the sedan.

"Merchant Hu came back and said you had disappeared," Lo recounted. "Then a week later, a message arrived—an imperial message!"

He inspected the automated sedan as well as Zuo in his official's cap and robe. The two men exchanged perfunctory bows.

"I suppose it was all true, then," Lo murmured.

I helped him up into the transport. It managed to carry the three of us, but the churning of the gears was markedly more labored.

"Is my family well? They knew I would come back for them, didn't they?"

Lo told of how the entire village had packed up at once to flee from the approaching army. Those with branches of family in other areas went to rejoin their kin while the rest came to Changsha.

"It hasn't been easy here," he admitted.

I could see where families had camped out in alleyways and alongside the street on bamboo mats. According to Secretary Zuo, the city was large enough to accommodate them, but supplies of fresh water and food were low.

"Able-bodied men were immediately conscripted into the militia. Some of them no more than boys," Lo said.

"Tian?"

"Heavens, no. Your brother was too young. But there were fourteen-, fifteen-year-olds conscripted."

"A necessary measure," Zuo said defensively. "There are many civil tasks that require manpower. Policing the streets, for one. The youngest won't be sent to battle unless there is no other way."

There was another door plastered with a red strip. I squinted at the writing on it but couldn't make it out.

"It's worse in the neighboring ward." Zuo tilted his head toward the blocked gate. "We believe it started with stray dogs scavenging in the alleyways."

"Dogs?"

"Mad dog sickness," Physician Lo explained.

I was confused. I knew that particular sickness could be spread to people, but why would entire residences need to be condemned?

Ahead of us, a lone boy stood at the street corner with his shoulders slouched, seemingly absorbed by some pattern in the road. Even from afar, I recognized the slight slouch in this stance. My heart swelled.

"Tian!"

I begged Zuo to stop the sedan. By the time my brother turned to us, I was already running toward him. I caught him up in my arms and squeezed tight.

"*Soling*," he squeaked out.

It was a long time before I let him go, and when I did, it was only so I could take a good look at him.

"You've gotten thinner. What are you doing out alone on the street?"

He was full of questions himself. "What took you so long? Were you really on a special assignment for the Emperor?"

There was a smudge on his cheek. Absently I wiped at it only to have him squirm away in protest.

"How is Mother?" I asked.

I saw how his expression blanked. He gave a shrug and nodded toward a nearby alleyway. "We have been staying down there."

I knew immediately why Tian was loitering in the street. It was the same reason he spent so much time wandering around the fish pond before trudging home from school. The same reason I had been dreading my return home even as I longed for it.

For the last month, a weight had been lifted off my shoulders. Now my heart was heavy with guilt because part of me had enjoyed the freedom of not watching, day by day, as the supply of rice and opium dwindled down to nothing. I had enjoyed the freedom of being responsible for no one but myself.

28

Physician Lo asked if I needed his assistance, but I declined. In Linhua, he had only a vague notion of Mother's situation. He knew I secretly purchased opium but never questioned it. I had asked him once about methods of treating the symptoms of opium withdrawal.

"There is nothing to be done but to keep the patient comfortable and wait it out," he had told me.

He was right, except there was no such thing as comfort. And I had never had the courage to let the withdrawal run its course.

With a mournful sort of silence, Tian led me down the alley where our family and many of the other families of Linhua had taken shelter. Mother's shameful secret was no longer a secret. From the moment I entered the narrow space, I could hear her moans of anguish echoing against walls.

I saw Nan first, huddled over a figure on the ground. The loyal maidservant was speaking soothing words, pressing a wet cloth to Mother's forehead. A makeshift shelter had been constructed around them, fashioned out of bamboo and wooden scraps over which a curtain could be hung.

"Your work?" I asked Tian.

He nodded wordlessly.

"It's very well made."

This is what we did. Talk of inconsequential things to reassure one another. As a distraction.

It never worked.

Nan looked up and her face brightened with relief when she saw me. Worry lines had carved deep grooves around her eyes and mouth, telling the story of all she had endured since I was gone.

"How long?" I asked.

She didn't need to ask what I meant. "Two days."

Two days since my mother had last had any opium. She lay curled into a tight ball now, her hands clenched into fists while she writhed in agony. Her clothes were soiled and her hair ragged about her face.

Suddenly, she lurched forward and Nan hurried to place a pot beneath her, holding her head while she was sick. I looked away. All around us, the other squatters from our village huddled silently in their corners, averting their eyes, out of respect, out of revulsion, out of pity. Perhaps all three.

When Nan laid Mother back onto the bamboo mat, I went to her, brushing back her matted hair with a shaking hand.

"It's me, Mother. It's Soling."

She shook her head back and forth, whimpering like a wounded animal. I hated feeling so helpless. Despite my study of healing and acupuncture and treating the symptoms of sickness, there was nothing I could do for her. The same thing had happened before when Mother had tried to wean herself off of opium. I had run to Cui's den to get the next dose myself.

But I'd been a child then. Sixteen and unsure of myself.

Out on the street, Zuo waited beside Physician Lo. For now the governor and his functionaries assumed I had the crown prince's favor. I could take my family away from this forsaken alleyway and provide comfort and warmth and a small measure of security. Yet, I hesitated. Even now, while Mother lay on the ground surrounded by refuse.

Though my eyes filled with tears at the thought, I wanted to send Zuo away. I would stay here with Mother. This was our burden to bear, not anyone else's.

Mother had once been the wife of a high-ranking official, a well-respected lady. She wouldn't want anyone to see her like this. Opium was her escape and her private shame. It was mine as well.

It had always been easier to scrape the coins together and buy the opium than face the reality of how low our family had fallen, but there was no hiding anymore. I was awake.

"Mother."

My voice caught in my throat. I didn't know if she could hear me or if she was too far gone.

"I'm going to take you somewhere. A safe place."

"I can't stand it," she moaned. For the first time, her eyes opened. They were swollen and glassy. "Please, Soling—"

Please bring more opium. Please ease the pain.

"No, Mother. No more." I took her hand firmly. Her fingers were cold in my palm. "It's going to get better, I promise."

But first it was going to get a lot worse.

WITHIN HOURS, Zuo had us situated in the governor's mansion. He arranged for a carriage and stood by respectfully as we helped Mother onto it with me beneath one arm and Nan on the other. When we arrived at the front gate, the governor's servants stood ready to receive us. Rooms had been prepared and tea set out. The efficiency of how everything was managed convinced me that Zuo wouldn't merely be a governor's assistant for long.

We brought Mother into the inner women's quarters and took to her care ourselves. The servants were of the proper and discreet sort, holding their tongues as they helped draw bathwater and bring fresh clothing. They saw to our needs while not interfering.

I was grateful. It still shamed me deeply to have to put ourselves in the hands of others.

Tian remained quiet in the courtyard, picking through the contents of his writing box. I went to him once Mother had settled down enough to sleep.

"What is that?" I asked, looking over the contraption he had set on the ground.

"Nothing," he murmured.

"Nothing?"

He had tied together several thin bamboo rods to create a frame and was attempting to attach one of his writing brushes onto it with a length of string.

"I don't want to say until I know the design is worthy," he amended.

"Is there anything you need, then?" I asked.

He shrugged. "Something to act as a counterweight."

My heart swelled for my brother, this quiet, thoughtful boy.

"I met someone during my trip," I told him. "Someone you might find interesting."

I wondered where Chen Chang-wei could be. Was he still in the war council, discussing the city's defenses? By now he would have told them of our encounter with Lady Su's faction along the river. Any day now, we would be under siege. Everyone was waiting for the inevitable, I could sense it in the air.

One would think that I would feel safe now behind the thick stone walls of Changsha, with the city guard and Banner army to protect us. But I didn't feel any more secure. The approaching army was one of thousands, and they were no longer afraid of imperial authority.

Nan was calling me back inside. I took one final look at Tian's invention—the writing brush was now dangling like a pendulum—and told him I looked forward to seeing it when it was finished.

Then I returned to Mother's vigil.

IT HAD BEEN A LONG TIME, I believed, since my mother had gotten any pleasure from opium's murky embrace. There were times when she seemed to hate it. There were times when she seemed to hate herself for wanting it. It had broken her down and stripped her of everything; this relentless hunger for a substance that would never leave her satisfied.

I was so tempted to believe, as Yang did, that someone else had done this to her. Or that even the opium itself was a monster, a malevolent and greedy thing.

But it was really just a vapor. A gas, formless and accommodating, flowing in to fill an empty space and taking on the shape of its container. Sometimes when I saw her in the midst of an opium stupor, her eyes vacant, I thought of her as an empty container that once held my mother.

As I sat beside Mother now, listening to her cry, watching her writhe and tremble, holding her head while she was sick, I forced myself to believe that this was a necessary phase and she would get better. There would be an end to this.

I hated to see Mother suffer, but she at least she wasn't empty anymore.

As the day wore on into evening, we tied her hands down to the bed. She had started clawing at herself as if she wanted to tear off her own skin.

"It itches, it itches," she wailed when we told her to stop.

After she'd torn a gash across her cheek, I had called for the servants to fetch rope. Then I held Mother's wrists while Nan bound her. Our old maidservant and I took turns sleeping beside her in fits and starts while Mother tossed about.

I wished that I had been selfish and asked Physician Lo to stay with us. I would have asked him whether it was possible to die from opium withdrawal.

We had an adjoining room where Tian slept. Whenever I slumped onto the bed beside him, he would ask me softly how Mother was. That's how I knew he could hear everything that happened in the next room. He slept no better than we did.

The next morning, Mother seemed a little better. I was able to coax her to take some water and broth, but she refused even the thinnest of rice congee.

When I sat with her, she was able to prop her back up against the wall and face me. There was a gray pallor to her complexion and her lips were pale. Her hair had been pinned into a bun, but the coils were now tangled like a spider's web on her head.

"While I was away, I met an old acquaintance of the family," I told her.

"Oh?" Her voice was strained and her hands remained clenched in her lap.

"Engineer Liu Yentai. From Peking," I added when there was no sign of recognition in her eyes.

Mother wasn't being deliberately dismissive. She was trying hard to take her mind away from the cravings. Every muscle in her must have ached to the bone.

"Old Liu," she conceded finally.

She didn't inquire about him, so I went on. "Liu Yentai told me stories of how you came to the Ministry disguised as a candidate for the science exams. He said you had a talent for mathematics. I never knew that, Mother."

Silence.

I cast my eyes downward. "I also saw Yang Hanzhu."

"Yang," she echoed, her tone flat.

"Yang the alchemist," I prompted. "He worked with Father on the gunpowder experiments. Father always spoke of how brilliant—"

"I don't want to hear about these people," she cut in irritably. Her hands curled so tight that the knuckles whitened. "I don't want to hear about anything having to do with your father or our past life."

"But what if we could return to the capital?"

"There's nothing for us in Peking," she retorted. "Why would we go back?"

Agitated, Mother lay back down and curled her knees up toward her chest. She looked so childishly small; my own mother.

When she didn't say anything for a long time, I came to touch her lightly on the shoulder. Any touch was an irritant in her condition.

"It pains me, Soling."

"The tea I brewed should dull the ache in your joints."

"No." She squeezed her eyes shut. "The memories. They hurt inside. Once they start, I can't stop them."

Though she didn't want any, I gave her more tea, spooning the brew into her mouth.

"The worst is over, Mother." I promised.

"I need time to pass by," she moaned softly. "For it to go by faster. Why won't it go by?"

Mother tried hard to fall asleep, and I said nothing more that might dredge up painful memories.

When she finally did sleep, I continued to watch over her fearfully. Mother looked much better now than the day before, but she looked far from well. Though opium had broken her down, she would take the drug in a heartbeat if it were offered to her. She would inhale it into her lungs more dearly than she did oxygen.

29

I stayed in the lookout tower until the battalion disappeared into the horizon. Chang-wei would be with them, trying to detect sounds of activity beneath the ground. If they suspected there was a tunnel underfoot, they would use explosives to try to destroy it.

The first explosion boomed like thunder in the distance. I jumped at the sound, my heart beating hard against my chest. I had no way of knowing whether Chang-wei had been successful, but another explosion followed a mere few minutes later. Each one shook me to my very core. Such weapons easily turned upon their masters.

I prayed for Chang-wei's safe return, and then forced myself down the stairs. My heart couldn't bear it any longer staring out into emptiness, waiting for the worst.

Chang-wei's workshop had been set up in a storage area on the ground floor of the fortress. I found my brother there, already focused on his task. An array of parts and tools had been laid out over the table. Tian was in the process of inspecting and categorizing each one.

I took a seat on the stool in the corner. "Do you need any help?" I asked after some time had passed.

Tian shook his head.

My brother was not formally trained, and he had never worked with such materials before. I hoped he didn't find Chang-wei's task beyond his capabilities.

"Mister Chen is a part of the Ministry of Science like Father was?" he asked.

"He once worked under our father."

Tian began sorting the materials into separate piles. His movements were methodical and deliberate, and his brow furrowed in concentration.

"I hope I don't disappoint him."

"You won't."

I remained there in the corner, quiet so as not to disturb him. But I wanted to be there to help in any way I could, even though I had no knowledge of engineering. It turned out that Tian's questions were not about machine work.

"Are you and Mister Chen friends?"

"Yes, we've become…friends."

The pause said more than I wanted to tell. Tian's focus remained on the device he'd started constructing, but I wondered what he was thinking.

"Is Mister Chen an honorable man?"

Was my eight-year-old brother being protective of me? I wasn't the only one who had grown during my time away.

"He looks at you," my brother said.

I chose to remain quiet on that. Tian and I were close, but ten years separated us, and he was also a boy. I couldn't confide in him about Chang-wei, but I did long for someone to talk to all of a sudden. I could still taste Chang-wei's kiss on my lips.

The frame of the detector had emerged when I next broke the silence. "I should return to Mother and Nan."

Tian didn't look up.

"Will you be all right here on your own?"

"I'm not a child," he said, irritated.

I was taken aback. Tian never spoke back to me like that, but I didn't reprimand him for his sharp tone. The situation was tense for everyone. At least my brother had his new project to keep him occupied, and, once again, I was grateful to Chen Chang-wei.

"I'll return later."

He mumbled a farewell as I left to find Zuo. My brother would be safe in the confines of the fortress, and I prayed that Chang-wei would return by sundown, unharmed. I pressed my fingers to my lips to recapture the imprint of his kiss.

Returning to fetch Tian would give me an excuse to seek Chang-wei out. I would have until then to figure out what to say to him. My pulse was still pounding too hard to figure it out at the moment.

SECRETARY ZUO SENT two armed guards to accompany me back to governor's mansion. We took the mechanical sedan, which sagged under the weight of heavy armor and weapons. The vehicle still managed to transport us at a good pace through the streets, but as we neared the mansion, I pulled the control lever to bring us to a stop.

My guards tensed within the sedan. They had heard the commotion, too; shouting on the next lane over and the stomp of feet. With more knowledge of the area than the guardsmen, I took over the controls and directed the sedan into a side street. Moments later, a huge crowd of civilians marched by as we crouched in the darkness of the alley. A mob had taken to the streets armed with clubs and knives.

The guards reached for their swords. "Miss, we should return to the fortress," one of them said.

He looked to be only a few years older than me. I ignored him and focused on the abacus control board, plotting out an alternative route. My mother and Nan were nearby and defenseless. I wouldn't leave them.

"We're closer to the governor's mansion than the fortress. His family and mine are there. They'll need your protection."

The governor was with his war council, planning the defense of the city. This left his mansion a vulnerable target.

Taking hold of the two levers at the control board, I backed the sedan out through the opposite side of the alleyway and started winding around toward the mansion. When we reached the far end of the street, I saw that reinforcements had already been sent to the residence. A line of city guards blocked the front gate with additional patrols around the perimeter. It was fortunate they were there, because the mob was rounding the corner and shouting for blood.

I left the sedan and darted for the gate while my guards shouted after me. I ignored them as I stood before the line of defense in front of the gate.

"Let me inside. My family is in there!"

There was little time to consider my request. The commander pounded on the gate and it opened, revealing another patrol stationed inside. I slipped into the courtyard while my guards moved to join the defenses.

The gate slammed shut behind me, followed by the sound of insults being hurled at the guards. I heard several thumps against the wall. The mob was throwing rocks while the patrol shouted at them to stop or face punishment.

I was relieved that everyone inside was still safe, but my relief didn't last long. Fighting broke out on the other side of the walls.

"Get inside the house," the guard captain barked at me. "Stay hidden until we get rid of this rabble."

The clash of metal outside the walls sent me running to the back of the house. The servants were in a panic, but there was little for them to do. They were trapped inside like we all were. I saw that some of the men had armed themselves with clubs. I wove past them all to search for Mother and Nan.

The two women were huddled in my mother's room, hands clutched together. My mother looked pale with ragged strands of hair hanging about her face.

Her eyes widened when she saw me. "What are you doing here? Why did you come back?"

Mother's sharp tone pierced me deeply, but a moment later she held out her hand to me. She was angry, not at the sight of me, but that I had rushed into danger to come to her.

I clasped her hand just as an explosion shook the walls. Startled, I fell forward and Mother wrapped her arms around me as we clung to each other. Beside her, I could hear Nan reciting a prayer to the Goddess of Mercy over and over.

When the rumbling stopped, the fighting outside sounded even closer.

"The rebels have broken through the outer wall," I cried. "We have to go."

At first neither Mother nor our elderly maidservant would move. They continued to huddle on the bed as another explosion rocked the governor's mansion.

"Mother, *please*."

I tugged on her arm and thankfully she rose, her legs trembling. She had spent the last days entirely in bed, rendered helpless by the opium sickness. I dragged her along now even as she stumbled. My actions may have seemed uncaring, but there was no time to be considerate.

The courtyard had become a battlefield. A hole had been blasted through the stone wall from which the rebels pushed their way inside. A scattering of city guards attempted to repel them while flames danced wickedly upon the rooftops. There was smoke everywhere, and I could feel the sting of it in my eyes and throat.

Perhaps the rebels had thought the governor was in residence or they didn't care. The mansion was a symbol of imperial authority and had to be destroyed.

Keeping to the outer perimeter of the courtyard, I ushered Mother and Nan past the battle to the opening in the wall. The edges were jagged where the rebels had blasted through the brick. With one eye on the skirmish, I grasped Nan's arm to help her over the rubble. Despite her thinness, there was a sinewy strength in the old woman, a strength I knew had helped my family through many difficult times.

My mother was trembling as I took hold of her, but there was a hard set to her jaw. For the first time in a long time, her eyes were clear as she looked at me. She had survived hard times, too, those eyes told me.

Nan steadied Mother from the other side, and I climbed over after her. There were more guards outside rushing toward the breach in the wall. I spied the sedan still partially hidden in the alleyway and guided Mother toward it. I could hear the shudder in her breath. The escape had given her a burst of energy, but she was fading now.

We had just climbed into the sedan when a stranger came out of nowhere, grabbing onto the side and shouting at us. My hand closed around the war fan tucked into my belt. With a flick of my wrist, I snapped it open.

The blades clicked as they locked in place. I slashed at the stranger's face. A thin line of blood appeared over his cheek, and he let go with a startled cry. With no time to waste, I pulled the lever into reverse.

The jolt of the sedan threw me back onto Nan and Mother, but the mechanical gears were moving us away from the site of the battle. When we reached the opposite street, I flicked the fan closed and righted myself enough to take the controls. I directed the machine back toward the fortress, haplessly bumping against the stone wall as I rounded the corner.

"My daughter," Mother said, her breath labored. "I never imagined."

Only now that we were clear of danger did my hands start to shake. I gripped the levers harder to steady myself. I would have never imagined, either. I was a very different girl from the one who had left our village a month ago. That other Soling was nothing more than a ghost to me now.

30

We were stopped at the fortress entrance, but not for long. The guards recognized the official emblem on the sedan as well as my face. I took some time getting my mother and Nan settled somewhere quiet to rest before seeking out a report on the governor's mansion.

The fortress was in disarray. Apparently more patrols had been sent out to the streets and I couldn't find the usual attendants at their stations. Secretary Zuo was also nowhere to be seen. When I went to Chang-wei's workshop, it was empty.

Where was my brother? I saw various sketches he'd made, but the detection device and tools were missing. I should have known not to leave him alone—as clever as he was, he was still only a child.

With my heart pounding, I set out to search for him, but was immediately intercepted by a man I recognized as one of Zuo's assistants. "Secretary Zuo is looking for you, miss."

I followed the messenger as he sparked a lantern and led me down a set of stairs into a passage below the fortress. The air was cool and the walls were made of pressed dirt reinforced with a layer of stone. These tunnels had been dug out of the earth and appeared to be used for storage, though the space might be large enough to provide a refuge during a siege. I shuddered at the thought of being trapped down here, encased in the ground.

There were voices around the corner. As we turned, the passageway opened up. A ring of lanterns had been strung up overhead and a group of authorities were circled around something. I tensed at their grim expressions.

As I came closer, I saw it was Tian standing at the center beside a lattice of metalwork. It was his device, but reworked with a sturdier frame and springs at the base. The basic design had been expanded in a radial pattern, with arms fanning out like the points of a compass.

Secretary Zuo stood protectively beside my brother as Tian stared at the scroll of paper laid out over the floor of the tunnel. In the center of the paper was a spiral of black ink. A tangled spider's web. No one spoke around them.

The earth suddenly wrenched beneath my feet and I lost my balance. The tunnel rumbled around us while a murmur went through the gathering. Someone muttered an oath.

With heart pounding, I braced my hand against the rough stone wall and counted the seconds until the tremors subsided. At that moment, Tian looked up, his eyes widening when he saw me. Beside him, the brush apparatus drew frantic spirals over the paper.

"The rebels are attacking from all sides, Soling. They're everywhere."

My brother looked up at me expectantly, as if I would have all the answers. All I could do was stare at the spikes of black of ink.

I let out a breath, struggling to steady my pulse. "We can't intercept them all."

Inevitably, one of those tunnels would breach the walls and bring the battle inside.

"We must try to stop as many as we can," Zuo said.

The war council considered using the volunteer militia to

bolster the Banner army, but I told them what had happened at the governor's mansion. There were insurgents within the city that also needed to be controlled.

"Danger from inside as well as outside," Zuo remarked somberly.

No wonder so many cities had fallen without warning. As Zuo and the commanders left to relay the new information to the governor, I took my brother's side.

"You did well, Tian," I said.

He looked solemnly at the ink pattern. "I could be wrong. These could be false alarms."

My instincts told me he wasn't mistaken. Chang-wei had trusted him, hadn't he? Another tremor rumbled beneath our feet, much fainter this time, and fear gnawed a pit in my stomach. Changsha was a death trap. Escape was no longer an option.

We chose to stay in the workshop rather than go back to where Mother and Nan were resting. At least here, we continued to receive reports from the battalions that had been sent out. Earlier that day, the soldiers accompanied by Chang-wei had detected two separate tunnels that they'd exposed using explosives. The ensuing battles had been brief as the tunnel only contained mining crews who were captured for interrogation.

Based on Tian's discovery, it was believed there were at least twelve such tunnels in various stages of advancement toward the city walls. It truly was an attack from all sides.

The battalions divided into smaller crews to try to locate the tunnels with listening devices from above ground. We continued to hear loud booms throughout the day as they detonated explosives over suspected dig sites. It was like hunting for pangolins burrowed deep inside their trenches; a frustrating and time-consuming endeavor.

Every so often, we heard news that another tunnel had been found. Some were abandoned; others had a few workmen. The bulk of the rebel force was still unaccounted for, which meant the threat was still crouched low, waiting to pounce.

Late into the night, I sent Tian back to see Mother while I stayed in the workshop. I ended up falling asleep on a mat in the corner while the oil lamp burned down. I didn't know how much time had passed before I was roused by the rustle of cloth and the sound of footsteps carefully navigating the room.

I thought I recognized Chang-wei's silhouette as I stirred.

"It's me. It's Soling," I called out softly.

"What are you doing here?"

"I was waiting for you."

My face flooded with heat as soon as I spoke, and I was glad for the darkness. The last time we had seen each other, I had lost my first kiss to him. The memory of it made my heart beat wildly.

Chang-wei raised his lantern as he came closer, revealing himself fully to me. My chest hitched at the sight of him. There was a smudge of soot on his cheek, and his eyes appeared drawn past the point of exhaustion, but he was safe.

"I heard the governor's mansion was attacked," he began.

"The mob was put down shortly after."

"You shouldn't have been anywhere near danger."

He had lowered himself onto one knee before me. Even though his tone was admonishing, it was only out of concern. I couldn't help but feel this was how it should be between us; each of us concerned for the other. Protecting each other.

"What's happening out there?" I asked.

His expression turned grim. "We're doing what we can. The battalion is still out, scouring the surrounding area. I only have two hours before I must rejoin them."

He had come back to create more explosive devices and to get some rest.

"Rest first," I insisted. He started to protest, but I raised a finger to quiet him. "You're more likely to make mistakes if you're tired."

My logic worked its way past his thick skull. He nodded and I moved aside so he could lower himself onto the mat. I should have left him there to rest, but I couldn't bear the thought of losing these moments. How long would it be before I saw him again?

Fortunately, he didn't ask me to leave. Instead, he laid his head back and closed his eyes.

"Does it have to be you out there?" I asked after I sensed he wasn't sleeping.

He inhaled and exhaled deeply before replying. "It should be me."

Just as he'd been the last one to man the cannons when Wusong fell.

"We'll find and destroy the tunnels," he assured me. "Changsha will not fall. Our spies have spotted the rebel army camp. There are over five thousand in number, and they will be here within days. It is critical we destroy their tunnels before then."

Five thousand above ground and how many below? Were the rebels strong enough to take the city even now that we knew their plan of attack?

The next part was difficult for me to say. "I couldn't bear it if anything happened to you."

"I couldn't bear it if anything happened to you," he echoed, his voice thick with emotion.

That was the reason why I didn't want him to go. And that was his reason for why he had to go. Chang-wei's hand came to rest just beside mine, the backs of our palms touching. He ventured no further than that, but it was enough to send my pulse racing.

When he rose half an hour later, I got up to work alongside him, measuring out gunpowder and filling the ceramic shells. Each explosive device we constructed left us with less gunpowder to use in the cannons for our defense. Each explosive had to be deployed judiciously.

This time, there was no time for anything more heartfelt than a slight bow as Chang-wei took his leave in the dim hours before dawn. But I felt every emotion in the way he looked deeply into my eyes before parting.

I will return, he told me with his eyes.

Promise, I tried to beg him. *Promise me.*

But we said nothing aloud, and then he was gone again.

THERE WERE MORE explosions early that morning, closer to the city than before. More tremors shook the ground. Reports came back that the battalions were actively engaging rebel troops now who had their own supply of cannons and gunpowder.

"Eight of their tunnels have been destroyed," Zuo told us. "The last one held over three hundred rebels armed for battle. There were casualties suffered on both sides."

I wanted to call after him to ask whether there was any news of Chang-wei, but he had hurried off. Zuo was constantly busy relaying information between the governor and the field commanders as well as maintaining order within the wards. A city under siege was a pot just beneath boiling. Changsha had been straining under pressure for weeks.

As to detecting the tunnels, there was no longer any need. The sounds of drills and shovels could be heard directly in the underground passages. Tian and I were ushered into the living quarters of the fortress where Mother was convalescing.

No one knew when or where it would happen, but an invasion was imminent.

When we had been at war with the *Yangguizi*, the battles had been far away, removed from us by hundreds of *li*. Now the fighting was right outside the gate. The enemy was right beneath our feet. I sat with Mother and Nan in the chamber where we had been placed and waited out the hours. My brother hovered at the window, though there was nothing to see outside but other refugees. The governor's wife and family had also been relocated nearby.

A gong sounded throughout the fortress, making us jump. The sound was deafening. Chang-wei had warned me of what the signal meant—they were calling all battalions back to fortify the city. Over the last days, Changsha's defenses had been spread thin. Guards had been stationed around the armories and gunpowder stores, and there were soldiers upon the wall to operate the cannons, but the bulk of the garrison had set out to hunt down the rebels.

"Tian, come back here and sit with your mother," Nan called out in a shaky voice.

"There has to be some way we can help," my brother insisted, refusing to move from his lookout point. "It's our duty to do what we can to defend the empire against these traitors."

Apparently, his taste of responsibility had brought forth a strong sense of duty in him. Mother wasn't happy to see it.

"What is there for you to do? You're just a boy," she snapped. "This war belongs to those men out there."

Though she seemed to have mastered the opium cravings, Mother's manner had become short-tempered and cutting.

"The burden belongs to all of us," Tian insisted. "This is our country."

Mother and Nan spoke at once. The elderly maidservant admonished my brother for being insolent while my mother dismissed him as being naive.

"Just like your father!" she hissed.

Tian blinked, stunned by the acid in her tone. "Then I should be proud then," he said finally.

At that, Mother's anger crumbled away, leaving her in tears.

Nan threw her arms around Mother and glared at the boy. "Apologize to your mother!"

My brother mumbled an apology, but Mother couldn't hear him. "I'm so tired. So tired," she whispered, rocking in Nan's arms.

I shot Tian a reprimanding look. Sullenly, he went to place a hand onto Mother's shoulder. I understood her desire to withdraw from the politics of the empire. If Father hadn't been entrenched in the war against the *Yangguizi*, he would still be here with us.

But then he wouldn't have been the same man that we called our father. For him, like for Chang-wei, there was no other choice. No other way.

Mother folded her arms around Tian to pull him close to her. At that moment, a deafening explosion rocked the fortress walls. The windows of the chamber flew open and a washbasin toppled over, shattering, while the walls shook.

"Evacuate!" the guards shouted from outside. "Evacuate now!"

My ears were still ringing, but I staggered to my family and grabbed onto them; a hand in Tian's shirt, an arm around Mother's shoulders. I shouted for them to head toward the door, but my voice was drowned out by another thunderclap.

When we finally stumbled out into the courtyard, there were people scrambling in every which direction. Acrid smoke and dust filled the air, clogging my throat.

The fortress was under attack. Even though I could barely see, I held on tight to my family. No matter what happened, we would not be separated again. I would not let go.

31

When Chang-wei came to visit the next morning, I felt as if I were nothing but skin stretched over bone. In addition to tending to Mother, another earthquake had shaken the city with enough force to knock items from the shelves. It had happened in the middle of the night during one of those rare moments when I had drifted off to sleep.

He was polite enough to say nothing about my appearance, but he did lean solicitously toward me, asking in a gentle voice if I needed anything.

"Perhaps something to act as a counterweight?" I said.

His eyebrows rose in confusion.

"Can we take a walk?" I asked instead of trying to explain.

Even from the parlor room in the front of the house, I thought I could hear Mother's moaning. She would be mortified if Chen Chang-wei knew anything of her suffering. He was one of Father's former associates and the man the two of them had selected in a bygone time to be my husband.

We started in a circuit around the surrounding streets. This area was one of the wealthier neighborhoods and showed none of the squalor or sickness of the refugee quarters. The morning air was clean and crisp, and I breathed it in deep, trying to banish the phantoms of the sickroom.

Chang-wei was dressed once more in an official robe and cap denoting his rank. Something about the clothing restored his sense of formality around me, or maybe it was our return to civilization. I wasn't certain of the cause, but he seemed different this morning.

"I hear you have found your family."

"Yes. We're very fortunate to have been reunited."

"I came to pay my respects to Jin *Furen*," he referred to my mother respectfully by her married title.

"Mother is resting now," I said quickly. "But...but perhaps you can visit her later."

"She is well?"

"Yes." A lie. "What did the war council say when they heard of Lady Su's faction?"

"The governor and his council are recruiting more men for the volunteer militia. They've also asked me to assess their defenses. A plea was sent out for imperial reinforcements several weeks ago, but it's unlikely any help will arrive in time for the initial offensive."

"Initial offensive," I echoed thoughtfully. "Oddly, I'm surprised there hasn't been an attack against Changsha yet. I thought for certain the rebel army would be upon us by now."

The rebels who had captured us were preparing for an attack on the city; I was certain of it. But why were they holding back? Every day that passed bought more time for reinforcements from the imperial army to arrive.

"No one knows when they will come, but they will," Chang-wei assured me. "Assistant Secretary Zuo has recounted their movements over the last year to me. At first they struck smaller cities, gathering supplies and troops. Changsha would be their largest target yet—I'm being tiresome, aren't I?"

I shook my head fiercely, mid-yawn. "It's not you."

He grinned and my stomach fluttered in response. Then his expression turned serious. "Soling, there is something I have wanted to say for a long time—"

When he came toward me, I practically jumped away. My back collided into the wall that surrounded the governor's mansion.

"You're very tired," he amended, stepping back. I immediately regretted my impulse.

"Chang-wei, we—" The words caught in my throat. How could one hope for something, yet fear it all the same? "We're friends now, aren't we?"

"Yes." His jaw tightened. "Friends."

He didn't know anything of my life or of my family's situation. How far we had fallen. Chang-wei had offered to help us, perhaps guided by his loyalty to my father's memory, but he didn't know what a burden that would be and why I couldn't accept. I was struggling to find the words to explain, when the ground lurched beneath my feet.

Chang-wei caught me as I stumbled. We held on to each other as the ground shook.

"Another earthquake," he murmured.

My pulse beat like a hummingbird's wings with his arms around me. Even when the trembling stopped, he held on; a single steady point in my world.

"Soling!"

I pushed against his chest, and Chang-wei released me just as my brother appeared at the gate.

"That was from the opposite direction of the last one!"

Only after he'd given his excited report did Tian notice Chang-wei beside me. My younger brother bowed awkwardly, unable to muster any proper greeting.

"This is Imperial Engineer Chen," I introduced.

"Sir," Tian mumbled, head still bowed.

My heart was pounding though the shaking had subsided.

There was nothing to feel ashamed about, I told myself. Nothing at all.

Except that I had liked the feel of Chang-wei's arms around me, even though we were out in the open where anyone could see us. Even though I was about to tell him that it was best we go our own ways from here forward.

"Young Mister Jin," Chang-wei greeted. "Tell me, how can you know the origin of the earthquake?"

Tian fidgeted, uncomfortable with such honorifics.

I was curious as well. "Show us," I told him gently.

Obediently, Tian turned and led us back into the courtyard. From there, he headed toward our private chambers, and my heart lodged in my throat. Mother was in the depths of her opium sickness and not fit for visitors.

To my relief, the garden was quiet for now. I prayed that Mother had fallen asleep. We followed my brother to the wooden pavilion. From there, one was meant to sit, have tea and enjoy a relaxing view of the manicured trees and carefully placed stones, but I saw that Tian had set a contraption onto the center of the stone table.

It was the bamboo cage he'd constructed the day before with a thin calligraphy brush dangling from the top of the frame. The base of the device had been tied onto a flat stone to keep it steady. White paper lay beneath with the tip of the brush just resting against the smooth surface. Black marks traced each movement of the brush.

There were two distinct spikes in the ink and then a lighter pattern of whirls as the brush settled.

"A pendulum." Chang-wei inspected the device from one angle and then another. "With a stabilizing mechanism."

Tian blushed a little. "I don't know what you call it, sir."

Chang-wei went on, inspecting the materials and how they'd been put together. "Magnets. Very clever usage."

At that moment, the ground shook once more in a single

shifting motion. Once again the brush created a spike. The pattern beneath it was starting to look like a flower with petals radiating outward.

"We've had a lot of earthquakes lately. Would you say more than usual for this province?" Chang-wei directed the question to Tian.

The boy nodded. I was grateful for the attention Chang-wei was showing my brother, and I made a note to thank him later. Tian was so often overlooked.

But Chang-wei's expression remained focused. That line that I had come to know formed between his eyes.

He straightened and turned toward me. "Rumor is that the rebellion started in the area of Thistle Mountain. There are many tunnels and caves there where they were able to hide."

"And mining pits." I froze and our gazes locked.

"The first to join the rebellion were miners with their shovels and drills and heavy excavating equipment. Powerful machines that can move rock and cut holes through mountains." Chang-wei glanced at the earth beneath his feet. "The attack has already begun. The rebels are digging tunnels."

CHANG-WEI LEFT IMMEDIATELY on a quest to rally the war council. Within three hours, I was summoned along with my brother to the fortress tower. Secretary Zuo came to fetch us in the automated sedan.

"The governor has given the order to clear the streets and lock down the city," Zuo told me as the sedan sped around the corner. "But Mister Chang insisted he be allowed to speak to you."

We passed by a guard patrol ushering civilians back to their homes. The market gong clanged loudly from the towers while signal drums beat out an incessant warning. As we neared the tower, the stone walls rose high before us. Changsha relied on its walls for protection. It was chilling to think that rebels were trying to tunnel beneath the fortifications this very moment.

Zuo led the way up the stairs to the lookout tower while Tian and I followed dutifully behind. My brother reached out for my hand. When he squeezed it, his grip was steady. The look he gave me showed no fear. We're together, it told me.

No matter what happened, I was home. We would face this together.

Chang-wei was looking out over the walls with his back turned to us. His hands were clasped behind him and his shoulders squared.

Zuo called through the beating of the drums. "Mister Chang?"

Chang-wei turned and I saw the grim set of his mouth. "Thank you, Mister Zuo. Tell the governor we'll be ready by the next hour."

The assistant left us. I saw that the rest of the war council had also left their positions. Presumably to prepare for battle.

"I need your help, young Mister Jin. Are you aware of what is happening here?" Chang-wei began.

Tian nodded solemnly. In that moment, I could see the sort of man he would become one day.

"The governor is sending out troops in the direction of the recent earthquakes. The rebels are digging tunnels toward Changsha. Once they've breached the walls from below, they'll march their army through. We must stop them before this happens."

"We?" I asked.

Chang-wei turned to me, his expression disturbingly calm. "I will be riding out with the garrison."

I started to protest but bit my tongue. I didn't want Tian to know how frightened I was. Whether or not I wanted any part of it, we were caught in the middle of a war. This was no place for fear or doubt.

"Sir, my invention is very crude," Tian confessed. "The readings aren't exact."

"I am aware of this." There was no insult in Chang-wei's reply. "Going out to intercept the attack is a risk. It divides our forces, and we don't have time or men to waste, but I convinced the war council that this is the best course of action. The rebels have divided their forces as well—they're digging from multiple directions. I wager there will be more earthquakes in the coming days. If we can locate the exact origins, we'll know where there rebels are. Young Mister Jin, can you build a more efficient model of your detector?"

Tian stood straighter. "I can, sir."

My chest welled with pride.

"I have prepared materials in my workshop for your use. I trust you will require no further instructions. Even if you did, there is no one to give them. The city is relying upon you."

Zuo returned to escort my brother to his work area. Only Chang-wei and I were left in the tower.

I could no longer remain silent. "You're no soldier, Chen Chang-wei."

"This is the best solution."

"You don't know how many rebels are out there or how well armed they are or where they're hiding."

"I have considered all these factors." He came closer, speaking in a soothing tone that made me even more agitated. "I need to determine the exact locations and set the explosive devices. The ones I've constructed are dangerous and, well, not as well tested as I would like."

I knew then he had been doing more than reviewing the city's defenses. He had been building weapons.

"If they catch you, they'll kill you," I choked out.

"If they take the city, I'll be executed anyway." He placed his hands over my arms. "You're angry at me?"

He spoke with surprise. I hated how calm he sounded. Chang-wei was utterly resolved, even if it meant death.

"Do you have to be so unquestioningly loyal?" I spat out.

My question took him aback. "You're upset with me because of my sense of loyalty?"

I thought of my father, kneeling with head bowed to surrender his life. Then there was Chang-wei, manning the cannons long after the battle was lost only to be taken prisoner by the enemy.

"The empire won't consider you a hero for your sacrifice."

"I'm not doing this to be a hero."

I looked away, bitter. "Then why?"

He cupped my face in his hands, gently lifting my chin so that our eyes met.

"This is who I am," he said.

Feebly, I nodded. I knew it was who he was and I hated him for it. But I was afraid that I might also love him for it as well.

"We don't have much time, Soling, so forgive me for being so direct."

Chang-wei had not brought me here to say some fatalistic farewell. I wouldn't let him.

"You're coming back," I told him fiercely.

He didn't answer, which made my stomach sink further. "What I wanted to say earlier—no, you'll let me speak this time, Soling. What I wanted to say earlier was that I thought about you, Soling. I thought about you often when I was imprisoned aboard the foreign ship."

"That's impossible. You didn't even know me."

I don't know why I insisted on being combative. Perhaps it was the only way to keep my tears from falling.

"I didn't know you," Chang-wei conceded. His thumb caressed my cheek. "Not the way I know you now."

His eyes were dark and endless above me. Chang-wei was always such a master of his emotions that seeing them displayed so clearly over his face was almost frightening. It took my breath away.

"Since the day your father promised you to me, I have never imagined myself with anyone but you, Soling. Yet I don't regret that we never married as your parents intended. I'm glad that we had to find each other in this way, so many years later. That we could share such adventures together. I'm glad that I was given the chance to see you as you really are." He exhaled deeply, letting the last of his resistance crumble away. "And that you could see me. Even if I'm not who you want."

I started to protest that wasn't true, but the words never left my lips. Chang-wei rested his hand against the nape of my neck, tilting my head upward. Before I knew what was happening, his mouth was pressed to mine in a kiss that was soft and searching. My first. The moment our lips touched, I knew that I had been waiting for a long time for this. My mind and body just didn't have the language to express it.

Chang-wei pulled away and the world spun around me. I had just lost my first kiss and it was already over? Before I could despair, he lowered his head to me once more. Harder this time, yet with a tenderness that made my chest ache. I kissed him back. I wanted Chang-wei to know what I felt for him. If anything happened to him, it would break me into a hundred pieces.

As I clung to him, I was painfully aware of my inexperience, but Chang-wei guided me gently against him. His lips caressed mine until my fear melted away and my knees weakened. I would have crumbled to the floor, but Chang-wei held me tight, surrounding me with his strength. When the kiss ended, we were both breathing hard.

For a long moment, we did nothing but look at each other. It was as if I was seeing him for the first time. His eyes captivated me. I had always thought him handsome, but now his face had become irreplaceable. Every line and contour was precious to me.

I wanted him to promise me he would return, but he said nothing beyond the way he looked at me with longing in his eyes before leaving. I watched his back until he disappeared down the stairs, and I followed him with my eyes as he rode out along with a battalion of soldiers, off to fight an invisible foe.

32

I could only ascertain what had happened in bits and pieces. The rebels had broken through the north wall. There was fighting inside the citadel.

There were no armed guards to guide the evacuation, and we were left to swarm like ants. Tian was small and able to squeeze through small spaces to act as a scout. He scurried forward and then shouted directions back to us.

"Through the corridor! The front hall is clear."

I pulled my mother and Nan along with my needle gun drawn. If we encountered any threat, there was little it could do besides incapacitate a single attacker, but I needed every bit of courage I could gather. A skirmish had erupted in the bailey, and I couldn't make out rebel from soldier in the confusion.

"Soling, let's go back!" Mother pleaded.

I was torn. Should we slip back inside and hide, hoping for reinforcements to arrive? Or should we try for the gates? A man was struck down right in front of us, his face covered in blood as he fell to the dust. I shrank back against the wall just as Tian broke away from me. I screamed for him to come back, but his thin figure disappeared, swallowed by the smoke and dust and confusion.

I had never been surrounded by so much violence and madness. The blood rushed through my veins so hot that the urge to run was overwhelming. All I could think was the vow that I had said to myself earlier: Stay together. Stay together, no matter what.

"Come on," I dragged Mother forward. "We have to go."

The citadel had become a death trap. If we could only get out of here, we had a chance.

I finally found my brother again crouching beside the arch of the gate. He turned back to wave us over. At that same moment, I saw rebels rushing through from outside. Long Hairs. Their weapons were drawn and their expressions feral with blood frenzy.

My heart bled out. Tian wasn't a threat to them, but it didn't matter. Kill or be killed; that's all anyone knew in battle. I tried to raise my needle gun, but my fingers had gone slack. My limbs felt like lead.

I was too far away to stop the attack. I knew that in my mind, but I had to do something. Had to. My vision sharpened, focusing starkly upon Tian. He looked so small, lost in the midst of battle.

A moment later, two loud cracks split the air like the pop of firecrackers. The rebels fell to the ground while Tian stood unharmed.

In shock, I scanned the gate and gasped when I saw Chang-wei, pistol raised. He'd come back for us. A rush of emotion swept through me and I sank to my knees, holding tight onto Mother, who was shaking so hard I thought she would fall apart.

"Tian isn't hurt," I murmured to her. "He's all right."

Soldiers from the city garrison spilled into the courtyard around him. Lowering the weapon, Chang-wei went to my brother. Then he looked to where I was huddled with my mother and Nan.

Armored guardsmen flanked either side of him as he approached.

"If you'll come with me, madame. We need to get you somewhere safe."

Chang-wei addressed my mother while more men came to form a protective barrier around our family. I grabbed hold of Tian's hand and didn't let go. His fingers were ice cold in my grasp, but they held on to mine with equal fierceness.

We moved as quickly as we could, the men clearing a path for us. The fight wasn't over, but as the men escorted us from the courtyard, the rebels were being routed by the rest of the garrison.

When we were finally clear of the fortress, I could see the hole that had been blasted into the city from underneath. The entry point was surrounded by armed soldiers who were already starting to barricade it.

"Is it over?" I asked.

Chang-wei tucked the firearm into his belt before turning to me. "No, Soling. I'm afraid it's just begun."

ONCE AGAIN, we were adrift like sparrows in the storm and seeking refuge. Zuo graciously took us into his home, which was a modest-sized residence compared to the governor's mansion, but we were grateful for his generosity.

Chang-wei stayed with us while the city garrison contained the rebel threat. He spent some time sitting with my mother, exchanging polite inquiries and asking after her health, though anyone with eyes could see how poorly she was doing. Cut Chang-wei was always the gentleman. Finally he excused himself under the pretense of needing to converse with Zuo. As he stood to exit the parlor, Mother rose and spoke quietly. Chang-wei had to bend down to hear her.

I leaned in to catch the conversation, but it was over before it started. Chang-wei straightened and nodded grimly before taking his leave. He met my eyes only briefly, giving me a curt bow before moving past.

If my family wasn't there watching I would have gone after him, but I had a responsibility to them now.

"How are you, Mother?"

I poured her more tea, but she waved the cup away. She wasn't yet able to stomach food or drink and could only take a little water without feeling sick. When Chang-wei was there, she'd had taken a few sips merely out of politeness.

"Chen Chang-wei." She spoke his name aloud, then waited for me to answer her unspoken question. I said nothing.

"You may not remember, but Mister Chen was once—"

"I know, Mother," I interrupted. "That's all in the past now."

"Interesting that the two of you should meet again like this," she murmured. "*Yuan fen*."

Fate.

My face heated beneath her scrutiny, and I bent to rearrange the tea tray, which didn't need rearranging. It had been years since my mother had been lucid enough to converse like this. We had never spoken as mother and daughter should.

"I hope you didn't say anything to him," I said, my pulse skipping. Chang-wei and I had reached an unspoken truce about our failed betrothal. Neither of us spoke of it. I couldn't bear the shame of dredging up the past now.

"I only thanked him for taking care of my daughter," Mother said quietly. "Your father was always impressed by that young man."

He had been right. After being imprisoned by the enemy, Chang-wei had managed to fight his way back and gain a respected position within the Ministry. He was intelligent and steadfast and loyal, but he wasn't for me. He was never meant for me. Chang-wei had his duty to the empire and a rising position in the imperial administration. I had my family to protect and a name that was still held in disgrace. We would be nothing but a burden to him.

Shortly after, I brought Mother to our room. She and I were to share the bed while a mat had been laid out for Nan and Tian on the floor. That evening we heard news that the rebels who had infiltrated had been subdued and the hole sealed off. The city wall was still intact.

"Changsha will now live or die on the strength of our walls," Zuo told us.

Just as we would live or die with the fate of Changsha.

In the days and weeks that followed, the city fell under martial law. The markets opened in the morning and closed in late afternoon, several hours earlier than it normally would. By sundown, all the streets were cleared.

There were more guards patrolling the city. No sign of disobedience or unrest was tolerated.

Food and water were rationed, but otherwise Changsha fell into a quiet routine with the inhabitants continuing on as they'd always done, although the mood was certainly subdued. At times, I could almost imagine there was no rebel army surrounding the city, but as soon as I began to relax, the ground would shake again.

Mother started to regain herself, bit by bit. One day, I came into our room to see her sitting beside Tian with a sheet filled with calculations between them. They both looked up and Mother appeared almost embarrassed. *An accomplished mathematician in her youth*, Engineer Liu Yentai had told me. This woman was a stranger to me, which made our reunion all the more awkward.

I took refuge in activity outside of our lodgings. Just as I'd done in our village. I joined Physician Lo in the refugee settlement to treat the sick and dispense herbal cures. What he had mistaken for mad dog disease we discovered was a violent form of opium sickness, similar to what Big Gao had suffered. The sufferers had to be tied down while seizures and tantrums wracked their bodies. I had yet to see anyone recover from it.

Though I hadn't believed him at the time, Yang had been correct. The affliction struck addicts as well as the occasional smoker. Specific batches of opium appeared to be tainted as the affliction came in clusters. Whether or not the opium had been deliberately manufactured had yet to be proven.

As morbid as it sounded, I considered trying to take samples of blood from the afflicted just as Yang had done. But I didn't have Yang Hanzhu's knowledge of alchemy. Even Yang had admitted that the practice of bio-alchemy was very much still a mystery. Blood was a much more difficult riddle to solve than the reactions of purer elements and compounds.

I found myself thinking of Yang and what he would have said about everything happening here. Is this the demise of the empire that he had predicted? Would he have joined the rebels in their cause or stood by us in our fight? There was no way to reach Yang to share my thoughts or discoveries. He was adrift on the open sea; a man without a country.

Whenever Lo and I weren't treating patients, we wrote up edicts for the street hoppers to paste up over the city warning people of the tainted opium. One afternoon, I had just finished loading the automaton with a stack of yellow notices and winding it up when I spotted an opium den right in the middle of the street. It had no shortage of patrons.

There was no stopping the tide. One would think after being under siege for so long, the supply of opium would have dwindled by now.

I tried to reach Chang-wei at least once or twice a week. I usually did so under the guise of inquiring about the siege because there was a deeper question I was afraid to ask. It was too difficult to speak of such intimate things in person, but I was no bolder in writing.

What of us? I wanted to write, but didn't dare. Was he thinking of me at all, or were his thoughts completely occupied with duty and the defense of the city?

At first his answers were brief. He was always detained by one task or another and when the replies stopped altogether, I had my answer. There was no *yuan fen* between us. We were only together due to circumstance and necessity.

Our kiss was just one of those moments to be lost in time.

But I couldn't forget the things he'd said to me. And the way his lips had pressed against mine, both hard and soft all at once. When I closed my eyes, I could almost feel his arms around me once more.

Yet when I opened them, I would always find myself alone, surrounded by the cool air as the summer turned to fall. The siege had lasted over a month.

Supplies were scarce and the marketplace hardly functioned anymore. People still bartered and traded for goods as needed, but the mood was becoming subdued. Sullen.

"Ripe for rebellion," Zuo observed.

He had been promoted to the position of councilman based on his valiant efforts organizing the volunteer militia. It seemed I still held a position of esteem in his eyes, so Zuo continued to give me reports.

They had intercepted ten separate tunnels, he told me as our respective families sat around the dinner table. Just that day, the scouts in the sewage tunnels heard digging and they sent an advance party to intercept the band of rebels underground.

"Engineer Chen was able to devise a strategy using controlled explosions to carve out a path to the rebels without causing the ground above to cave in. He is quite resourceful."

I nodded, ducking my head to scoop rice into my mouth. I could feel my mother's knowing gaze on me. The woman who had emerged from beneath the opium haze was entirely too perceptive.

Then again, she *was* my mother with a mother's sharp eye. And after hearing nothing from Chang-wei for so long, I wasn't hiding my emotions very well.

Later that night—because I was desperate for some word from him, because I missed him—I handed a letter to Zuo with hopes that he would be willing to act as messenger for me.

The letter was different from the others. I didn't write about the state of the city or everyday events.

Tell me how you are, I wrote him. *We worry about you.* Then boldly, *I worry about you.*

The next evening, the councilman let me know that the letter had been delivered. He said nothing of a reply. I waited two days before sending along another. If one letter wasn't impertinent enough, two was a scandal. After that, I forbade myself from writing again.

33

I was assisting Old Man Lo one morning in the refugee settlement when the mechanical sedan rolled up to us carrying a functionary in a black robe. He appeared no older than I was as he bowed low and addressed me formally.

"You have been summoned to the citadel, miss."

Physician Lo dismissed me with a wave. "Go on."

I climbed into the transport, noting that the dents and scratches from my haphazard driving had not yet been repaired. The directions back to the citadel were already set on the abacus, and one pull of the lever set the sedan in motion. The appointed messenger sat opposite me, his shoulders stiff and chin high.

"May I ask who has summoned me?"

"You have been summoned to the citadel, miss."

No help there, then.

The entire way to the citadel, I wondered what could be so urgent. When we reached the gates, the guards parted to let the sedan enter, and I was lead up the stairway and onto the fortress wall once more.

A tall figure stood waiting for me in the lookout tower with his back turned to me.

Chang-wei. My heart nearly stopped and I could hardly breathe.

"Come see," he said gently, beckoning me over.

I had feared there would be awkwardness between us; a rift that would take too long to repair. But he looked the same to me. He *felt* the same as I took his side. I was the one who was different. I felt as if my chest would burst and I didn't know what to do with my hands. They wanted so desperately to reach out and touch him.

I clasped them in front of me as we both turned to look out onto the surrounding area. What I saw made my stomach drop as if I were plummeting to the ground.

The city was surrounded by the rebel army. There were *thousands* of them. Tens of thousands. The camp formed a new horizon stretching out to where land met sky.

"I received your letters," he confessed. "But the war council had a strict order of silence. We had made the decision that none of the civilians could know of what we faced out here. It would incite the people to panic."

"Or encourage any rebels within the city to rise up," I murmured. Just looking at the force gathered around us made me sick with fear.

"But see there?" He handed me a spyglass and pointed. "They are moving on."

Indeed, through the spyglass, I saw that the western part of the camp had been disassembled and packed. The others were doing the same, taking down tents, hitching up wagons.

"How can you be certain they're leaving?"

"We've destroyed their tunnels," Chang-wei replied. "That was their element of surprise and their main advantage."

I would have thought their sheer numbers would be their main advantage. We would have to arm every man in the city to match such a force. No one in the imperial court anticipated the rebel army would grow so strong.

"There is something else."

Chang-wei reached around me to angle the spyglass upward. His arm brushed against my shoulder as he did so, sending a shudder down my spine.

He had to know how I felt about him. He'd read my letters—letters in which I'd said nothing of an intimate nature, but I'd rambled on with no purpose. And when he'd kissed me, I'd returned it.

Standing next to him now, I could feel every pulse, every breath elevated within me. It felt so good to finally be beside Chang-wei once more, speaking to him.

He was not unintelligent. He was brilliant! Yet he made no mention of anything that had passed between us. Maybe none of it was worth mentioning. Chen Chang-wei was meant for greater things.

I squinted into the spyglass and tried to target the point Chang-wei had directed me to. The tiny smudge came into focus, and I saw a great dragon in the sky, its mouth gaping and scales gleaming red. No, not a dragon, but a dragon boat floating in the air.

"The *Yangguizi* are not the only ones with airships," he said with an air of satisfaction. "But we've kept our fleet hidden until now. The rebels will have seen the dragon ship. They know the imperial eye is trained onto them, and they've decided to move on to an easier target.

"Imperial ground troops have been unable to penetrate through rebel territory," he continued. "With the airships, the Emperor can bypass the blockades at the rivers and byways. Imperial battalions can be maneuvered and positioned deep into enemy territory. With any luck, the imperial army will be here soon to help restore order."

"But you had meant to use these weapons against the *Yangguizi*."

"Doesn't this army pose just as much of a threat?" he indicated the rebel horde.

"Is Changsha safe, then?" I asked.

"I hope so. Soon we'll be, but the Long Hairs are moving their fight elsewhere. This rebellion is far from over."

And he would continue to defend the empire, whether it be from rebels or foreign devils or anyone else who threated the land.

I looked up at him, tracing the line of his profile to commit to memory. My chest squeezed painfully. This is where we parted. Chang-wei to his imperial cause and me to Mother and Nan and Tian. Our family might not be able to return to the village, but we would find a place somewhere.

"You know that you have a hand in this victory," Chang-wei said as I returned the spyglass to him. "You and your brother have done the empire a great service."

So formal once more. "It was merely our duty to the throne," I replied sullenly.

"Do you mean that, Soling? About duty?"

I frowned at him. Was he expecting an oath of loyalty from me here and now?

"Come with me."

My heart leapt. He wouldn't ask it if he didn't mean it, and in that moment, I wanted to. I truly did.

"I can't."

"The empire needs good minds. People who are willing to think and adapt."

Just as quickly my heart sank. I didn't want to hear about the empire right now.

"The Emperor had all of the great thinkers exiled or executed," I pointed out bitterly.

"Soling, the Emperor is dead."

At first, I didn't believe him. After everything that happened here, it seemed impossible there were even larger catastrophes.

"We received a message this morning." Chang-wei said. "Prince Yizhu must now take the throne. He was the one who dispatched the airships, but everything is being kept secret until he can gather his forces."

"Then why are you telling me?"

He looked at me, his gaze holding onto mine. "Because I trust you."

My pulse skipped and I had to look away.

Even though I claimed no love for the Emperor, I still felt the loss deep inside. This was the man who had my father executed out of ignorance. Why should I mourn for him?

But to us, the Emperor was both a man and the Son of Heaven. For his death to happen now, right as this rebellion was taking root and foreigners had invaded our port. The entire kingdom would be thrown into turmoil.

Chang-wei was relentless. "Prince Yizhu needs strong counsel, now more than ever, Soling. He's willing to listen. The Emperor's death at this time can either destroy our kingdom, or it can be the beginning of a new era."

"The empire will rise or fall without me," I muttered.

What I said must have sounded like treason to him. How could I not want to redeem my family name in the eyes of the throne? How could I not want to serve the glory of the empire?

Nothing he could say would ever bring my father back or destroy the empty, cynical demon inside of me.

"I have to think of my family," I told him. "My mother finds memories of Peking too painful. She can't return there."

The dragon airship flew closer with each moment. I could make out its shape with my naked eye. The sentries on the wall straightened, gasping as they spotted it.

"Then think of your family," Chang-wei insisted. "Think of your brother. I can see to his education in Peking. I can guide him. He's capable of so much more."

"That isn't fair."

Tian had sprouted like a young tree under Chang-wei's brief tutelage. He was no longer acting like a timid, shrinking shadow. I wanted a future so much for my brother, but I had to resist.

Let the imperial court and the *Yangguizi* fight it out. Neither of them cared about the people of the land. We were merely dust to them.

"I can't let him get involved in the Emperor's war," I argued, my voice trembling.

"Soling, have I told you why I came back?"

I shook my head, pressing my lips together stubbornly. A rift was forming between us. Didn't he realize that if he had just asked me, not as some appeal to my loyalty to the empire, but just as Chang-wei to Soling, I would have gone with him willingly?

But there was no speaking of the two of us in that way. Country before family. Family before self. That was the way of things.

"You returned because you're loyal at heart," I replied. "More loyal than I am."

He shook his head. "I didn't return out of a blind sense of loyalty. All those years while I was a prisoner, while I watched our ports being carved up and opium forced upon our shores, I wanted only one thing: To not be a slave."

"But you were a slave to the Emperor and are now to Prince Yizhu."

"I give my loyalty freely, as your father did. It doesn't have to be suffering and subjugation, Soling. We can learn. We can adapt. We can fight back."

The red dragon was upon us, looming overhead. I quivered at the sight of it, and the urge to fall to my knees overwhelmed me. The dragon was the symbol of the divinity of imperial power. And we had all been groomed to worship the Emperor like a god. In return, the dragon granted our land his protection.

But did I truly believe it anymore?

Things were going to get worse, Yang had warned. The Emperor was dead and the rebel army was growing.

"Come with me," Chang-wei implored. He held his hand out to me. "I've seen what we're capable of together. Come with me."

I thought of Yang Hanzhu in exile upon the seas, loyal to no one but his own heart. I thought of Mother enslaved by opium. I thought of Tian, merely a boy now, but one day he would be a man and able to stand tall.

For so many years, I had been hiding. Everyone I loved was a fugitive.

My eyes were open now. I knew that the dragon before me was carved of wood. His scales were painted. His belly was a furnace and it was physics and mathematics and alchemy that gave him the gift of flight.

But in spite of all I *knew*, I wanted to believe in the vision that Chang-wei had presented to me. My father had fought his battle too soon. The empire wasn't ready and he knew it, but he had no choice but to fight on.

Chang-wei took my hand, his strong fingers curling around mine. He appeared so confident beside me. Unwavering.

A rope ladder descended from the airship, and he continued to hold on to me.

I trust you, he'd said.

I trusted him too. With my life, and at the moment with my heart.

His thumb stroked over mine, telling me the things I'd longed to hear, but not in words. Would he ever speak them out loud?

It would tear out a piece of my soul to let go at this moment, never knowing. I knew then that I would step onto that dragonship with him to rise into the clouds. I was ready to learn from our past mistakes. I was ready to adapt.

Most of all, I was ready to fight.

THE WARLORD AND THE NIGHTINGALE

A GUNPOWDER CHRONICLES SHORT STORY

PROLOGUE

It is said the story of "The Warlord and the Nightingale" was once on display in six painted panels that decorated the keep of Koriya Castle. A mad tale of a mad world, with illustrations of fierce samurai and clever mechanical creations. To our sorrow, the castle has been reduced to nothing but rubble and ash.

There were also rumors that the story was passed on to Dutch traders on Dejima Island who, over time, adopted a happier version of the tale.

Lovers of legends insist the karakuri maker in the tale is an ancestor of esteemed inventor Takeda Hideyori. When asked whether there was any truth to the connection, Takeda-san merely stated with the flare of an illusionist, "There is no such thing as truth."

Yet a clockwork nightingale with copper feathers and jeweled eyes can be seen on the upper shelf in his workshop. Its beak curves upward in a mysterious smile.

CHAPTER ONE

The tick of the lantern clock counted out the minutes. The system of weights and gears had been adapted from a Western design, but the exact hour hardly mattered. Hanzo would be working until the sun came up just as he had the night before. It wasn't any decree that drove him. His own mind goaded him on, refusing to let him sleep while there was a problem to be solved.

Before him stood a steel cage frame and an assortment of metal gears. Not the natural wooden parts that karakuri were traditionally made of. This task required strength. This creation would be more than an amusing parlor trick.

Several months ago, in the heart of winter, Chancellor Sakai had traveled through the snow to reach Hanzo's humble shack hidden in the mountains. Surprised to have a visitor, Hanzo had invited the official inside and offered what hospitality he could. His workshop had been strewn with tools. Puppet heads with painted smiles had witnessed the curious exchange from the shelves.

"Karakuri no Hanzo has become well-known throughout the province," the gray-haired official declared, referring to Hanzo by his formal title: Hanzo the Karakuri maker. "The great Lord Mizunaga desires one of Hanzo-dono's wondrous machines for his court."

Chancellor Sakai had then laid down enough silver to feed Hanzo for a year.

This had all come as a surprise to Hanzo, who, though a young man, rarely left his workshop. His youth had been spent in apprenticeship, taking devices apart and putting them back together. With his sensei gone, he'd taken over the practice. The mechanical karakuri dolls kept him company and, when patrons came to take them away, he made more.

Flattered to receive such praise, Hanzo had worked through the winter and into spring to finish his most intricate design. Two miniature samurai engaged in a mock duel, directed by the clockwork hidden inside. There were no strings on these puppets.

"A clever toy," Chancellor Sakai had pronounced when he returned. "Fit for a child."

But Lord Mizunaga was no child.

Hanzo was far from devastated. Instead, a fire lit in his chest. New challenges meant opportunity for new discoveries.

The chancellor brought Hanzo to Koriya Castle, the seat of the Mizunaga's domain, and installed him in a workroom in the main keep. It seemed a trivial task for the chancellor to oversee himself, but Hanzo didn't ponder it for too long. He had work to do.

Hanzo started to design an automaton on a grand scale. One worthy of being presented before the proud daimyo who ruled the province.

"The karakuri should be a warrior," Sakai insisted. "Fearsome to behold."

The chancellor had a full suit of samurai armor brought in. It lay on the workbench like a fallen soldier while Sakai lifted a long bow that stood taller than Hanzo.

"What a great tribute this will be to Lord Mizunaga, who is

known for his archery skill." He entrusted the bow ceremoniously into Hanzo's hands. "Only samurai are allowed weapons, Hanzo-dono. Treat this one with care."

Once Sakai left, Hanzo lifted the weapon and drew the bowstring back with all his might. The bamboo frame barely yielded beneath the full force of his effort.

The karakuri he needed to build would be no lightweight puppet. It would require a warrior's strength. In his head, Hanzo envisioned a series of cogs and wheels interlocked. Springs wound tight to store the force required.

Now with the frame built and the gears cut, the thing was heavy. Too heavy to lift itself, let alone wield a weapon. Hanzo stared hatefully at the ugly cage of metal. The thing was hard and lifeless to behold when his aim was always to create something cleverly crafted and whimsical.

To be a karakuri master was to be part engineer, part artist, part illusionist. Right now he was none of those things. He was just a blind fool trying to stumble upon a solution. All the while, he could hear Chancellor Sakai's snide tone ringing in his ears. "A clever toy. A toy for a child."

The lantern clock chimed evening hour three.

Hanzo started to attach a spring to an arm joint only to have the metal tear into his palm. A jolt of pain shot through him. Cursing, Hanzo pressed a rag to the wound. It wasn't a deep cut, but a sudden wave of despair washed over him. It was followed by an unreasonable surge of rage—at himself.

It was all wrong. From the very foundation upward, every bolt and wire was wrong.

Gritting his teeth, Hanzo tore himself away from the monstrosity and pushed himself out into the cool air. He breathed in the night in one long inhale and exhale. If he'd stayed inside a moment longer, he would have dismantled everything and scattered all the parts out of frustration. Then he would have burnt every single one of his sketches and started over.

Instead he walked. It was an aimless, driven sort of pacing meant to rid himself of his doubts. In the mountains, it had been easy. Go outside, climb up into the rocks. Clear his head. Here, he was trapped in the walls of the castle. His mind was trapped as well.

The courtyard ended and another began. And then another. He'd wandered into an unknown part of the fortress while pondering counterweights and spring mechanisms. There were lanterns glowing up ahead, but it was the singing that drew him. A voice, cutting and clear in the middle of the night. He followed it.

The melody rose high, the sound of it so pure it pierced deep into his chest. Hanzo passed through an archway that led into a garden where the trees twisted low to the ground. Pebbled pathways wound through the grass and a raised rock formation lay silent on a bed of sand. The moon cast a murky reflection upon the waters of a koi pond. The song had grown as soft as the evening breeze.

A set of rooms stood at the far end of the garden, and light glowed through translucent panels that formed the outer wall. The outline visible through the mulberry paper was unmistakably feminine. She stood as still as a statue while she sang of a young maiden's plea to her lost lover. Her kimono flowed around her, the obi outlining a slender waist. The woman appeared uncommonly tall, but it may have been a trick of the light lengthening the shadows.

She must be one of Lord Mizunaga's *oiran*, a prized entertainer in the daimyo's court.

The courtesan wasn't aware of Hanzo's presence. For now, she remained a creature of pure sound and shadow that he could mold into anything in his mind. A karakuri maker was a storyteller at heart. The woman could be a moon goddess, a divine spirit of the woods.

Hanzo's trance was broken by the sound of footsteps. Rough hands grabbed onto his arms and forced him to the ground. The stones of the walkway cut into his knees.

In a daze, he stared up at the guardsmen. Firelight gleamed off of black armor.

"Trespasser," the guard captain proclaimed. He grabbed a fistful of Hanzo's topknot and dragged his head back to bare his neck. "State your name."

He trembled. "Kara—Karakuri no Hanzo—"

"Lord Mizunaga's honored guest," another voice interrupted.

Hanzo hazarded a sideways glance and relief flooded him when he saw the chancellor. Sakai's manner was always courteous, with an understated air that was in contrast to the rest of Mizunaga's samurai.

The gray-haired official approached with a stately stride. At his approach, the guardsmen loosened their hold on Hanzo and bowed. Hanzo was finally able to draw breath, though he thought it wise to keep his head lowered.

"Lord Chancellor," the captain greeted. "Entrance to the daimyo's private courtyard is strictly forbidden."

The singing stopped. From where he knelt, Hanzo could see the courtesan's outline turn toward the courtyard. Her hair ornament swung with the movement, a disrupted pendulum measuring time. A sharp command came from within the chamber, and she immediately resumed her song.

"Indeed entrance to this courtyard is forbidden," Sakai agreed. "But Hanzo-dono is a guest, unaware of our rules. Whose responsibility is it that he unknowingly ventured so far? Does the night patrol not guard the entire perimeter around Lord Mizunaga's private domain?"

At that, the captain backed away and fell to his knees. "Forgive me, Chancellor."

"This oversight will be seen to in the morning. Continue with your duties."

With a wave of his hand, Sakai sent the guardsmen away while Hanzo remained on his knees, unsure of whether he was absolved.

"Hanzo-dono, accept our apologies." Sakai touched a hand to his shoulder to bid him to rise.

"Lord Chancellor, I'm grateful for your mercy—"

Sakai hushed him, ushering him away from the courtyard. "Quietly, lest Lord Mizunaga's slumber be disturbed any further. He is most unforgiving in this matter."

The chancellor took his side even though Sakai was far above him in status. Only when the courtesan's song faded away did the chancellor speak again.

"You are a guest here, Hanzo-dono. But be careful where you wander." He glanced back toward the daimyo's private quarter. An unreadable expression flickered over his face. "Lord Mizunaga is right to fear assassination. Even more so since his brother's untimely death."

CHAPTER TWO

A group of children chased Hanzo's clockwork nightingale around the courtyard outside his workshop. All around, the plum trees burst with blossoms, signaling the height of spring. The mechanical bird hopped from branch to branch, lifting its wings made of copper feathers. After each landing, the bird paused to chirp out a tune before making the short flight to another branch, sending the children into peals of laughter.

Hanzo was so focused on scribbling out a new design that when he raised his head, a stranger had slipped into the courtyard. A young lady holding a silk parasol stood just beyond the trees. From the elaborate leaf pattern and gold threading of her kimono, Hanzo guessed she was one of the ladies of the castle, yet no one attended her as she watched the children play.

Her face remained hidden beneath the shade of the parasol. What he could see of it was moon pale, as if she rarely saw the sun. At first the lady did nothing more than watch, absently twirling the handle of her parasol in a lazy circle. Gradually, she edged closer.

The children were circling the trunk of a plum tree and trying to shake the branches. The nightingale perched above them while blossoms fell from the tree like snow.

"Come down! Come down!" they called up to the mechanical bird.

The nightingale chirped out a taunt before taking off to land on another branch. The lady lowered her parasol to track the flight, and Hanzo's heart skipped a beat.

For a moment, he forgot about mechanics and joints and wires. Instead, a new weight pressed over his chest. A hint of a smile touched her lips, and it was like a breeze drifting over still water, stirring gently. Setting things in motion.

Yet the children were oblivious to her presence. They swarmed past her to chase the nightingale. To Hanzo's surprise, the lady pursed her lips and whistled at the mechanical bird, imitating the warbling call of a nightingale.

"Hoo—hokekyo..."

"Hoo—hokekyo...Hoo—hokekyo..."

The nightingale whistled back and the children erupted into more laughter. The older ones attempted to imitate the call themselves while the younger ones continued to run and run. The lady's face brightened, and he lost all sense of equilibrium. She was beautiful, the most captivating woman he had ever seen.

Hanzo found himself rising to his feet, though for what purpose, he didn't know. The lady turned to meet his gaze, and for the first time, he saw the dark circles beneath her eyes. Her startling beauty faded into something more flawed and vulnerable, which only fascinated him more. He'd never seen her before, but perhaps that had something to do with the circles under his own eyes. His waking hours were spent shut away.

It took several moments before Hanzo realized he was staring. He averted his eyes and tried to form a proper greeting, but by the time he turned back, the mysterious lady had disappeared.

THE ARRIVAL of Lord Itô along with his retainers warranted a feast day. Mizunaga's fields were cleared for a tournament of both mounted and target archery.

"You should come, Hanzo-dono. A good opportunity for you to study a warrior's technique."

Sakai seemed in good spirits as he delivered the invitation. The chancellor delivered all of his communications to Hanzo in person. It was an anomaly that Hanzo acknowledged only briefly before shuffling it away. Chancellor Sakai had taken special interest in his endeavor and it wasn't for him to question.

On the day of the celebration, Hanzo hovered at the edge of the target area, making sketches in his notebook. The postures of the archers, the position of the hand before and after release. Some of these movements would be important for designing the machinery. Others would go toward creating the illusion — an archer should stand in this way, head and shoulders back, and lift his arms just so.

Hanzo didn't realize he'd ventured close to the warlord himself until he looked up to find the daimyo looming before him. It was the first time Hanzo had seen Lord Mizunaga up close, and the sight of the warlord made the hairs on his neck stand on end.

Mizunaga shifted to reveal a thick black beard matched by a pair of eyebrows that slashed sharply downward. A scar cut across the bridge of his nose. Hanzo cowered instinctively, though it wasn't he who had drawn the daimyo's attention. Lord Itô was in conversation with Lord Mizunaga, but not about battles or government.

"Lady Yura is known throughout all of Edo. I heard her sing once! Ah, a voice like a summer breeze through the trees, that one."

With his gaze fixed onto Lord Itô, Mizunaga handed his bow to a page as he lowered a hand to his belt. While the vassal continued to speak, Mizunaga unsheathed a dagger and approached Itô with a slow, deliberate stride.

And proceeded to slice the man's ear off.

Hanzo stared as Lord Itô reeled backward with his hand clutched to the wound. Blood poured over his face, flowing so freely that Hanzo's mind told him it must be paint. Red paint, and this was a drama being performed on stage. But this was no performance.

Itô's screams split the air, pitching high into delirium. His men reached for their swords at the same time Mizunaga's men reached for theirs. A mixture of anger and horror was etched upon every face. Chancellor Sakai rushed to the center of the impending battle to call for restraint.

Hanzo remained crouched between the two factions with a charcoal stick clutched in his hand.

Lord Mizunaga turned. For a moment, his black eyes fixed onto Hanzo's like an eagle who had spotted a mouse. This was a man who'd known battle and death. This was a man who had no interest in anything so frivolous as a mechanical puppet to entertain his guests.

Hanzo held completely still, willing himself to become nothing. To disappear. The scent of blood hung in the air, and death was waiting to pounce. While Hanzo's heartbeat thundered in his chest, the warlord turned back to the archery target and held out his hand for his bow.

The crowd hushed and the atmosphere took on the gravity of a funeral procession. Then the unthinkable happened. Lord Itô, with his hand held to the gaping hole that had been his ear and his fingers soaked in blood, knelt down before the daimyo—and bowed in apology.

This was a code of behavior Hanzo did not understand and

would never understand. Was this what a samurai's honor and loyalty demanded of him? Flesh and blood and silence? Lord Mizunaga fitted an arrow to his bow, drew back until his arm was held taut, and let it fly as if nothing unusual had taken place.

CHAPTER THREE

"Karakuri-sensei is younger than I imagined."

A melodic tone broke through Hanzo's trance. He'd spent the rest of the day after leaving the archery grounds with his head down, hard at work. It wasn't the study of the archers that inspired him. Rather it was the thought that the sooner he completed his work, the sooner he could leave the madness behind and return to his hut in the mountains.

He looked up from his work to see the lady from the courtyard. She'd managed to enter his chamber unnoticed to stand before him with her hands folded in her sleeves.

"They said there was a karakuri master at Koriya," she continued, her tone and inflection immediately marking her above him. "They say he is clever. They say he is *tensai-desu*."

Heat rose up Hanzo's neck at the compliment. A quick glance over the lady's shoulder showed the shoji door closed behind her. He'd been so absorbed in his task, he hadn't heard a rap on the frame or the slide of the panel.

"Hime...Hime-sama."

Perhaps he was being overly polite to address her so, but she made no introduction. Her lips curved ever so slightly, a smile and not a smile, like the faces of his puppets. Able to portray a multitude of meanings by not committing to any one.

Hanzo managed an awkward bow. A strand of hair fell from his topknot to cover his face while his pulse raced. Hanzo ran his hands over the fold of his yukuta in an attempt to straighten it. Surely she was a noble lady, able to come and go as she pleased. Yet why was she alone in his quarters?

"Your puppets are so charming." She bent to touch a light hand to the tea-bearer's tray.

"They're—" He had to swallow to find his voice. Everything about this visit was so confusing. "They're not puppets, hime-sama. I don't control them. They move themselves."

"Machines," she murmured. "But you do design their movements. You grant them your intentions when you make them."

Her interest had moved on to his more complex designs. A magician performing a magic trick. The two dueling samurai. She paused at a figure of a dancer on a wooden platform. The doll rose only to the height of the lady's knee.

"How does one make her move?" she asked.

"The winding mechanism is hidden beneath the wooden platform."

Hanzo considered winding the machinery himself, but the lady was standing too close to the mechanical dancer. He would have had to move past her, brushing against the silk of her sleeve. The scent of her perfume would surround him like fog, making him lose his way.

She shouldn't be here. With him. Alone at this hour...what hour was it? Hanzo looked at the clock to see that it was evening seven. Almost time for sunrise.

The lady knelt to wind the device, appearing no less enchanted for knowing its secrets. The doll came to life, drawing the red fan open. Then she lifted her arm to wave the fan in a graceful arc.

"There were machines in the tea houses in Edo that would sing songs," the lady remarked as she watched the dancer. "They were quite delightful, but could only sing the same songs over and over. Inevitably the patrons grew tired of them."

"New songs could be added," Hanzo proposed, remaining at a respectful distance. "Or one might create a karakuri capable of picking up an instrument and playing back what it has heard."

"Is that truly possible?"

With the dance complete, the doll returned to its starting pose. The lady moved on to the shelf where the clockwork nightingale was perched. The creature opened its onyx eyes and cooed as she stroked its metallic feathers. She imitated the nightingale's call as she had done in the courtyard.

"*Hoo-hokekyo...*"

The gears hummed as the mechanical bird answered back.

A thoughtful look crossed the lady's face. She tapped the bird on the head, and the creature hopped back and forth on the shelf, chirping happily.

"A puppet that responds to commands. So clever. *Tensai-desu*."

Hanzo knew little of courtly etiquette and even less of conversing with women, but by now he was certain she was no noble lady. Her manner, speech, the elegant way which she held herself—she had indeed been taught these skills and taught well. As a master of artifice, Hanzo saw her manner for what it was. An illusion. She was not a noblewoman, but rather the faithful recreation of one. The realization made his skin prickle.

The lady had reached the archer, or what was to become an archer. A metal cage stood at the center of the workroom. Two skeletal arms stretched out from the frame. As the lady passed by, they appeared to reach for her. It was grotesque, practically menacing.

"Is that how they all appear underneath?" she asked in awe.

"It's...it's unfinished. The noble lady shouldn't be looking at it in this state."

His palms begun to sweat. Her inspection was too invasive. As if it were his skin that had been peeled away and his open chest she were peering into with such curiosity. If she could see his heart, it would be throbbing, throbbing and unable to find a steady rhythm.

"You don't have any apprentices?" she asked, while he stood frozen behind her. "No one to help you?"

He swallowed. "A karakuri maker is protective of his art."

As a young boy, Hanzo had knelt before his sensei's door for five days and five nights without food and water before being allowed into the workshop. Once inside, he'd had to prove himself, taking apart karakuri piece by piece and recreating them. There had been no books, no stern words of instruction.

"A courtesan must be protective of her art as well."

The lady turned to reveal a playful tilt of her chin and a quirk in her left eyebrow that transformed her previously pleasant expression into something sly and mysterious. It was said that a courtesan's every look and gesture was practiced. Perfected. In many ways, she was like his karakuri dolls. Acting in a specifically crafted fashion.

"When they brought the song machines into the tea houses, we laughed and clapped with delight along with the guests. But late at night, my courtesan sisters and I rose to stab our hairpins into the controls. Did they think our hard-won skills could be replaced so easily?"

As she approached, Hanzo noticed the lady was uncommonly tall. She was as tall as he was and as graceful as her silhouette had appeared though the paper screen around Mizunaga's chamber.

"You are Lady Yura...from Edo."

Her pretty eyes didn't blink. "Yes."

"The lady shouldn't be here."

She didn't appear insulted. Instead Lady Yura glanced back at the steel skeleton. "There are also machines in Edo that can be used to execute a man," she went on. "Kill him quickly and soundlessly. Do you think such a frightful act should be taken over by something without a soul, Karakuri no Hanzo? By something without a heart?"

Hanzo's own heart was pounding, his skin cold. Despite her talk of death, her voice remained like water and silk. He finally recognized the source of his fear. It was only partly due to the image of Lord Mizunaga slicing off his vassal's ear at the mere mention of Lady Yura's name.

Hanzo understood now why the chancellor had brought him here, and why Sakai showed such interest. Hanzo also knew what a warlord would want from a puppet maker. Karakuri were nothing but harmless parlor tricks. It was easy to hide something more sinister within them.

"You shouldn't be here, Lady Yura," he repeated with more conviction.

A look of loneliness crossed her face before her expression became blank, as smooth as a still pond. With a graceful bow, Yura turned to leave. The edge of her kimono whispered over the tatami mats as she departed. Her feet barely made a sound.

Lady Yura didn't come again. The next time he saw her was at the tail end of one night, before darkness faded into morning. He had stayed up assembling and disassembling, caught up on yet another one of the chancellor's demands. When he stepped out of his workshop for fresh air, he'd spied a pale figure in a kimono moving through the courtyard.

He started to watch for her, so often was he up during this time. Hanzo soon found that she would often return to her quarters after the Hour of the Tiger, in the gray silver light of the coming dawn. Sometimes later, sometimes a little earlier, but always when the night was nearly done.

She hadn't come to him with any mischief or motive in mind. Lady Yura had simply been drawn to the lamplight of his workshop. She'd seen his silhouette through the paper window, just as he'd seen her. Here was another soul who was still up.

Hers was a life lived alone and in the dark, awake while others slept, asleep while the world exchanged courtesies and shared food and laughed. It was a life too similar to his own.

The courtesan belonged to Lord Mizunaga, who had her sing for him like a bird in a cage. For Hanzo to seek her company would be an insult to his host — or rather his master now that he was in the daimyo's service. In any case, Lady Yura was beyond his reach.

So he merely waited for her every day as the night edged close to morning.

One time, she was already out in the courtyard when he opened his door. She was sitting upon the stones in the miniature garden with her lantern hung upon a tree branch. Though Lady Yura wasn't looking at him, he could see her face, pale and lost and lovely. Her gaze was directed upward, perhaps at the moon as it departed. Perhaps she was listening for the sound of the carp in the pond, swimming in endless circles.

Hanzo ducked into his workshop, but only for a moment to retrieve the clockwork nightingale from the shelf. He returned to the doorway with the bird in both hands.

The internal logic of its gears was intricate in design, yet simple in function. If tossed into the air, it would open its wings and fly until finding a perch. Hanzo did so now, hefting the creature gently upwards. He'd seen a hundred models crash to the ground in order for this one to be created.

The little nightingale took flight and the whir of its rotors hummed softly as it circled. The bird settled on to the branch above Lady Yura. She glanced up and greeted it with the nightingale's song. The bird answered back in kind.

"Hoo—hokekyo...Hoo-hokekyo..."

Yura looked toward Hanzo then. It was too far away for him to be certain, but he thought she smiled. He didn't dare go to her, but from where Hanzo stood, he smiled back.

CHAPTER FOUR

Hanzo fell upon his work in earnest like a soldier rushing headlong into battle. If Chancellor Sakai intended him to create a weapon, how was he any different from a swordsmith or a fletcher crafting arrows? Their work was honorable work, valued by the daimyo.

And machines were meant to *do* something. He'd long felt a dissatisfaction for his work. Ever since his sensei had passed away and Hanzo was left to discover on his own, he'd pushed the nature of his creations, not knowing quite what he was aiming for. Perhaps what he was aiming for was purpose — something beyond trickery and amusement.

So now he had a purpose and a practical application to drive him. His archer was not yet strong enough to pull back a samurai's bow. The counterweights to perform such a task would be heavy. Or they would need to be dropped from a great height, requiring the archer be raised onto a towering platform.

He could do away with the archer's facade, but then the device would be a simple war machine. It would not be karakuri with the illusion of being alive.

The force would have to reside within the automaton, wound

into gears and springs the same way an archer's strength was stored within tendon and muscle. But how to generate such force? The karakuri was larger than any of the wind-up contraptions he'd built in the past.

His hands were raw with scrapes and wire cuts by the time the lantern clock struck evening five. His supper lay cold upon a tray, uneaten. He didn't recall seeing sunlight that day.

Hanzo let the cords snake from his hands onto the floor. The walls of his workshop had become a prison. He was used to solitude, sustained by his own work, but maybe a man needed more. Sliding open the door, he stepped outside to absorb the spring air.

Lady Yura would be singing.

He shouldn't have allowed himself that thought, but there it was. Echoing in his skull. He wanted to talk to her — speak to her about coils and springs and weights. Not that Lady Yura would have any understanding of such things. He just wanted someone to talk to. If she laughed at his absurdity, then he would get to hear her laugh.

Just wait, fool.

Hanzo berated himself even as he stepped through the garden. He didn't want to wait. At the end of the night, he would get nothing but a glimpse of Yura retreating to her room. Now that he knew the way to Lord Mizunaga's private courtyard, perhaps he could get close enough to hear her voice carried on the breeze. Just one soothing note to untangle the knots inside his head.

He moved without a lantern using the walls for guidance. Just as before, he encountered no guard patrols as he neared the courtyard. Realizing he'd gambled too much already, Hanzo paused outside the courtyard and pressed himself into a dark corner to listen.

There was nothing. Silence. He was a fool. Lady Yura was a

very beautiful woman who was trained to engage in a pleasant conversation with even the likes of him.

Hanzo was about to sneak back to his workshop when shouting came from the inner courtyard. And then he heard what he'd longed for: Yura's voice, but not in song. She was crying, broken.

His palms dampened. Lady Yura was pleading for mercy. His throat seized tight as he heard her cry out again.

Hanzo had never thought himself a brave man. He was certainly no hero, but he ran toward Lord Mizunaga's chamber anyway with his heart pounding.

As he entered the courtyard, something swung out and struck him hard in the chest. Hanzo staggered, gasping for breath as strong hands took hold of him.

"The karakuri maker," the guardsman announced, giving him a rough shake. "You are forbidden to enter here."

The night patrol had assembled in the courtyard, explaining their lack of presence on the outer perimeter. They formed a semi-circle around Mizunaga's chamber like an audience watching a shadow play. The lanterns inside illuminated two figures, one massive and broad-shouldered. One as slender as a reed.

"Worthless!" the shadow warlord growled as he struck Lady Yura across the face.

Hanzo's stomach plunged. He surged forward out of reflex only to feel the hands on him tighten. All around him, the other guards stood motionless.

Lady Yura huddled low with her head pressed to the floor. "*Tono*," she wept. "I apologize. Please have mercy."

Hanzo struggled against his captors. "Help her!"

His words had no effect on the guardsmen, but Chancellor Sakai arrived and the patrol parted to allow him entrance.

Sakai surveyed the scene and then looked back at Hanzo. His expression was remained impassive.

"Come with me," Sakai commanded the soldiers.

The captain and two others followed. The moment they entered the daimyo's chamber, they too became part of the shadow play.

The men bowed low, apologizing for interrupting Lord Mizunaga's rest. Sakai addressed his daimyo with his usual calm, pausing only for a moment to flick his hand toward Lady Yura. It was the smallest of gestures, but one of the guards moved to lift her to her feet and take her from the room.

A knot formed in Hanzo's chest when she emerged into the courtyard, her hair askew. Her face was wet with tears as she sagged against the soldier who held onto her.

At least she was no longer a shadow held beneath Mizunaga's thumb. At least she was outside and flesh and blood.

A moment later, the door slid open once more. Sakai peered out and searched until he found Hanzo being held in the corner.

"Take her," the chancellor directed with a nod of his head.

Sakai disappeared back into Lord Mizunaga's chamber and Hanzo suddenly found Lady Yura thrust into his arms.

WITH NOWHERE ELSE TO GO, Hanzo took Lady Yura back to his workshop. Though his tea was cold, he poured it for her while she remained seated on the mat, head down. A curtain of dark hair shielded her face.

He set the cup onto the floor and slid it before her. When she wouldn't touch it, Hanzo did the same with a handkerchief, pushing it forward until it lay beside the tea. After a long pause, she reached for the cloth and pressed it to her face.

"I don't want you to see me like this," she said, her voice small.

Hanzo stood and dimmed the lanterns until only a faint glow illuminated the room. Then he remained at the wall with his hands by his sides. Helpless.

"Lord Mizunaga doesn't sleep," she choked out. "He's plagued by nightmares. They've driven him mad."

Yura stifled a sob, pressing the handkerchief to her mouth. Hanzo turned away as she fought her tears. He wasn't certain whether to stay or go, but as hard as it was to see her so broken, he didn't want to leave her alone.

Gradually her breathing became steadier. Hanzo lowered himself to the floor, but remained where he was so she could have her privacy. It would have been impolite to ask what had happened, so he didn't ask. He didn't say anything.

"One day, he's going to kill me."

She was no longer crying. Instead her tone had become flat and chilling in its finality.

"It will be because I've lost my voice or I choose a song that doesn't please him or simply because the moon is full. He'll lift his sword and strike me down—"

"No."

Hanzo could hear the rise of his own breath stirred into a panic.

"No," he repeated.

"I will finally be free."

She brushed her hair back revealing a blank expression. The side of her face was swollen and she bled from a cut on her lower lip. Hanzo's hands curled into fists.

How badly had Mizunaga hurt her? How often did he do this? All questions Hanzo wanted to ask, but they would have been useless things to say, dragging up hurt and hopelessness without offering anything in return.

"I wish I could—" Hanzo paused. What could he possibly tell her? "I wish I could help you be free."

I'm hurting because you're hurting, was what he truly wanted to say. He wasn't at liberty to throw such sentiment at her. They hadn't spoken a word since that night she'd wandered into his workshop.

Lady Yura smiled faintly at him. "You can come sit closer."

He moved across from her and settled down onto the tatami mat. They faced each other as if at a tea ceremony, but the lonesome cup remained between them, untouched.

"When I was brought to Koriya from Edo, I thought it an honor," she confessed. "I was to be courtesan to a great lord. My future would be so bright. But all I do every night is sing. I stay on one side of the screen, singing one song after another. Lord Mizunaga doesn't even see me. Sometimes, I wonder if he even listens, but if I stumble or falter, he becomes agitated. If I stop, he wakes up enraged. Only when he is completely still am I allowed to slip away."

"You keep the nightmares away," Hanzo suggested.

"Nothing can keep them away," she retorted. "Lord Mizunaga is haunted by ghosts only he can see. I'm afraid to move or take one wrong breath, lest he awaken with sword drawn. Lord Mizunaga may seem like a fearsome warrior, but he's afraid all the time."

Her bitterness tainted the very air around them. Hanzo glanced to the windows, hoping no one happened to overhear them. To accuse a daimyo like Mizunaga of being afraid, of being weak in any way was an unspeakable insult.

Hanzo recalled what Chancellor Sakai had told him. "Lord Mizunaga must have become more fearful after his brother's death."

Yura glanced up sharply. "His brother was daimyo of this domain. Lord Mizunaga was the one who had him killed."

They both fell silent once more.

"Tell me something, Hanzo-dono," she implored. "Anything. For a year now, I've barely seen the sun. Lord Mizunaga's chamber has become my cage."

He cast about his workshop until his gaze settled on the shelf behind his workbench. "The nightingale," he began.

"The nightingale." Yura waited.

"There is a small device inside him, like a metal comb pressed very thin. The teeth of the comb vibrate in the presence of sound. That is how the nightingale is able to sing back when one imitates his call."

He demonstrated the nightingale's song and the clockwork bird dutifully responded.

Yura frowned, her eyebrows arching. "But I don't understand. How can the bird hear you?"

"Each tone causes a different part of the comb to vibrate. The same thing that happens when one speaks." Leaning forward, Hanzo took hold of her hand to place her fingers lightly over her throat. "Can you feel it? Here?"

Her lashes fluttered as she met his gaze. "I can."

He could feel the beat of her pulse where his hand was pressed against hers. "The mechanism triggers when specific parts of the comb vibrate, causing the nightingale to sing in response," he explained, his throat suddenly dry.

Her gaze fixed onto him, her eyes dark and wide. They were close with hands touching, yet he longed to be closer still.

"You have a kind heart, Hanzo-dono," she said, her voice low and soft.

"So do you, O-Yura."

"No." She shook her head. "I don't."

Lady Yura was an experienced courtesan while he had never been so close to a woman before. Recklessly, Hanzo pressed his lips to hers and kissed her. Gently. As gently as he could. She was bruised and he couldn't bear to hurt her any more than she had already suffered.

If Lord Mizunaga cut off a man's ear for having listened to Yura sing, what would he cut off for this? But none of that mattered here, in these stolen moments inside a madman's castle.

When Yura didn't pull away, Hanzo kissed her again. And felt his blood soar.

CHAPTER FIVE

Chancellor Sakai had the training yard cleared for a morning demonstration. The official attended alone, situated in a covered chair as Hanzo positioned his archer. The target lay directly ahead at the far end of the yard.

Hanzo had fashioned a suit of armor out of lacquer and paper mâché to cover the frame. From afar, the karakuri was a samurai warrior from its very stance to the ornate helmet and mask it wore. The trigger mechanism was hidden beneath the shoulder plate of the suit of armor. Hanzo reached inside to pull the lever down before standing back.

In one fluid movement, the automaton lifted the bow and fixed its stance in an archer's pose. The mechanical arm pulled back to its farthest point before the jointed fingers released the arrow, sending it home to the center of the target.

The chancellor watched from his seat, unmoved.

The karakuri pulled another arrow from its quiver and repeated the first shot without error. Then a third arrow joined the first two inside the target.

Chancellor Sakai rose to his feet. "Very good, Hanzo-dono."

He moved closer to inspect the target before nodding. Despite all the outward signs of approval, a knot formed in Hanzo's stomach. He'd come to know the chancellor's carefully measured expressions.

"An exceptional recreation," Sakai remarked, approaching the automaton now. He circled the armored figure. "At the start, what was Hanzo-dono adjusting behind the machine?"

"A dial used to set the distance from the target, Chancellor."

"Hmm." Sakai ran a hand over his beard. "Then your archer is only able to hit a target directly in from of him?"

"Yes."

"Ah, but what if the target was set off to one side? Wouldn't it be beneficial to allow one to direct the arrow?"

This was what Hanzo had come to expect from Sakai. Always another suggestion, another improvement. But now Hanzo knew why. The chancellor had always been designing a weapon.

"Chancellor Sakai is very wise," Hanzo admitted. "Such a feature would vastly improve the design."

Already his mind was working. A change to the structure to allow the archer to pivot. The replacement of several joints with a ball and socket fixture. He had the human body as a model.

"This is why I value your skill, Hanzo-dono. Every challenge is an opportunity to you."

Hanzo bowed in a proper show of humility.

"There is a feast planned for the next full moon. The daimyo's most loyal vassals have been invited. It would be a great service to show off the archer at the banquet."

"Of course, Chancellor." Once again he bowed, keeping his expression veiled.

Only a few months at Koriya Castle and Hanzo was no longer blind. Chancellor Sakai had an intended target in mind. Someone who would be attending that banquet.

Weapons-making was an honorable trade, but there was no honor in assassination. His creation would be used to cheat someone out of his life. It would appear to be an unforeseeable accident. The misfiring of a mindless machine.

In that same moment, Hanzo would lose his life as well when he was held responsible. His name, his honor, his future...all gone to dust.

You grant them your intentions, Yura had told him.

If he was to be made complicit either way, then Hanzo could very will choose his own target. One worthy of his sacrifice, and one that would allow Lady Yura to think well of him.

He would move mountains for her. He would touch the sky. He would keep her safe, the only way he knew how.

"I will begin work immediately," Hanzo promised. The full moon was less than two weeks away.

Attendants came to drape a canvas over the karakuri to transport the machine back to the workshop. Hanzo meant to take his leave, but Sakai stopped him.

"A final word, Hanzo-dono." Once they were alone, the chancellor spoke in a lowered tone. "I say this as a friend. Lord Mizunaga is very protective of what belongs to him.

Hanzo stiffened and Sakai detected the change.

"Be careful of your friendship with Lady Yura. She is one of Lord Mizunaga's most prized possessions."

"I understand, Lord Chancellor."

Every challenge was indeed an opportunity.

In many, Hanzo spoke through his karakuri. They were an extension of his own hands, his own arms. This newest creation would be the same, accomplishing what he could not. Accomplishing what everyone else was afraid to do.

HANZO DIDN'T KNOW how Yura had slipped once more into his room, or for how long she had stood in the corner watching him. Only when he heard his name did he look up.

"When did you last sleep?" She looked over his ragged appearance. "When did you last eat?"

Yura was only ever released from Lord Mizunaga's service when morning neared. If she was here, then Hanzo had reached the end of another night without success. He stared back at the archer. Half of the armor had been stripped away and he had his hands deep within the nest of control wires. "You shouldn't be here, O-Yura."

What had seemed like a simple addition to Chancellor Sakai, had in fact required the entire construction to be rebuilt. Now that it was done, the aim remained inconsistent. Each snap of the bow rattled the frame, requiring the entire assembly to be re-calibrated. Hanzo needed to work and think of nothing else. The moon was waxing full.

"Hanzo-dono."

He'd found what was wrong. A socket joint that had come loose. Perhaps he could tighten it there, or would it be best to disassemble the entire section?

"*Hanzo-dono.*"

Yura was still there. She gestured towards the lanterns and Hanzo stared at them for several long moments before he understood. Everything within the chamber cast shadows onto the paper panels. They could be seen.

Once he extinguished the lanterns, she came to him. "You're making yourself ill, Hanzo."

He gripped her upper arms, fighting against her as she tried to draw him away from the karakuri. Away from his work. Yura was stronger than he expected, or perhaps he'd become weakened.

"If Mizunaga finds you here, he'll kill us both," he said grimly.

"Is that why you've been hiding away? Every night, your lanterns are lit, but your door remains closed."

She had known about all those times he'd stood in the doorway to watch for her. Hanzo closed his eyes. He was exhausted, and the scent of her skin was making him light-headed.

"It isn't why. I have to finish this."

He wasn't only talking about the karakuri. Over the last week, he'd finally seen what he'd been blind to all along. The entire castle was terrified of Mizunaga. They all lived in silence with their heads down. The only one who seemed clear-eyed and unafraid was Chancellor Sakai.

"I know why I was brought here." Hanzo let out a long sigh. It was fate. "I know what I must do."

"This task will be the death of you."

Yura touched her hand to his face. They hadn't done any more than kiss before she had disappeared into the night. Out of instinct, out of longing, his arms wrapped around her, sliding over warm skin and smooth silk. He'd touched nothing but sharp and cold metal for days.

This was what human hands were meant to touch, but he'd denied himself, reaching out instead through his karakuri. Only allowing himself to connect with others from afar.

Hanzo rested his head against Yura's hair, letting the strands brush against his cheek. "Then let it be a good death, Yura."

She drew him trembling into her arms. "It doesn't have to be like this," she whispered into his ear.

Yura took him by the hand. Hers was delicate and soft, while his were calloused and scrubbed raw by copper wire. Hanzo let her lead him to the sleeping compartment in back. Even in the dark, with the workshop strewn with tools and parts and devices, she never faltered.

By the time she untied his yakuta and pushed the cloth from his shoulders, Hanzo was breathing hard.

"You'll go mad if you don't sleep." Her feather-light lips pressed against his shoulder, then his throat.

Yura was a courtesan, more worldly and experienced than he was. He was grateful as she helped him with the ties of her kimono. Then she guided his hands to her bare skin, sighing as his palms curved over her breasts.

It was his first time with a woman, but Hanzo learned as he always did. Through exploration, first with his hands and then his mouth, knowing each sweet, stolen moment could mean his death.

~

HANZO HELD Yura naked in his arms, surrounded in darkness. In the aftermath of their joining, he'd confessed everything to her. The creation of the clockwork assassin and his suspicions about Chancellor Sakai.

"Why are you telling me this? I am nothing but a lowly servant here. I could inform the chancellor of your treachery and you'd be executed."

Yura was tucked into the crook of his arm with her head against his chest. He couldn't see her face as she spoke, but he didn't need to. He'd watched her for a long time now, with more care than he'd spent on any other subject.

"I don't believe you're just a servant." He threaded his fingers through the black silk of her hair. "If I succeed, I die. If I fail, I also die. I have nothing left to fear."

He was condemned either way, but now that Hanzo had resolved to aim the machine at Lord Mizunaga himself, all knowledge and skill had failed him. The karakuri was broken. It wouldn't work.

"Are you doing this for me, Hanzo-dono?" Her fingers trailed a line over his chest to hover over his heart.

"You will be free."

She fell silent. The tick of the lantern clock out in the workshop continued to count down the minutes. Hanzo was content to let time pass, breathing in the jasmine scent of her hair.

"When I first came to Koriya, I thought I would be brought to Lord Mizunaga's bed," she told him.

Hanzo tensed at the thought of the warlord's hands on her. Yura had known men before him and there would be others when he was gone. He tried not to let that thought poison this moment. This moment was theirs, his and hers alone.

"But the daimyo is too cautious to take a mistress so carelessly. I've become his shield. Another one of his many guards. While I sing, he believes all is well."

Hanzo glanced at the windows. "It's almost morning, Yura."

She went on regardless. "Mizunaga fears assassination with good reason. Many men have tried to kill him. They all failed because they either lacked the skill, or the patience to wait for the right moment to strike. Most men, however, are not meant to kill another man. It's important that you hear this, Hanzo-dono."

Yura raised her head to look into his eyes. Hanzo would have liked nothing better than to remain as they were, even if the talk was about treachery and death. As long as she stayed, and as long as she kept on looking at him like that.

"You are a good man, Karakuri no Hanzo. There is a cost to taking a life, and the reason that you struggle now, the reason you cannot build this machine when you have created so many other miraculous devices is because your heart will not let you. You do not hate Lord Mizunaga enough, nor do you hate yourself enough to kill him."

His heart pounded as he struggled with Yura's words. He wanted to argue with her: she was wrong. Mizunaga was a tyrant. He was a lunatic who killed family, friends and strangers with the same impunity. One day, Mizunaga would kill her unless Hanzo stopped him.

But Hanzo said none of those things. Yura sank back against him, bringing warmth back to the part of him that had started to go cold.

Cold, but not cold enough.

He held on to Yura while the light filtering in through the windows went from silver to gold. The sun was rising. She would have to go, and he would have to let her.

"Sing for me," he implored.

Pressed close to his side, Yura hesitated. "Lord Mizunaga doesn't allow me to sing for anyone but him."

"Then softly, so no one else will hear."

She did sing for him, very softly, while Hanzo closed his eyes and tried to absorb every sound inside himself. He could feel the melody resonating inside of her while they embraced.

When the song was done, he sent her away and forbid her to come to him in his chamber ever again. He had much work to do.

CHAPTER SIX

Just before dawn, the karakuri master's shadow could be seen inside his workshop, bent over some task with a tool in hand. Once in a while, the figure would lay down his tool, pause, and pick up a new one.

In Lord Mizunaga's chamber, Lady Yura stood on her feet, singing from dusk till near dawn as she always did. Her silhouette was visible through the translucent panes of the mulberry paper with her silk kimono draped over a willowy form. She'd been in that same position for hours now. While she sang, the guardsmen knew not to disturb their master.

In the glare of the morning light, the courtesan was still singing a melody sweeter than any she'd ever sung. Mizunaga must have found it quite pleasing. He slumbered past the early morning, something the restless warlord was never known to do.

But the lateness of the day and the unwavering nature of the courtesan's song soon become suspicious. By the Hour of the Dragon, Chancellor Sakai commanded the guards to do the unthinkable and breach Lord Mizunaga's sleeping chamber.

Upon entering, they saw the beautiful courtesan was made of wood and wire draped in a silk kimono. The melody came from a wind-up box, much like the song machines popular in the tea houses of Edo. Once close enough, they could hear the click of the gears as the song changed.

A further inspection inside the chamber found Lord Mizunaga indeed in a slumber, a perpetual slumber, with a long, thin needle jabbed into his left eye deep enough to touch the brain. The other eye was blissfully closed.

And the clockwork courtesan sang on.

HANZO WAITED by the river bend. He'd burned his designs and dismantled his automata before sneaking away from the castle while the inhabitants were asleep. Hanzo only took a single horse with him for the journey. All of his beloved tools and creations had been left behind, save for one.

The mechanical nightingale lay tucked beneath his arm. Its eyes were closed and its gears silent.

As the moon rose and began to fall, Hanzo wrapped his cloak tighter around himself and huddled close to the trees. He prayed the castle guards were not yet aware he had fled, but it wouldn't be long before his ruse was discovered. In a few more hours, it would be morning and the world would awaken.

He started to doze off when a warble came from somewhere out in the darkness. "Hoo—hokekyo!"

In his arms, the clockwork nightingale sprang to life. "Hoo—hokekyo...Hoo—hokekyo..." It stretched its wings as it answered.

Hanzo snapped the beak closed with his thumb and forefinger. With his heart pounding, he looked in the direction of the initiating call. The leaves around him rustled as if visited by a soft breeze. A moment later, Yura appeared through them, pale and luminous like a night spirit kissed by the moon.

"Yura." His heart burst with joy.

She wasn't smiling. "We must go quickly."

They mounted the horse with her at the reins. Lady Yura was a more experienced rider than he, and the journey ahead of them would be long and hard.

"If Mizunaga's men find us, they'll kill us," he said.

"They won't find us." Yura's voice was set with steel.

He closed his arms around her, grateful that she had made it out of Koriya Castle safe. No matter what happened now, they would face it together.

For a moment, she let her cheek rest against his arm. She touched her hand to his. "How did you know about me, Hanzo?"

Kunoichi. The word filtered through his mind. It was a taboo word, more mysterious and shadowy than even its counterpart: *shinobi.* Secret assassin. All the others had failed because they didn't have the skill or were not patient enough to wait for the right moment. Yura was apparently both skilled and patient.

He had known there was something different about Yura from the very first time they'd spoken. He'd known that some part of her was an illusion, but he hadn't understood the exact nature of it. Perhaps he never would.

"I study the art of movement," Hanzo replied, a little bit afraid of her, but also very much in love. "And you always move without making a sound."

AUTHOR'S NOTE & ACKNOWLEDGMENTS

Thank you for reading *Gunpowder Alchemy* and the companion short story "The Warlord and the Nightingale". Please consider taking the time to leave a review online. Whether positive or negative, reviews help readers discover new books. I do appreciate each and every review.

These stories are set in the Opium War steampunk world of *The Gunpowder Chronicles*. The first book, *Gunpowder Alchemy*, is set in China and the adventure continues in the second book, *Clockwork Samurai*, which ventures into 19th century Japan.

The series was originally published in 2014-2015 by InterMix Books. The re-release of this series has allowed me to commission artwork that is aligned with my vision of the series as well as provide additional stories and content within the *Gunpowder Chronicles* world.

Steampunk author Suzanne Lazear was the one who told me there should be an Asian steampunk and that I should write it. At that moment, I hadn't even considered the possibility. However, the more I thought of it, the more the idea started taking shape until I absolutely had to create this world. All the pieces fit so perfectly: history, science and the dystopia of the Opium War period.

This series would have not been possible without my agent, Gail Fortune, who wholeheartedly championed this project from the beginning. Also I must give a big thanks to Cindy Hwang for her editorial guidance and support. Last, but not least, thank you to Dayna Hart for lending me her critical eye as well as holding my hand through the rough spots.

In addition to the two originally published books, there is a *Gunpowder Chronicles* novella collection and additional full-length novels in the series to come.

For more information about the series and other books or to receive updates on future releases, sign up for my newsletter at:

www.jeannielin.com

HISTORICAL NOTES

When I set about creating the world of the Gunpowder Chronicles, I wanted to base the steampunk inventions on the technological advances and scientific philosophies that existed in China during the early 19th century – much like how a good portion of Western steampunk is inspired by a Victorian mindset. Chinese learning at that time was not completely closed off to the world, as often cited. Far from it. In fact, the Chinese had been exposed to Western technology and learning through many sources, one of which were Jesuit scientists who had served in the imperial court.

Gunpowder was famously invented by the Chinese and its many uses in warfare were documented in a 14th century text called the ***Huolongjing*** or the Fire Dragon Manual. There was no record of gunpowder being used for engines by the Chinese, though gunpowder combustion engines were explored by Western scientists as early as the 17th century. No official record of a working engine exists and the concept was apparently busted by the Mythbusters. However, the central idea of an internal combustion engine powered by gunpowder seemed a natural fit for a culture that was familiar with gunpowder.

Along with the technological and scientific component, I also wanted to interweave the actual history of the time into a re-telling. Readers may be surprised to discover how little I had to make up. Crown Prince Yizhu is a real historical figure who inherited an empire in turmoil at the age of 19.

The Ministry of Science and Engineering was added as a seventh ministry to the existing Six Ministry system with an imperial examination process in the sciences that parallels the existing Chinese civil exams.

The uprising at the center of the series is based on the Taiping Rebellion, which did feature several notable female leaders. Lady Su was based on Su Sanniang, a rebel leader of over two thousand people who became an outlaw after her husband was killed by Qing forces.

The Emperor never executed the imperial scientists after the losses of the first Opium War. It was thought that the Chinese had underestimated the technological advancements of the west and despite losing to the "devil ships". Any call to learn from the Western technology and science continued to be shunned after the First Opium War. The execution of the scientists was a representation of the hubris of the imperial court refusing to accept that it could be bested in any way by Western developments. The push to study and learn from Western methods did not take root until later after the Second Opium War during the self-strengthening movement.

The execution of the high ranking scientists was also inspired by conflicts between Western and Eastern learning happening in Japan at that time – a concept that is explored further in the next book in the series, *Clockwork Samurai.*

NEXT BOOK: CLOCKWORK SAMURAI

***The Gunpowder Chronicles* continue as a woman left adrift by a dynasty in decline attempts to reclaim her family's honor...**

Appointed to the Court of Physicians, Jin Soling can see that the newly-crowned Emperor is cracking, relying on opium to drown his troubles. The Qing Empire is failing, and war with the British is imminent, but the man to whom Soling was once engaged has a bold idea to save it.

A leader within the Ministry of Engineering, Chen Chang-wei suggests an alliance with the isolated island empire of Japan, whose scientists claim to have technical advancements that could turn the tide of the war.

Seeking to escape the politics of the imperial court, Soling arranges her own passage on the airship to Japan. But once they land, Chang-wei and Soling become targets of the shogunate's armored samurai assassins. Caught in an age-old battle between the feudal tradition and innovation, and stranded in a land distrustful of foreigners, Soling and Chang-wei search for a path toward the future—the survival of both Qing Empire and the island nation of Japan depend on it.

OTHER BOOKS BY JEANNIE LIN

The Gunpowder Chronicles

Gunpowder Alchemy (#1)
Clockwork Samurai (#2)
The Warlord and the Nightingale (short story)

The Lotus Palace Mystery Series

The Lotus Palace (#1)
The Jade Temptress (#2)
The Liar's Dice (novella) (#2.5)

Harlequin Historicals

Butterfly Swords
The Dragon and the Pearl
My Fair Concubine
The Sword Dancer
A Dance with Danger
Silk, Swords and Surrender (a novella collection)

ABOUT THE AUTHOR

USA Today bestselling author **Jeannie Lin** grew up fascinated by stories of Western epic fantasy, Eastern martial arts adventures, and romance novels. Formerly a high school teacher, Jeannie is now known for writing groundbreaking, award-winning historical romances set in Tang Dynasty China, including her Golden Heart Award–winning debut, *Butterfly Swords*, as well as *The Dragon and the Pearl*, *My Fair Concubine*, and *The Lotus Palace*.

You can find out more information or contact Jeannie online at her website: www.jeannielin.com.

Printed in the USA
CPSIA information can be obtained
at www.ICGtesting.com
LVHW071158170923
758443LV00031B/186